S0-BFB-118

Praise for the Cat Star Chronicles

FUGITIVE

"A fabulous book with the galaxy's most enticing heroes… the Cat Star Chronicles is CATegorically the best exotic and sensuously erotic science fiction in the market. If you haven't read them, buy the whole series and give yourself a treat."

—Star-Crossed Romance

"Just the right blend of science fiction, romance, and erotica."

—This Book for Free

"Another stellar book in this phenomenal series that just gets better and better. Awe inspiring… It's sexy space travel at its finest."

—Night Owl Romance

"A steamy, action-filled ride. Ms. Brooks' world-building is impressive as well as creative."

—Anna's Book Blog

"Cat Star Chronicles has become one of my favorite futuristic series… There's plenty of kick butt action as well as laugh-out-loud moments."

—Romance Junkies

"The hottest one yet… Cheryl Brooks continues to delight with her alien races and sexy Zetithian men."

—Moonlight to Twilight

Other books in the
Cat Star Chronicles series:

THE CAT STAR CHRONICLES

HERO

CHERYL BROOKS

sourcebooks
casablanca

Published by Sourcebooks Casablanca, an imprint of Sourcebooks, Inc.
P.O. Box 4410, Naperville, Illinois 60567-4410
(630) 961-3900
FAX: (630) 961-2168
www.sourcebooks.com

Printed and bound in the United States of America
QW 10 9 8 7 6 5 4 3 2 1

For that spark of heroism in all of us

Prologue

TRAG KNEW IT WAS A MISTAKE TO ATTEND THE WEDDING. Not that he begrudged Manx and Drusilla their new state of wedded bliss or that he didn't enjoy seeing his old friend again, but because he knew he'd be sitting just exactly where he was right now; on Kyra's left while his brother, Tychar, sat on her right. She was as warm and lovely as she had been on the day Trag left Darconia, but just as firmly fixed as his brother's mate as she had been on the day they met. There was no getting past fate, destiny, or Zetithian visions, particularly when they involved a future mate. Tychar had known Kyra would be his long before he ever saw her; he just hadn't bothered to mention it to Trag.

Trag was thankful that he was wearing clothing, which he hadn't done when he and Ty had been slaves to the Darconian queen, because his reaction to her scent was the same as always; his cock was so hard he couldn't think about anything else.

He stared at Jack in a desperate attempt to divert his thoughts as she performed the wedding ceremony. It gave Jack great pleasure to be able to have all of the remaining Zetithians aboard her ship, and gave her even greater satisfaction to be tying the knot between the last known Zetithian and his Terran mate.

Finding Manx had been nothing short of a miracle, and though Trag had prayed to the Great Mother of the

Desert for one more, so far she hadn't been attending to him. He tried turning away from Kyra, but her scent lingered in his head until the shallow breaths he'd been taking finally caught up with him and, inhaling deeply, he succumbed to the memory...

He and Tychar had converged on Kyra immediately. She had said yes, so there had been no point in waiting any longer. He fed her fruit while Tychar wiped the sweat from her body, and Trag tasted her sweetness in every way he could. He licked her lips after each bite until she kissed him, sucking his tongue into her mouth and driving him insane with desire. Her intoxicating kisses soon had him purring like mad as his hands caressed her body. She tasted like hot, wet love and her aroma was like nothing he'd ever imagined, igniting flames of passion that threatened to consume him. When Tychar pulled her thighs apart and urged him to taste the source of her scent, Trag licked her soft, wet lips, thrusting his tongue deep inside her, devouring her until, with a gush of creamy wetness, she came in his face. A triumphant snarl erupted from the depths of his throat, and when Ty pushed her beneath him, Trag didn't hesitate; he buried his stiff shaft in her soft warmth and felt love for the very first time.

Trag lost control after that, fucking her harder than he'd ever fucked anyone in his life. It took a while to regain that control, and when he did, he used every move on her he could think of, purring with delight and enjoying the vision of her lovely eyes and gentle smile.

And then, at his suggestion, she'd sucked Tychar. Trag's balls tightened at the memory of it... He'd never seen a more erotic vision before—or since—and it was a wonder he hadn't lost it right then, but Ty got there ahead of him, spraying her face and tongue with his sweet snard. It was one race Trag didn't mind losing though, for her orgasm seized his cock and sent him over the edge. Trag had felt that ejaculation clear down to his toenails and the double dose of Zetithian semen had Kyra babbling on about something—just what, he couldn't recall—but his satisfaction had been complete. He had given joy to a beautiful woman—a woman he now loved, but knew he could never call his own.

It was Trag's first, last, and only time with Kyra. After that, it became clear that she loved Tychar, not him, and when Queen Scalia's death freed the two men from slavery, Trag had tried to make the best of it. He might have withdrawn from Kyra and never tasted her love again, but he certainly hadn't forgotten it.

He tried to imagine what it would be like to love another woman but it was difficult. Any Terran woman would remind him too much of Kyra, if for no other reason than her scent. Telling those who urged him to find a mate that he was holding out for a Zetithian woman made it easier, first, because it gave him breathing space, and second, because he knew in his heart he'd never find one. He was certain they had all perished when Zetith exploded, and if any had been living offworld, the Nedwut bounty hunters had surely killed them all by now. He and his brother had only survived because of Queen Scalia's protection. What chance would a lone Zetithian female have against such determined killers?

Though he visited brothels from time to time, he never recaptured that feeling, and Trag's secret devotion to Kyra never wavered—at least in his waking moments—but his dreams were confused. Whenever he tried to recall them, the image seemed blurred, as though his own mind was uncertain of whom he should love. Was it Kyra, or was it someone else?

Trag didn't know for sure, but with the marriage of Manx to Drusilla, he was now the last Zetithian without a mate, and he was no closer to finding love than he had been as a slave living among the reptilian Darconians. It shouldn't have been that hard for the pilot of a starship to find the woman he was destined to meet, but, then again, it was a very big galaxy…

—∿∿—

Micayla's earliest memory was of a smothering darkness. She could sense her mother's terror as she fled through the crowded spaceport, but wrapped in the folds of Jenall's cloak, she was unable to see the source of it. Nevertheless, she could feel Jenall's sweat and hear her pounding heart and gasping breaths as her mother pushed herself to the limits of her endurance and beyond. Later, Micayla would understand what it meant to be running for one's life, but at the age of two, the concept of fear meant very little.

There were loud noises and the sound of people screaming, but her mother ran on, bumping, jostling, her feet slapping against the smooth floor. Suddenly, Jenall halted and opened her cloak, and Micayla found herself looking up into the face of an odd being—smooth-skinned and dark, with almond-shaped eyes and softly curling ringlets framing her face.

"Take her," Jenall rasped. "Hide her and keep her safe."

The response might have been unintelligible, but the intent was clear: the woman opened her own cloak and Micayla was thrust into her waiting arms. As they watched, Jenall turned and ran on, but though her brief pause might have saved her daughter's life, it didn't save her own.

Micayla heard her father's roar as Jenall fell into a nerveless heap and saw him whirl around, his long dark hair flowing out behind him as he set his two sons on their feet and ran to his mate's aid. Micayla didn't see any more, for her rescuer turned and hurried away with her precious bundle—leaving the scene as quickly as any prudent bystander would do. Micayla heard three more shots and then silence.

Chapter 1

HIS SWIRLING CLOAK WAS WHAT CAUGHT HER EYE, BUT even from across the crowded park, his aura of sadness and regret went straight to her heart. A little girl ran after him as he walked away, and when he stopped and knelt beside her, she held out her hand, offering him something. His long curling hair fell forward as he accepted it, revealing a streak of orange in the otherwise black locks. There was a brief exchange that Micayla couldn't hear, but whatever the girl had given him must have been quite a treat, for his smile after tasting it was a mixture of wistfulness and delight.

Micayla had never seen him before, but, being a newcomer to Orleon Station, this wasn't surprising. So far, Windura was the only one she saw on other than a coworker basis, and that was mainly because their quarters were next door to one another.

"Hey, Micayla," Windura called out from the corridor behind her. "Let's meet for lunch, okay?"

"Yeah, sure," Micayla replied. Tearing her eyes away from the man, she turned to greet her Vessonian friend. "Lunch would be great."

"The main dining hall at eleven hundred?"

"Fine," Micayla replied, forcing herself to smile. Glancing over her shoulder, to her dismay she saw that the man had already gone. She strained her eyes to find him among the huge potted plants and benches of the space station's "park." "Did you see that guy—the one in the cloak with the long black hair?"

"A cloak?" Windura echoed. "Why would *anyone* be wearing a cloak? It's hot as hell in here!"

It wasn't the first time she'd heard Windura complain about the heat, but then catering to the preferences of a variety of different beings made the choice of ambient temperature difficult. "Maybe so," she said doubtfully. "But some people are just cold-natured…" She stared off in the direction he must have taken. "What's back that way?"

"Some of the more disreputable parts of the station," Windura replied, flipping her long blond hair over her shoulder. "You're better off not going down there."

Micayla nodded absently. "I'm sure you're right," she said, but something about him was so compelling that if Windura hadn't intervened, she'd have gone running after him in a heartbeat.

"We've got to get you better oriented to this place," Windura went on. "A girl like you needs to know the ropes."

Micayla frowned. "What makes you say that?"

Shaking her head, Windura replied, "If you don't know that by now, then I can't help you." With a quick grin, she added, "See you at eleven," and was gone.

Micayla stood gazing blankly at the throng of children, unable to recall why she had gone to the park in the first place. Ordinarily it would've been a cold day in hell, let alone Orleon Station, when a man distracted her *that* much, but then she remembered: *Tea. You're here to get tea.* Getting in line at Starbucks, she ordered a tall cup of hot, foaming chai and then headed off to work.

The communications center was a hive of bustling activity, and Micayla had to squeeze past several other officers to get to her station, nearly spilling her tea as she finally plunked down in her seat. The guy from the previous shift had left his candy wrappers scattered about, and she gathered them up, grumbling as one of them stuck to the console.

"Sorry about that," he said from behind her. Reaching over her shoulder, he retrieved the last of them, his chest pressing lightly against her back.

Micayla shifted away from him slightly. Scott was Terran and an attractive fellow with a terrific smile, but he was getting a little too... chummy. As a female of an unknown species, if there was one thing Micayla had learned, it was that Terrans and whatever she was weren't compatible—at least, none she'd met so far— and having grown up on Earth, she'd met quite a few.

"That's okay, Scott," she said. "I'm sure I leave tea stains for Xantric to wipe up when she comes on duty."

"Not sure she'd notice," Scott said with a shrug. "And if she did, you'd never know it. Twilanans never complain about anything." He turned to leave, but then paused, adding, "Not much traffic on the system for the past couple of hours, but I'm sure it'll pick up for you."

Micayla took a sip of her tea and nodded. "It always does," she agreed. "Get some sleep."

Scott sighed. "Too bad you and I work different shifts. Otherwise, we could spend a little more time together—instead of me just going back to my quarters and dreaming about you."

Micayla felt a pang near her heart and wished she could have felt something other than regret when a man said such things to her. Steeling herself against his inevitable reaction, she purposely avoided his eyes, focusing instead on resetting the instrument panel with her fingerprint on the log entry. "Dreams will have to suffice, big guy," she said. "I'm not looking for a boyfriend."

"You always say that," Scott grumbled. "Sure I can't talk you out of it?"

"You could try," she said, wishing it really *would* work, just once, "but it probably won't do you any good."

"Ice Queen," he muttered.

"I've been called that before," she said wearily.

"Treacherous Temptress?"

"Been called that too."

"You're kidding me, right?"

"You'd be surprised." Micayla sighed. "And believe me, it's nothing personal, Scott. I have no problem with being friends, but if you want more than that, I'm simply the wrong species."

Seeming to take this as an invitation, Scott turned and leaned against the partition that divided the workstations. "What are you, anyway?"

"No idea," she replied. "But I'm not human, that's for sure."

"No shit," Scott said. "You're better looking than any Terran I've ever seen. I love those cat-like eyes of yours. The elfin ears are nice too, and the *fangs…*" His voice trailed off there as though indulging in some erotic fantasy.

"The better to bite you with, my dear," Micayla quoted. When her stepmother had first read her that story, she probably never realized that Micayla identified much more with the wolf than with Little Red

Riding Hood—though, in truth, she looked more like a lion or a panther than a wolf.

If Scott's response was any indication, being savaged by a lioness was the answer to his wildest imaginings. "Would you?" he asked eagerly. "Please? Pretty please?"

"Absolutely not," Micayla said firmly as a hail came through the system. "Get going, now," she added, shooing him away. "I've got work to do."

Scott withdrew with obvious reluctance, mumbling imprecations under his breath as he went.

Micayla redirected the hail and wondered if it would be worth it to try to spend a little more time with Scott. He was a nice guy and it would take no encouragement whatsoever to—no, she decided. It wasn't worth the pain. Her lack of interest in the opposite sex wasn't her fault, but he would end up despising her for it and then she'd be right back where she started.

Her attitude wasn't precisely a lack of interest, however; it was more a lack of desire, and though she knew what desire was supposed to feel like—she had one fantasy that never failed to elicit that response—it never seemed to work with a flesh and blood man. The man she'd seen in the park might have been different, though; she'd at least felt something for him, if only compassion. Had the little girl been his daughter, telling him good-bye as he left on a journey through space? Was she a friend or a complete stranger? Micayla had no way of knowing, but the more she thought about it, the more she itched to find out.

She glanced up as Dana took her seat at the next station, apologizing to Roxanne for being late. "I had such a tough time getting Cara out of the park!" Dana was saying. "She started talking to someone and didn't want to leave. I'm surprised she didn't go running after him."

Micayla had never met Dana's daughter, but she knew the feeling. It had taken every bit of her strong work ethic to remind her that running after men in cloaks wasn't in her job description. "A stranger?"

"Yes, and you'd think I'd have taught her not to do that by now, wouldn't you?" said Dana. "But since I talked to him myself, I can't say I've been setting a very good example, can I?"

Micayla couldn't help but laugh. Dana was probably the friendliest person she had ever met. Talking to anyone—stranger or not—seemed to come very easily to her.

"And he looked so sad," Dana went on. "I think she cheered him up a little."

Micayla felt her pulse quicken. "Why? What did she do?"

"Climbed up in his lap and wiped away his tears," Dana replied. "She made him smile, too—she gave him a strawberry."

Her heart was pounding now. "What did he look like?"

Dana cocked her head to the side, gazing thoughtfully at Micayla. "You know, he looked something like you," she replied. "I don't know why it didn't occur to me at the time, but he had the same kind of cat's eyes, and his eyebrows were upswept like yours. He even had fangs." Dana laughed softly. "And he could purr like a kitten."

"Did he say anything else—like who he was or where he was from?" Micayla asked breathlessly.

Dana's soft brown curls bounced as she shook her head. "No, he just got up and left."

"I—I think I saw him too," Micayla said. "He had long black hair and was wearing a cloak, right?"

Dana nodded. "Do you know him?"

"No, but I wish I did. There was something about him that got my attention."

"He probably gets plenty of that," Dana said with a giggle. "He was *very* handsome—especially when he smiled."

Micayla felt a surge of emotions. Regret for not having run after him, despair that she might never see him again, and envy that Dana had actually spoken with him—and all this because of a man she'd never even met. How very odd…

———

Trag went back the way he'd come with a heavy heart. Nothing in his entire life had prepared him for the way he'd felt that morning, and he'd spent twenty years of that life as a slave. The fact that he'd been a free man and the pilot of a starship for the past three years didn't matter—he still felt trapped.

"Inheriting" a fortune in jewels from his former master might have provided him with the means, but something was missing from his life and until that space was filled, he felt adrift. He'd opted to take the job as Lerotan Kanotay's pilot, mainly because he couldn't come up with a better plan. Living among Lerotan's rough, uncouth crew was nothing like he imagined freedom would be, though his years of slavery might have had something to do with why he felt that way. Lerotan had teased him more than once about having been the Darconian queen's pampered pet.

Unlike Trag, his brother, Tychar, had done something far more interesting with his life, but he had talent as a singer and a woman who loved him. Trag could have gone on tour with Ty's band, but playing the flunky younger brother to a rock star didn't appeal to him in the slightest. There would always be a place for him aboard Jack Tshevnoe's ship, but Trag thought it was a bad idea for so many of the few remaining Zetithians to be together on one vessel. If the Nedwuts attacked and blew the *Jolly Roger* to bits, it would wipe out half of the six that were left of his species.

At least the six that were known. There could have been others in hiding, but with the increased bounty being paid on Zetithians, the Nedwut bounty hunters were more determined than ever to capture the remaining few. This meant that Trag often had to fight to stay alive and though he hoped to find other survivors—perhaps even a female—the odds were slim. Just that morning at the breakfast table while their ship cruised toward Orleon Station, Lerotan had teased him that perhaps this was the day. Trag, however, had not been quite so optimistic.

"Maybe," he had said. "But knowing my luck, even if we *did* find a Zetithian woman, she'd probably already have a mate, or she'd be the wrong age for me."

"And she'd automatically want you if she *was* the right age and not taken?"

This comment hit Trag like a stun blast to the chest. "I hadn't thought of that."

Lerotan roared with laughter. "Let's say we *do* find one that's eligible, what's to say she'd be so desperate that she'd want you?"

"Well, I—if I'm the only one left that doesn't have a mate," Trag sputtered, "she'd *have* to take me!"

"Oh, yeah. I'm sure *I'd* want a woman who only took me because of a lack of options."

Trag scowled at Lerotan but knew he was right. "I didn't mean it that way," he said. "What I meant was that if she's Zetithian, she wouldn't want anyone *but* another Zetithian."

"Oh, so it's different with the women?" Lerotan said skeptically. "You can do the Terran female/Zetithian male thing but not the other way around?"

"That's right," Trag said, crossing his arms firmly. "Hell, they didn't want *us* half the time, and we're irresistible. What makes you think they'd want anyone else?"

"You cocky Zetithians," Lerotan said with a wag of his head. "Always think women will want you no matter what. Well, let me tell you something, Trag. The males of other species have cocks as big and fancy as yours— some even have more than one. You aren't *that* special."

"Well, someone must've thought we were hot shit or they wouldn't be so set on making sure we were all dead," Trag grumbled. "That's Jack's theory, and I'd be willing to bet she's right."

"Suit yourself," Lerotan said, leaning back in his chair. "But I can do things with a woman that you can't, and you don't see anyone trying to crash asteroids into *my* planet, do you?"

Trag knew it was true but hated to admit it. Dark-skinned and handsome with a long, black braid that hung over one shoulder, Lerotan looked human, except for the tail, and the rune tattooed on his left temple only added to his allure with women. Trag hadn't seen a woman turn him down yet; in fact, they tended to line up for the chance to be part of a threesome or get double-fucked when he used his tail on them. Trag had had the misfortune of walking in on him once; the tuft of his tail had opened at the point, enabling the erectile tissue inside to protrude, looking for all the world like a spare cock. He had almost as much control of it as Trag had with his own penis—which was considerable. Trag was good—and it was a given that no woman had ever complained—but he certainly couldn't do two of them at the same time.

Still, he couldn't let Lerotan think he was better at pleasing one woman than he was. It was a matter of pride. "I know you've essentially got two tools, but can your fluids trigger orgasms?"

Lerotan took a sip of his drink and smiled. "I like to think it's my own efforts that make women scream for more, rather than drugging them with some kind of orgasmic cock syrup."

"Yeah, well, somebody else must have felt that way too, but trust me, it wasn't a woman!" *And especially not Kyra.* Trag pushed himself away from the table and lunged to his feet. "We're coming up on the space station."

"Well, be careful," Lerotan warned. "I don't want the paint scratched."

Trag rolled his eyes and headed off to the helm, not bothering to reply.

Orleon Station was about the size of a small moon but was shaped like a crystal with points in every direction, its growth seemingly haphazard as new sections were added on. Once the pride of the sector, it had become seedier with age, and those of Lerotan's ilk frequented the dingier bars seeking the illegal goods that had been banned from the station in the beginning but were now the more common merchandise.

It was rumored that the new commander was attempting to clean up some of the corruption, but Lerotan had made the comment that it was probably too late for that. Trag avoided arguing with Lerotan about what he sold, but also knew from having met Jack that it was possible to amass a small fortune by dealing in legal commodities. Unfortunately, while Jack had a knack for knowing what would sell on every planet she visited, from medical supplies to exotic cuisine, Lerotan just knew a good weapon when he saw one.

The first hail from the station brought Lerotan to the communications console to respond. "Captain: Lerotan Kanotay. Ship: *The Equalizer*. Cargo: weapons of all kinds for all kinds of buyers." He said this last with the same smirk as always, and Trag suspected he derived some sort of pleasure from putting it that way. No, Lerotan would never give up the arms game—at least not until someone killed him.

"Permission granted to dock on level ten, section thirty," the reedy-voiced Kitnock said. "Follow the beacon."

Trag stared at the viewscreen wondering how anything that looked like a collection of twigs could possibly need a mouth that big in order to feed itself, but he was distracted when a red light began pulsing at one of the points of the crystal. Aiming the ship toward it, he was momentarily startled by a soft jolt on the controls. "Looks like someone installed a damn tractor beam since we were here last," he growled in disgust. "You can't blame me for scratched paint this time."

"Lucky you," Lerotan said. "Guess I'll have to find something else to blame you for."

"Like what?" Trag demanded.

Lerotan cocked his head to one side and pursed his lips as though trying to remember. Then his eyes widened in surprise. "Do you know, I've never had the slightest bit of trouble with you? Never had to bust you out of jail, patch you up after a fight, or pay off a woman you got too rough with."

"No shit," Trag grumbled. "If I'm so wonderful, then why the hell don't you pay me more?"

"I suppose I should," Lerotan said amiably. "Doesn't mean I will, but—"

"Just forget it, Leroy. You pay me plenty."

"No, I don't."

"Yeah, but I get to see the galaxy."

Lerotan laughed. "Now that you mention it, I'm probably paying you too much—and don't call me Leroy."

Trag leaned back in his chair and scowled up at his boss, but his expression brightened as the ship slid into the airlock with a loud screech. "There goes the paint. *Leroy*."

Lerotan shrugged and tried to hide his displeasure, but the twitching of his leonine tail gave him away.

Trag tried to focus his mind on shutting down the engines, but Kyra's memory was still there to tease him. Smiling at him. Laughing at one of his jokes. Rolling her eyes at what a poor musician he was. He was fairly certain no one suspected—certainly not any of his shipmates, who were as rough a band of mercenaries as you might find anywhere in the galaxy—but he was beginning to tire of the charade. He was tired of going into spaceport bars and feigning interest in the women who frequented such places. Tired of going through the motions when one of them smelled good enough to give him an erection. Sometimes he fucked them just because he could, but it wasn't what he was looking for, mainly because what he wanted apparently didn't exist—a woman who could make him forget Kyra.

Chapter 2

MICAYLA MET WINDURA FOR LUNCH AS PROMISED, BUT her hopes that Windura might help her hunt for a man she'd only seen for a moment were dashed in light of the direction he'd taken.

"You need to steer clear of sections twenty-eight and twenty-nine," Windura warned briskly. "The worst scumbags in the quadrant hang out down there."

Micayla looked over at her new friend with a slightly jaundiced eye. "I've seen scumbags before. This isn't my first post, you know. Besides, you've been down there and you obviously survived."

"Yes, but I'm a bit more streetwise than you, and not nearly as pretty. You might get kidnapped and sold as a slave."

Confident in her fighting skills, Micayla snorted her skepticism. "You've got to be kidding me."

"Oh, no," Windura assured her. "There are slave ships that dock here. It isn't advertised, of course—and Commander Beontal would have a fit if he knew about it—but it happens."

"Well, maybe you should tell the commander that," Micayla suggested. "If he's trying to clean up the corruption here, getting rid of the slavers would be a good place to start."

"Yes, but it might also get me in trouble with the slavers," Windura pointed out. "And they are *not* the kind of people you want to piss off."

"You're probably right about that," Micayla agreed, "but at least they don't come to this part of the station." Sighing, she went on, "I'd really like to find that guy, though—if for no other reason than to get a closer look at him."

Windura cocked her head to one side. "Why—was he that handsome?"

"I couldn't tell," Micayla replied. "Dana said he was, but what's even more interesting is that she thought he and I might be the same species."

"Really?" Windura said, her curiosity clearly piqued. "I know you don't know what you are, but there's something about you that seems so familiar to me." She stopped there, shaking her head. "I just can't seem to remember…"

"Got a cat?" Micayla prompted.

"No," Windura replied. "Why do you ask?"

"The kids back home always said I looked like one."

"And this man did too, huh?"

"Yes, and according to Dana, he could purr like a kitten."

"And you can do that?"

"Sometimes," Micayla replied. "But I have to be in a certain mood." There was only one thing that could put her in that mood, but this was a subject she preferred to avoid. She focused on Windura instead, noting her slanted ears and forehead ridges. "Can Vessonians purr?"

"No," Windura replied with a giggle. "And we don't have any magical powers, either—although some people think I have a positive effect on their computers. What about you? Can you do anything besides purr?"

"If I tell you, you'll think I'm crazy," Micayla said, shaking her head.

"Try me," Windura said, taking a bite of her sandwich. "I've met lots of crazy people."

Micayla ran a finger down the side of her frosty glass. "Well, as long as you don't mind one more," she began tentatively, lowering her voice.

Windura leaned forward, clearly intrigued, and Micayla glanced around at the crowded cafeteria, hoping the general din of a hundred other conversations was enough to drown out the one in which she was currently engaged. "I sometimes know things and I don't know how I know them. Does that make sense?"

"I dunno," said Windura. "What sort of things?"

"Like this station, for example. I'd never been here before—never even seen a hologram of it—but I knew what it looked like before I got here. Even knew where things were without looking at a diagram."

"That's pretty weird," Windura admitted, "but convenient. At least you'll never get lost—and you'll always know where sections twenty-eight and twenty-nine are."

"I suppose so."

"Ever see the man of your dreams?"

"Only in my dreams," Micayla said with a rueful smile.

"Or the park," Windura suggested.

"I don't know that he was the man of my dreams," Micayla said. "I just noticed him, that's all." She couldn't help but think there was more to it than that, though. That arrow to her heart had to mean *something*…

"Ever been in love?"

Micayla ran a hand through her curls, feeling the sting of tears just as she always did when she thought about Adam. He was cute and funny and she'd liked him a lot—perhaps even loved him a little—which made it that much harder to bear when he told her he was going to look else-where for love. She couldn't blame him for wanting to find a girlfriend who actually appreciated his lovemaking efforts rather than merely tolerating them, but it still hurt. "Not really," she replied. "But I keep looking."

"Might help if you could find a male of your own species," Windura said, "which might also explain why you'd feel so compelled to find that man you saw this morning." Tapping her chin thoughtfully, she added, "Too bad you don't know what to look for. Ever done any research?"

Micayla laughed shortly. "Are you kidding? Of course I have! And my stepmother did too. She tried to discover what I was when she first brought me to Earth, but she never found a thing. I was practically a baby at the time, so I couldn't tell her much."

"And how did she wind up with you?"

"My real mother handed me off to Rulie just before she and the rest of my family were gunned down in a spaceport. Rulie never told me where it was. I think she was afraid I'd go looking for the killers or something."

"How awful!" Windura exclaimed. "I—I can't imag-ine what that would feel like." Windura sat quietly, as though playing the scenario through her mind. Then her expression darkened and she shuddered slightly. "I know one thing; I'd want to hunt down whoever did that to my family." She took a bite of her sandwich and chewed it thoughtfully before she spoke again. "Still, if you were a baby at the time, that had to have been at least twenty years ago. Have you checked into it lately?"

"No," Micayla replied. "I'd love to be able to write something other than 'unknown' in the slot for Planet of

Origin on an application, but to tell you the truth, as I've gotten older, I've begun to wonder if it's such a good idea. I mean, what if it turns out that I'm descended from an ancient species of killer cats—the kind that have been hunted down and shot on sight for centuries?"

"Well, that might explain why there are so few of you left," Windura agreed, "and I can see why it would make you a bit leery, but nobody is going to be hunting someone like you, Micayla. You're no killer."

Micayla shrugged. "True, but Rulie wasn't crazy about me taking a post so far from Earth, which makes me wonder if she knows something I don't."

Windura laughed. "My mother didn't want me to work here either, so it's not like you're alone in that." Downing the last of her Rubean punch, she went on, "I still think it's worth looking into. Computers are my thing; I might be more successful—and who knows? I might even be able to find your mystery man."

"But you might also find trouble."

Windura eyed her speculatively. "Willing to take that risk?"

A hazy memory of that tragic day when she lost her family in the spaceport surfaced briefly, only to be replaced by the compelling image of the man in the park. Micayla felt a pang near her heart and, suddenly, her concerns vanished without a trace. If nothing else, *he* was worth the risk. "Yes," she said firmly. "I believe I am."

~~~

As always, Trag's initial thought when he entered Orleon Station a few hours before had been that the place was trying too hard not to stink. A potent perfume wafted from the ventilators as he and his shipmates stepped through the double hatch on the airlock, and Trag's sensitive nose was the first to rebel. Sneezing violently, he motioned for the others to go on without him.

"What the hell's the matter with you?" Rodan had asked. "Don't like what you smell?"

"No!" Trag exclaimed. "And you wouldn't either if you had any sense of smell at all."

Rodan just grinned, revealing several large gaps in his stained teeth. As the ship's first officer, Rodan was as coarse as Lerotan was charming. Big, bald, tattooed, and fond of wearing leather and chains, Rodan hailed from a planet that must have smelled even worse than the station because the natives never seemed to notice just how bad they smelled themselves. At least, Rodan didn't. Trag had a hard time being in the same room with him. Most women didn't like him and even though he was rumored to be extremely well-endowed, they usually steered clear of him after one encounter. Apparently there was such a thing as being *too* big.

His other companion, aside from Lerotan, was Hidar, *The Equalizer*'s medical officer and cook. Hidar was Scorillian—a hideous species of tall bipedal insects with translucent green wings and a triangular head—and, as such, had women the galaxy over avoiding him like the plague for which his planet was famous.

Having recovered from his sneezing fit, Trag followed the flashing lights on the walls of the corridor advertising the various shops on the main deck. He had no use for most of their wares; all he really wanted was some fresh fruit, though he doubted he would find it so deep in space. Darconians were vegetarian and ate their food fresh and uncooked, and, as their slave, he had been fed the same way. As a result, Trag had a hard time adjusting to the uncertain diet on board *The Equalizer*; he had to be almost starving before he ate anything Hidar cooked. It was always spicy, greasy, and sat in his stomach like a grenade just waiting to explode. Trag had always considered it ironic, but convenient, that Hidar was both the ship's cook and medic; after his cooking made you sick, he could treat your bellyache.

Another relic of his life on Darconia was that Trag was cold all the time. After twenty years on a hot, desert planet where he wore nothing but two jeweled collars— one around his neck and the other around his genitals— he still hadn't acclimated enough to wear anything less than two layers of clothing and a heavy cloak. His brother performed on stage stripped down to nothing but a pair of low-slung, skin-tight pants, but rock stars like Tychar had hot lights and plenty of physical activity to keep them warm. Off stage, he was usually freezing his nuts off too.

Reaching the end of the corridor, Trag's senses were assaulted by the noise, smoke, flashing lights, and mingled odors of a variety of different life-forms all mixed in together. Despite the immense size of the place, it seemed crowded as beings of all kinds jostled their way through the wide aisle between the vendors. There were hideous Cylopeans selling what appeared to be shrunken heads, Drells demonstrating the virtues of their hair tonic, a black-scaled Nerik hawking tracking devices, fish-lipped Norludians beckoning to customers with their sucker-tipped fingers and urging them to buy a vial of Essence Preservative (which, rumor had it, was simply their own urine), Kitnocks selling clothes that wouldn't fit any other species, and of course, numerous merchants selling weapons, along with spare parts for just about any type of starship made in the known galaxy. The booths selling food had the most disgusting array Trag had ever seen—some of it still alive and wriggling.

"Great Mother of the Desert!" Trag muttered. "Doesn't anyone have any fuckin' fruit?"

Then there were the hookers. Their alcove was draped with rich fabrics beyond which he could see the plush cushions that covered the floor. Painted, jeweled, and, for all intents and purposes, naked, these exotic beauties hailed from almost every planet in the quadrant and shook their tits at him as he approached. Most had the usual two, but some had four, and one bizarre-looking woman with big, dark eyes had eight.

"My darling Trag, at last!" the woman said sidling up to him.

Trag grinned. "Hey, Layha. How are you and the girls doing these days?"

"Oh, same as always," Layha said with a wave that made her breasts jiggle enticingly. "We put up with the rest of the damn johns and dream about you."

"You can't fool me," Trag said as he gave her a hug. "You say that to every man who walks by."

"Do not," Layha insisted. "Only you. You just get your sweet little ass in here and give us some joy. Lerotan already paid your shot."

"He paid you?" Trag echoed incredulously. "Wonder why—unless it's his backhanded way of giving me a raise."

"No clue," Layha replied. "He ought to know we never charge you." Taking his hand, she attempted to pull him into the alcove, but Trag resisted.

"Not right now," he said. "What I really want is something to eat. Know where I can get any fresh fruit?"

Layha's eyes narrowed and she faced him with her fists firmly planted on her lush hips. "I've got the hottest ladies in the sector here in my brothel—I've even got an Edraitian now—and all you want is *fruit?* What the hell is wrong with you? Are you sick?"

"No," said Trag. "I'm just not in the mood right now—especially for an Edraitian, or anything else that's blue—blue eyes, blue hair, blue anything!"

Layha grimaced. "Forgot about that little peculiarity of yours." She laid a hand on his forehead but didn't seem reassured. "You still ought to come in and let us take care of you."

"I'm not sick," Trag insisted. "Just hungry!"

"Want some of my milk?" Layha suggested, offering one of her large breasts.

Trag shook his head. He'd tried it before and though he knew it was tasty, he also knew that getting anywhere near her nipples would lead to something else entirely. Her scent was already wafting through his nostrils, and the effect was going straight to his groin. Layha had a Terran girl in her stable too, and her scent was guaranteed to keep Trag hard long enough to do the whole lot of them—something Trag knew from past experience.

Hidar came sauntering up, his antennae puffed out like plumes above his head. "I would like—"

"No Scorillians allowed," Layha said firmly, barring the way as the blue-skinned Edraitian and three other exotic beauties ganged up on Trag and pulled him inside, yanking him down on the cushions so hard it nearly knocked the wind out of him.

"Since you've paid, we're obligated to do *something*," Layha said as she entered, pulling a heavy curtain down behind her, "unless you want a refund."

Trag shook his head, knowing that Layha needed the credits far more than he did. "Keep it."

"Can't do that," Layha said firmly. "Not even as a tip since we haven't done anything. Station regulations and all. How about a massage?"

"That I'll take," said Trag. "But I really don't want anything else."

Layha surveyed him with concern. "Maybe you should have Hidar take a look at you—or one of the doctors here on the station. That's just not normal!"

Trag knew she was right but wasn't about to say so. "No, really, I'm fine," he said as a tall brunette pulled off his cloak and the Edraitian went for his shirt. His exposed skin reacted to the chilly air with a shiver and he sucked in a ragged breath as Layha's warm hands settled on his shoulders, only then realizing how tense and sore he was. Stretching his arms behind him, he felt the joints popping all up and down his spine.

"Don't worry," Layha said. "We'll fix that."

"Okay, but no sex," Trag reiterated. "We're clear on that, right?"

Blowing out an exasperated breath, she agreed, though reluctantly. "Some days it's just no fun being a hooker."

~M~

Trag caught up with Lerotan, Rodan, and Hidar outside a booth selling engine parts. "I hope you paid them really well," he said.

"Enough," Lerotan replied. "Why? How many of them did you do?"

"All of them," Trag said with a grin. "You know how it is. Once one gets a taste, they all join in."

Lerotan's brow rose slightly, displaying his skepticism. "Liar. You haven't been gone long enough for that. You didn't do any of them, did you?"

"Hey, if you don't believe me, then maybe you should quit wasting your money on them and pay me directly."

Hidar made a loud clicking noise with his mandibles.

"Don't start with me, Hidar," Trag warned. "It's not my fault nobody will fuck you. Besides, I could have gotten past them if they hadn't been looking for me. Remind me never to let you guys get ahead of me again." He paused as he realized it might have been worth it if he'd gotten something to eat. "I'm starving! I've got to find something decent to fill my stomach instead of that crap you try to pass off as food."

"It doesn't pay to piss off the chef," Hidar cautioned, his antennae beating the air with fury.

"You call yourself a *chef?*" Trag shot back. "I think you're a—"

"Now, boys," Lerotan said, doing his best to suppress a grin. "You stop that fighting right now!"

Rodan let out a loud guffaw, slapping his leather-clad thigh and setting his chains to rattling.

"Shut up, Rodan," Trag growled. "And yes, *Mother*, we will stop fighting if that asshole would just—"

"Just what?" Hidar said menacingly.

"Let me do the cooking once in a while!" Trag spat out. "Why is that so hard for you?"

"What makes you think you could do any better?" Hidar demanded.

"Great Mother of the Desert!" Trag exclaimed, yanking his hair in frustration. "There's no way I could possibly do any worse!"

"Okay, okay," Lerotan said, raising a hand. "Trag can fix one meal a day. That way he'll always have something he likes."

"Thank you!" Trag said fervently, then added under his breath, "Only taken me three *fuckin'* years…"

Hidar clenched his mandibles so tightly that they should have cracked under the strain, but the Scorillian just walked away, his wings fluttering out behind him the way they always did when he was angry.

"Why, *why* would you ever let some *insect* be the cook on your ship?" Trag said in an aside to Lerotan. "I mean, really, what were you thinking?"

Lerotan shrugged. "What can I say? He likes to cook, and no one else wanted the job. Now that he's got it, it hurts his feelings when you don't like what he fixes—you *know* how touchy he is!—and besides, he makes a good stew."

"If you've got a stomach made out of stone it might be good, but—"

"Calm down, Trag," Lerotan said evenly. "I know we've been stuck on the ship for a long time, so let's just try to make this visit to the station as pleasant as possible."

"Okay, I'll try," said Trag, "but at some point can we please go to a nice, green planet that has fruit?"

"Want to go back to Darconia for a visit?"

Trag let out a sigh. Darconia wasn't exactly verdant,

but it was better than a lot of places they'd been, and Earth was out of the question. "Maybe. You know, I never thought I'd want to go back to a planet where I was a slave, but those are starting to seem like the good old days." The good old days when Kyra was— "No, not necessary," Trag said abruptly. "Any planet with fruit will do."

Lerotan grinned. "I'll ask around."

Trag had ventured on, wandering through the station still looking for fruit, mainly because there wasn't anything else in the whole damn place he wanted to buy. Never one to fritter away his pay, he had money, but despite drinking the occasional bottle of ale, he didn't particularly enjoy getting drunk, gambling appealed to him even less, and the hookers never charged him. The truth was, he was restless and dissatisfied, and, though he hated to admit it, he was also bored out of his mind; he just didn't know what to do about it.

He walked on through the station, taking several turns at random until the next corridor opened up ahead of him and he heard the joyful shouts of children at play. It was cleaner there, more colorfully decorated, and brightly lit. The ceiling had been painted to resemble a blue sky with puffy clouds, and the "sun" hovered off to one side as though just beginning to rise to its zenith. Potted plants, tall trees, and benches were scattered about while jugglers, acrobats, and musicians moved through the throng providing festive entertainment. Food vendors, candy stores, and toy shops were spread out along the circular outer wall. Women sat on the benches chatting while their children played nearby on swings, slides, trampolines, and monkey bars, and a teenage girl was making glowing balloon animals for the little ones to their collective delight. Boys were tossing balls and then tackling whoever caught them as a toddler licked a messy, creamy confection from a cone. The air was filled with sounds of laughter, music, and squeals of glee.

Trag sat down on an empty bench to watch. It was a sight he'd rarely seen before—not as a slave and certainly not since taking the job with Lerotan. Though he didn't know it, the setting was patterned after Earth— many of those present were Terran—but, even so, it reminded him of Zetith. Closing his eyes, he could almost feel the green grass between his toes, smell the sweet scent of flowers in bloom, and feel the warm breeze on his skin. His mind drifted back to a time when he played with Ty in the shade of the trees near his home, each of them wielding a blunt wooden sword and laughing when they scored a hit. His sister was playing with her friends nearby—girls who stole glances at the two boys from time to time but seldom got caught at it.

Trag ventured on to his favorite fantasy, imagining that he and Kyra were in an orchard picking fruit, then making love beneath the trees when their work was done. He didn't indulge in it very often because it always filled him with regret, but just this once he didn't think it was possible to feel any worse.

Lost in thought, Trag didn't notice the child approaching until she tugged at his hand. Upon opening his eyes, he found himself being regarded by a pair of emerald green orbs set in a cherubic face framed with dark, riotous curls.

"Are you okay?" the little girl asked.

"Cara, don't bother the man while he's resting," her

mother called, hurrying over to take her daughter's hand.

"She's not bothering me," Trag said, looking up at the mother, a Terran woman with the same eyes and softly curling hair as her child.

Cara twisted away from her mother and proceeded to climb up in Trag's lap. Her tiny fingers reached out and touched his face. "You're crying," she said as she wiped away tears that had fallen unnoticed. "Why are you so sad?"

"I'm not sad," Trag said, giving her his best grin.

Cara smiled back at him. "That's better," she said approvingly. "You're very pretty when you smile. You shouldn't be sad."

"No, I shouldn't be sad, but sometimes I feel that way. Everyone does."

"I know," Cara said. "I was sad when my kitty died. She had eyes like yours, 'cept they didn't shine like that."

"I don't suppose they did," said Trag.

"I miss my kitty," Cara mourned. "She used to sit beside me and purr all the time."

"I can purr too," Trag said. "Would you like to hear it?"

"Oh, yes," Cara replied.

As Trag began, Cara pressed her ear to his chest and then giggled with delight. "You sound just like her!"

"And you look just like my sister," Trag said wistfully. "She died too."

As she raised her head, Cara's guileless gaze seemed to peer into his soul. "Is that why you were crying?"

"Maybe," he replied. "I'm not sure. She died a long time ago." Trag started to put his arms around the child but paused, glancing up at her mother for permission. There were tears swimming in her eyes as she nodded her reply.

As Trag enfolded the little girl in his arms, he felt a tear run down his cheek.

"You miss your sister, don't you?" Cara's mother said.

"Yes," Trag replied. "But there's so much more, I can't even comprehend it sometimes." He stood up, still holding Cara for a moment before giving her back to her mother.

Trag waved good-bye and turned to go back the way he'd come—back where he figured he was supposed to be, whether he truly belonged there or not.

He hadn't gone far when he heard Cara call out as she ran to him.

Trag stopped and knelt down beside her as she held out her hand. "Here," she said. "Maybe this will make you feel better."

"What is it?"

"It's a strawberry," she giggled. "Don't you *know?*"

Trag shook his head. "They don't have these where I come from."

"They're from Earth. You eat them!"

Trag took a bite and a sweet, delicious juice ran down his chin. "You know something, Cara?" he said, wiping his mouth with the back of his hand. "This is exactly what I needed."

"Feel better now?"

"Yes," he replied. "I believe I do."

But as he walked away he realized that strawberries were just one more reason to want to visit Earth—a planet where he was not welcome.

Chapter 3

RUTGER GREKKOR SAT OPPOSITE THE NEW ORLEON Station commander, studying him closely. The best he could tell, Beontal's personality, like the décor of his sparsely furnished office, had come straight out of a book of regulations. With an expression that was perfectly correct for the situation, he was stiff even when attempting to be friendly; the typical Edraitian snobbishness multiplied in him by a factor of ten. This would not be easy.

"You will not find me tolerant of bribes or any other forms of persuasion," Beontal was saying with a smile that showed every one of his even, white teeth. His shaved head revealed no trace of the red hair of his kind, and he regarded Grekkor with a gaze that seemed capable of seeing past any form of concealment. "Anyone not following the regulations set down by the Council will be expelled from the station. That is my final word on the subject."

"But Commander," Grekkor said smoothly. "Many of the more successful merchants on this station rely on the, shall we say, *byproducts* of the less desirable."

"I don't believe I know what you mean," Beontal said.

"Oh, surely you realize that those who are here to trade in unapproved commodities—"

"By that you mean illegal weapons, drugs, and slaves?" Beontal interjected.

"There are no slaves being bought and sold here!" Grekkor asserted. He took a deep breath and composed his chiseled face into the disarming smile he'd so carefully cultivated, rather than the murderous glare he would have preferred to direct at the station commander.

"So you say," Beontal said with obvious skepticism. "But I have heard otherwise."

"Your sources have been misinformed," Grekkor said. "What I was about to say was that *all* tradesmen benefit from traffic through the station—whether it be within the regulations or not."

"Let me make this perfectly clear," said Beontal, sitting up straighter—if that was possible. He already looked like he had a rod stitched into the back of his uniform. "I will not tolerate illegality—of any kind—on my station."

"And the brothels?" Grekkor said, tilting his head back to look down his nose at Beontal. He had control of himself now. "Will *they* be allowed to continue?"

"They are legal, approved, and follow their specific regulations as set down by the Council. I see no reason to remove them from the station."

"Hmm," said Grekkor. "There are those who would disagree."

Beontal smiled again. "But they are not on the Council, are they?"

"Go by the book, then, do you?"

"Always."

"Well, then," Grekkor said lightly, "it's fortunate that I am not personally involved in any illegal trade—far from it, in fact. I merely wished to point out to you that there are those who will object to being banned from the station."

"I'm sure there will be," Beontal said. "And as the head of the regional Commerce Consortium, I would expect you to sympathize with their situation but not cater to their whims—particularly when those 'whims' are contrary to the law."

Grekkor smiled, but without any pleasure whatsoever. "I do my best to see to it that all commerce is conducted in the proper manner."

"I'm glad we understand one another."

"Oh, to be sure," Grekkor said, rising to his feet. His powerful but elegant form was accentuated rather than concealed by the shimmering cape he wore over his carefully chosen attire. Rich, but not ostentatious. It wouldn't do to appear to possess more wealth than was appropriate for his standing in the Consortium— just enough to look the part, and no more. "I'll pass the results of our meeting along to the members. Perhaps, knowing your stand, those who are in violation of the regulations will leave voluntarily."

"I certainly hope so," said Beontal. "But I wouldn't count on it."

Grekkor's smile turned grim. "Neither would I."

Nor would he count on Beontal remaining alive for long if he maintained this stand. Grekkor had gone up against far more formidable opponents than the stiff-necked Edraitian and emerged victorious. He might even kill Beontal himself… and with a great deal of pleasure.

Windura headed back to her post after lunch still convinced that she'd seen someone like Micayla before; she just couldn't remember where. One thing was certain—she'd never met one in person, and in her ten years on Orleon Station, she'd met beings from a hundred different worlds, though very few that were as attractive as Micayla's kind.

Normally, she wouldn't have had the chance to become well acquainted with a communications officer like Micayla, who was among the station's elite; Windura was just the computer whiz who kept everything running smoothly—most of the time. She and her team were constantly putting out fires and were at virtually everyone's beck and call—with the result that Windura had at least a passing acquaintance with nearly everyone on the station, and that included the hookers. She'd revamped their "john" tracking system more than once, and Windura had to admit, it was pretty effective. Once a man entered their lair his biometric imprint was recorded into the Hooker's Network, and from then on, they knew who to kick out and who to invite back. They might not have actual names listed, but they knew every customer's preferences and habits, as well as his tipping record. The network wasn't advertised—in fact, Windura had been sworn to secrecy—but wrong one hooker, and you've wronged them all.

Micayla's situation intrigued her. Windura couldn't begin to fathom what it would be like to feel as alone in the universe as Micayla must. Her own parents were teachers on Vessonia, and Windura knew exactly where they were and what they were doing, receiving deep space missives from them on a regular basis. She understood what it meant to be the only one of her kind on the station, but at least she knew what "kind" she was.

Sitting down at her desk, she switched on the Orleon music loop's rock station and logged on to her computer.

After an hour's fruitless search of the standard database, she was about to give up when she decided to try a different tactic. Logging into the Hooker's Network with the password Layha had given her, along with the retinal scan the system required, she simply typed in the word "fangs."

Holograms of some of the fiercest-looking creatures she'd ever seen popped up, some of which had actually passed through Orleon, but one in particular stood out from the rest. Yes, he was the one she remembered seeing before—probably during a previous check of the system. Male, of course, but his features were similar to Micayla's and he was every bit as handsome as she was beautiful, the orange streak in his black hair only adding to his attractiveness. The description of his sexual abilities was remarkable to the point of sounding like fiction—body fluids that could chemically trigger orgasms? That couldn't be true! But the hookers were known for their strict adherence to the facts. His performance and genitalia were second to none and he wasn't the kind to get too rough, but he had one other interesting talent: he could purr.

A song began playing just then, one performed by a band Windura had never seen but had heard about. The lead singer was supposed to be the sexiest thing to hit the galactic music scene in a hundred years, one of a lost race of feline humanoids…

Switching to the entertainment database, Windura finally found what she was looking for. Why it wasn't in the standard files was a mystery, but there he was, one of the few survivors of the destruction of the planet Zetith. According to a footnote, there were only six adult males known to exist. Any other remnants of that civilization had been tracked down and presumably killed by Nedwut bounty hunters. Though some had produced offspring with Terran mates, there was no mention of any female survivors; apparently none had ever been found—until now.

—⁓—

Lerotan viewed the list of new station regulations with distaste. "We'll have to leave soon," he told Rodan. "According to this, we can resupply and buy anything we like on Orleon, but we can't sell any of our weapons."

"Since when has that ever stopped you?" Rodan countered.

"Since now," Lerotan replied tersely. "It's not worth the trouble. Pick up what we need and let the rest of the crew know we'll be leaving again in a couple of hours. If anyone wants to buy arms, they'll just have to buy them from me somewhere else."

"You aren't going soft, are you?"

"No, just getting older and smarter," Lerotan replied. "And besides, it's a big galaxy. There are plenty of other places we can operate without being hassled."

—⁓—

Micayla's shift had been busy, but not busy enough to divert her thoughts completely. During the occasional lulls, she asked Dana enough questions to irritate the most obliging person imaginable—but fortunately, Dana was just such a person. She filled Micayla in on the entire exchange, from the man's eye color to the loss of his sister, and by the time Micayla relinquished her post to Xantric, she was ready to go charging down to sections twenty-eight and nine alone, in spite of Windura's dire warnings.

"She's going hunk hunting," Dana said when Xantric remarked on her haste. "I've seen the guy, and trust me, I'd be running out of here too."

Xantric's bald pate gleamed as she shook her head at Micayla. "Scott will be *so* disappointed if you find someone else."

"Something tells me he'll get over it," Micayla said.

"I don't know," Xantric said. "To hear him talk, the two of you are already an item." She took in Micayla's attire with a swift, assessing glance. "Not going after hunks dressed like that, are you?"

"Why—what's wrong with my uniform?" she asked, making a quick check for tea stains.

Xantric rubbed the horn at the end of her rhinoceros-like snout contemplatively. "Don't you have anything prettier to wear?"

"No," Micayla replied, "at least not what you'd call pretty." Micayla rarely wore anything aside from her uniform, and even when she did, it was certainly nothing like the colorful, voluminous dresses and gaudy earrings that Xantric favored.

"Just a suggestion," Xantric said kindly. "I could loan you something if you like."

Since Xantric was well over two meters in height with a much broader build, Micayla would have been swallowed up in one of her dresses.

"I've got a dress that would look fabulous on you," Dana said. "I could run and get it real quick."

Micayla was about to refuse both offers when Windura interrupted them.

"No time for that," Windura said as she approached. "We really need to get going." The urgency in her voice and the gleam of excitement in her eyes spoke volumes.

"You found something?"

"You bet I did," Windura replied. "Something *very* interesting."

"Like what?" Dana asked.

"I'd rather not say until I'm sure," Windura said evasively.

"Oh, come on, don't keep us in suspense," Dana urged. "Did you at least find out his name?"

"No," Windura replied. "But—"

"Never mind that," Xantric interjected. "And never mind changing clothes," she said to Micayla, giving her a push toward the door. "Get going, girl!"

Micayla had a million questions buzzing through her head as they hurried along the concourse, but one of them stood firmly in the forefront.

"Did you find out what I—?"

Windura put a finger to her lips and shook her head. "I'll explain in a minute."

The reason for secrecy wasn't clear, but Micayla somehow managed to hold her tongue until they reached the lift, which was also crowded with various station residents. When they finally got off the lift, the corridor ahead was chilly and dimly lit and their footsteps echoed eerily off the dull grey walls. "I've never been on Level One before," she said. "It's kinda creepy, isn't it?"

"Yes, but it's the best way to get to section twenty-nine," Windura assured her. "Much safer than the main commerce deck."

"Can we talk now?"

Windura nodded. "I didn't want anyone to overhear us."

"Why not?"

"Remember what you said about maybe being the kind of species that was hunted down and shot on sight?"

"Yes, but surely you don't think…"

"Listen, if you're what I think you are, that possibility definitely exists, and I'd rather no one else knew about it until we're sure."

Micayla's hands turned to ice. "So I really *am* some sort of evil cat?"

"Probably not, but apparently someone thinks you are. We need to get Layha to run a scan on you to see if you match up."

Micayla's disappointment was profound. "You mean we're not going looking for the man in the park? And who is Layha anyway?"

Windura grinned. "She's a hooker—a *Delfian* hooker."

Micayla blinked hard. She'd heard enough about Delfians to know she didn't want to meet one—particularly a hooker who probably didn't wear very much.

"If I'm right—and I'm pretty sure I am," Windura continued, "we'll have the answer to all of your questions pretty soon. Ever hear of a rock band called Princes & Slaves?"

"Should I have?"

"Maybe not," Windura admitted. "They're very popular in the Andromeda quadrant. Some in the Terran quadrant have heard of them, and since we're on the border between the two, I've heard their music and know a bit about them, but I'd never looked up a picture until now."

"And this is important because…?"

"The lead singer of Princes & Slaves is a guy named Tycharian Vladatonsk," Windura replied. "Women all over the quadrant are hot after his ass. But so is someone else. Seems their species was nearly exterminated—about the same time you lost your family—and there are only a handful of them left. Some Nedwuts tried to kill him during a performance a few weeks ago, but his fans mobbed them and tore them to pieces."

"Dedicated fans," Micayla remarked. "But I still don't understand—"

"The connection?" Windura said. "The connection is that he's got the same pointed ears, fangs, and feline eyes that you have—and the curly hair. Granted, his coloring is different, but I think you're the same species."

Micayla felt her heart try to leap out of her chest, but she somehow managed to keep walking.

"There was another one too, but he was only in the hooker's database," Windura went on, directing a triumphant glance at Micayla. "Long black hair and wears a cloak. Sound like someone you might have seen?"

The implication struck Micayla dumb for a moment. "Did he—does he have an orange streak in his hair?" she asked, surprised at how faint her own voice sounded.

Windura nodded. "Yes, he does, and, like I said, I knew there was something familiar about you, I just couldn't place it. I must have seen him before when I'd run a check of the network."

"So what do we have to do?"

"Layha will run a scan on you to see if there's a biometric match in her system. I'm willing to bet there is—and if he's still here on the station she just might know where to find him."

———∿∿∿———

Grekkor was beyond furious. He was livid. "But do you mean to tell me, Tilat, that even after I warned you to keep a low profile, you went and spouted off to the section chief that you were selling Friotian cocaine?"

The sniveling Kitnock spread his thin, bony arms in protest. "He asked to buy some! We've never been the subject of any stings on this station. How was I to know?"

"If you had listened to me, you would have," Grekkor seethed. "Now I'll have to go see that cursed commander again and explain that you are a stupid fool and thought that the man was joking with you."

"But—"

"And then you will leave this station and never return. Do you understand?"

Tilat was taller than Grekkor by about ten centimeters, but Grekkor was powerfully built and probably outweighed him by half, and his thug was even bigger. Dolurp was a big, hairy, ape-like humanoid from Herpatron who, rumor had it, enjoyed breaking fingers—especially those of Kitnocks; he liked the sound they made when they snapped.

Whirling away as though he could no longer stand the sight of the Kitnock, Grekkor stormed off down the narrow corridor, his cape billowing out behind him and Dolurp at his heels.

He hadn't gone far when he saw two females approaching, both in the uniform of station staff. He automatically began to smile, but it was wiped from his face as he recognized one of them. Not her, specifically, but her kind.

As they passed, his icy blue eyes met the darkly glowing feline orbs of the woman in question. Hatred for her and all her kind blazed up in him. However, he managed to hold his comment until they passed.

"As if this day hadn't gone badly enough," he growled. "I thought we'd killed all those cats."

"Want me to go get her?" Dolurp inquired, plainly itching for some action.

"Don't bother," he said, tossing a glance over his shoulder. "Without one of their males, the females can't repro—" He broke off as he saw that the woman had turned and was staring after him. "—duce."

―∾∾―

"Whoa, shit!" Windura exclaimed as the two men began to race toward them. "We're in trouble now!"

Micayla had been on the alert from the moment that venomous gaze had locked onto hers and, pivoting on one foot, she snatched Windura's hand and sped off down the passageway, dragging Windura behind her.

"'Stay away from sections twenty-eight and twenty-nine,'" Micayla quoted as she ran. "Why the hell don't you pay attention to your own advice?"

"Trust me, he doesn't belong here either," Windura gasped. "I know who he is."

"Tell me later," Micayla said, picking up speed. Rounding a corner, she almost ran into a load lifter carrying three huge barrels.

"No shooting!" the Norludian driver exclaimed, waving his sucker-tipped fingers in alarm.

"We don't have weapons!" Micayla shouted as she passed. A pulse beam struck the barrels and they burst open, flooding the corridor. "But I guess *they* do," she added.

"I'll bet they have friends around to head us off," Windura said darkly. "He's a very powerful man. We've got to get to another level. Someplace where there are more people."

They heard the sounds of a crash and a scuffle behind them. Apparently the bad guys had slipped on whatever the Norludian had in the barrel. Micayla could hear shouted curses and insults. "Too bad they didn't break their necks," she muttered. "There's a lift up ahead."

"How the hell do you know?" Windura demanded.

"Remember what I told you before about knowing where everything is?"

"Yeah, right. I remember now. Oh, joy."

"You don't sound very happy about it."

"Hey, I thought you were crazy at the time," Windura explained. "Any premonitions that we get out of this alive?"

"Uh, no. Not really."

"Make one up then."

They reached the lift, Windura pounding on the control buttons and cursing it for being so slow. When the lift finally jolted to a halt, the doors slid open with a hiss to reveal two huge Darconians. "I *told* you we exceeded the weight limit," one of them said. "You never listen to me."

"Aw, shut up," the other said as the dinosaur-like creatures lumbered out of the lift with their tails swinging behind them.

Micayla and Windura dove into the lift and they both shouted out, "Level Ten!" The doors remained open for what seemed like an eternity before finally closing just as their pursuers came into view.

"Shit!" Windura exclaimed. "This was a bad idea. They'll know what level we've gone to. All they have to do is look at the console!"

Fortunately, the lift stopped on Level Five to allow three Drells to get on before continuing on to Level Ten uninterrupted. Being Drells, they insisted on getting off first when the ladies tried to push past them. Shuffling slowly with their all-concealing locks dragging along the floor, Micayla was about to rip their hair out in frustration before they finally got out of the way. "Rude little rats, aren't they?" she observed.

"Can't stand them," Windura agreed. Glancing around, she read: "Level Ten, section thirty. Great. This is one of the docking rings. The station dead-ends here. Sections twenty-eight and twenty-nine are that way," she said, pointing to the right. "Come on," she said, motioning for Micayla to follow. "We've got to keep moving. This is where we were headed to start with, so maybe we'll be safe. Lots of people here."

"What about trying to find a guard?"

"Against those two? You don't know who we're up against, do you?"

Micayla shook her head.

"That was Rutger Grekkor," Windura said. "He's the head of the Commerce Consortium—has an interest in all sorts of things: jewelry, building materials, pharmaceuticals, food processing, you name it. His official record is clean, but rumor has it that he heads up the biggest ring of drug smugglers in the galaxy."

"Oh, great," Micayla groaned. "He's probably got

henchmen all over this station. And did you hear what he said?"

"Yeah, I heard. You are in deep shit, my friend."

"Well, what about you? You heard what he said too. You're a witness. He said he had 'killed all those cats.' You realize what that means, don't you? He killed off everyone on my planet!"

"Looks like I'm in deep, deep shit right along with you."

Micayla took a hasty breath. "I know next to no one on this station and certainly nobody who works down here. Is there anyone you can trust?"

Windura looked uncomfortable. "Well, there's you... and the, um, hookers."

"Well, that's just great," Micayla said with disgust. "You know practically everyone and the hookers are the only ones you trust?"

"And you," Windura reminded her. "I trust you. You're too new here to be corrupted."

"And you, who knows everyone, *aren't* corrupt?"

Windura shrugged. "What can I say? I'm a computer geek. I can't be corrupted because I don't have any vices."

"No addiction to drugs, sex, or gambling?"

Windura shook her head.

"Not even food or alcohol?"

"Well, I *do* have to eat, but—"

"Never been bribed to fix a computer with expensive jewelry or sexual favors?"

"Sexual favors? Come on, Micayla! Who on this entire station would *anyone* want to have sex with? The Norludians? I'm the only Vessonian that I know of, and even if there were others… well, maybe I'm just too choosy—I mean, the Terrans aren't bad looking as a species, but most of the single ones on the station seem kinda skuzzy, except maybe that one guy you work with, but—"

"Oh, crap!"

"What?"

"Look," Micayla said, pointing.

Shouldering his way through the crowd ahead of them was Rutger Grekkor, his shining blond hair in sharp contrast with the unkempt locks of those surrounding him.

"How the hell did he do that?" Micayla demanded as the two women turned tail and started running again, which was difficult because the place was crowded with some of the most disreputable-looking creatures Micayla had ever seen in her life. Windura hadn't been kidding about it being a good place to avoid.

"God only knows," Windura replied as she pushed past a smelly Cylopean.

"Did you see that gorilla with him?"

"You mean the Herpatronian?"

"Yeah, I guess." Micayla had never heard of the planet or the species and was beginning to wish she didn't know about them now.

"Didn't see him."

Micayla stopped short. "I do. There he is. Ahead of us."

"No, wait, there's a guard," Windura said. "Maybe—"

"Yes, I see him," Micayla said with a sinking feeling, "but something tells me he's not on our side." The tall, muscular Terran looked, if anything, even more forbidding than the gorilla. "Commander Beontal really has his work cut out for him, doesn't he?"

"You could say that," Grekkor said in Micayla's ear as she felt his arm grip her around the waist. The guard and the gorilla began to close in on them from the only other way out. "Don't make a sound or your friend dies."

Chapter 4

"WHAT ARE YOU DOING?" MICAYLA DEMANDED AS THE two women were wrestled back toward the docking ring. "Where are you taking us?"

"I should have thought that was perfectly obvious," Grekkor said smoothly. "The slavers will soon be banned from this station—at least temporarily—but one of their ships is still docked here. You, my dears, are about to become their passengers."

"You'll never get away with this," Windura growled, struggling in the hold of Grekkor's gorilla.

"I'd rather die than be anyone's slave," Micayla said with an angry glare.

"That is easily arranged," Grekkor said. "No trouble at all, really. In fact, I believe I would enjoy watching you die. You are an abomination to this galaxy and should not be allowed to exist."

"And just what makes me such an abomination?" Micayla demanded.

Hatred flashed in his eyes, but he managed to control it enough to continue. "Your males," he spat out. "They are the most disgusting displays of carnal lust ever conceived."

"What's the matter?" Micayla taunted. "Have they got bigger balls than you?"

"They do *not*," Grekkor said, his voice cutting through her like a shard of ice. "For your information, I killed the one my wife consorted with. Slit his throat while she watched—and do you know what she did then?"

"Cut *your* balls off?" Micayla suggested sweetly. "It's what I would have done."

"Boy, you sure know how to placate the enemy, don't you?" Windura muttered.

"No!" Grekkor snarled. "She escaped from me and took the first ship she could find to go back to that cursed planet for another one!"

"Not very particular, was she?" Micayla said, adding, "But then, she did marry *you.*"

Grekkor seemed to ignore this jibe, continuing on as though Micayla hadn't spoken, his eyes taking on a maniacal gleam. "I knew then that they all had to die. Other males couldn't compete. Theirs was a newly discovered world—no more than a few years on the star charts and relatively unknown—backward, too. Not possessing the capability for interstellar travel if it hadn't been handed to them. I had to act quickly, and I did. It was not difficult to recruit an army against them. They were a threat to men of every mammalian species."

"And to the drug trade," Windura said getting into the spirit. "I know some women in the brothels. You're talking about Zetithians, aren't you? Their penile secretions and semen act like drugs, triggering orgasms and euphoria in females. Let them spread across the galaxy and they could easily eliminate half of your drug sales— maybe even some of the legal ones—and even more if it affected males."

Sneering at the Vessonian woman, Grekkor got right in her face and spoke very deliberately, enunciating each emphatic word. "I do not sell illegal drugs."

"No, you probably just take your cut of the profits from all of those who do," Windura countered.

"You know nothing!"

"Hey, if I'm going to die or become a slave, it doesn't matter what I know, does it?"

Micayla felt the man holding her shift slightly and waited for the opportunity. If one of them could escape and sound the alarm...

"You there!" the Norludian shouted as he rounded the corner. "No shooting in the station! You spilled an entire shipment of Essence Preservative! You will have to pay for that!"

"Now!" Micayla shouted, stomping down hard on the Terran guard's foot as she elbowed him in the throat. Spinning on one foot, she slammed the other foot upside the Herpatronian's head and then kicked Grekkor in the groin.

"Come on!" Micayla yelled as she took off running.

"Not that way!" Windura protested. "It just circles around. All they have to do is wait for us."

They both began to stagger as a strong vibration hummed through the ring. "What's that?"

"A ship firing up."

"Where?"

"There," Windura pointed as they raced toward the hatch.

Micayla hammered on the control panel, pushing every button there was. Suddenly, the hatch rolled back with a screech and they both jumped into the airlock. "This could be a very bad place in a minute when that ship leaves," she said as the hatch closed behind them.

"There's a force field on the airlock," Windura said, shaking her head. "We won't get sucked into space. If we're lucky, they'll think we've kept on running and might not find us for a while. That Norludian was pretty pissed too," she added before beginning to laugh uncontrollably.

"What's so damn funny?" Micayla demanded.

"That's what Essence Preservative is," she gasped as she wiped away tears of mirth. "It's their piss. They've probably been collecting that for months!"

Micayla couldn't help but laugh at the thought of their captors having slipped in a lake of urine. "I thought those guys smelled weird."

"They sure did," Windura agreed. "By the way, where the hell did you learn to do all of that self-defense stuff?"

"Martial arts training, courtesy of my stepmom," Micayla replied. "She thought it would help keep me safe—something she promised my real mother."

"Well, you're damn good at it," Windura said with unconcealed admiration. "Ever have to use it before?"

"Just on a few amorous boys from time to time. After a while, they decided it might be best to leave me alone."

"Did they teach you to antagonize the enemy like that?"

"Throws them off balance sometimes," Micayla said with a nod. "Other times it just makes things worse. I don't know—"

"Holy shit," Windura whispered as she peeked through the porthole. "They're coming this way!"

Micayla didn't hesitate and began pounding on the ship's hatch with all her might.

Just as Grekkor's face appeared in the porthole, the hatch opened with a hiss and they both tumbled inside to land at the feet of a male Scorillian.

"Close the goddamn hatch, Hidar!" someone called out from beyond the huge insect. "What are you trying to do—get us all killed?"

"But what will we do with these?" the Scorillian asked.

"These, what?" the other man demanded, coming closer.

Micayla looked up into the flashing black eyes of a tall, dark-haired Terran with a Ralayan rune tattooed above his left eye. "Well, would you look at what the bug let in," he said with a slow smile. "This trip might have been worth something after all."

Micayla's first thought was that, in spite of their escape, they'd managed to end up on the slave ship. "We are *not* slaves!" she said indignantly.

The man laughed. "Nobody said you were." The ship shuddered as it broke free of the force field and slowly rotated away from the dock. "Seems arms dealers are no longer welcome at Orleon, so we're heading back into the Andromeda quadrant. Hope you girls remembered to bring along your spare undies."

"Can I fuck them?" the Scorillian asked eagerly. "They are stowaways and must pay for their passage. I'm allowed to fuck stowaways, right?"

Micayla felt all the blood drain out of her face as she looked up at the tall, green Scorillian who was now eagerly rubbing his barbed forearms together like a gigantic praying mantis.

"Naw, we'll let Trag fuck them," the tattooed man said. "We'll have less trouble with them that way."

Micayla felt her feeling of faintness give way to nausea. She had no idea who or what "Trag" was, but she had no intention of letting him anywhere near her. "I don't intend to let anyone fuck me."

"We'll see about that," he said as his long, leonine tail snaked out from beneath his robes.

"He can fuck with his dick *and* his tail," the Scorillian cackled with apparent delight. "Both of you at the same time."

"Damn!" Windura said, speaking up for the first time. "I've heard about you. Lerotan Kanotay, right?"

"You have the advantage over me," the Terran said. "You are…?"

"Windura Rhidal," she replied. "Orleon's computer specialist."

"I see," he said with a raised brow. "And just *where* did you hear about me?"

"From the hookers," Windura said. "You're a Terran/ Xuerreldian cross, aren't you?"

"And if I am?" he said ominously.

"Nothing," Windura muttered, looking away quickly. "Just wanted to verify that."

Lerotan came closer, peering down at the two women sprawled on the floor of his ship. "What about you? Vessonian?"

Windura nodded. "And this is Micayla Johnson," she added, gesturing toward her companion. "She's the new communications officer."

"Officer?" Lerotan echoed. "Does that mean I should give up my quarters for her?"

The Scorillian cackled again. "Let me have them, Captain! I will keep them in my quarters. I will take good care of them. I need some females."

"Shut up, Hidar," Lerotan said absently. "I wouldn't give them to you even if they *were* slaves."

Micayla was momentarily heartened by this but

paled again at the thought of being at the mercy of a male with two cocks, which would undoubtedly double her displeasure.

"Why did you jump on my ship if you both work on the station?" Lerotan asked.

"I—I'd rather not say just yet," Windura replied. "Not until I'm sure whose side you'd be on."

"Fair enough," Lerotan said with a shrug. "But I warn you, my men are, shall we say, a bit rough."

"Meaning we should stick with you instead of the crew?"

"Exactly," Lerotan said. Holding out a hand, he took Windura's and pulled her to her feet. When he reached down to do the same for Micayla, he froze. "Who did you say this was?"

"Micayla Johnson," Windura repeated. "She's from Earth, but I'm pretty sure she's—"

"Zetithian," Lerotan whispered as Micayla rose from the floor.

"You know about them?" Windura asked with surprise.

"You could say that," Lerotan replied. "Did you know there's a bounty on them? The Nedwuts are collecting five million credits for each male."

"And—and the females?" Windura stammered.

Lerotan grinned. "They're worth nothing to anyone but a male Zetithian."

Windura breathed a sigh of relief. "Good. Then you won't turn us in."

"You'd make good bait for a male, though," Lerotan mused, looking Micayla up and down. "I could catch plenty of them with a beautiful specimen like you. One whiff of your desire and they'd come running. I could make millions."

Micayla swallowed hard as she regarded him. "I don't think I'd be any help to you in that respect."

"No?" Lerotan said. "You might be surprised." Turning to the Scorillian, he said, "Hey, Hidar, do me a favor and go get Trag."

Hidar's mandibles clicked sharply as though he resented being used as a messenger boy, but he went anyway, returning a few moments later, followed by a man wrapped in a heavy cloak. His long black hair hung to his waist and he was *not* happy.

"Couldn't you at least let me get the course set before sending Hidar to drag me off?" he complained. "What the devil do you want?"

"Just wanted you to see this," Lerotan said, stepping aside. "What do you think?"

Micayla's reaction was immediate and instinctive. Drawing back with a snarl, she let out a loud hiss.

The one called Trag stared at her in dismay. "Great Mother of the Desert!" he exclaimed. "That's just fuckin' great, Leroy. You finally find me a Zetithian girl and she turns out to be a hissing, spitting bitch!"

Chapter 5

MICAYLA WAS MORTIFIED. IN ALL HER BORN DAYS she'd never hissed at anyone, and now, here she was, snarling at a complete stranger on sight—and to make matters worse, it was *him!* Windura was looking at her as though she might bite too.

"Sorry," she muttered. "Don't know why I did that." She stole another glance at Trag and fought the urge to hiss again.

"Trag, this lovely young lady is Micayla Johnson," Lerotan said with a chuckle. "Should have known it wouldn't be that simple."

"No shit," Trag said. "I never expected it to be easy, but—"

"And this is Tragonathon Vladatonsk," Lerotan said to Micayla.

This information didn't immediately register with Micayla, but it did with Windura. "No kidding?" she squealed. "Tycharian's brother?"

"In the flesh," Lerotan replied.

"Wow!" Windura began to say something else but was cut off by Trag.

"Don't *do* that!" Trag exclaimed, giving his hair a yank. "I'm not just his brother. I'm a person too, you know!"

"Now, Trag," Lerotan soothed. "We all know that— but she *did* ask. No need for you to get so upset."

Trag shot a glowering look at Lerotan and growled. "I'm not upset, I'm just sick to death of being referred to as Old Blue Eyes's brother all the time!"

"Did I call you that?" Lerotan chided.

"Well, no, but—"

"I don't think you need to worry about standing in your brother's shadow," Windura said. "From what I've heard, you've got a few claims to fame of your own."

"Layha been talking to you?" Trag said with a wince.

"In a manner of speaking," Windura replied, licking her lips. "I heard it all."

Trag groaned and tugged his hair again, this time spearing his fingers through it near the scalp as though trying to pull it out by the roots. Micayla wondered how he managed to keep from going bald.

Lerotan shook his head sadly. "The guy's got a famous brother, a dick that's the most lethal weapon for light-years around, he's piloting a starship after being a slave for twenty years, and he's *still* not happy." Throwing up his hands in a gesture of futility, he added, "I don't know what to do with him."

"Maybe he just needs to find the right girl," Windura suggested. "I'd be happy to audition."

Micayla whipped around to glare at her friend. Windura, who claimed to have no interest in any of the men stationed on Orleon, was now coming on to the one man Micayla had been anxious to meet. Granted, she'd hissed at him, but even so, it showed a decided lack of camaraderie.

Trag dropped his head and let out a sob of frustration. "I get that wherever I go, too," he muttered.

"Sorry," Windura said with a shrug. "I figured it wouldn't hurt to try."

Trag combed his hair back with his fingers but didn't pull on it this time. "I'm sorry too. There was a time when I'd have given anything to hear a woman say that, but now—"

"He's holding out for a nice Zetithian girl," Lerotan explained.

Trag sighed deeply. "Yeah, and what's the first thing she does? She hisses at me. Guess I'll just go back and fly the fuckin' ship." With that parting shot, he turned on his heel and left.

Micayla stared at his retreating figure, again feeling an overpowering urge to run after him, but her feet refused to move. All she could think was *Oh, my God! It's him, and I freakin' hissed at him!*

"Ladies," Lerotan said with a sweeping gesture. "Allow me to escort you to the bridge."

"Blew that one, didn't you?" Windura observed dryly as they followed Lerotan down the passageway.

Micayla's gaze was focused on Lerotan's tail, which danced behind him as though luring them into a trap. Hidar's lurking presence intensified the feeling. "I didn't *mean* to hiss at him," she protested. "It just… popped out."

"You could have at least *talked* to him," Windura went on. "I mean, he's one of your own people—not to mention the handsomest man I've ever seen in my life. Come on, girl! Get a grip!"

"It's been a very odd day." Micayla sighed. "I find out what I am, find a man who's like me, and also find out who tried to exterminate my people. How am I supposed to act?"

"Uh, what was that last bit?" Lerotan inquired, pausing to look back at them.

"You mean the part about the exterminator?"

"Yeah," he replied. "That part. Anyone we know?"

Windura nodded. "You've probably heard of him," she replied. "Name's Rutger Grekkor—a Terran, I think."

"You mean that big, blond sonofabitch who runs the Commerce Consortium?"

"I take it you don't care for him either," Micayla observed.

"You could say that," Lerotan agreed. "I've had run-ins with him before—and yes, he's Terran. He's also a pompous asshole who has amassed way too much money for what he does for a living, and he's not very kind to his competition."

"No shit," Windura said. "We just heard him admit to having killed everyone on Zetith because his wife had a Zetithian lover. Oh, and he killed the lover too."

"That doesn't surprise me a bit," Lerotan said. "What does surprise me is that he isn't out there boasting about it. After all, destroying an entire world is quite a feat."

"Wait a minute," Micayla interrupted. "Destroyed? You mean the *whole planet?*"

Lerotan nodded. "A Nedwut ship somehow managed to redirect an asteroid into Zetith's orbit, causing it to explode—or so I've heard."

Micayla's chest felt as though that same asteroid had just crashed into it. It was one thing to not know where you came from, but to suddenly discover that it no longer existed was shocking. "It can't be!" she protested.

Lerotan's smile was grim. "Yes, it can. It was assumed to be a natural occurrence until Cat had a vision."

"Vision?" Micayla echoed. "And who is Cat?"

"Cat's another survivor. He had a vision—Zetithians are known to do that—which showed that the Nedwuts were responsible. No one ever doubted him, but how those thugs ever had the know-how or the money to pull off something like that has always been something of a mystery. Now we know. Grekkor's probably made enough money selling illegal drugs to finance the whole thing."

"He wouldn't admit to that," Micayla pointed out.

"No, he wouldn't," Windura agreed. "Odd that he'd admit to genocide but not drug dealing. Go figure."

Lerotan shrugged. "Everyone has their standards, I suppose."

"That's a laugh," Windura said. "Everyone knows he's involved in the drug trade somehow, but it really doesn't matter what else he does; blowing up a planet has got to be against the law."

"You'd think so, wouldn't you?" Lerotan agreed. "Trouble is, with Zetith gone, I'm not sure who would prosecute him."

"And we have no proof other than what he told us," Micayla pointed out. "We might not be considered adequate witnesses against someone like that. I mean, it's his word against ours."

"And if we were dead or sold as slaves..." Windura added.

"Well, we'll try not to let that happen," Lerotan said. "They'll have to catch us first."

"Fast ship?" Micayla said hopefully, glancing about her. It didn't look like much, but sometimes it was hard to tell from the inside.

"Faster than anything he's got, I can promise you that," Lerotan replied. "Better weapons, too."

"So they are to remain on board?" Hidar asked expectantly.

"Yes," Lerotan said firmly. "Do you really think I could just toss one of the last remaining Zetithians out on her ear? Jack would make me miserable for the rest of my life!"

"I appreciate that," Micayla said. "But who is Jack?"

"Captain Jack—actually *Jacinth*—Tshevnoe," Lerotan replied, "but don't call her that to her face. She's a trader—in legal goods, by the way—and she's married to a Zetithian she calls Cat—the one who had the vision. Anyway, they travel with Leo, another Zetithian, and his wife, Tisana. Tisana is a witch who can communicate with animals and set you on fire with a glance, but she's a good witch. Jack, on the other hand, is, well…" Lerotan paused as though at a loss for words. "You'd have to meet her to understand. And speaking of Jack, we'd better let her know we found you. She'll be delighted to hear the news."

As they arrived on the bridge, Hidar began clicking his mandibles again, drawing Micayla's attention. His antennae were rubbing together in an anticipatory manner that sent shivers down her spine.

"So no, you do *not* get to fuck the stowaways, Hidar," Lerotan said. "You can bunk with Rodan and the ladies will share your quarters."

Micayla wasn't sure she wanted to use a room so recently vacated by an insect but decided it might be preferable when a large, odoriferous male of unknown origin approached, apparently having heard at least some of the conversation.

"I have to share quarters with Hidar?" he demanded. "No fuckin' way! I'd rather sleep with a—"

Lerotan's pointed look cut him off. "That's enough, Rodan," he said. "It's only temporary."

Rodan managed a weak smile. "Sorry. Oh, and just so you know, we're being hailed."

Lerotan rolled his eyes. "Let me guess. Rutger Grekkor?"

"Well, no," Rodan admitted. "Just someone from the station who wants to know if we took on any, uh, passengers," he added with an eye toward the ladies.

"I'll talk to them," Lerotan said. "You two stay where you are and keep quiet."

Micayla didn't need the warning. By this time she was barely able to think, let alone talk. Her planet of origin was called Zetith, and it wasn't just remote, it no longer existed. But having visions was normal. Then there was Trag. Dana hadn't been kidding when she said he was handsome—though in her eyes, he went far beyond that. He was absolutely gorgeous and to top it off, she'd made him mad right off the bat. All of this, coming on the heels of the discovery that the demise of her people had been instigated by one man—one incredibly ruthless man who would now be hunting her down with the same cold-blooded vengeance that had destroyed an entire planet—rendered her speechless.

As Lerotan took his seat in the captain's chair, Micayla couldn't help but be grateful for the miracle that they had somehow managed to board the right ship. She wondered if Trag would see it the same way. The rest of the crew appeared to be every bit as rough as Lerotan said, but at least Lerotan seemed trustworthy.

He handled the exchange with the station official with casual indifference and if Micayla hadn't known better she'd have believed she wasn't on board either.

The new station commander might be trustworthy too, but even admitting they were on Lerotan's ship—which Grekkor had to have realized they were—was risky unless Beontal was told directly. There was a chance that Lerotan's ship hadn't been the only one leaving port at that time, but even so, Grekkor had known what docking bay they'd disappeared into. What story had he told? What lies about them?

This question was soon answered. "They are wanted for questioning in the death of a Norludian merchant," the station official said sternly.

Micayla nearly screamed out a protest but somehow managed to keep her outburst to a hoarse whisper. "What?"

Windura covered her hand and gave it a meaningful squeeze. Lerotan's reply was as smooth as they could have hoped—the proper mix of regret and concern, but not changing his story one iota in light of this new information.

Signing off, Lerotan turned to them. "Okay, then. I've lied for you. Now would you mind telling me the whole story?"

"They must have killed that Norludian," Windura began. "I never heard a shot, but—"

"We had no weapons," Micayla said bitterly. "How could *anyone* believe such an accusation?"

Lerotan gave Windura a knowing look. "Not been on Orleon for very long, has she?"

"No, she hasn't," Windura replied, "but neither has Commander Beontal. He's here to put an end to the corruption, but what he might not know is that it goes all the way to the top—or at least it did until he took over. It wouldn't surprise me if he ended up dead too."

"So no one on the whole station will believe we didn't kill that Norludian?" Micayla gasped.

"Probably not," Windura said. "Especially if Grekkor tells them to believe otherwise."

Micayla slumped back against the bulkhead and closed her eyes. She could have taken a nice, cushy job at Earth's diplomatic station on Velasia, but instead she had opted for Orleon because it sounded more challenging. Knowing what she knew now, she'd have given a lot for a nice, boring post on Io. "Why on Earth didn't I listen to my mother?"

Trag went back to the pilot's console on the far side of the dimly lit bridge. Sitting in the small alcove with his back to the others, he could almost pretend he was flying alone through space; master of his own destiny with the whole galaxy to explore and no one's orders to follow but his own. He had other dreams too, and though he might have told himself he wasn't interested, he'd also spent a fair amount of time imagining what it would be like to meet up with a Zetithian girl—one he really could fall in love with. Someone who could make him forget Kyra.

They were typically idle daydreams of rescuing damsels in distress, or even a chance meeting in a bar on some backwoods planet, but he'd never imagined anything comparable to actually meeting Micayla for the first time. She'd actually hissed at him! He'd never heard of such a thing, though, granted, he'd been raised offworld and wasn't well-versed in traditional Zetithian culture, let alone the courtship rituals. Judging from Micayla's apparent age, neither was she; she had to have been a baby when Zetith was destroyed. He had all kinds of questions about her—which was understandable—but he found it difficult to even consider discussing past histories with a girl who obviously couldn't stand the sight of him. He tried to tell himself it didn't matter—he was only feigning interest in finding a mate, anyway—but he was still affected by it. Most of the time he had women crawling all over him, and though there was the occasional woman who wasn't smitten with him on sight, they certainly didn't spit at him like an angry cat.

Still, he found it intriguing that she would respond to him in that manner. She'd apologized immediately, seeming to be as shocked by her reaction as the others had been—which led him to believe that it wasn't typical behavior for her—but why had she done it?

His uncle could have told him if he'd still been alive; as captain of a space freighter, he'd been around an awful lot. Trag had too, but he had never been with a Zetithian woman. Actually, the person he probably needed the most right now was his mother, but she'd been killed long ago.

Trag tried to ignore the others as they came onto the bridge, but he couldn't help but overhear the exchange between Lerotan and the station official. He wasn't surprised that Lerotan would lie so easily to protect them. His captain might have been ruthless when it came to dealing with customers, but women had always been Lerotan's soft spot. Trag was amazed that it had never gotten him into trouble before, but there was a first time for everything. Trag was fairly certain that the women hadn't been responsible for a murder, but if anyone else believed it and came after them, things could get nasty. Trag knew that *The Equalizer*'s weapons system was second to none—and that knowledge alone was enough to keep most ships from firing on them—but he wasn't so sure they could count on it this time.

Chapter 6

"RODAN, SEND OUT A DEEP SPACE HAIL TO JACK," Lerotan said as the ship quickly left Orleon Station behind. "No, wait. I was forgetting we have a communications officer now," he added, grinning at Micayla and gesturing toward a station. "We've had to double up on duties. Not many of my men can handle the more technical end of things, unless it has to do with a weapon."

"Good," Rodan said, appearing relieved. "I've always hated doing that shit. I'd much rather fire the pulse cannons."

"Well, then, that's settled," Lerotan said pleasantly as Micayla took a seat at her new post.

Glancing at the controls, she commented, "Outdated, but functional."

"Tell Jack we've found you," Lerotan said, ignoring her remark. With a nod toward Windura, he added, "You might want to take a peek at our computer system too. It's been a bit temperamental lately." Looking pointedly at Hidar, he went on, "And now that you ladies both have jobs, you can't be considered passengers *or* stowaways, so Hidar might not feel the need to fuck you."

"I will always feel the need," Hidar said morosely. "I haven't fucked anyone in many years."

"Sorry about that, Hidar," Windura said cheerfully. "I'd help you out if I could, but something tells me—"

"Don't give him any ideas," Lerotan warned. "He's hard enough to control when we make port. He's been kicked out of more brothels than anyone in the sector, and with two females on board, he might be more of a problem."

Not looking up from her console where she was engaged in the search for Jack's hailing frequency, Micayla said absently, "Are your testicles well protected, Hidar?"

"Oh, yes," Hidar replied. "They are deep inside my exoskeleton—unlike those of mammalian bipeds."

"Pity," Micayla said. "Any other sensitive parts?"

Finally suspicious, Hidar trained his antennae on her. "Why do you ask?"

"Just wanted to know in case I ever decide to fuck you," Micayla replied. "Wouldn't want to hurt you." Actually, she was seeking a way to do just that, but Hidar didn't need to know it—yet.

"My wings are very sensitive," Hidar admitted, rustling them gently. "But if you wish to stroke them…"

"I wouldn't do that if I were you," Lerotan advised.

"And why not?" Windura asked before Micayla could reply. "They're actually very attractive."

"It's part of the Scorillian mating ritual," Lerotan replied. "It makes his dick hard—well, no, actually it just makes his dick pop out. It's *always* hard."

Obviously viewing her as a more likely candidate than Micayla, Hidar sidled up to Windura, rustling his wings again. "Would you like to see it?"

"Maybe later," Windura replied. "Nice wings, though." Glancing around, she added, "I can look into your system anytime you like, Leroy. Got a tech station somewhere?"

"Over there next to Trag," Lerotan said with a nod. "It's probably safe. Never saw him bite anyone, though he is a bit surly these days." He paused for a moment before adding, "What did you call me?"

"Leroy," Windura replied. "Seems less formal than Lerotan. Do you mind? Or would you prefer that I call you Captain?"

"Never mind." Lerotan sighed and shook his head. "And I thought it was just Terrans…"

———

Micayla found the frequency signature and sent out the message that a Zetithian female named Micayla Johnson had been found, which was odd since she had never considered herself to be lost. After that, she worked on familiarizing herself with some of Lerotan's other contacts. The designations were certainly colorful, as one might expect from an arms dealer—Gunrunner Gereg, Swordmaster Sakram, and so on—which led her to believe that no one ever used their real name in the weapons trade. She'd found Jack Tshevnoe listed as Jack of all Traders.

From time to time she stole a glance at Trag. He was just sitting at his station with his back toward her, but she still felt like hissing at him. Weird. She didn't know enough about him to take an immediate dislike to him. And she *didn't* dislike him, it was just that from the first moment she'd seen him, even at a distance, he had affected her like no man ever had.

Windura leaned over and said something to Trag that actually got a chuckle out of him, causing Micayla to experience a sharp pang of jealousy. It was difficult for her to joke around with men; everything had to be strictly business or they had a tendency to get the wrong idea. While this wasn't ordinarily a problem, Trag was actually from her homeworld! She had so many questions she didn't know where to begin, but she couldn't blame him for not sticking around to chat after she'd behaved so badly. She'd already apologized, but he still seemed angry; he hadn't said a word to her since they came on the bridge. Perhaps talking to this "Jack" would be easier.

─〜〜〜─

It was obvious that Micayla would have gladly continued her perusal of the ship's com system without interruption, but Lerotan felt that some further discussion was required. "So, Micayla," he began. "Tell me, did Grekkor say *how* he destroyed Zetith?"

"No," Micayla replied. "Just that he had."

"Too bad," Lerotan mused. "That information might come in handy sometime."

"What?" Trag exploded, spinning around in his chair. "You know who did that?"

"Oh," Lerotan said innocently. "I was forgetting. You didn't stick around for the rest of the story, did you?"

His jibe was not lost on Trag, who replied with a mumbled, "No, I didn't."

Satisfied that he had made his point, Lerotan continued, "Shifting an asteroid's trajectory would be tough." Tapping his leg with his tufted tail, he added, "I wonder if they used explosives or just rammed it with a large starship. Either one would probably work, but explosives would be tricky on an asteroid with no oxygen atmosphere to support the explosion, and sacrificing a ship that big would be damned expensive."

"Could have been more than one ship," Windura suggested. "They could have towed the asteroid with tractor beams."

"Still wildly expensive," Lerotan said, shaking his head. "I can't imagine why anyone would go to that much trouble."

"I think Grekkor is a little on the crazy side," Windura said. "You should have seen the look on his face when he was telling us what he'd done." Shuddering, she added, "He gave me the creeps."

"Let me get this straight," Trag said, looking back and forth at the two women. "You know who destroyed Zetith, and he *knows* you know he did it?"

"That's right," Micayla chimed in without looking up. "And if he catches up with this ship, we're all dead meat."

"Fuck!" Trag exclaimed. "Why the devil didn't you tell me we needed to hurry?"

"Trag," Lerotan said with a grin, "we need to hurry."

"No shit," Trag said, turning back to the controls, muttering, "You might have at least *mentioned* it."

Lerotan shrugged. "Well, now you know. Full speed ahead and all that crap." Glancing at Rodan, he added, "And you might want to get the big guns warmed up."

Windura gazed at Lerotan with frank admiration. "Do you *ever* get bent out of shape—about anything?"

"Not often," Lerotan replied.

"Just don't step on his tail," Rodan put in. "He gets really pissed when you do that."

"Would you like it if someone stepped on your spare dick?" Lerotan countered.

Rodan grinned, showing the gaps between his teeth. "I'd probably enjoy it."

"Well, unless you're serious about that, you'd better keep away from Micayla," Windura warned. "You should have seen what she did to Grekkor and his two thugs. Their nuts will be sore for a month!"

Rodan swiveled his seat around and spread his legs apart as though welcoming the attention. "I'd like to see her try."

"Keep it up and I might," Micayla warned.

While the rest of the crew roared with laughter, Rodan growled something that Lerotan didn't catch, though it was apparent that Micayla had. Only a flick of an eyebrow indicated that she'd heard him at all, but Lerotan could see the tension building.

His gaze shifted to Trag, who was already coming out of his seat with fire in his eyes. Deciding he'd seen enough, Lerotan said, "Simmer down, kids. There will be none of that on the bridge. Oh, and Micayla, you might want to send out another hail to tell Jack about Grekkor. Not sure which bit of info will make her day more—finding you, or finding him."

Lerotan leaned back in his captain's chair with a smirk. Under different circumstances, having two women on board could have spelled trouble, but though Micayla was quite beautiful—and the little Vessonian was cute too—these ladies were obviously more than a match for his crew. What was even more revealing was Trag's reaction. So, he was willing to go up against Rodan in Micayla's defense, was he? Even though she'd hissed at him? *Interesting…*

At the end of what was perhaps the second most eventful day in her life, Micayla's brain was still humming, making sleep highly unlikely. Hidar had moved out of his quarters as ordered but had done nothing to hide his displeasure—nor had he backed off in his attempts to persuade the women to accept him as a roommate. Windura thought it was funny, but Micayla was not amused.

"So, what do you think of him?" Windura prompted.

Micayla paused as she peered at the sheets provided for them with frank distaste. "Which one?"

"Any of them," Windura replied. "They're an interesting bunch, don't you think?"

"Maybe," Micayla said cautiously. "If you enjoy living among the riffraff of the galaxy."

"Aw, come on, Micayla!" Windura argued, punching her pillow. Unfortunately, this action did more to raise a cloud of dust than it did to soften the pillow, nor did it smooth out any of the lumps. "They're a nice bunch of guys."

"If you think they're nice," Micayla said dryly, "you've obviously been on Orleon for too long."

"Well, maybe I have," Windura admitted, "but it could have been a lot worse."

"How?"

Glancing about the tiny cabin, she said, "We could be sharing this room with Hidar."

The Scorillian must not have had much in the way of personal possessions, because the steel plating showed no marks where any photographs had been hung, nor were there any odds and ends left in the drawers of the battered dresser in the corner. The overhead light was dimmed with a coating of grime, and an odd-looking strip of what Micayla suspected was some of Hidar's dead "skin" dangled from the edge of the metal bed frame. Yes, it could have been much worse.

"Better than sharing one with Rodan, though," Micayla said. "What a jerk!"

Windura shrugged as she flipped the sheet over the bed and began tucking it in. "You just need to loosen up a little. They don't mean any harm."

"Maybe, but what if Lerotan wasn't in charge?"

"We probably would have been fucked by at least one of them by now," Windura admitted. "I wouldn't mind if it was Trag," she added wistfully.

Micayla didn't reply. She didn't want to admit that she was thinking the same thing, despite her visceral reaction.

"He seemed like the nicest one," Windura went on. "Handsome devil, too. Don't know why you'd want to hiss at him. Don't you like him?"

"I don't want to talk about it," Micayla said flatly.

"Lerotan's okay too," Windura said. "I mean, a guy with two dicks? Sounds fabulous."

"To you, maybe. Sounds like torture to me."

"You just need to get out more," Windura suggested. "Or talk to some hookers. They'll tell you what's good and what's not."

"I really don't want to know," Micayla said evasively as the sudden image of an aroused, nude Trag flitted through her mind. That, combined with Windura's earlier rundown of Zetithian sexual attributes, nearly overwhelmed her. Pressing her fingertips to her temples, she added, "Can we talk about something else, like what the hell we're going to do when the bad guys catch up with us?"

"You think they will?"

"You think they *won't?*"

"Leroy did say this was a fast ship."

"Oh, come on, Windy!" Micayla chided her. "Someone with the money to finance the destruction of an entire planet would have the wherewithal to buy the fastest ship in existence. Maybe even one of the big Arconian ships."

Windura shook her head. "No, he doesn't, at least not that I've ever heard. He's just got a little Rutaran Runabout. They aren't that fast."

"But I'll bet he's got access to others you don't know about."

Windura finished making the bed and flopped down on it, stretching out with a sigh. "Maybe so, but right now I'm too tired to give a damn. Sure you don't want the bed?"

"I'm sure," Micayla said with a shudder. "No way am I sleeping on anything that bug's been in."

"Better than the floor the bug's been walking on," Windura pointed out. "But you do whatever makes you happy."

Micayla stared down at her companion, who appeared to be quite comfortable in Hidar's bed and not at all concerned with their situation. "So, you're just going to go to sleep and trust these guys to keep us alive?"

"Well, yeah. You heard Leroy. That Jack will make him miserable if they don't."

"Maybe so," Micayla said. "But we don't know anything about Jack. How can we be sure?"

"I guess we can't," Windura replied. "But I'm perfectly willing to let these guys protect us for a while. I mean, they're arms dealers, Micayla! If they can't fight off the bad guys, who can?"

Micayla couldn't find fault with her friend's reasoning, and since she had no other choice, she reluctantly nodded her acceptance. "I just don't like relying on them for anything," she said. "It's not what I'm used to."

"Well, they probably aren't used to it either. Did you notice we're the only women on board? I get the impression that rescuing damsels in distress isn't exactly in their line."

"And we didn't plan to be here ourselves," Micayla said with a wry smile. "It's not like we booked passage with them. I wish you could've asked Layha more about the others. I'm sure she could have told you all kinds of things."

"Too late now," Windura said with a shrug. Glancing up at Micayla who was now pacing the floor like a caged animal, she added, "You might as well learn to go with the flow, girlfriend."

Micayla paused, letting out a long sigh. "I know I should. But it bugs the hell out of me to have to depend on someone I'm not sure I can trust."

Windura looked thoughtful for a moment. "I think you could trust Trag," she said at length. "If anyone would see to your welfare, it would be him."

"I wouldn't count on it," Micayla said ruefully. "I didn't exactly make a good first impression with him."

Windura grinned. "You might be surprised."

Chapter 7

"HOLY COW!" JACK EXCLAIMED AS SHE READ THE DEEP space missive her son, Larry, had just handed her. "Will you listen to this? Leroy has found a female Zetithian! Says he picked her up on Orleon Station, and get this: she's from Earth!"

"How is that possible?" Cat asked his wife.

"I have absolutely no idea," Jack replied. "But I intend to find out." Consulting her star charts, she quickly located Orleon. "Hmm, yeah, that's right... near the border," she muttered, "and a long damn way from here. Wonder which way he's heading?"

"Knowing Leroy, it's probably the wrong direction," Tisana quipped.

Grinning at her shipmate, Jack agreed. "He never could stay out of the Andromeda quadrant for long. Too many places this side of the border he can't go."

"And there are too many places on the other side that we shouldn't visit," Cat reminded her. "We should not try to find them."

"My God, Cat! Don't you want to meet her?"

"Yes," Cat replied. "But not to risk our children. We should be more cautious."

"Like *trying* to stay out of trouble would help," Jack scoffed. "Trouble follows us wherever we go. The damn Nedwuts would probably find us on Earth too, and it chills my bones to think that they almost got to Tychar.

Wish we could just get some of the hairy bastards to talk. I'd give a bundle to know who Mr. Big is."

"Uh, Mom, there's another message here," Larry reported from his station.

"From Leroy?"

"Yeah," the boy replied. "It says that someone named Rutger Grekkor blew up Zetith."

"What?" Jack exclaimed. "Let me see that."

Shaking his head, Larry handed her the pad. "I always thought the Nedwuts did it."

"Great balls of fire!" Jack whispered when she read it. Spearing her fingers through her short, dark hair, she spun on her heel toward her husband. "We've got to get there, and fast."

"Why?" asked Cat.

"Because this Grekkor fellow knows they're on to him—and he knows whose ship they're on too." Turning to her son, Moe, she said, "Fire up the power boosters, kiddo. We're gonna need 'em." The *Jolly Roger* was Jack's ship and though it wasn't her usual style to bark orders, everyone knew it was pointless to argue when her dander was up. Turning to the tall, golden-haired Zetithian at the weapons console, she went on, "Leo, we're going to need weapons too. Run checks on the system. Tisana, if you haven't already figured out how to shoot fireballs in space, now would be a good time to do it."

"Jack," Tisana said patiently, "you know very well I'd have to stick my head out the hatch to do it. I don't think that's a good idea."

"Very true," agreed Jack. "We just need some kind of torpedo tube that you can fire them into, and then we could use them to blast another ship."

Tisana couldn't help but laugh. "Really, Jack. Don't you think Lerotan's weapons are enough?"

"Can't be too careful," Jack said earnestly. "When it comes to protecting our Zetithians, we must exercise constant vigilance, Tisana. Constant!"

"Bet Trag's exercising some constant vigilance too," Tisana said thoughtfully. Her jewel-green eyes were focused on Jack, but fortunately without the intensity required to set her on fire. Brushing aside a stray lock of her dusky hair, she added, "Did they say how old she was?"

"Nope," Jack replied. "See? We need more information. All the more reason to try to rendezvous with them."

"Terra Minor is not far from here," Cat said slowly. "If we will be going into battle, perhaps—"

"You are *not* leaving us behind on Terra Minor!" Larry and his brother, Moe, chorused.

Cat looked at his sons with a mixture of pride and concern. With their black hair and equally black eyes, they favored him far more than they did their mother, but they had all inherited Jack's indomitable spirit. Keeping them out of harm's way might prove difficult. "This battle could be deadly," he said grimly. "You will be safe there."

"Fine," said Larry. "We can drop off the little ones, but Moe and I are going with you—and so is Curly."

"I'm going where?" asked Curly as he walked onto the bridge.

"With us," Larry said eagerly.

"Into battle!" added Moe.

Jack chewed on her lip. "If we left the other kids with

Bonnie and Lynx, they would be safe, but if this turns out to be a battle in space, we might need these guys to man the stations."

"You are pilot and navigator, I am tech and communications, Leo is weapons, and Tisana is medic," Cat said. "We would not need them."

"But what if we need replacements?" Jack argued. "Curly is getting to be a whiz at piloting, Larry could get a message through to the devil himself, and Moe can navigate his way through a nebula blindfolded. Aside from that, Althea is one talented little witch, and all the kids are good shots with a pulse pistol."

"You would have our children fight?" Cat began, but he obviously changed his mind as soon as the words were out of his mouth. "No, you are right. They must be allowed to fight for their freedom from this cursed bounty, just as we have done."

"But the babies—" Tisana interjected.

"Should stay with Bonnie and Lynx," Jack agreed.

"What about Lynx? Would he want to come?" Tisana asked.

"Probably," said Cat, "but he and Bonnie have just had their first litter, and if we're going to leave our children with them, they will need him."

"True," Tisana said. "What about Manx?"

"Too far away," Jack said. "We can't sit on this forever. If only we had more time…" Tapping her chin, she continued on, thinking aloud. "Wonder if anyone we know is already on Orleon. It would help to have someone there—even as a spy. Veluka said he was headed that way a while back. I wonder…"

"Not him again!" Tisana exclaimed.

"Maybe," Jack replied. "He's got one helluva fast ship, too—even has a cloaking device. He'd be very useful."

Making a quick decision, Jack turned to Larry. "Send out hails to Veluka, Leroy, and Lynx. We need to get organized."

"Too bad most of our 'friends' are people you can't trust," Tisana said, shaking her head sadly. "Veluka will cause trouble, you wait and see."

"Aw, I can handle Veluka," Jack said with an impatient gesture. "He's always come through for me."

"Like those tracking nanobots he sold you on Barada Seven," Leo snickered. "They didn't function for more than a week."

"Got us through a tight spot, though, didn't they?" Jack countered.

"Yes, but we couldn't track the Nedwuts with them afterward," Leo pointed out.

"Yeah, that would have been nice," Jack agreed. "I'd have stuck a whole lot closer to Klarkunk if I'd had a cloaking device myself. Maybe I should look into getting one."

"If we ever catch Grekkor," Tisana said quietly, "you won't need it."

"Good point," Jack conceded. "Well, if we need stealth, Veluka can handle that part. And if we need firepower, we've got Leroy—better tell him where we are, Larry, and find out where he's headed—and for sheer guts and determination, we've got Zetithians."

She just hoped it would be enough.

"Any sign of pursuit?" Lerotan asked Trag.

"I've been running continuous sensor sweeps," Trag reported. "Nothing yet."

"Well, maybe it's time we looped back around and headed the other direction."

"Back to the station?"

"Not exactly," Lerotan replied. "If Jack has received our hail, she'll be headed this way. I'd bet my life on it. We need to find out where she is and meet her somewhere."

"Last I heard, Jack was in the alpha portion of sector six," Trag said, consulting his charts. "If we loop around we could meet her on Darconia, which is near the outer rim of sector nine. We're three sectors in the other direction, and it's not on a direct route, but at least we know Darconia is safe."

"Sounds good," Lerotan said. "Make it so."

Trag rolled his eyes. "You've been watching some of Jack's old movies, haven't you?"

Lerotan shrugged. "Got nothing better to do." Standing up, he gave his leather tunic a tug at the hem. "Almost got that Picard maneuver down too."

"Jack will be thrilled," Trag said dryly.

"Ha, ha," said Lerotan. "Rodan, send out another hail to Jack telling her to meet us on Darconia. Trag, you plot the course and then get some sleep. We can set the sensors to sound the alarm if anything shows up."

"I don't trust that system," Trag grumbled.

"Yes, but I don't trust you when you haven't slept. Makes you cranky and your eyes get all fuzzy." Lerotan paused a moment before adding, "I'm going to bed too. Hidar, you have the con."

"But I have not slept either," Hidar complained, clicking his mandibles in protest.

"Yes, but since you're sharing quarters with Rodan, you two will need to sleep on opposite shifts—and besides, bugs like you don't need that much sleep."

"I will die a painful death," Hidar mourned. "Lack of sleep, no proper food—"

"Bitch, bitch, bitch…"

"No females—"

"My quarters are next to the women," Lerotan warned. "I'll hear them if they start yelling."

"Never get to fuck or cook again. Why do I go on living?"

"Because you've got a two hundred year life span?" Trag suggested.

"That might be it," Hidar admitted. Spreading his wings over the back of the command station, he slumped down in Lerotan's chair, his feathery antennae drooping down over his eyes. "Only a hundred and twenty-five left to go."

Trag went to bed as ordered but the image of Micayla hissing like a demon cat kept him awake—her high cheekbones; straight, aristocratic nose; sensuous lips that should have smiled at him but had snarled; and rich brown hair he could get lost in forever.

"Why couldn't she at least have had blue eyes like the damned Davordians?" he grumbled, punching his pillow. "I could have stood it, then—no problem at all— but noooo! She had to have fabulous, dark, sexy eyes! I wouldn't give a shit if it weren't for—no, scratch that, I don't give a shit, anyway. Don't want her and don't want her to want me—not that she ever will. Go right ahead, sweetheart, hiss away." He told himself he didn't mind, but he also knew that Leroy would probably give him hell about it forever—and so would Jack. He finally fell asleep while trying to decide which was worse.

—∿∿—

He might have told himself he didn't care, but sitting across the breakfast table from Micayla the next morning was nearly Trag's undoing. He was trying to avoid looking at her, but he was picking up the scent of feminine desire from someone; he wasn't sure which of the women it was. Windura seemed quite friendly—not gorgeous or anything—just a regular girl who could probably get along with the devil himself, but Micayla was as cold as the far reaches of space. His only consolation was that she'd managed to say "Good morning" without hissing at him.

Hidar had gone off to bed after working the night shift, leaving Trag to prepare the meal, and so far, no one was complaining. Not praising him to the skies, precisely, but at least they were eating it. Windura had even thanked him.

Windura, who was now smiling at him over her coffee cup. It had to be her. Getting too friendly with a shipmate was probably a bad idea, but when she offered to clean up, he got a big whiff as she came around the table to take his plate. Generally speaking, Vessonian women had never been among his favorites, but she was nice—and funny too. Of course, having heard about Zetithian men from Layha, she was bound to be interested. He knew he should have tried to ignore her scent, but it was making his dick hard.

Thankful that his nose wasn't nearly as good as that of his friend Manx—who only had to be downwind of a

receptive female to get it up—and that his current style
of dress camouflaged his reaction, Trag went off to his
station. Performing another manual sensor sweep, he
still didn't pick up on anything, which was odd. Still,
they had a good head start and Lerotan's ship was one
of the fastest he knew of—only Jack's ship was faster—
having been modified by some Delfian mechanics who
knew a few things most others didn't. Apparently their
loop back toward Darconia was a move that Grekkor
hadn't anticipated either. Trag chuckled to himself
thinking that anyone following their last known trajectory was bound to be getting pissed by now.

Later on, Windura brought him a cup of coffee at
his station. Her scent was softer now—not enough to
evoke a response—but it was still there. She liked him,
all right, and when she squeezed his shoulder just before
she took her seat at the tech station, he was sure of it.

—⁓—

Micayla watched Windura with a pang of envy. There
she was, talking to a guy she'd just met the day before,
and she wasn't afraid to get friendly with him either. Not
that she was being as friendly with Rodan—after all, who
would want to be?—but she did speak to him, whereas
Micayla was reluctant to open her mouth for fear that
Rodan would start harassing her again. Trag, on the other
hand, seemed to be very likable, and Windura wasn't
being flirtatious either. She'd gone after her own coffee and had brought some back for Trag. Just a simple,
friendly gesture, but the way he smiled at her…

It wasn't the first time Micayla had ever considered
having a closer relationship with a man, but so much more

seemed to be riding on it now. Maybe it was just because he was a fellow Zetithian, which was also odd; she'd never had that much in common with anyone before.

Lerotan's voice startled her out of her thoughts. "Guess we ought to let Wazak know we're coming. Micayla, send out a hail to Darconia, and ask if Tychar is there while you're at it."

"Be great if Ty *was* there," Trag said wistfully. "Haven't seen him in ages."

"We're going to see *him*?" Windura gasped. "Really? I can't believe—"

Her excitement was cut short by an exasperated grumble from Trag.

"Sorry, Trag," she said meekly. "Don't know what came over me."

Trag laughed it off, but Micayla suspected that living in the shadow of a famous sibling bothered him more than he let on. Micayla could imagine it would be difficult, although she certainly didn't know from personal experience. Her stepmother, Rulie, had never married, and though Micayla suspected that it had something to do with her alien stepchild, Rulie had never admitted to wanting a husband—or other children.

"I have you to love," she often told Micayla. "I don't need anyone else."

Statements like that had made Micayla think long and hard before leaving Earth behind, but Rulie understood. "Your destiny awaits you," she had said the day Micayla left for her first post. "Don't waste the opportunity."

She'd never said specifically, but Micayla wondered if Rulie had known that the day would come when she would begin to seek the answers to the questions of her past. Now

many of those questions had been answered, but Micayla
still didn't understand much about her own personal
makeup. Was it common for Zetithian women to feel so
little desire for men? And if so, what was the reason for it?

She continued to ponder this while preparing the
hail to Darconia, and sent it off with the hope that she
would find someone—*anyone*—who could help her
understand more.

Micayla had just sent the hail when the ship gave a
sudden lurch, nearly throwing her out of her seat.

"What the hell was that?" Lerotan demanded.

"Nothing on the sensors," Trag yelled as the ship took
another hit. "The fuckers must have a cloaked ship!"

"And a damned fast one too," Lerotan added. "Rodan,
fire anything you've got in the direction that pulse blast
came from!"

"Already on it!" Rodan shouted.

The third round blew out half the lights and sent
Micayla sprawling onto the deck with Trag on top of
her. The impact knocked the breath out of her, and she
pushed against him, gasping for air.

"Don't you *dare* hiss at me," Trag warned as he rolled
away. "I'm really *not* in the mood!" Scrambling to his
feet, he returned to his post and waited until Rodan had
fired the pulse cannons before sending the ship on an
evasive maneuver, muttering, "Nobody has ever caught
us with this gambit; this better not be the time they do."

"Keep firing aft, Rodan!" Lerotan ordered. "Don't
stop until something explodes."

Micayla clambered into to her seat, barely able to
breathe as her console began flashing. "It's a hail!"
she gasped.

"I don't want to talk to them!" Lerotan yelled.

Another pulse blast rocked their vessel and Micayla's arm hit the receiver control. The viewscreen flickered to life with the image of a snarling wolf-like creature staring at them.

"Prepare to surrender your vessel and be boarded!" he said. "We are only seeking your passengers."

"We don't *have* passengers!" Lerotan growled. "Only crew!"

Glancing at Windura, Micayla shook her head, feeling completely confused. It wasn't Grekkor. It was someone else entirely.

Lerotan obviously knew something about him, though, because he snarled: "No Nedwut *ever* will board my ship."

"Then we will destroy it," the Nedwut said.

"Like hell you will," Lerotan shot back, but the viewscreen went blank as Rodan fired another round. Trag was still engaged in evasive maneuvers that, coming on top of getting the wind knocked out of her, were making Micayla want to throw up, but at least the blasts weren't hitting them anymore. If nothing else, she had to admit that Trag was a darn good pilot.

It was all Micayla could do to hang on to her station—let alone her breakfast—when Trag finally let out a shout of triumph. "You got him!" he crowed as he set the ship on a straight but divergent course.

"Great shot, Rodan!" Lerotan said with a grin as the shock wave buffeted the ship.

"You don't suppose Grekkor was on that ship, do you?" Micayla said hopefully.

"I doubt it," Windura commented. "He doesn't strike me as the type to do his own dirty work."

"What I'm wondering is where that last blast came from," Rodan said, scratching his shiny bald head.

"You mean you didn't fire it?" Lerotan demanded.

"That's exactly what I mean," Rodan replied. "Unless it was a delayed reaction."

"Hmm," said Lerotan. "Perhaps we have a friend out there somewhere."

"If we do, they're cloaked too," Trag reported. "Because according to my sensors, there's nothing out there but debris."

"And since when do Nedwuts have cloaking technology on their ships, anyway?" Rodan said, shaking his head. "I never heard of that."

"Makes keeping Zetithians alive a bit more difficult," Lerotan said grimly.

"Sorry to be so much trouble," Trag grumbled. "Guess I'll just go jump in an escape pod and eliminate the problem."

Lerotan rolled his eyes. "Forget it, Trag. We need you. And besides, you aren't the only Zetithian on board anymore."

"No way am I sharing a pod with *her*," Trag said, pulling his cloak around his shoulders. "It's cold enough in space as it is."

Safely aboard the cloaked *Okeoula*, Veluka was chuckling his scaly, black head off. Jack would *really* owe him now.

Chapter 8

"HMM, DARCONIA, HUH?" JACK MUSED AS SHE READ THE deep space missive Larry had just given her. "Been needing to go there anyway. It took some doing, but I finally found that video I promised Dragus."

"A video for Dragus?" Cat drawled. "I cannot imagine what *that* would be."

"It's not *that* kind of video," she said with a quelling glance. "Dragus has more things on his mind than you might think."

"You astonish me," Cat said dryly. "I cannot recall anything being on his mind but—"

"Not in front of the children," Jack cautioned.

"Aw, Mom!" Larry complained. "We know all about Dragus."

"Yeah, he's that guard who's got the hots for Earth women," Moe said.

"Who told you that?" Jack demanded.

Moe looked at her as though she'd lost her mind. "Dragus," he replied. "Who'd you think?"

Jack shook her head ruefully. "The things you kids have been exposed to! Maybe I should have left you on Earth to be raised by my parents."

"Yeah, right," Larry chuckled. "No way would Grandma *ever* be able to put up with us."

"She told you that?"

"Sure did," Larry said with a nod of his curly head.

"Said she didn't want to be responsible for a bunch of precocious boys." Larry seemed puzzled, adding, "What's precocious mean, anyway?"

"That's an English word which means that you're advanced for your age," Jack replied, "which is certainly true. I don't know many seven-year-olds who could do what you guys do. Must be a Zetithian thing."

"Nope. It's the Terran/Zetithian cross," Moe said knowledgeably. "'Least that's what Dad said."

"He only said that because he wants me to feel like I had something to do with it," Jack said roundly. "Don't believe everything he tells you." For her part, it was difficult *not* to take everything Cat said as the gospel truth. One glimpse of his long, lean body and beckoning smile would have her buying bridges in Brooklyn and lakes on Darconia in no time. Good thing he was so honest…

"I have never lied to our children," Cat insisted, his black eyes flashing with indignation. "They are very intelligent, and I believe it is because of you."

"I know you *think* that, Cat," Jack said impatiently, "and neither of us are what you'd call stupid, but I wasn't flying a ship at that age."

"Did you have the opportunity?" Cat countered. Moving closer, his eyes began to glow and Jack had no doubt that this was one disagreement he was going to win.

"Well, no," Jack admitted. "I don't suppose I did, but—"

"I have no doubt that you could have," her husband said firmly. "Therefore it is no surprise to me that our children can."

Jack's eyes narrowed. "You're sweet-talking me again, Kittycat. You want something, don't you?"

Cat smiled wickedly. "Can you doubt it?" he said, beginning to purr.

"Maybe later," she said with a grin. Actually, there was no "maybe" about it. Jack knew he would work his magic on her just as he always did. He was completely irresistible, and he knew it. Damn him.

Larry and Moe returned to their stations giggling. They knew a whole lot more than their parents thought they did.

———

Trag sat down at the dinner table feeling slightly unsure about the meal he'd prepared. In a fit of pique, Hidar had not only refused to fix dinner but had also refused to explain what was what in the galley, so in some cases, Trag was forced to make a guess.

"I can't wait to get to Darconia," Rodan said, sitting down next to Micayla, who shifted away from him slightly. Though Rodan's stench had improved considerably since the ladies joined the crew—a side effect for which Trag was extremely grateful—Micayla obviously wasn't longing for a closer relationship, no matter what Rodan might have in mind.

"And why is that?" Micayla asked, cocking her head toward him. "Got a thing for big, scaly lizards?"

"No," Rodan replied. "You don't have to wear clothes on Darconia." Leering at her, he added, "And once you see me naked, you'll want me so bad you'll be down on your knees begging."

Micayla let out a sardonic laugh and rolled her eyes. "I doubt it, Rodan, but you can keep dreaming, if you like. I'm just not interested."

Rodan snickered. "You haven't seen me naked."

"And I hope I never do," she said smoothly, "though I'm not sure it would make any difference."

Rodan laughed and dug into his dinner, obviously not the least bit discouraged.

Trag was looking forward to visiting Darconia himself, partly for the chance to see Kyra again, but mainly for the warmth. He'd spent years wishing for a cooler climate, only to discover that "cooler" meant he was uncomfortably cold most of the time. He also missed the freedom of being nude, and without missing a beat his mind made the leap to Kyra and how he'd teased her to stop wearing her long dresses and wear nothing but jewelry like the Darconian females did. She had finally given in but had never seemed very comfortable with it—no matter how terrific she might have looked.

Trag considered his two new shipmates carefully and decided that while Windura might adopt the Darconian style eventually, he couldn't see Micayla ever doing it, no matter how hot it was. She wore that space station uniform as though perpetually anticipating a formal inspection; everything tucked, buttoned, and zipped up tight. She wasn't what you'd call timid, though—the exchange between her and Rodan proved that—but she did seem awfully quiet sometimes—even aloof—especially around Trag.

This irked Trag because she seemed able to talk to everyone else on board, which didn't make a bit of sense. She was Zetithian, for heaven's sake! He ought to at least be able to talk to her. Peering at her surreptitiously across the dinner table, Trag pondered this until he simply couldn't stand it anymore.

"So, Micayla," he began. "You're from Earth, right? Any idea how you got there?"

⁓⁓⁓

Never having encouraged him to speak to her, Micayla glanced up at Trag in surprise. Unfortunately, she now had to fight the urge not only to hiss at him, but to bite him as well. The desire to sink her teeth into his succulent flesh was almost overwhelming. In fact, the only way she could answer his question without attacking him was to avoid looking at him entirely. "My family was being chased through a spaceport," she replied, staring down at her plate, "and my mother handed me off to a stranger—my stepmother, Rulie—and told her to keep me safe. She took me to Earth."

"And your real family?" he prompted. "Do you know what happened to them?"

"They were killed," Micayla said, still keeping her head down.

"I'm sorry about that," Trag said warmly. "I was lucky that way—Ty and I were captured and sold together. You must feel very lonely."

This sounded like another version of Rodan's approach, but rather than getting into a lengthy discussion, Micayla opted to cut it short, replying with a terse affirmative. She couldn't deny that she felt something for him—though she wasn't quite sure what it was—but talking to Trag made her uncomfortable. She didn't trust the unfamiliar reactions triggered by his presence.

"I'm surprised Jack never found you though," Trag went on. "She's put out the word all over the galaxy about what happened to Zetith and that the Nedwuts were responsible. I can't believe you didn't know you were Zetithian."

"My stepmother did her best to keep me safe—from everyone," Micayla replied. "If she heard anything about it, she would have assumed it was the bad guys looking for survivors."

"True," Trag agreed. "I'm not sure I would try to contact Jack if I'd been in hiding like that. Of course, Earth's a pretty safe place to hide—even from us."

Micayla's curiosity got the best of her. "What do you mean by that?"

"We can't land there," Rodan chimed in. "We're all *undesirables*." The emphasis he put on that last word, along with the accompanying chuckle, suggested that he was either proud of the fact or thought it was ridiculous—Micayla wasn't sure which.

"Can't go to Terra Minor either," said Trag. "The toughest immigration and landing regulations in the galaxy, though Lynx did get them to allow any Zetithians needing refuge to go there—with the exception of me because I've been hanging out with these guys."

"Which means we'll be considered undesirables too, I suppose," Windura said bleakly, "or murderers."

Micayla started to ask what she meant but then remembered Grekkor's accusation implicating the two women in the death of the Norludian. "So we're outlaws now, huh?" Micayla mused, shaking her head as she stabbed at the food on her plate. "Guess we'll be on the run until we can clear our names—which, under the circumstances, doesn't seem very likely." She paused with a forkful poised before her lips. "What *is* this anyway? Fish?"

"Um, that's part of the problem," Trag said. "Hidar used to do all the cooking—I've only recently started doing it myself—and there's some stuff in the stasis unit I'm not sure about. I thought it might be Kreater beast, but—"

"If it's Kreater beast, then it's okay," Windura said soothingly. "This is what it's supposed to taste like."

"Yes, but what if it isn't?" Micayla said, still scrutinizing the bit of meat on her fork.

"I guess outlaws like us can't be too choosy," Trag said with a shrug. He appeared nonchalant, but something in his tone of voice told Micayla that it had been the wrong subject to broach—maybe even worse than hissing at him. Then his expression clouded and she was sure of it. *Way to go, Micayla*.

"Hasn't killed us yet!" Rodan said cheerfully. Downing the last bit on his plate with gusto, he upended his bottle of ale, draining the contents before letting out a satisfied belch.

"I'm not sure you're the best one to judge, Rodan," Windura said. "Something tells me it would take more than rotten Kreater beast to kill *you*."

"He actually *likes* Hidar's cooking," Trag whispered to her, "if that tells you anything. It's nearly killed me several times."

"Well, I don't think this would kill anyone," Micayla said. "But *I* certainly wouldn't kill for it."

Trag's eyes darkened ominously. "I'd like to see you try figuring out what all that shit is," he snarled. "Maybe if you go rub Hidar's wings he'd tell you."

"I'd rather not," Micayla shot back.

"Well then lay off, Ice Queen."

Micayla knew she'd hurt his feelings, but the attack hardly seemed warranted. "Ice Queen?" she echoed indignantly. "And just what do you mean by that?"

"That you're cold as ice?" Trag suggested. "The kind of girl who can make men's dicks shrivel up with one glance—or should I say, one hiss?"

Micayla stared at him in disbelief. All she'd done was question the menu—and even he'd admitted he wasn't sure what it was. It shouldn't have been enough to set him off, unless he was a whole lot more sensitive than any other man she'd ever met. Without warning, her temper flared. "Well, you can just keep your shriveled-up cock to yourself, Trag," she spat out. "I don't want it!"

"Yeah, well, maybe I will—*Mick*," Trag said with a sneer. Pushing away from the table, he left without another word. Rodan followed in his wake, though somewhat sheepishly, Micayla thought. Perhaps Rodan would think twice about pursuing her if the shriveling effect was widespread.

"Guess it's up to us to do the dishes," Windura observed, "seeing as how you've managed to run the guys off." With an exasperated shake of her head, she went on, "What *is* it with you two? One minute you seem to be getting along fine and then, wham! You're at each other's throats!"

"Guess I made him mad when I asked about the food," Micayla muttered. "It was all downhill after that."

"You could be a little nicer to him, you know," Windura chided. "I mean, I could understand if you couldn't stand the sight of him, but—"

"That's just it," Micayla moaned. "I *can't* stand the sight of him!"

"He's even more gorgeous than you are," Windura said frankly. "What's the matter? Are you jealous?"

"No," she insisted. "I'm not! I just, well, all I have to do is look at him and I want to bite him or at least snarl at him. It's all I can do to control it. It's very strange."

"That *is* weird," Windura agreed. "Glad you can keep from biting him, though. With those fangs of yours, you'd probably have him bleeding to death with one bite. Of course, that would give me an excuse to baby him a little."

Micayla's eyes widened. "*You want to baby him?*"

"The truth?" Windura stood up and faced Micayla squarely. "I'd like to do just about anything with him. I'm not picky. I'd take whatever I could get."

"Really?"

"Yeah, really," Windura replied. "Is that so hard to believe? I mean, he's a nice guy and he's gorgeous. What's not to like?"

Micayla was hard-pressed to reply. "I don't know," she said slowly. "I can't really say I don't like him—I don't know him well enough for that—it's just this compulsion I feel to scratch his eyes out just for looking in my direction. But at the same time, I can't take my eyes off of him—like the first time I saw him."

"Well, do me a favor and keep your claws out of him," Windura said. "I don't want him all ripped up."

Lerotan walked in just then seeming a bit harassed. "I got busy updating my logs," he began but stopped short at the sight of the empty plates. "Don't tell me I missed dinner!"

"We saved you a plate," Windura said, setting it down on the table.

Lerotan looked at it suspiciously, his raised eyebrow wrinkling the tattoo at his temple. "What is it?"

"We don't know," Micayla replied. "But it might be Kreater beast."

"Really?" he asked tipping up the plate. "Looks sort of like it—but then, I'll eat just about anything." Pulling up a chair he sat down and picked up his fork. "By the way, I passed Trag just now. Mind telling me why he looks like he wants to kill someone?"

"Probably because he does," Windura said. "Micayla pissed him off."

"Picked on his cooking, did you?" Lerotan said genially.

"Well, not exactly…" Micayla replied. "I just wanted to know what it was. Things deteriorated after that."

Lerotan folded his hands piously and gazed upward. "May the gods deliver me from sensitive cooks."

"And sensitive cats," Windura added sagely.

"Especially sensitive cats," Lerotan agreed.

"Go on," Windura said to her friend. "I'll finish this up."

"Hold on a second," Lerotan said. "As I recall, you ladies boarded my ship without any luggage. There are some women's clothes stored down in the hold. One of the men can show you where they are. Help yourself to anything you want."

"Thanks," said Windura. With a barely suppressed smile, she added, "I can't imagine how someone like you could have wound up with clothes but no females to go with them."

Lerotan shrugged. "You collect lots of things in my business. Some you need, some you keep in the hope that you might need them someday."

"Not a lot of room for extras on a ship, though," Windura commented.

"True," Lerotan agreed. "You just have to decide what's most important to you."

Micayla and Windura exchanged a look. Neither of the women understood why those particular items would have been important enough for him to keep but left it at that.

—◦◦◦—

"Sir," Worell reported, "we have received word that *The Equalizer* has been engaged and that the Nedwut ship is under fire from them and possibly another ship which may also be cloaked."

Grekkor glared at his chief assistant, fighting the urge to kill the messenger. "Idiots!" he spat. "When I find who *neglected* to tell me that we were sending only one ship full of those fool Nedwuts after a known arms dealer…" Taking a deep breath to calm himself, Grekkor added. "Find out who that was, would you please, Worell?"

"Yes, sir."

"And while you're at it, find out everything there is to know about Lerotan Kanotay—his ship, his contacts, his friends—anything that might help us track him down."

"That will be difficult, sir," Worell said candidly. "He deals in arms—illegally on many worlds—and there is no registry of such merchants."

Grekkor gripped the arms of his chair so tightly that the thin metal gave way beneath his hands. "Then find out who he's fucking!" he snarled as he released his grip—not so much to avoid damaging the armrest, but because his rings were cutting into his fingers. Smoothing out his sleeve, he added, "We all know that says more about a man than anything."

"The Hooker's Network is impossible to hack into, sir," Worell pointed out. "Many have tried, but—"

"Then find me a fucking whore who can tell me to my face!" Grekkor snarled. "Send Dolurp back to Orleon in a shuttle. Tell him to bring one of them in for questioning." Grekkor laughed pleasantly as another thought occurred to him. "They might even know something about the women who killed that poor Norludian."

"Sir, shall I give that as a reason?" Worell asked.

Grekkor glanced suspiciously at Worell, briefly noting that the man was as impassive and colorless as ever. "It *is* the reason." With a flick of his wrist, Grekkor added, "Just get one. I don't care how."

"Sir, we also have new information from the station," Worell went on. "A Nerik ship made an unscheduled departure from the docking ring not long after *The Equalizer*."

"And?"

"It left on the same heading."

"Interesting. A Nerik ship, you say—not one of ours?"

"No, sir," said Worell. "It is registered to a Nerik called Veluka."

"Could it have overtaken Kanotay's ship?"

"Possibly."

"Hmm, the plot thickens... wouldn't you say, Worell?"

Chapter 9

THE VOYAGE TO DARCONIA HAD TAKEN THREE WEEKS, and Micayla's first glimpse of that world had been the waves of heat rising from the desert floor as they landed at the spaceport. "Not exactly your tropical paradise, is it?" she said to Windura.

"No, but get a load of that," Windura replied, pointing with a gesture toward the city. "It looks like the whole place was carved out of stone."

This was true. From what Micayla could see, there was nothing to break the monotony of the dull yellowish brown of both the desert sand and the buildings in the city.

"The palace is over that way," Lerotan said with a gesture past the jumble of stone structures.

Micayla peered into the distance. The huge palace sat right in the center of a vast stretch of green farmland and looked like something straight out of *1001 Arabian Nights*. "Is it cooler there?" she asked hopefully.

Lerotan nodded. "It's not too bad once you're inside. Being built on the oasis source helps too."

Micayla was encouraged, but Windura was skeptical. "I don't know," she said. "Looks pretty hot to me."

They rode to the palace in hovercars which provided some relief from the heat, and upon their arrival, they were met by Tycharian and Kyra. Lerotan was right; it was cooler in the palace, but not by much.

Introductions were made and during the happy re-union which followed, Micayla studied Trag's brother, deciding that while they were both equally attractive, there were still differences. Seen together, they reminded her of two tigers. The white streak in Tychar's otherwise black hair and his china blue eyes made her think of a Siberian tiger, while Trag, with his orange streak and green eyes, was reminiscent of the Bengal variety. Their personalities were different too—Tychar was more cultured and charming, while Trag was a bit rough around the edges—but the most surprising thing was that she could talk to Tychar without feeling the need to hurt him. This made her wonder what would happen when the others arrived. Would she hiss at them? Or was it only guys with green eyes and a streak of orange in their hair that aroused her ire? On the other hand, it might not have had anything to do with how he looked; maybe it was the way he smelled.

She wished she could have tested that theory in some reasonable way, but other than saying flat out that she wanted to compare their scents, she didn't think it was likely. She'd kept as clear of Trag as she possibly could during their journey to Darconia—which was difficult on a ship that size—but she was no more comfortable in his presence than she had been from the start. If anything, the feeling had intensified.

⁓

The Darconian desert hadn't changed one iota since Trag had left it; still hot and desolate with nothing but rocks and sand all the way to the distant mountains. Kyra, however, was even more beautiful than he remembered.

They'd arrived in the early evening, and laughing joyously, she'd run to him and hugged him hard. His eyes stung from the desert glare—at least, that's what he told himself—but the effect of her scent on him was unmistakable; something told him that nudity on this visit was not an option. Perhaps it would be best to wear loose trousers and tight underwear because she still smelled like love, whether she was his brother's mate or not, and worst of all, except for a few jewels, she was naked. She still wore her long, dark hair in a braid, and memories of what it was like to free those tresses and feel them on his skin made him wish he'd stayed away.

"Wow, Trag," she exclaimed. "I almost didn't recognize you under all those clothes. Aren't you hot?"

"Been freezing to death ever since I left here," he replied. "I'm just starting to feel warm again."

"I don't suppose Jack is here yet, is she?" Lerotan asked.

"No, but we expect them soon. They had to go to Terra Minor to drop off the young ones, so you have no reason to gloat, Leroy," Kyra added, obviously noting his smug expression. "It's going to be so great having all of you here!"

"In the meantime, we have plenty of time to relax and plan our strategy," Trag said. "Got any fruit? I haven't had decent food since I started hanging out with these pirates."

"Pirates?" Lerotan echoed. "We are *not* pirates."

"Oh, lighten up, Leroy," Kyra said. "He's just kidding you, and you know it. Come on, Trag," she said kindly. "Let's go get you something to eat. You'll want to see the kids too." In an aside, she whispered, "One of them looks just like you."

Trag's heart nearly stopped at the thought of Kyra having his children. It wasn't possible, of course—she hadn't conceived until long after he'd left Darconia with Lerotan—but the idea still made his head swim.

He must have looked odd too, because Kyra took his hand, saying solicitously, "It's the heat, isn't it? You aren't used to it anymore. Remember how wilted I was when I first arrived?"

"How could I forget?" Trag said, trying to sound more cheerful than he felt. "You were fainting all the time."

"Oh, I was not," she said, giving his hair a tug. "But I *was* kinda puny," she admitted. "I'm pretty tough now."

Tough wasn't the word he would have used to describe her, but it didn't matter. Nothing did as long as she was in love with Ty.

Trag let her take him by the hand, inhaling her fragrance as she led him and the others through the maze of corridors to the dining room of their quarters. Trag was a little surprised to find them living in the palace, but apparently Queen Zealon had insisted. *Just like Scalia*.

Trag certainly hadn't been in love with the late queen, but he'd liked and respected her and the palace just didn't seem the same without her. But for Dobraton's failed coup, he would be there still, he and Ty sharing Kyra's love, and Kyra teaching piano to the princess.

So much had changed. He was free, but not truly free to go anywhere he wished, or to be with whomever he chose. Being Scalia's slave hadn't been hard, but being free was difficult. All of the other Zetithian survivors had found mates and had begun new lives. He had chosen a new life, but without love, there was no satisfaction in it.

—m—

Micayla watched the others interact during dinner, old friends and family enjoying a reunion that she only wished she could feel a part of. True, they were strangers, but she ought to have felt a sense of kinship or camaraderie at the very least. Instead, she felt on the outside, like the friend of a friend who had nowhere else to go for Thanksgiving dinner and was invited out of pity. Windura had even less of a connection to the group, but she seemed to be having a great time—though perhaps it was just from having a bunch of hulking Darconians around to protect her from Grekkor. The one called Dragus seemed quite taken with her and didn't bother to hide it, hitting on her unabashedly throughout the meal, which added to the fun. Micayla thought it would be much easier to parry comments from a guy who looked like a snub-nosed, upright *Tyrannosaurus rex* than it was to hold her own against someone like Rodan, who at least *looked* human—sort of.

It was Dragus who escorted the ladies to their quarters in the palace later that evening, explaining the workings of the glowstones—"You only have to think you need more or less light, and they'll do it"—and scrail cloths—"No water for baths; you wipe yourself off with these"—as well as the comstones. "If you ladies need anything—and I do mean *anything*—you be sure to let me know." He gave them each a necklace consisting of one small stone on a fine chain. Placing them around each of their necks, he went on, "You need to wear these at all times, and if you need me, just tap the stone and call my name and I'll be right there."

Micayla turned her back, pretending to be fascinated with the view from the window while trying very hard not to laugh. Rodan practically made her sick, but Dragus was kind of cute.

"I'll be happy to do *anything* for you," Dragus reiterated, his suggestive meaning perfectly clear. "Call me anytime."

"I'm sure we'll be just fine through the night," Windura told the amorous lizard before practically shutting the door in his face. The echoes of his ponderous tread had just begun to fade away when they both dissolved in giggles.

"Do you believe that?" Micayla said, wiping her streaming eyes. "A horny dinosaur!"

"I must admit, that's a first for me," Windura said. "Can't say I've ever been propositioned by a lizard before."

"First time for everything, I guess. I haven't laughed like that in a long time."

"Me either," Windura agreed. She was smiling when she said it but sobered considerably before she spoke again. "So, did you notice anything odd at dinner?"

"Like what?" Micayla returned. "I mean, other than the fact that our host and hostess weren't wearing clothes and some of the guests looked like prehistoric monsters?"

Windura shook her head. "No, I mean Trag," she replied. "He was acting very strangely." Pausing for a moment, she ran her hand through her hair and sighed. "If I didn't know better, I'd say he's in love with Kyra."

Since Micayla had done her best to avoid looking at Trag at all cost, these slight differences in his behavior were lost on her. "What makes you think that?"

"Well, every time I looked at him, he was looking at her," she said morosely. "The way his eyes were glowing was hard to miss. So much for *my* chances. She's freakin' beautiful."

"But she's also his brother's wife," Micayla pointed out. "It's not like he's going to marry her or anything."

"Yes, but before Kyra and Tychar were married, she apparently did a little something with Trag—at least, that's the impression I got. Maybe I should get a string of beads and dress like the Darconians," she added pensively. "It was weird having Tychar and Kyra naked all the time. He's completely stunning, of course, but—"

"Not starstruck anymore?" Micayla ventured.

"More like I'm stuck on the star's brother," Windura said lamely. "I know I don't stand a chance, but he is so totally hot, I just can't help it…"

"Well, I'm certainly not going to stand in your way," Micayla said briskly, "and I hate to say this, girlfriend, but if he's still all dreamy-eyed over Kyra, you probably *don't* stand a chance."

Windura sighed again. "Yeah, I know. Story of my life. If there's one thing I've learned, it's that hunks don't notice geeks like me until their computers break down—and then it's just a pat on the back on my way out, or on the ass if I'm lucky."

"There's nothing wrong with being appreciated for your talents," Micayla said wisely. "Trust me, being attractive to men isn't all it's cracked up to be."

"Yeah, maybe," Windura grumbled. "But just *once* I'd like to have a problem like that."

Micayla couldn't help but laugh. "There's always Dragus."

"He's a hoot, isn't he?" Windura agreed. "Of course, given the size of the rest of him, he must have a dick as long as your arm. He'd probably kill me with it."

"Still, he might be better than Rodan," Micayla said with a shudder. "I don't even want to *think* about that."

Windura was laughing too, but reluctantly. "Yeah, or Hidar." Shaking her head, she went on, "I see what you mean, but if Trag was nuts about you, wouldn't you at least talk to him?"

"You've seen what happens when we try," Micayla said with a shrug. "We're like oil and water. We just don't mix."

"Well, I think you should try harder," Windura said bluntly. "He doesn't deserve to be treated like that."

"I know," Micayla moaned. "But I just can't help it. The funny thing is, I keep thinking he should be doing something."

"Like what?"

"I don't know," Micayla replied. "Something to make me change the way I feel about him—but whatever it is, he's not doing it."

Windura stretched out on her bed and stared up at the ceiling. "Maybe it's a Zetithian thing. There's lots of things you don't know about them."

"Yeah, like damn near everything," Micayla agreed. "And it's for sure Trag won't enlighten me."

"Maybe you should talk to Kyra or Tychar," Windura suggested, sounding rather sleepy.

"Yeah, maybe," Micayla agreed. "But right now I'm too tired to think about it."

"Me too," said Windura. Snuggling down into her pillow, she added, "You know, this living in a palace could grow on me. I've never been on a more comfortable bed. It sure beats that cot of Hidar's—although, after seeing everything else around here, I was afraid we'd be sleeping on a bed of rocks."

"Me too," Micayla agreed. "Want to try the lights?"

"Go for it."

Micayla directed her thoughts to the glowstones set into the ceiling and wished it was dark. The stones slowly dimmed in response. "Now *that's* cool," she remarked.

Unfortunately, it was the only thing cool on Darconia, which they discovered the next morning.

"My God, it's hot here," Micayla said over breakfast. "I'm already thinking about stripping down and the sun's barely up yet."

"It takes a while to acclimate," Kyra said, passing her a glass of fruit juice. "Just be sure to drink plenty of fluids and wear whatever you feel comfortable in. I'll be happy to loan you some beads if you like."

"I'll keep that in mind," Micayla said, pausing to take a sip. Just then, Trag walked in wearing nothing but a pair of low-slung, loose-fitting shorts, nearly causing her to choke on her juice.

Windura was less subtle, letting out a low whistle. "Damn, Trag, you look—well—*fabulous*."

"Handsome devil, isn't he?" Kyra said proudly. "Overdressed, of course, but still very handsome."

"I, um, thought this was best, under the circumstances," Trag muttered as he took a seat next to Kyra. "Nice to feel warm again, though."

Kyra leaned over to give him a one-armed hug. "Nice to have you here," she said warmly. "We hardly ever get to see you anymore. You should visit more often."

"Yeah, I know," Trag said, piling his plate with fruit. "It's the only place I can feel warm enough *and* get decent food."

"You know, you don't have to leave," Kyra reminded him. "You could stay here from now on."

Trag shrugged. "I'll think about it."

Micayla was staring at Trag's bare chest as though her eyes were stuck to it. Sitting at the table, he might as well have been naked except for the comstone hanging from a chain around his neck, and though his certainly wasn't the first perfect male body she'd ever seen, she felt an overwhelming urge to bite him. She'd just picked out a spot on his shoulder to sink her fangs into when she was distracted by the arrival of Lerotan, who was dressed in the same kind of shorts as Trag, except that his were made from a thin, gauzy material that left very little to the imagination and had a slit up the back to accommodate his tail. He was followed by Hidar who, having never worn clothing of any kind, looked the same as always, and by Rodan, who was completely naked. Windura let out a shriek and fled from the room.

"Was it something I said?" Lerotan inquired blandly.

"I think she's gone to find Dragus," Micayla said, noting that she had to swallow some excess saliva before she spoke. "They had an appointment. She must have just remembered it."

"Uh-*huh*," Lerotan said, sounding unconvinced. "Must have been important."

"Oh, it was," Micayla assured him. "*Very* important."

Lerotan was still staring out the open doorway at Windura's retreating figure, his tail lashing back and forth like that of an angry lion.

"I don't think Vessonians are comfortable with nudity," Kyra said, filling in the awkward silence. "We've had a few Vessonian traders here, but they never seem to stay very long."

"That must be it," Lerotan said absently. Frowning, he took a seat across from Micayla and bit rather savagely into a large peach-like fruit. Rodan sat down next to him—thankfully out of Micayla's line of sight, though it wouldn't have mattered anyway because her gaze was once again riveted to that succulent spot on Trag's left shoulder.

Deciding that Lerotan had the right idea, Micayla picked up a fruit that looked a little like an apple and, though it wasn't quite as satisfying as she'd hoped, sank her fangs into it, letting the juice run down her chin. She'd eaten several bites before she noticed Kyra's giggles.

She glanced at her hostess questioningly, but Kyra only shot a look at Hidar before staring back down at her own plate.

Following Kyra's glance, Micayla saw that while all three of the men were attacking pieces of whole fruit as if they were starving, Hidar was delicately slicing his with a knife and fork held in his claw-like forelegs. Skewering a tiny bit with the fork, Hidar then held it up to his bony mandibles, his antennae beating furiously as he nibbled off an infinitesimal amount.

"I cannot eat this," Hidar announced, putting down his fork. "I need cooked food."

"You ate it last night," Lerotan said, "didn't you?"

"I did not," Hidar said petulantly. "I was very hungry, but I did not eat."

"Sorry, Hidar," Kyra said, "but hardly anybody cooks their food here—not in the palace, anyway."

"Then I will starve," Hidar said, his voice sounding even more high-pitched and piteous than usual. "Or I must return to the ship for sustenance."

"You could go to the McDonald's," Micayla suggested. "I saw one on the way from the spaceport. I'm sure they can cook something up for you."

"After all we went through to get that McDonald's, I can't believe I didn't think of it first," Kyra exclaimed. "Great idea!"

At the mere mention of the name, Hidar's antennae had stopped waving and now stood straight up. "A McDonald's?" he said. "I must have missed it. Where did you say it was?"

"It's not far," Kyra replied. "Just beyond the outer edge of the farmland that surrounds the palace. One of the guards could take you there in a hovercar."

Hidar stood up, fluttering his wings. "No need," he said. "I will fly." Perching briefly on the casement, he launched himself from the open window and was gone.

"Good thing there wasn't any glass in those windows," Micayla muttered.

"I don't remember this being a problem the last time you were here," Kyra said, clearly puzzled by Hidar's behavior.

"I think he's going through the change," Lerotan replied. "It's a Scorillian thing. They get really picky when they're about to molt."

"Ah, I see," said Kyra. "Well, if he doesn't want to fly over to McDonald's for every meal, we can have it delivered." Grinning at Micayla, she added, "It's one of the perks of living in a palace. Free delivery." With a quick glance in his direction, she went on, casually, "Trag, you need to take Micayla and show her The Shrine."

"The Shrine?"

"Yes," Kyra replied. "It's where the slaves used to live, but it's the most beautiful part of the palace. Actually, there are two of them; one is the oasis source and one is like a huge greenhouse. You need to see them both."

Micayla tried to think of a reason to say no, knowing that Trag wouldn't like the idea any more than she did, but couldn't come up with an excuse. Instead, she stammered out, "I—I don't think—I'm not sure he would want—"

"I'll take you," Rodan volunteered eagerly. "I know where it is."

The thought of being escorted through the palace by a nude Rodan nearly sent Micayla into shock. "Don't bother, Rodan," she began, "I'm sure I can—"

"I'll do it," Trag said shortly, cutting off her protest as he got to his feet. "Come on."

He was quick on his feet—was almost to the door by the time Micayla got up to follow him—but even so, she thought he was moving rather stiffly.

"I'm only doing this so you won't have to go with Rodan," he said over his shoulder as soon as they were out of earshot. "I wouldn't wish that on anybody."

"Even me?" Micayla said grimly.

"Even you," he said shortly. "Even though you *were* sitting there looking like you wanted to take a piece out of me." Scowling at her, he added, "I've already figured out that you can't stand the sight of me, but do you have to keep rubbing my nose in it?"

"I can't—"

"Help it?" he finished for her. "Yeah, I've figured that out too."

Micayla tried counting to three but only made it to two before retorting, "You're pretty damned obvious yourself. I saw the way—"

Rounding on her with fangs bared and eyes glowing like an inferno, he said tersely, "Don't say it."

"Windura noticed it too," she went on. "You should be more careful."

"It's none of her business either," he said, turning on his heel to charge off down the corridor again. "Come on, *Mick*. Let's get this over with."

He'd already taken so many turns, Micayla was sure she'd never find her way back to her room or anywhere else, so she had no choice but to follow him. He seemed to be walking better, but unfortunately, his shoulder looked like it needed biting again. She could almost feel herself running toward him, pouncing on him, digging into him with her nails and fangs. She was just about to lose all control and do just that when the guard posted by an ornate set of doors called out:

"Hey there, Slave Boy! I heard you were back. How the hell you been?"

"Just fine, Hartak," Trag replied, wincing as the huge Darconian pounded him on the back in greeting. "This is Micayla," he said, cocking a thumb at her. "Okay if I show her The Shrine?"

"Oh, yeah, sure," Hartak said. "Anybody can go in now. I've got the easiest job in the palace." Grinning at Micayla he added, "'Course, I used to have the *best* job in the palace."

"Oh," Micayla said with a questioning look at Trag. "Really?"

Trag laughed. "He was Kyra's guard."

"God, I loved that job." Hartak sighed. Shaking his fearsome head, he added longingly, "Those were the days."

"Well, for *you*, maybe," Trag conceded, "but I was a slave. Remember?"

"And now you're a pilot," Hartak said with frank admiration. "You always said you could fly anything. Looks like you've proved it."

"Yeah, I guess so," Trag said, seeming slightly embarrassed. "We're just going to have a look around. Is the stairway open?"

"Yeah," Hartak replied. "It's even clean." With a sweeping gesture, he added, "Welcome to The Shrine of the Desert, Micayla. Enjoy your visit."

Micayla was already uncomfortably hot, but as soon as she passed through the entrance, the heat became even more pronounced and the humidity level quadrupled. It was like trying to breathe through hot, wet cotton.

"You used to *live* here?" she said incredulously. "I can barely breathe! How did you stand it?"

"I lived here for twenty years," Trag replied, taking a deep, obviously satisfying breath. "You get used to it."

"Now I understand why you're so cold all the time," she said, fanning her face, "but I don't think I'd want to spend much time in here myself." Walking toward the middle, she turned slowly, taking it all in. They were standing inside an enormous clear bubble set against the back of the palace, which afforded a breathtaking view of the distant mountains. Just inside the doors to the left, water cascaded from a carved niche high up in the stone wall, while blooming, tropical plants grew in profusion all around her. Beyond the glass dome was a walled patio sitting on top of the portico that encircled the palace, half of which was sheltered from the sun by a domed roof supported by six stone columns. "It *is* pretty, though."

"Yeah," Trag said with a quiet sigh. "A beautiful cage for Scalia's little slave boys. I'll say this much for her—she kept us alive and gave us a nice place to live. Too bad she had to die to set us free."

Something in his tone struck her, and she looked over at him, suddenly seeing him in a completely different light. "You were fond of her?"

Trag nodded. "We *all* liked her. Hell, Sladnil was in love with her—and he's a Norludian. I know it sounds weird for slaves to actually like their master, but we did. She was quite a queen."

"I can't imagine what it would be like to be a slave," Micayla said slowly. "It must have been horrible."

"Not really. We were well treated; we just couldn't leave the palace. That was the hard part." Laughing mirthlessly, he added, "Trouble is, now that I'm free, there are *still* places I can't go."

"The bounty?"

Trag nodded. "That and other things."

She thought she understood him, which prompted her to ask, "What do you think our chances are going up against someone like Grekkor?"

"Not good," he replied. "Though Jack's a tough one to cross. She knows an awful lot of people throughout the galaxy—some allies and some enemies—and with her on our side, our chances improve significantly." He paused, then added, "I don't know about you, but I'd rather not have to spend every minute my life wondering when I'm gonna get shot in the back. I think we at least have to try."

Nodding, Micayla said, "Or end up in another cage."

"Yeah. No matter how big or how beautiful it is, it's still a cage." Motioning toward the outer doors, he said, "Come on, I'll show you the rest."

Micayla followed him down a spiral staircase built inside one of the gleaming columns to ground level. Trag led the way underneath the portico to an open chamber below and to the east of The Shrine they had just left.

"I saw this for the first time the night we escaped from the palace after Scalia was assassinated," he said. "I'm not sure the effect will be the same in daylight as it was in the dark, but the whole room is lined with glowstone."

It was dazzling enough by day with the eruption of water in the center basin spilling over the smooth stones, but Micayla could only imagine what it must have been like to come out of the darkness into the light of such a shrine. She had to shade her eyes for a moment even after adjusting to the blazing sunshine outside. There were several Darconians there, some carrying water away in large flasks, some just gazing in awe at the power of the life-giving water. "This looks more like a shrine, doesn't it?"

Trag nodded. "It was the original one, but it was closed for years until Zealon became queen." Gesturing toward the water, he added, "You should get a drink while you're here. It's supposed to be good luck to drink from either of the fountains."

"And we need all the luck we can get, don't we?" she said with a grim smile.

Micayla stepped up to the water's edge, momentarily mesmerized by the clear water flowing smoothly over the polished stone. Taking a cup from the low shelf carved beneath the lip, she scooped up a portion and drank, feeling the cool strength of it flowing throughout her body. "It certainly makes you feel better," she commented. "What's in it?"

"Nothing," he replied with a shrug. "It's just water."

Noting that he seemed to be making no move to take a cup of his own, she prompted, "Aren't you going to have some?"

Trag shook his head. "I used to drink from the one upstairs all the time," he said. "Any luck I might have gotten from it has probably all been used up by now."

"All the more reason to drink some more," she urged. Dipping her cup once again, she offered it to him.

Trag took the cup, albeit reluctantly, and began to drink.

"Ah," said a nearby Darconian woman. "You are lovers. I thought as much."

Upon hearing this, Trag choked and began coughing violently while Micayla drew back in surprise. "Oh, no we aren't!" she protested.

"But you have given water to him from a cup that has touched your own lips," the Darconian said. "There can be no doubt."

"Maybe she did," Trag gasped between coughs, "but we aren't Darconians—different rules!"

The Darconian woman laughed. "The Great Mother of the Desert does not recognize those distinctions," she said archly. "What the water of The Shrine bestows cannot be denied."

"What are you, the High Priestess or something?" Micayla demanded, still aghast at the notion that she would ever mate with Trag, whose effect on her was anything but lover-like.

"Yes," the woman replied. "I am Shentuk, Keeper of The Shrine of the Desert."

"Must be a new job," Trag muttered. "I never heard any of that when I lived here before."

"Many of the old beliefs were lost when this shrine was closed," Shentuk explained. "When it was reopened, ancient texts were discovered that described the powers of the water." Smiling, she shook her head, causing the beads of her many necklaces to clink together. The sound echoed throughout the chamber even more than their voices had done, and when Shentuk spoke again, her words were strangely amplified. "As The Great Mother of the Desert has willed it, so shall it be."

It may have just been a trick of the acoustics in The Shrine, but to Micayla, it sounded disturbingly like a prophesy.

Bowing his head as though in acceptance, Trag whispered, "Let's get out of here—now!"

"I'm with you on that one," she whispered back.

Aloud, Trag muttered his thanks to Shentuk and then hustled Micayla toward the door.

Chapter 10

"YOU DON'T REALLY BELIEVE ANY OF THAT MYSTICAL crap, do you?" Micayla said as she headed back toward the stairs, Shentuk's laughter echoing behind them.

Taking her by the arm, Trag muttered, "Not that way," pulling her in the opposite direction. "Might be bad luck. Maybe taking the long way around will cancel it out."

"I suppose I can take that as a yes," Micayla said dryly. "Trag, I'm surprised at you!"

"Listen," said Trag, "I've seen a lot of strange stuff—prophesies, visions, and such—and if there's one thing I've learned, it's that you can't always dismiss them as mystical nonsense."

"So, what are you saying?" she said, jogging to keep up with him. "That we're cursed or something?"

"Shit, I don't know," Trag said. "But it sure as hell sounded like it to me."

Micayla remained skeptical. "Mind telling me just what visions you've seen?"

"I haven't had any myself," Trag said, striking off again at a fast pace through the portico, "but Ty has. He had a vision that Kyra would come and that his life would change."

"Oh, surely you don't believe that!" she scoffed. "Did he tell you that before or after she arrived?"

"After," Trag replied, "but—"

"Well, that was convenient," she said mildly. "I'm not sure I'd believe it myself unless he told me ahead of time."

"Yes, but Cat does it too," Trag countered. "He had a vision that Nedwuts blew up Zetith, and that one turned out to be true—just wish he'd had one about Rutger Grekkor! He also knows when women friends are pregnant—even the sex of the children—and Leo's had a few mystical experiences of his own. It's a Zetithian thing," he added, looking nervously over his shoulder as though the curse was somehow following them.

Following his glance, Micayla saw Shentuk standing by the entrance to The Shrine, waving at them in farewell. "Oh, really?"

"Yes, really," Trag assured her.

"Well, be that as it may, *I've* never had any visions—well, not like that, though I do have a sort of déjà vu thing now and then—and you say you haven't either, so…"

"No, I haven't," he admitted, "but that doesn't mean I can't start, and right now, I'm seeing disaster."

"Disaster?" she echoed. "Being my mate would be a *disaster?*"

"What—you think we'd be the happiest couple in history?"

"Well, no, maybe not, but—"

"I'm not chancing it," he said roundly. Reaching the corner of the palace walls, he turned quickly, breathing a sigh of relief as though escaping Shentuk's line of sight made such a horrendous calamity less likely.

Trag walked on in silence after that but at least slackened his pace. Micayla had no idea what he was thinking, but she was trying to understand why his flat refusal irked her so much. After all, practically every man she'd ever met would have given his left nut for the chance to—

That was it, she decided. She wasn't feeling hurt because he didn't want her—and it wasn't vanity, either. It was simply that, having had to refuse so many men in the past, it seemed odd when she didn't have to. The novelty of it appealed to her for some reason, and she smiled to herself.

—⁓—

Trag happened to glance at her just then and caught her smile. "I really mean it, Mick," he said. "Not a chance."

"That's fine," she said, still smiling disturbingly. He must have appeared skeptical, for she added, "No, really, I don't mind at all."

"Good," he said shortly.

"In fact," she went on, "I think we should make a pact *not* to be lovers."

"I like that idea," Trag said with a firm nod. "We will not be lovers, no matter what The Great Mother of the Desert has to say about it."

"Agreed," she said, holding out her hand. "Pact?"

"Pact," Trag said, gripping her hand tightly. "And don't hiss at me anymore."

"I only did that once, Trag!" she protested. "I still don't know why, either—but I'll try not to."

"And while we're at it," he said as another thought occurred to him, "don't tease me about Kyra. I know it's not right, but I can't help how I feel."

"Okay," she said, "but can I make one request?"

"Maybe," he said cautiously. "What is it?"

"Rodan," she said with a shudder. "Just don't leave me alone with him if you can help it."

"You aren't afraid of him, are you?" Trag asked in surprise. "I thought you were tough."

"Maybe so, but that doesn't mean I want to be alone with him. Especially not when he's naked."

Trag chuckled knowingly. "Scary, isn't it?"

"You know, on Earth, a well-endowed man is generally referred to as being hung like a horse, but he's more like a bull elephant."

Trag couldn't help but think that Rodan would be proud of this analogy, but he kept that opinion to himself. "Okay. You don't tease me about Kyra, and I won't give Rodan the chance to try anything funny."

"Good," she said, "because if I have to, I'll rip his big, hairy donkey balls off and feed them to the rats—or whatever they have around here."

Trag also promised to warn Rodan not to suggest anything that might put said balls within the range of Micayla's fangs. Trag was thankful that his own jewels were hidden securely inside his pants. After all, he didn't want her getting any ideas.

―⁂―

Several days later, the palace received a message that the *Jolly Roger* was on its way.

"They've left the younger ones on Terra Minor with Bonnie and Lynx as planned," Tychar said as he read Jack's missive to the group. "Lynx wanted to come here, of course, but Bonnie needs him."

"I'm sure she does," Kyra said. "That would be six babies to care for—along with her farm. Still, I wish

Jack had been able to bring everyone," she added wistfully. "I'd love to see them."

"It's probably best that they stay on Terra Minor," Tychar said. "Better climate, not to mention very strict landing regulations."

"Yes, but we live in a palace with guards," Kyra reminded her husband. "Scalia kept you guys safe for twenty years, and we've got a whole lot more room than Bonnie does."

"She lives on a farm, for heaven's sake," Trag pointed out. "They've probably got tons of room."

"Well, she did say that she and Lynx had built on to the house," Kyra admitted. Sighing, she added, "Wouldn't it be great if we all lived on the same planet?"

"Perhaps when this matter is settled, we will be able to," Tychar said soberly. "But until that time, as Jack always says, it's best not to put all of our eggs in one basket."

"And Terra Minor is the safest basket there is," Kyra agreed. "Maybe someday."

Micayla listened to this discussion with interest, the idea of a whole planet populated by Zetithians capturing her imagination. Always considered an oddity before, in present company she was among the majority for the first time since that fateful day when she was separated from her family, and she was already beginning to realize what it would it be like to be a part of that culture and not feel quite so alone in the universe.

Even so, as the only Zetithian female, there was no one with whom she could truly relate. Kyra knew firsthand what it was like to love a Zetithian, whereas Micayla and Windura could only guess at it, and now that Micayla had made her pact with Trag, Windura probably stood a better chance of being Trag's lover than she did.

Micayla leaned back in her chair, her eyes widening in shock. She was actually thinking about it! Was she already regretting their agreement? Stealing a glance at Trag, she found she could easily restrain herself from biting or hissing at him now, but just then he grinned at something Tychar said and the feeling returned.

"I still do," Tychar was saying. "Think you're up to it?"

"I feel pretty good," Trag replied. "I think I could handle it."

"Tonight, then," Tychar said.

Having lost the thread of the conversation, Micayla looked questioningly at Tychar, who explained, "We used to run on top of the portico at night when we were slaves. It kept us from going crazy."

"And made them that much more irresistible to the poor, unsuspecting piano teacher," Kyra added. "I nearly fainted when I first saw them—though the heat might have had something to do with my reaction."

"I can imagine it would," Windura said frankly. "It's taking a long time for me to get used to it too."

Since she and Windura had been taking it easy since their arrival in an attempt to adjust to the Darconian climate, Micayla hadn't done anything more strenuous than walking the corridors of the palace, but she was already beginning to feel the sluggishness she normally associated with inactivity. "I could use a run," she said. "If the heat doesn't kill me, that is."

Tychar eyed her speculatively, but it was Trag who commented. "She's tough enough," he said, "as long as we don't spend too much time in The Shrine."

"I don't do very well in there either," Kyra agreed. "It's much too humid!"

Micayla knew quite well that Trag hadn't been referring to the humidity level since she'd been giving both shrines a wide berth following their meeting with Shentuk. If his initial reaction to the "prophesy" was any indication, she suspected that he was doing the same. And she didn't blame him one bit.

The three Darconian moons were shining down on the stone portico as Micayla emerged from The Shrine. Tychar led the way, but nothing in his perfect male form affected her the way the presence of Trag walking beside her did. His eyes glowed in the moonlight when he happened to glance at her, sending tendrils of carnivorous urges wending their way through her brain. She should want to kiss him. There was nothing about him that should have made her feel so vicious. She should be admiring him.

"You aren't going to run like that, are you?" Tychar asked with an amused twinkle.

She glanced at Trag and then back at Ty. "Like what?"

"With clothes on," he replied. "You won't make it halfway around the palace."

Out of the corner of her eye, she could see Trag stripping off his pants before skimming off his stretchy undergarment. She averted her eyes abruptly, not wanting to see his cock. It would look just like Tychar's, after all, she reasoned. No need to look at it. Certainly no need to *stare*...

"What about you?" Tychar asked her.

The clothing she wore would have been comparable to a bikini on Earth, but on Darconia it was more like wearing a cloak. "I think I'll keep it on," she replied. "It's not that hot, really."

Tychar smiled. "Not until you start running," he said. "Then you may realize just how hot it truly is."

"I'll take that chance," she said.

"Okay, then, let's go."

The two brothers sprang forward as though on springs and began running lightly over the smooth stone surface, and Micayla was right with them. The three of them ran abreast of each other for a while, but Micayla couldn't help but be distracted by the way their dicks swung back and forth with each stride. Finally, she decided it was either run on ahead or drop behind. Knowing that running any faster would be a mistake, she slowed down and let them pass her, but it wasn't much better. Trag's bare butt was begging to be bitten even more than his shoulder had.

They didn't let her stay behind for long, but slowed enough for her to catch them.

"You okay?" Trag asked. "Want us to slow down?"

"I'm fine," Micayla replied. "Just pacing myself." *And trying very hard not to stare at your ass.*

―――

Trag would have preferred that she run ahead or at least abreast so he wouldn't have to worry about her, but he came to the conclusion that being able to see her was getting to him. Granted, she wasn't naked and didn't smell of desire—which would have been difficult to assess since his nose wasn't all that sensitive for a Zetithian's—but he knew that just one tiny little whiff of desire would have his cock bouncing like a drumstick. *No,* he thought with an inward groan, *I am not attracted to her. I do not mean to entice her. I will not do it…*

Trag dropped back and fell in behind her. *Bad move,* he chastised himself. *Now I can see her ass.* He may not have liked her—well, he couldn't even say that now—but he had to admit, she had a damn fine hind end on her. He shook his head, trying to dash away the vision. Nope, still there and still looking like it needed… What? No, not that. She'd kill him if he tried it. Then he remembered that if she didn't want him, it wouldn't matter; without the scent of her desire, his limp noodle wasn't going anywhere. Not for the first time in his life, he cursed that particular trait of Zetithian males. He could have had sex every single day of his twenty years of slavery if he'd been able to get it up without the right scent. Scalia had tried many times to get him hard, but nothing ever happened. Instead he lived in a palace, wore a collar and a cock strap made of jewels, did a little light housekeeping, and kept Scalia company while freaks like Sladnil and Refdeck fucked her. Not that he'd really wanted to, but just possessing the ability would have been nice.

He knew that, unlike Zetithians, males of other species only had to *think* about sex to get a stiff dick and could even make themselves ejaculate. Trag used to think this was ridiculous and had once made the statement that having sex without a woman was like trying to eat rocks, but getting his rocks off now and then might have made life more tolerable—might have made him less inclined to beg Kyra to take pity on him too.

Now there was a perfectly good Zetithian girl running just ahead of him and he'd made a no-sex pact with her. "Brilliant move there, Trag," he muttered to himself. "Fuckin' brilliant!" There wasn't a single female on the whole damn planet he could fuck except Kyra. He knew Windura liked him well enough, but he wasn't about to mess with a nice girl like that if he couldn't love her. Wincing, he realized that just as before, any time spent on Darconia would be lacking in sex.

His feet fell into a steady rhythm on the stone as he remembered the hookers, which were all he'd ever had except for Kyra. Hookers were good. They provided a valuable service. He'd have to remember to tip them better in the future—especially if whoever it was had an ass like Micayla's. In the end, he just gave up and stared at it—which was fortunate because when she stumbled and nearly fell, he was right there to catch her.

He knew what was wrong as soon as he pulled her into his arms. "Damn! I knew we should have brought along some water!"

"We are almost to The Shrine," Tychar said. "Can you walk?"

"I—don't know," Micayla mumbled. "I was doing just fine, but all of a sudden…"

"Yeah, it hits you like that," Trag said knowledgeably. "No warning and then—bam!—you're on your ass."

His choice of words may have reflected the body part he seemed to be preoccupied with, but no one else noticed.

"I will get some water," Tychar said before sprinting off toward The Shrine.

Sweeping Micayla off her unsteady feet and into his arms, Trag thought he was okay with it—until he looked down. Holding her against his chest, her breasts were pressed together with the end result that they were almost fully exposed in the moonlight.

Silently cursing the Darconian moons for being so illuminating, he stared straight ahead and marched onward, trying to ignore Micayla's frequent, though decidedly feeble, protests.

"You don't have to carry me," she said faintly. "I—I can walk."

"Aw, just shut up and let me be heroic for once," Trag said after listening to several pleas. "Ty got to carry Kyra when she was fainting all the time. Now it's my turn."

Micayla giggled softly. "You *want* to be a hero?"

"All guys do," Trag said with a firm nod. "And you don't get the opportunity very often. You gotta grab it while you can."

To his surprise, she laughed again. "I'll try to faint more often."

"No need to make a habit of it," he said. "I'm sure I'll survive."

—∿∿—

Micayla wasn't sure she would, though. Then it hit her: she was being carried around an exotic desert palace by a very handsome naked man—and she *still* wasn't turned on. *What is* wrong *with me? This is every girl's dream and I might as well be in Dragus's arms for all the effect it's having!* For the thousandth time, she wished there was at least one other Zetithian female around for her to talk to—preferably one that was older and had at least had children. After all, she couldn't very well ask Trag why she felt no sexual attraction to him; it would certainly kill any heroism inherent in their current situation, not to mention the severe blow to his ego. The worst part of it was that she was much too close to his shoulder for comfort. Her mouth had been dry as a bone while she was running, but now she was salivating so much she had to swallow to keep from drooling. And he smelled so... bitable. Not edible, precisely... just something she wanted to—

"Here," Tychar said as he approached and held a cup of water to her lips. "Drink this."

Micayla drank it gratefully, hoping it would wash away whatever it was that was making her feel so strange. She'd been overheated and dehydrated before, but this was different.

"You go on, Ty," Trag said. "She can rest out here where it's cooler."

Tychar nodded and disappeared inside the transparent bubble as Trag lowered Micayla to a nearby bench. He was right about it being cooler there; she was even shivering slightly.

"It always amazed me the way the temperature would drop so quickly at night and then heat up almost immediately when the sun comes up." Sitting down beside her, he gestured toward the sheltered patio. "I used to sleep out here all the time."

The space beneath the dome was shaded from the moonlight, but she could still see the soft glow of his eyes, and, at least for the moment, she wasn't hissing and he wasn't angry or irritated with her. Now that she had him at her disposal, numerous questions resurfaced, beginning with: "What was Zetith like?"

Trag shook his head. "I hardly remember, but from what Jack tells me about Earth, they were pretty similar—some parts of it, anyway. Cool green forests with trees so big you could live in them, some open grassland, lakes and rivers, blue sky—that sort of thing."

Micayla nodded. "On Earth I lived near the redwood forest—the tallest trees on the planet. I always felt best when I was beneath those trees. Maybe that's why."

Trag turned away from her abruptly but said "yeah" in an odd tone that had Micayla peering curiously at him. He leaned back, resting his weight on one hand while spearing the fingers of the other so forcefully through his hair it was a wonder he didn't pull out a whole handful of it.

"And neither of us can go there anymore," she said with a wistful sigh. "Can we?"

"Nope," he replied. He hesitated a moment before turning his gaze on her once again. "Mind telling me why you left?"

Micayla shook her head slowly. "I don't know," she said. "It just seemed like something I needed to do. Maybe I thought I could find out who—or what—I was."

"Well, now you know."

"Yeah, now I know," she began, but added, "and I still don't know very much. Just enough to know I'll never see my homeworld or any family I might have had there."

Trag waved a hand at the starry sky—a sky almost as clear as the view from a starship. "I used to lie out here and look up at the billions of stars up there thinking just how small and insignificant this planet—hell, this whole solar system!—was in comparison to the rest of the universe. And me least of all; one tiny little being on a world where I didn't belong." Gripping another handful of his hair, he exclaimed, "God, I wanted to get off this rock! And now, it's the only place I feel at home—but it's still not right."

"I think I know what you mean," she said. "Earth is my home, but I never felt as if I belonged there; I was always an outsider. Remember what Kyra said about all of us living on one planet? It'd be nice, wouldn't it?"

Trag laughed scornfully. "There aren't enough of us left to fill a space cruiser, let alone a planet. I think we're a lost cause."

"Jack—it *was* 'Jack' wasn't it?—doesn't seem to think so. Tell me about her."

Trag chuckled. "She bought Cat at a slave auction so he could pose as her master when she went to Statzeel to try to find her sister who was a slave there. In fact, *all* Statzeelian women are slaves. Does that tell you anything?"

"That she's completely crazy?" Micayla suggested with a wry smile.

"Probably," Trag admitted. "But she loves Cat to pieces, and he—" He stopped abruptly, his expression sobering as he bit his lip and looked away again.

"What is it?" she prompted, noting his sudden change of mood.

"Nothing," he replied. "Just—nothing." He surged to his feet and turned, holding out his hand. "Come on. You'll be all right now. Let's get you to bed."

In any other context, his words might have been suggestive, and when spoken by a naked hunk, the effect
tripled, but if he was intending to share that bed with her,
it wasn't obvious. His long, thick cock was right at eye
level, displaying a decided lack of interest—something
that, if all the talk meant anything, most men's would have
done. She wasn't interested either, though she thought she
should have been, but the reason for that escaped her.

"Tell me something else," she began. "When I landed
on Lerotan's ship, even though we didn't exactly get
off to a good start, he seemed to think you'd be glad to
see someone like me, and yet you weren't—at least, it
didn't seem that way—and you probably should have
been. Why were you looking for a Zetithian woman if
you didn't want—"

Trag's stormy expression cut her off, but instead
of yelling at her, he let out a resigned sigh. "Because
I knew I'd never find one," he replied. "I could keep
on feeling the way I do about Kyra while pretending to
want someone else and no one would ever realize it."

"But you did find one."

"Yeah, I did." Pinning her with a look, he added,
"Jack won't like this a bit."

Micayla didn't have to ask what he was referring to.
"Don't tell her."

"If you think that'll make any difference," Trag
snickered, "then you've got a lot to learn about Jack."

Later that night, Micayla lay in her bed staring up at
the ceiling. Thanks to the moons and the lack of cloud
cover, it was rarely completely dark on Darconia, but
it really didn't matter; she wasn't looking at it anyway.
She was thinking.

That little bit of time spent alone with Trag had changed her opinion of him. She was even beginning to suspect that they could become friends. She'd eventually get over the need to tear hunks out of him; she only needed to get used to being around him. Then it would go away.

Windura's steady breathing indicated her deep slumber, but Micayla was as far from sleep as she'd ever been. She couldn't see herself as a member of Lerotan's crew forever, even though it wasn't much different from her previous post. She was, after all, doing the same kind of work, just in a different setting. Pretty soon she'd feel like one of the crew, Rodan would prove to be nothing but hot air, and Hidar—well, Hidar would molt and would hopefully be more chipper. The men would eventually understand that she wasn't like other women and would quit teasing her. She'd just be one of the guys.

Right. If only it didn't feel so wrong.

———⁓———

Beontal faced the viewscreen with casual indifference. "Let me be sure I understand this, Mr. Grekkor. You want a hooker to question regarding the death of the Norludian merchant?"

"Yes, I should have thought that was self-evident when Dolurp asked for one."

Beontal went from casual to skeptical in a heartbeat. "And would you be so kind as to tell me why a hooker— *any* hooker—would have the information you require?"

"It has to do with someone else involved in the case," Grekkor said, reluctant to reveal anything further, but doing his best to conceal that fact.

"Ah, so the two women had an accomplice?"

"I believe so," Grekkor replied. "You need only to allow my man to bring one of the hookers to me for questioning."

Beontal's smile was decidedly chilly. "I should have thought that was *my* job."

"I only wish to be of assistance," Grekkor said. "I don't understand why—"

"Why I wouldn't allow a possible witness to be extradited from my jurisdiction—a case that took place *within* that jurisdiction?" Lowering his head, Beontal eyed Grekkor with reproach. "Really, Mr. Grekkor," he chided. "Your ignorance astonishes me."

"But I—" Grekkor felt that control of the conversation had definitely gone over to Beontal. It would have to be regained carefully.

"Would it interest you to know that I've done a bit of checking into several backgrounds since you left the station so abruptly?"

"I cannot imagine why."

"There were witnesses to the fact that you were seen chasing those two women through the station—*prior* to the death of the Norludian."

"I hardly think—"

"That the testimony of others aboard this station would carry less weight than your own—or that of certain security officers who are no longer employed at this facility?"

"No longer employed?" Grekkor tried to hide his reaction, but control was slipping again.

"Yes, and I'm also beginning to question the wisdom of having allowed you to leave the station before this matter was settled."

Grekkor's laugh was intended to be disarming but ended up sounding hollow. "Surely you don't suspect that I had anything to do with that unfortunate man's death, do you?"

Beontal smiled again. "Let's just say I'm not ruling out any possibilities at this point in the investigation." He appeared to consult something on his desk before adding, "I am aware of your current heading and destination. When you decide on another, you *will* keep me informed, won't you?"

"Most assuredly," Grekkor replied. "I wish to be of any assistance I can."

"I'm sure you do," Beontal said pleasantly. "In the meantime, I'll be sending your man back to you soon—oh, and *without* any of the ladies you requested." His smile was quite genuine this time. "They are all needed here on the station—absolutely essential personnel, you know. I'm sure you understand."

"Completely," Grekkor said, doing his best to match Beontal's tone. "I will keep you informed. Please, let me know when the mystery is solved."

"Oh, there's no mystery," Beontal said. "It's only a matter of collecting the right… *evidence*." The weight he placed on his last word left Grekkor with no doubt that Beontal suspected that the evidence he had given was false.

Grekkor signed off with the usual pleasantries before Beontal could see that he was beginning to sweat. If the station commander had believed him in the beginning, he certainly didn't believe him now. He had only to find evidence to support that belief.

It was now more imperative than ever to find the Zetithian bitch and her Vessonian friend.

And kill them both.

How he had ever let them escape was beyond him. The disgusting Zetithian had been arrogant and deceptively dangerous. His mouth watered briefly at the thought of the pleasure he would have had in killing her. The fact that there were more of them out there—they'd even been reproducing!—was like an itch he couldn't scratch. He'd poured more money into eliminating that race of cats than his legitimate business dealings could provide. The drug and slave trades were more lucrative, and though they did provide the needed funds, he was anxious for all Zetithians to finally be killed and the matter settled forever. The fact that many of them were on ships wasn't comforting—it was extremely difficult to track them—and he liked them better on the ground. He'd already sent Nedwuts to Terra Minor several times, but they'd always been caught before they reached their target. The survivors who lived on Earth could be dispatched by paid assassins, but even that was tricky. Earth wasn't the planet it once was, and villains were scarce there—those he could hire, that is.

If only his minions had succeeded in killing that rock star! That would have been a coup, indeed. And that other hideous being whose wife painted portrait after portrait of him—Grekkor longed to kill him too. He'd spotted a painting in the office of one of his female competitors, and he was forced to admit that though it was indeed a fine work of art, the subject matter nearly had Grekkor vomiting all over the woman's carpet.

Women. They were the root cause of his hatred. Grekkor shuddered at the thought of his wife with one of those cats. Amelyana had been a prize—a trophy of a wife and the most stunningly beautiful woman Grekkor had ever seen. She'd been his to possess—until that scum of a Zetithian had crossed her path. He could still recall the day they'd met. He'd taken Amelyana with him to a formal consortium dinner, proud to have her at his side and taking due note of the envy in other men's eyes. The elderly Zetithian ambassador had brought his son with him—a tall, handsome man with long blond hair and glowing green eyes. Grekkor should have killed him on the spot, if only for the way Amelyana had looked at him...

Chapter 11

WHEN THE *JOLLY ROGER* LANDED, MICAYLA'S FEELING that being just "one of the guys" was wrong intensified. Micayla had already seen how much in love Kyra and Tychar were, but the tie between Cat and Jack was even more pronounced. She later learned that this was partly because they'd been bonded together by a Zerkan healer, but Tisana and Leo were just about as tight.

The ship had landed in the late afternoon, and the new arrivals gathered in the main room of Tychar and Kyra's living quarters. It was a large, boisterous party with children laughing and playing while the adults attempted to catch up on each other's news. After dinner, the adults remained at the table to talk, but even though she was sitting with the group, Micayla found herself withdrawing from the conversation, observing rather than participating.

Having already met Trag and Tychar, Micayla had assumed that all Zetithian men had similar coloring, so she was unprepared for just how different they were from one another. Cat may have had long black hair like the two brothers, but he was more like a big, black leopard than a tiger. He looked older too, and if the scars on his body were any indication, he had seen some harsh treatment in his life as a slave, as had Leo, whose golden hair and eyes were like those of a lion.

And the two women were complete opposites. Jack was tall and athletic-looking with short dark brown hair and brown eyes and looked tough as nails, but Tisana had a more feminine aura, and her long black hair and green eyes only added to her mystique.

Micayla had been pelted with a million questions, leaving her little opportunity to ask many of her own, and feeling as if she needed a break, she had elected to have dinner sitting between Lerotan and Hidar—who was pushing his untouched plate of fruit away with distaste.

"You aren't eating anything again," Micayla scolded him. "That can't be good for you. You're starting to look sort of... dried out."

"I am fine," Hidar said firmly.

"But you've got to eat *something*," she insisted.

"I did," he said with a tiny burp. "I had a Big Mac and a large order of fries earlier. I am fine."

"Well, you certainly don't look it," Micayla said briskly. "Your skin, or whatever you call it, is getting all dull and cracked. Lerotan said you were getting ready to molt, but is there anything that might help? I mean, you look like you could use an industrial strength moisturizer."

Hidar's antennae began trembling and his wings sounded raspy as they fluttered nervously. "It is nothing to worry about," he said. "I require nothing."

"You're *sure* you don't want me to put some lotion on your wings?"

"Not now," Hidar said irritably. "But perhaps in a few days." Getting up from the table, he added, "I must fly now."

Micayla wondered what he would be like after he had shed his old exoskeleton, but suspected that his personality wouldn't change appreciably. She turned away to hide her smile only to find Lerotan watching her.

"You've got all these Zetithians hanging around and you're sitting there chatting with Hidar," he said as he leaned toward her. "What's the matter? Feeling left out of the family reunion?"

"I wouldn't say that," she replied. She'd been hugged until her eyes felt loose in their sockets, and though she felt like less of an outsider than she normally did in a crowd, they were still strangers to her. "A little over-whelmed, perhaps."

Lerotan smiled. "That's not surprising. Jack can do that all by herself."

"She *is* different," Micayla agreed. Tisana had a dry wit and a slightly acidic tongue, and the men all seemed very nice and friendly, but the force of Jack's personality hit like a sledgehammer.

"Better watch out for Jack," Lerotan warned. "She'll have you and Trag married before you know it. Manx and Drusilla were married on her ship, and, as captain, Jack performed the ceremony herself. There were other reasons for that, but personally, I don't think she trusted anyone else to do it."

"I can't marry Trag," Micayla said flatly.

"Oh, and why not?" he asked with a wicked grin. "What's the matter—got the hots for Rodan?"

"Oh, God, no!" she exclaimed with a quick glance at the other end of the table where Rodan sat chatting with Jack. Shuddering slightly, she added candidly, "As a matter-of-fact, I don't have the hots for anybody—never have. I mean, I *want* to—and *believe* me, I've tried—but I just don't feel it."

"Ah, I see," Lerotan said. "Well, believe it or not, from what I hear that's supposed to be typical for a Zetithian female."

Micayla stared at him in surprise. "You mean it's *normal* for me to have no desire for men?"

Lerotan nodded. "Not sure how they ever got the job done on that planet. 'Course, that might be why they always have triplets and why the men are so..."

"Irresistible?" Micayla said with a grim smile. "I'm sure they are, but not to me. Trag just—well, I'm beginning to think I might be able to be friends with him, but no more than that."

Lerotan shook his head. "That's amazing. You should see what happens when he walks into a bar or a brothel. In less than ten seconds he's got women crawling all over him. Hell, most hookers'll do him for free."

Micayla glanced at Trag, who was laughing at one of Cat's comments and looked as though he *should* have been irresistible to her—but he wasn't, at least not sexually. "Thanks for telling me that," she said absently. "About the Zetithian women, I mean. I've spent half my life wondering why men left me cold."

She was gazing at Trag as she spoke, but her thoughts were elsewhere. She was remembering all the boys who had teased her mercilessly because she refused to go out on dates with them. Then there was Adam. She'd liked him and they'd had fun together, but the sexual nature of the relationship had eluded her. She'd always thought she was an aberration of some kind—no matter where she came from—and though it explained a great deal, it also raised questions. "So, did they have to kidnap females and force them into marriage?"

"I don't really know," Lerotan admitted, "and I'm not sure Trag does either. He was raised offworld, you know; was just a kid when he left. You might ask one of the others, but I've never known one of them to have to use force on anyone. Like I said, Trag usually has to fight to keep them away… which makes *you* unique." He gazed thoughtfully in the direction of the children, who were playing a game with Windura that involved scattering glowing gems on a carved stone surface and trying to get them to stay in the niches. "Kyra was in love with Tychar," he went on, "but even she was willing to give Trag some relief—something that a Zetithian woman wouldn't have done." His expression never changed as he added, "Wish *I* was that irresistible."

"I don't think you have anything to worry about," Micayla said, forcing herself to smile. "You're what the girls on Earth would call a hunk."

"Really?" he said lightly. "You might be surprised—but then, this isn't Earth."

Something in his tone aroused her curiosity. "Think you'd have better luck with humans?"

"I'm not saying I don't have *any* luck," he replied. "Just not the right kind."

"Could be the company you keep," Micayla suggested. "It's hard to find a nice girl in the places you do business. I mean, let's face it; the night life at Orleon Station isn't exactly a church social."

Lerotan rolled his eyes. "If I didn't know better, I'd say you'd been talking to Jack. She's been telling Trag that for ages."

"It applies to you too," Micayla said. "And this planet *definitely* isn't the place to look, unless you like

Darconians, and somehow I just can't see you living happily ever after with a lizard."

"Not likely," Lerotan agreed. "But then, so are a lot of things." Pushing back his chair, he stood and gestured toward the bar. "Want another drink? That Darconian wine is pretty good stuff."

She shook her head. Letting down her guard while Rodan was nearby—and naked—was a bad idea. "I'm sticking to water. Something tells me that getting tipsy on this planet would be a mistake."

"Suit yourself," he said with a shrug. "One glass of water coming up."

———

Trag looked up from his discourse with Cat just as Lerotan handed Micayla a glass of water and felt as though someone had just grabbed his heart and given it a quick twist. That brief feeling of shock was replaced by a surge of rage that shocked him even more. He'd never felt anything like it, and he was nearly coming out of his seat before reason prevailed. There was no reason why such a simple act of courtesy should arouse such a feeling of… what? Jealousy? He was about to dismiss it as nonsense when he remembered what Shentuck had said, though, upon further reflection, he doubted that Lerotan had given her a cup that he'd already drunk from—which unexpectedly eased his mind.

He was relieved when Lerotan wandered over to where Windura was playing with the kids, which left Micayla alone. She sat staring off into space, her expression blank and her finger tracing the rim of her glass—until Rodan got up and moved to a seat across the table from her. Rodan, as usual, had opted not to dress for dinner and seemed to be enjoying liberal amounts of the local wine—and was obviously delighted to have Micayla to himself. Thankfully, there was a table between them, but Micayla's distress was obvious. She seemed to withdraw; her shoulders hunched forward and her eyes cast down. Normally, she could give as good as she got in a verbal exchange with Rodan, but something had changed—

"Shit," he muttered, remembering his promise.

"What?" said Cat.

"Nothing," Trag replied. "I'll be back in a minute."

Approaching Micayla, Trag did his best to ignore Rodan's drunken suggestions and took the seat that Lerotan had just vacated. "How's it going?" he asked her. "I saw Leroy getting you a drink. You feeling okay?"

She nodded. "I'm fine," she replied, but Trag saw her eyes dart toward Rodan.

"Listen," he said quietly, "if he's bothering you, why don't you come over here and sit with me?" She looked uncomfortable at the suggestion, so he added, "I know we'll probably talk your ear off, but it's got to be better than listening to Rodan."

"Anything's better than that," she agreed.

"Well, you don't have to make it sound like such a chore," he grumbled.

"I'm sorry," she said quickly. "I didn't mean it that way."

"Sure you didn't." Getting to his feet, he held out his hand. "Come on, Mick, let's go."

She looked up at him with something in her eyes Trag hadn't seen before. The rest of her hadn't changed—though she *was* wearing different clothes. Someone—Jack, he suspected—had provided her with shorts and a tank top in a soft peach color that might have been less revealing than what she'd worn running, but it made her seem more feminine somehow. She looked stronger in her Orleon uniform—as though able to draw strength from its tailored fabric and insignia that denoted her rank—but now she struck him as vulnerable and a little lost, as though she'd given up part of her identity along with her job.

Micayla stood without the aid of the hand he'd offered, which made Trag feel like someone had taken a cheese grater to his nerves. She was a hard woman to rescue. Trag's previous experiences with damsels in distress had been much more rewarding. It wasn't that she was being deliberately insulting; she just didn't seem to understand how to act when rescued—like she'd never learned the rules of the game.

"Look, you asked me not to leave you alone with him, remember?" Trag prompted. "That's all I'm doing."

"I know," she said. "It's just that—well, Leroy told me something just now that has me a little… off balance."

He might have been irritated before, but suddenly he felt murderous—though it wasn't Micayla he wanted to kill. His eyes shot daggers at Lerotan's back. "What's he been telling you?" he demanded.

"Something I wish I'd known a long time ago," she replied.

Whatever it was, it hadn't made her angry; she seemed more perplexed than anything. But her befuddled expression did nothing to diminish her beauty; in fact, it enhanced it. Her eyes were wide and guileless;

her face seemed softer, less like a tough cookie able to hold her own with anyone and more like a lost child. Something snapped inside him and it was all Trag could do to keep from pulling her into his arms.

"It's nothing bad," she went on, "just something that explains a lot of things. I need some time to process it."

"Process it?" Trag echoed. "I can't imagine Leroy ever saying anything *that* profound."

"But he did," she replied. "I just need some time…" Her voice trailed off as her brow furrowed. She was thinking hard about something—but Trag had no idea what it could be.

"Well, just come over here with me," he urged. "You can sit and think and not say a thing if you don't want to—but at least you'll be away from Rodan."

She nodded and Trag snagged her chair and carried it over to where the others were engaged in lively conversation. He was glad for the excuse to do something other than follow his strongest inclination, which was to touch her in some way—an arm around her shoulders or a hand on the small of her back; something to comfort her and let her know she wasn't alone—but she probably wouldn't have liked that. She wasn't his mate, after all; she would see it as being possessive or encroaching rather than reassuring. Trag wished she'd get woozy again so he could have an excuse to pick her up and carry her.

As they approached the others, Kyra caught his eye and beamed at him, nearly taking his breath away—something she'd always been able to do to him. With a smile pasted on his lips, he gestured for Micayla to take his seat next to Cat while he sat on her right, turning the chair sideways to keep her in his line of sight.

Mick was nervous about something. She sat next to Cat—who was probably the nicest guy in the bunch, not to mention the wittiest—as if he was the enemy. Granted, he was a stranger to her and the scar on his cheek made him look a little intimidating, but there was something else going on there, something that hadn't been evident earlier. What *had* Lerotan said to her?

"Hey, Micayla," Jack began as Micayla took her seat. "Tell me more about this guy Grekkor. I've never heard of him."

"Windura actually knows more about him," Micayla replied. "I'd never seen him or heard of him except for that one time."

"Hmm, and he said his wife had a Zetithian lover—is that right?"

Micayla nodded. "He said he killed him and then she went back to Zetith to find another one."

The men all smiled smugly, but Jack didn't seem to notice. "That's not too surprising," she said in a matter-of-fact tone. "If I'd lost Cat and I knew there was a whole planet full of these guys somewhere, I'm pretty sure I would have tried to get there myself. Wonder whatever happened to her. Did he say?"

Micayla shrugged. "No—though I suppose it's possible she was on Zetith when the asteroid hit and was killed along with the rest."

"Seems like he would have gloated about that a bit, doncha think?" Jack mused. Not giving Micayla time to respond, she went on, "Of course, it wasn't as if you had a lengthy conversation with him—and he might not actually *know* what happened to her, but—"

   The topic must have caught Windura's attention, for she left off playing with the kids and headed back to the table with Lerotan following right behind her. "If I'd been her, I'd have gotten as far away from that creep as I could," she said firmly. "I don't know a whole lot about him, but the rumors are pretty scary. He's not the kind of man you'd want to cross."

   "I think we can all agree on that," Jack said. "I just wish we knew more about him—like how to find him. If we could get rid of Grekkor, call off the Nedwuts, and get the word out that it was safe, more Zetithians might turn up."

   "Grekkor would be a hard man to get to," Windura said. "We barely got off that station alive—and I wouldn't have if I'd been alone. Micayla's the only reason we escaped."

   "And the fact that you did get away from him and lived to tell about it is very fortunate," Cat said with a warm smile at Micayla. "This could mean a lot for those of us who are left."

   "Yes, but we're wanted now," Micayla said soberly. "We didn't kill that Norludian, but if he says we did, no one would dare contradict him—or believe us."

   "Norludian?" Jack echoed. "Obviously I need to hear more!"

   Micayla remained silent while Windura related the entire episode, including the part about finding Trag in the hooker's database.

   "Trag, what have I told you about that?" Jack said accusingly. "You need to stay away from those places from now on. You might catch something fatal." Softening her tone, she added, "Still, their data would be very useful. It might help us find more of you."

"Maybe," Windura admitted. "But it's mostly just faces and notes about how the men behave in the brothels— what they like or don't like, whether they tend to be violent or not—that sort of thing. They put in the names and species if they know them—and their location—but most guys don't give out a lot of information. Trag was the only Zetithian in the files."

"True," Jack admitted. "But it'd be nice if we could use it to find out where Grekkor is. Don't suppose you noticed him in there, did you?"

"No, but I wasn't looking for him either."

"Any chance you could hack into it and find out?"

"They've got it locked down pretty tight, but I was given a password." Windura paused as Jack looked at her expectantly. "I'm pretty sure I could get in."

Jack grinned. "That's just what I wanted to hear."

—◦◦◦—

Jack may have been pleased, but Micayla was focused on something else entirely. Lerotan's revelation had been distracting enough, but the longer she sat with the group, the more something else became clear to her— something even more significant. Cat's nearness wasn't bothering her anymore, nor had the smile he'd given her. Experimentally, she took a peek at Leo, noting that nothing registered, nor did she feel any reaction when she took a good, long look at Tychar.

The implication was disconcerting, to say the least. Pleading fatigue, Micayla went off to bed feeling more confused than ever. She'd now met four of the six surviving male Zetithians, and, as luck would have it, the only one who made her want to hiss and bite was Trag.

Chapter 12

MICAYLA'S ABRUPT DEPARTURE DIDN'T AROUSE ANY-one's curiosity but Trag's—or so he thought. He made it appear to be casual and unplanned, but Cat lingered briefly after Jack had gone to put their three sons to bed, taking Trag aside with a meaningful nod. "You need to purr," he said.

"Purr?" Trag echoed. "What for?"

"To entice Micayla," Cat replied.

Trag might have expected something like that from Jack, but coming from Cat, it took him by surprise. "Look, Cat," he said evenly. "I know she's pretty and all, but when a woman hisses at you on sight, I don't think enticement is what she has in mind."

"You might be surprised," said Cat. "She is a potential mate."

"So what?" Trag argued. "They're *all* potential mates." He'd certainly fucked enough of them to know that by now. He could have had his choice of a lot of women—women who claimed to worship the ground he walked on and might even have loved him—but he couldn't mate with someone he didn't love in return. It just seemed wrong.

"But Micayla's reaction to you means she is interested."

Trag's jaw dropped. "What? I've never heard that."

"You were just a boy when you left Zetith," Cat reminded him. "Mating rituals were not high on your list of priorities then."

"But someone should have told me about it—Ty, or my uncle, or *somebody!* I've never heard of such a thing!"

Cat shrugged. "Well, now you know."

"So, you're saying it's a *good* thing when a Zetithian girl hisses at you?"

"I am saying that there is a strong potential there. It is now up to you to entice her."

Trag rolled his eyes. "What if I don't want to?"

"Enticement is your choice," Cat replied. "If you do not want her, then do not purr."

"Simple as that, huh?"

"Simple as that." Cat peered at his friend closely. "But tell me, Trag, why would you not want her? She is beautiful, strong, intelligent—and Zetithian."

"Yeah, she's all that," Trag admitted, "but I'm just not sure she's the girl for me."

"She is too young, perhaps?" Cat suggested.

"No, it's not that," Trag began slowly. He knew the reason; it was because she wasn't Kyra—didn't act like her or even look like her. They were as different as two women could be; Kyra was sweet and warm, whereas Micayla was more like frozen steel—though since they'd made their pact she was decidedly less icy. Still, the only thing she and Kyra had in common was their long dark hair. "It's hard to explain."

"But you have searched for a Zetithian woman, have you not?" Cat inquired. "Now that you have found one, you realize that they are far more difficult to entice than human females. You know this from your experience with—"

"My brother's mate!" Trag snapped. "Don't go there, Cat."

"It was very kind of Kyra to ease your suffering," Cat said wisely. "But not every human female would have done the same, and a Zetithian woman would never—"

"Don't I know it!" Trag exclaimed. "Just—" He paused, letting out a long, rueful sigh. "Let's leave it be, okay? I'm already regretting a lot of things I've done in my life, and badgering Kyra to fuck me is the one that really stands out." Trag fought the urge to tear his hair out in frustration. The taste of Kyra was still on his lips, and whenever he slid into a woman, it was her face he saw. He could still feel her—like hot, sweet love wrapped around his cock. Trag had never felt the same way with any other woman, and God knows he'd tried to recapture it, but now that Micayla had tumbled onto Lerotan's ship, he had no desire to try again. If he enticed Micayla and mated with her, it would be for life, and he didn't want to spend the rest of his life wishing his mate was someone else. No, the pact they'd made not to become lovers was the best idea yet. He would stick to it.

The next day the men took the children to visit the military training grounds, giving the women a chance to become better acquainted. In a spacious divan, Windura sat at an ornately carved stone desk near a window that looked out toward the distant mountains while the other women lounged on two large, comfortable sofas. The breeze blowing in through the open windows carried the scent of flowers and ripening fruit, but Windura didn't seem to notice, nor did she appear to be relaxed by it. Using Kyra's computer, she was doing her best to get into the hookers' network, but thus far, she hadn't had any luck.

"They've changed the password," she grumbled.

"Can you still hack into it?" Jack asked.

"I don't know," Windura replied. "But I can try."

Jack, Tisana, and Kyra went on to trade anecdotes about their children while Micayla sat trying to figure out a way to bring up the subject of female Zetithian sexuality without giving Jack the wrong idea. She had just about decided to blurt out a question when Veluka was ushered into the room by Dragus, effectively halting the flow of conversation.

Micayla ignored Dragus and focused her gaze on Veluka. She'd known he was coming and that Tisana considered him untrustworthy, but she'd never met a Nerik before and, having heard a little bit about them, wasn't sure she wanted to. He was tall and broad-shouldered and covered with shiny black scales, but his eyes were his most prominent feature. The large white ovals dominated his flat, angular face and had no irises, a circumstance which made his pupillary reactions disturbingly obvious.

Tisana had stiffened beside her as Veluka arrived, and Micayla instinctively studied him for weaknesses. She knew his scales would provide protection against many conventional weapons, but his eyes seemed vulnerable and certainly provided a large target. His musculature was clearly visible beneath the rippling scales that weren't covered by the light tunic he wore, and if there was a gram of fat on his body, it didn't show. Micayla had been up against some formidable opponents before, but never one like this.

"About time you got here," Jack said without preamble. "I thought that ship of yours was fast."

Veluka shrugged and then blinked slowly, drawing attention to his eyes. "I did my best."

"Yeah, right," Jack scoffed. "Knowing you, you probably fiddle-farted the whole way here just so you could make a few deals while you were at it."

Veluka pressed a hand to his chest. "Your lack of faith wounds me deeply."

His voice, though smooth as glass, may have sent chills running down Micayla's spine, but he obviously didn't intimidate Jack in the slightest. "You'll get over it," she said carelessly.

Glancing sideways at Tisana, Micayla could almost see the fireballs forming in her eyes, and a quick look at Kyra confirmed that she wasn't happy about having the Nerik in her living room either. Even Windura's eyes had narrowed slightly.

"Have a seat, Veluka," Jack said with a casual wave. "We need to talk."

Dragus lingered at the doorway, grinning unabashedly at the women gathered there. Having heard Kyra's stories about how much he admired human females, Micayla wasn't surprised that he wanted to hang around, but when he reluctantly turned to leave, Jack called after him.

"Hold on a minute, Dragus!" she said. "I forgot to tell you I got that video you wanted."

With a quick shake of his head and a furtive glance, Dragus put up a hand to silence her.

"Oh, yeah, right," Jack said with a nod. "Forgot that part too. I'll give it to you later."

Dragus nodded and departed, his huge flat feet slapping on the stone floor as he moved off down the corridor.

Micayla felt the hair on the back of her neck prickle as Veluka laughed at the exchange between Dragus and Jack. It was not only the most intimidating laugh she'd ever heard, but it also caused his scales to rise, lifting the rough tunic, which was his only garment, making him seem larger, more imposing—fearsome, even.

Shaking her head, Jack grinned as Dragus's tail disappeared from view—a grin that faded slightly when she faced Veluka.

Veluka's pupils constricted to the point that they almost disappeared. "You seem displeased with me for some reason, Jack."

"Why—whatever gave you that idea?" Jack said with a sardonic smirk.

Glancing around the room, he said, "My reception seems a bit chilly."

"Tisana wouldn't trust you not to steal an old shoe," Jack said blithely, "but unless I miss my guess, the rest of these ladies just haven't seen a Nerik before. That's what you get for being so creepy looking."

Windura covered her mouth in a vain attempt to stifle a laugh as the Nerik sat down on a straight-backed chair near the door—obviously not wanting anyone between him and the nearest escape route.

"You never were one to mince words, were you, Jack?" Veluka commented. His smile made a clicking sound as his facial scales shifted, making Micayla wonder what would happen when he got mad.

Jack shrugged. "Don't see the point."

"I assume you asked me to come here for a reason," Veluka began. "Was it something I did?"

"Nope," Jack replied. "We need your help with something."

"Ah, do you now?" Veluka said with another crackly smile.

"What would you say if I told you we knew who was behind the vendetta against the Zetithians?"

Veluka's huge eyes opened even wider. "I would assume you would want this person dead."

Jack nodded. "Or at least brought to justice."

Veluka's eyelids lowered a fraction and his pupils dilated slightly. "To catch the one responsible for destroying an entire world would be... difficult."

"But not impossible," Tisana interjected. "We can't begin to pay you what you probably think—"

Jack put up a hand. "Easy, Tisana. I know you think Veluka is a liar and a cheat, and you're absolutely right, but—"

To Micayla's surprise, Veluka laughed. "I *do* enjoy doing business with you, Jack," he said. "It's so... refreshing."

"Aw, cut the crap," Jack said. "You only like it because I don't try to cheat you."

"You *are* one of the few that doesn't," Veluka admitted.

"Wish he would return the favor," Tisana muttered.

Micayla caught Tisana's eye with a questioning look.

Seeming to take this as encouragement, Tisana glared at the Nerik. "Those tracking nanobots you sold Jack on Barada Seven only lasted a week!" she said hotly. "If their lifespan had been just a little shorter, Leo and Cat might have been killed!"

"But they weren't," Jack said soothingly. "Chill out, Tisana. He never said they would last forever!"

"True," Tisana conceded, "but if the nanobots had died before we caught those Nedwuts—well, I don't want to think about what might have happened."

"Then don't," Jack retorted.

Micayla suspected that this was an argument of long standing between the two women, and a conspiratory glance from Kyra suggested that she felt the same way.

"Would you like a drink?" Kyra asked Veluka. "I'm sure you must be thirsty."

"I'd appreciate that," he replied. "But none of the local wine for me. I'll have water, please."

As Kyra left to get Veluka some refreshment, Micayla eyed him shrewdly. He was a scoundrel, all right, but not above being cheated himself and, therefore, very cautious.

"What we need is a fast ship with a cloaking device," Jack was saying. "And you've got that."

Kyra returned with a tall glass of water which Veluka received with a gracious nod, draining the contents before responding. "Do you only want to hire my ship, or do you need me to fly it?"

"Both," Jack replied. "We'll need you to carry some passengers."

"Where to?"

"That's something we don't know yet," Jack admitted. "But we hope to find out soon."

"Cloaked ship?" Micayla echoed as a thought struck her. "Just where *were* you when you got Jack's hail?"

To her surprise, Veluka's scales flattened. "That would be none of your business."

"Maybe not," Micayla conceded, "but on the way here from Orleon Station, a cloaked ship fired on us—one that had Nedwuts aboard—and from what I hear, Nedwuts don't have that technology."

"It can be bought," Veluka said, his voice as flat as his scales, "for the right price."

"I'm sure it can," Micayla said with a nod. "Anyway, we fired back, and *something* exploded, but our gunner didn't think he was the one who hit it." She looked at Veluka searchingly. "Any ideas as to why that was?"

"None," Veluka replied.

"The Nedwuts didn't possess the technology to destroy an entire planet either," Windura chimed in from her desk, "but they did it anyway. Our 'friend' has a vast amount of money—more than anyone could earn by honest means—and he's obviously willing to spend it to eliminate every last Zetithian in existence."

"And now he seems to be equipping the Nedwut bounty hunters," said Jack. Her expression darkened. "This is *not* good."

"He saw Micayla and captured us," Windura explained to Veluka. "He told us what he'd done, but we escaped—and now he'll come after us with everything he's got."

"I hate to say this," Kyra began. "But if he's heard anything about Tychar, he'd have to know Darconia was a safe haven for Zetithians. He could have ships on the way here right now."

"All the more reason why we've got to find out where he is and put an end to this," Jack said earnestly. With an eye toward Windura, she went on, "Any luck with that hacking job yet?"

Windura shook her head. "No, but I've been thinking. We might be able to recruit some help with that."

"How so?" asked Jack.

Windura took a deep breath. "We'd have to go back to Orleon Station to ask the hookers for help," she said. "And I really don't see how we can do that—at least, not openly."

"I know you said we could trust them, but do you really think the hookers would stick their necks out to help us?" Micayla scoffed.

"Oh, yeah," Windura said. "Trag's probably very popular with them. I'm sure they'd be more than willing to help him out."

Micayla blinked. Suddenly, all the little bits and pieces she'd heard about Trag and the other Zetithians fell into place. "Is he—I mean, are *they*—really that good?"

Jack, Kyra, and Tisana all exchanged meaningful looks, but it was Kyra who spoke. "Oh, yeah," she said as the other two women nodded in agreement. "They *all* are."

"Having grown up on Earth, I don't suppose you could have known," Tisana said kindly. "But Zetithian males are—" She paused, seeming to be at a loss for words.

"Absolutely incredible," Kyra finished for her.

Jack gazed at Micayla with sympathetic eyes. "You don't care much for men, do you?"

"Well, no," Micayla admitted. "I mean, I do, but not like that."

"It's only because you've never been around any of your own kind before," Tisana said bracingly. "What they're capable of is overkill for most other women—though *highly* addicting!—but for you, it's probably a necessity."

Kyra nodded in agreement. "And when they say 'I will give you joy unlike any you have ever known,' they aren't kidding," she said fervently. "Believe me, once you go cat, you *never* go back."

Micayla wanted to scream in frustration. Between this and what Lerotan had told her, she was finally beginning to understand why she felt the way she did. Obviously, for a Zetithian woman, only a Zetithian man would do—and she'd already made a no-sex pact with the only available one left alive.

Chapter 13

A ZETITHIAN MAN WHO, UNFORTUNATELY, MADE HER long to bite him and was also in love with his brother's wife. Micayla closed her eyes and waited for the thrumming inside her head to pass.

"Uh, maybe we shouldn't be discussing this right now," Windura said awkwardly. "Not with *him* here, anyway."

Micayla's eyes flew open. Windura was, of course, referring to Veluka, who was following the discussion with undisguised interest. "Forget I'm here," he said with an expansive wave of his hands. "I won't say a word."

Tisana snickered. "If you think we'll believe *that*…"

"It's okay," Micayla said. "Keep talking. I think I need to hear this."

"Obviously we should have had this conversation sooner, but the guys have always been hanging around," Kyra said. "You've seen them, of course, so you know how gorgeous they are—and you've seen them naked, so you know what they've got—but what you don't know is the effect one of them can have on you. They excrete a fluid from the penis that triggers orgasms in females, and their semen has the most euphoric effect— they've even got a sort of ruffle on the head that undulates after they ejaculate. It feels fabulous!"

"And afterward, you get this feeling they call *la-etralance*," Tisana put in. "It's the most peaceful, fulfilling, blissful thing you'll ever experience. There's not even a word for it in Stantongue—"

Windura had rattled off something similar when they were confronting Grekkor, but it had sounded too fantastic to be true. Micayla hadn't believed it at the time, but still, it would explain quite a bit.

"Yes," Windura said eagerly, "and Mr. Big sells drugs—though he won't admit to it—so it would cut in on his business!"

"I have *always* believed it was something like that!" Jack declared. "But he also said it was because his wife had a Zetithian lover."

"Ah, a crime of passion then?" Veluka suggested.

"A premeditated, highly organized, extremely well-funded crime of passion," Jack said roundly. "He's even confessed to it. We just have to get him to do it in front of witnesses."

"I realize I said I wouldn't say a word," Veluka said hesitantly, "but just who is it we're talking about? Someone I might know?"

Micayla looked at Jack, who merely shrugged.

"He'll find out eventually anyway." Tisana sighed. "You might as well tell him now."

"It was someone named Rutger Grekkor," Micayla said. "Ever hear of him?"

Veluka's pupils dilated to the point that his entire face went dark and his scales lost their shine. It was a long moment before he spoke. "And I blasted one of his ships…" he said faintly. "Jack, you *really* owe me this time."

"Ha!" Micayla exclaimed. "So it *was* you!"

"Yes," Veluka said, visibly shuddering. "It was." His

broad shoulders drooped and he hung his head. "I'm dead meat in a can."

"Not if we get to him first!" Jack exclaimed. "Oh, Veluka! I could kiss you!" She had already jumped up from the couch and was heading toward him when she stopped short. "Then again, maybe not."

"That's okay, Jack," Veluka said. "I understand completely." He took a deep, fortifying breath—presumably to steady his nerves—and held up a hand. "Just give me a moment."

Micayla looked at him curiously. "I can understand why Zetithians would be afraid of him, but is everyone?"

"No, just people who have sense enough to stay out of his way," Veluka replied. "I've managed to do that—up until now. I thought I was doing you a favor, Jack. Now I've probably signed my own death warrant."

"No you haven't," Jack said cheerfully. "If we don't tell him, he'll never know who did it. It's not as if there were any survivors."

Veluka shook his head sadly. "If only I could believe that."

"What? Which part?" Jack asked.

"Doesn't matter," Veluka replied. "Is it okay if I just stay here for a while? Somehow I feel safer among these Darconians than I do anywhere else."

The fact that Veluka was completely unnerved to discover that Grekkor was involved made Micayla reconsider their plan. She was beginning to think it would be easier to assassinate him than it would be to get him to confess again—especially in front of witnesses.

"How is it that you don't know Grekkor, Jack?" Veluka asked suddenly. "I thought you knew everyone."

"No, obviously I don't," Jack said. "He's a little out-side my usual territory and I don't deal in drugs."

"Or slaves," Micayla said. "I forgot to mention that he was going to put us on a slave ship."

"Yeah, well, that doesn't really matter now," Jack said. "What matters is that we find out where he is."

"And the hookers might not be any help if he doesn't ever visit them," Tisana pointed out.

"I really don't want to waste time going back to Orleon if that's the case," Jack agreed.

Windura smacked herself upside the head. "I can't believe I'm sitting here trying to hack into the hook-ers' network when all I really have to do is something much simpler."

"Like what?"

"Like hacking into the Orleon Station docking log!" she exclaimed. "I set that system up myself. It will tell us where he went when he left Orleon—*if* he left Orleon. Sorry it took me so long to figure this out. Don't know what I was thinking!"

Windura tapped furiously at the viewscreen for a few moments and then let out a groan.

"What is it?" Jack said.

"You aren't going to like this, Veluka," Windura warned.

"Oh?" Veluka said wearily. "And why not?"

"He went to Nerik."

The silence in the room was so complete that Micayla could have sworn she heard bees buzzing in the orchard beneath the palace windows. Then she realized it was Veluka; his scales were flapping up and down so fast he sounded like a hummingbird on the wing.

"It has to be a coincidence," Kyra insisted. "He couldn't have known Veluka had anything to do with us. Maybe he's just going there to buy more cloaked ships for his Nedwuts. By the way, Veluka, does it *have* to be a ship, or is it just a device?"

Though she'd never seen if for herself, Micayla knew how the technology worked—at least, in theory—but waited a moment for Veluka to respond to the question. He didn't say a word but kept right on humming.

"The technology is *very* expensive and retrofitting a ship with it is prohibitive," Micayla said. "They have to be built with it. Essentially, the ships are covered with small scales that can be flipped over when cloaked. The surface is designed to allow light to slide over and around it, rather than be reflected, which renders the object essentially invisible—both to the naked eye and to any type of scan."

"And the Neriks are the only ones who can make ships like that?" Kyra asked.

"They're the only ones I know of," Micayla replied. With an eye toward Veluka, she said, "Think he'll ever stop doing that?"

"No clue," Jack said, shaking her head. "Never saw him do it before."

Tisana rose from the sofa to study him more closely. "Looks like he could use a sedative."

"I wouldn't get too close to him, Tisana," Jack warned. "He sounds like he's about to explode."

Trag walked in just then. "Who's about to explode?" he asked.

"Him," Micayla said, pointing at Veluka.

"Nah," said Trag. "He just needs a good smack to

reset him." With that, he slapped the top of the Nerik's head and the humming ceased immediately.

"Thank you," Veluka said hoarsely.

"Don't mention it," said Trag.

"And just *how* did you know to do that?" Tisana demanded.

Trag shrugged. "I fucked a Nerik once. Had to do that twice before she stopped humming."

Micayla groaned inwardly, closing her eyes as her head began to pound again. She was within a hairsbreadth of asking Trag to break the no-sex pact right then and there. After all, if he could do it with a Nerik, he could certainly stomach doing it with her. But no, that wasn't the reason. He loved Kyra. Yeah, that was it. The Nerik was just—

"A Nerik?" Kyra echoed. "You're kidding us, right?"

Trag shook his head. "No," he replied. "I forget where I was at the time." Scratching his head, he added, "Maybe Hidar remembers. He was with me."

"I can't *believe* you would—" Kyra stopped there, rolling her eyes. "Oh, I *really* don't want to hear this. A *Nerik!*" she said again, this time with a visible shudder.

Trag threw up his hands. "Well, you *did* ask!" Eyeing her curiously, he went on, "You aren't jealous, are you?"

"Hey, what's wrong with Neriks?" Veluka spoke up. "I fuck them all the time."

Kyra ignored this, save for a withering glance in Veluka's direction, and stared at Trag as though he'd just sprouted horns. "Jealous? Why on Earth would I be jealous? Grossed out, maybe, but certainly not jealous!"

Trag felt like his nuts had just been grabbed—and not very gently, either. He'd just asked Kyra—his brother's wife!—if she was jealous of him being with other women! Swallowing hard, he wondered how he was ever going to talk his way out of this one. "I didn't mean—"

To Trag's surprise, Micayla came to his rescue. "You were in a brothel, right?"

"Well, yeah," Trag replied. "Hidar thought if I was with him he wouldn't get thrown out—which he usually does. I mean, *nobody* wants to do it with a Scorillian! Where else would I...?"

Micayla shrugged nonchalantly. "I don't see the problem." Looking at Kyra, she added, "Why would it bother you?"

"It shouldn't—um, doesn't," Kyra stammered. "I mean—I don't know *what* I mean, but do you really have to go to brothels and *pay* for it, Trag? I wouldn't think—"

"Well, why *wouldn't* you think that?" Trag shot back. "After all, I had to practically beg *you*."

"No you didn't!" Kyra insisted. "I was perfectly willing to—" Kyra stared beseechingly at Trag, but there was something else in her expression that he couldn't quite figure out. He blinked hard and peered at her again. Then it hit him. She wasn't jealous; she felt *sorry* for him!

"Look, Kyra," Trag said, his temper rising. "You may have given me a pity fuck once, but that doesn't mean I *only* get it out of pity—or that I can only get it from Neriks! Some women actually *like* me."

"And he doesn't always have to pay them either," Micayla put in. "I have it on good authority that not only will the hookers do him for free, most of them *volunteer*."

Micayla's comment stopped Trag from launching into a full tirade, but when he looked at her, all he wanted to do was scream—or purr. It was as if a veil had been pulled away from his face and his vision was now clear. No, she wasn't like Kyra at all. She was better—stronger, sexier, more beautiful—and she'd just stood up for him. Cat was right. The fire was right there in her eyes; he couldn't understand why he hadn't seen it before. She was strongly attracted to him; he knew that now—whether she realized it or not. According to Cat, all he had to do was purr and she'd be all over him—but could he risk it? Could he violate the terms of their agreement without considering her feelings?

As their eyes met, Micayla felt her mouth watering and practically had to bite her tongue to keep from hissing. If he moved or said a word, she knew she'd jump up from her seat and sink her teeth into him. Suddenly, it didn't seem like such a bad idea—quite pleasurable, in fact. She felt her upper lip beginning to slide up to reveal her fangs and could almost taste his blood…

Then she realized that snarling at him probably wasn't the best move at the time—not when she was trying to be supportive. Kyra didn't love him—and didn't need his love—not when she already had Tychar. Trag deserved more than her pity. He really needed to let her go.

Kyra was protesting that she had meant no such thing, but Micayla ignored her as she got up and crossed the room to stand squarely in front of Trag. They were almost exactly the same height; she didn't even have to lift her head to look straight into his fierce green eyes. "Hey, Trag," she said gently. "Got a minute? I think we need to go for a run or something. You know, to work off a little steam?"

His eyes widened as his jaw dropped. "Uh, yeah, sure, Mick," he said. "Whatever you want."

———

Glancing sideways at her as they walked down the corridor, Trag still didn't fully understand what had just happened. "You didn't have to do that," he said. "I'm a big boy. I can take a little heat."

"Who says I did it for you?" she said, staring straight ahead.

"Well, it sure seemed that way to me," he said roundly. "Nobody was questioning *your* sex appeal."

"Oh? Is that what it was?"

"Well, yeah," Trag said, beginning to question it himself, "wasn't it?"

"Not really. I think it was more a matter of you being your own man." With a backward glance, Micayla added, "She doesn't own you, Trag. You can do whatever you want. You don't have to answer to her—and you don't have to please her either. You can fuck as many Neriks as you want."

"Don't believe I'd care for that, actually," Trag said thoughtfully. "It was okay once, but—"

Micayla gave an exasperated snort. "You *do* see my point, don't you?"

"Well, maybe," Trag began.

"She doesn't love you, Trag," Micayla said earnestly. "She loves your brother. I'm sure she's fond of you, but—"

"She may not love me, but at least she's never *hissed* at me," Trag said. His tone was careless, but he followed it with a careful glance to gauge her reaction. Something told him it was the right thing to say, but he wasn't completely sure…

She reacted all right; it stopped her right in her tracks.

"Dammit, Trag! I *said* I was sorry! Are you going to keep throwing that in my face forever?"

"Maybe," Trag said with a nonchalant shrug. "Let's just say it made a big impression on me."

"Impression, huh?" she echoed. *"Impression?* I'll give you an *impression…"*

Trag had one brief moment to brace himself before she sprang at him with a snarl and sank her teeth into his shoulder.

———

Trag tasted like hot, molten sex—the tang of his blood, the salty flavor of his sweat—and as Micayla inhaled the pleasing aroma of his skin, she was sure he'd knock her on her ass, but he didn't. Against all odds, he began purring.

The vibrations seemed to settle into her chest as she licked the wound she'd made, and suddenly, she didn't just want to bite him and lick him, she wanted to *devour* him… pull him in and make him part of her.

Trag pushed her against the stone wall of the corridor, his eyes glowing like green embers. Licking his lips, he leaned in slowly and kissed her, but unlike the other times with other men, Micayla actually felt pleased by it and growled her approval. Desire washed over her like a tsunami. Her nipples tingled as they hardened against his chest, and as his tongue delved into her mouth, instead of feeling invaded she reveled in it; he was hot and delicious and sent flames racing through her body. The more she inhaled his scent and felt the vibrations of his purr, the more aware she became of the place between her thighs—a place that had previously felt empty and barren. As his kiss deepened, her clitoris tightened painfully and her vaginal mucosa began to swell and moisten, aching with a need too fierce and overwhelming to be denied. Suddenly, she felt his erection pressing into her stomach, a pressure that filled her with passion and made her long to rip off his clothing with her teeth, baring his body for her to feast upon. She'd already seen his cock. Now she knew what she wanted to do with it.

I want to suck it. The words were not spoken aloud but pounded in her head, urging her into action. She tore her lips away from Trag's and was about to sink to her knees to kiss his thick penis when a voice called out, "Hey, don't stop on my account. This is fabulous!"

Trag caught the expression of speechless horror on her face just as Micayla spun away from him and sprinted off down the corridor to disappear around the next corner.

"Way to go, Trag!" Dragus said gleefully. "She's just as hot as the Terrans!"

"I'm gonna kill you, Dragus," Trag snarled, "and then I'm gonna rip you limb from limb and roast you over an open fire. Very slowly."

"Ha!" Dragus laughed, clearly not the slightest bit worried. "Want me to catch her for you?"

"Yeah, like you could really do that," Trag scoffed. "I'm not even sure *I* could catch her now…"

"Just watch me," Dragus said, tapping the comstone on his breastplate. "Hartak," he said pleasantly, "bring Micayla back here, will you please?"

Trag waited for a moment and then heard a distant scuffle and a muffled scream, followed by Micayla shouting, "Put me down, you big snake!"

Moments later, Hartak appeared, carrying a kicking, cursing Micayla, his tail sweeping back and forth across the stone flags as he swaggered toward them. "Been called a lot of things in my day, but never a snake," Hartak commented. "Where do you want her?"

Without a moment's hesitation Trag held out his arms. "Right here."

Chapter 14

NEVER BEFORE HAD MICAYLA FELT SUCH AN ONSLAUGHT of emotions. She was angry, embarrassed, terrified, and turned on—all at the same time—and to top it all off, she'd just been captured by a dinosaur.

"You really need to learn to hold on to your woman, Trag," Hartak advised as he placed her in Trag's waiting arms. "She'll get all wilted from the heat if you keep letting her run off like that."

"Thanks," Trag said sardonically. "I'll try to keep that in mind."

Putting her arms around his neck, Micayla clung to Trag a little tighter than she needed to, her face buried in his hair. She felt like an absolute idiot for running and was trembling uncontrollably—though whether from fear or passion, she couldn't tell—but Trag obviously felt it too, and he gave her a reassuring squeeze.

"Of course, if you two would just quit *scaring* her to death…"

"Sorry, Micayla," Dragus said with an apologetic smile. "Me and Hartak, well, we just love Terrans, and you're real pretty too. We've been begging Kyra to see if she could get more Terran women to come here—"

"Some that like lizards!" Hartak said eagerly.

"But she won't do it."

"Why am I not surprised?" Trag muttered. "Listen,

guys, why don't you two run along and guard the palace? I think she'll be okay now."

"You're sure you won't need us?" Dragus said helpfully. "We could stand guard while you—"

"Dragus," Trag said in a dangerous voice. "Get *lost*."

"What? Lost? In our own—oh, I get it."

"Then *do* it," Trag said firmly. "*Now*."

"No need to get all huffy about it, Slave Boy," Dragus said. "We're leaving."

"Call us if you need us!" Hartak said cheerfully.

Micayla bit her lip as the humor of her predicament suddenly struck her and her body shook with suppressed mirth.

Trag held her tighter. "Hey, don't cry, Mick," he said soothingly. "The big, bad Darconians are gone now."

Silent giggles gave way to howls of laughter as Trag looked down at her with surprise. "Oh, my God, that was funny! You—a former slave in this palace!—ordering those big guys around like a couple of pups!"

The sound—and feel—of Trag's laughter as he held her against his chest warmed her to her toes. "Yeah. Times have changed." Sighing deeply, he said, "Now, where were we?"

"Um, I believe we were kissing each other."

"You didn't mind that, did you?" Trag asked cautiously.

"No," she said simply. "Not at all."

"Think you could bite me again?"

"You actually *liked* that?"

"My dear Mick," he said with fervor. "You have no idea."

"To tell the truth, I've wanted to do that for a while now," she said candidly, "but I didn't think you'd like it, so I've been trying not to."

His purring began again, making his voice deep and rough. "You can bite me anytime you like, Mick."

"What about our pact?"

"What pact?"

"The no-sex pact."

"Oh, yeah. *That* pact," he said. "Stupid idea, wasn't it?"

"Regretted it almost immediately," she agreed. "Don't know why, but—"

"What do you say we go somewhere and discuss it?"

"Where did you have in mind?"

Not bothering to set her down, Trag started walking. "Someplace private, where we can talk and not be disturbed."

"Sounds wonderful," she admitted.

"You're sure about this?"

Sighing, she said, "I think I was sure the moment I laid eyes on you; I just didn't realize it. But talking to Leroy helped."

"Oh, and what pearls of wisdom did Leroy have to share with you?"

"He said that the way I felt toward men was normal for a Zetithian woman. I've never felt *normal* in my whole life! It made a big difference."

Trag nodded. "So *that's* what you were talking about! I wondered. I guess that makes two of us who didn't know what we were doing. I never knew being hissed at was a good thing until Cat told me."

"Think we'd have ever figured it out on our own?"

"No clue," he said. "But I guess that's what friends are for."

"We need to be sure and thank them."

"Later," Trag said. "How far do you want to go?"

She certainly hadn't wanted to stop until they'd been interrupted. God only knew what the two guards would have seen if they'd happened upon them a few moments later. "All the way, I suppose," she replied. "Or do you think we should wait?"

Trag grinned but shook his head. "That's not what I meant, but I'm glad to hear it anyway. No, what I meant was, do you want to stay here or go on to your quarters?"

"Oh," she said, glancing up at the open doorway they were approaching. "Is this your room?"

"Uh-huh," he replied. "I'm sharing it with Leroy."

"Well, at least it's not Rodan," she said thankfully. "Can we lock the door?"

"We can bar it if you like, but if I know Hartak and Dragus, I doubt we'll need to. Hartak used to be Kyra's guard, remember?"

"Yes, but—"

"I'd bet money they'll both be back just as soon as this door closes and, trust me, Leroy won't get past them."

The thought of doing anything intimate while two huge lizards were listening didn't appeal to Micayla in the slightest. "I don't think I can…"

"Kyra didn't either," Trag said. "You'll get used to it."

"Look, maybe we shouldn't jump into this," she began. "I really—"

Trag set her on her feet in one swift motion. "You can stay or you can go, Mick. It's your choice. I'm not going to beg, coerce, or badger another woman ever again."

"I'm not Kyra," she reminded him. "I'm not in love with your brother or anyone else."

"And you aren't in love with me either."

"What do you mean?"

"This is just physical attraction," he said miserably. "It's got nothing to do with love."

Micayla closed her eyes and exhaled sharply. She was right back where she started. The only difference was that now she knew what if felt like to want a man—a real live man who wasn't part of a fantasy.

"Go on and leave if you want," he said. "But either way, I've *got* to get out of these pants. My dick is killing me."

"Really?"

"Yeah, but once you're gone, I won't be able to smell you and it'll go away." Spearing his fingers through his hair, he muttered, "Story of my whole fuckin' life."

"What do you mean, it'll go away?"

Trag laughed mirthlessly. "Didn't know that either, did you? Zetithian men can't get it up without the scent of a woman's desire. You have to smell right or it just won't work."

Glancing down at his groin, she said, "I guess that means I smell okay then?"

"Ty once told me that Kyra smelled even better than Zetithian women—"

"And—?"

His gaze met hers and held it for a long moment before he spoke. "He was wrong about that."

Micayla was having a hard time processing the meaning of it all. "So you're saying it's all just chemistry? Receptors and pheromones that trigger emotional and physiological responses?"

Trag winced. "Sounds even worse when you put it that way, doesn't it?"

"Sorry," she said wearily. "I've never been much of a romantic, but I'm trying to understand. I've been… well, I don't know *what* I've been, but I'm so tired of not feeling anything and wondering why I don't. But I really *felt* something with you—and I liked it." Studying his face, she realized that wasn't the only thing she liked. "I like *you* too," she went on. "Maybe I didn't at first, but I do now."

"I've had it in my head for so long that if I couldn't have Kyra, I didn't want anybody—and then when you hissed at me, it just made it that much easier *not* to like you, but I do. That sounds really stupid, doesn't it?"

"No it doesn't," Micayla replied, shaking her head. "I've spent most of my life trying to avoid men." She felt her eyes stinging with unwanted tears. "It wasn't so much that I didn't like them as it was that I didn't feel anything for them—and I wanted to, I really did!—and I tried, but I just couldn't do it! Then you—all I had to do was *look* at you and I felt more than I ever had before. Granted, it didn't seem like such a good thing at the time, but today they were all telling me how incredible you guys were, and then Kyra was talking like you were maybe not as good as the others, and I just couldn't sit there and let her do it. Maybe she didn't mean it that way, but it sure seemed like it."

"What about you, Mick?" he asked gently. "Do *you* think I'm not as good as the others?"

"I have no way of knowing that for sure," she admitted. "But no, I don't—and I really *did* enjoy kissing you."

A smile tugged at the corner of his mouth and he seemed to relax slightly. "I may not have to kill Dragus after all," he said. "If he hadn't interrupted us, I might never have heard you say that."

Micayla smiled back at him. "So what do we do now?"

"Still your choice, Mick," he said, moving further into the room. "You do what you want."

"And what you want doesn't count?"

"Oh, it counts all right," he said. "And I think I made my wishes perfectly clear."

Micayla stood at the threshold of more than just a room where a man was waiting for her answer. It was a turning point, and once she crossed over, there was no going back.

She looked at him as though seeing him for the first time. He was lean and muscular with eyes that burned like a green flame and his hair hung in thick, shining spirals, just waiting for her fingers to delve into it. In her eyes, the only thing wrong with him was that he was still dressed. Her mouth watered at the thought of tasting him again and without another moment's hesitation, she entered the room and closed the door behind her.

Her back was toward him as she slid the bolt into place, but she knew precisely when he began purring. "Do you have any idea what that does to me?" she asked, still facing the door.

"No," he purred. "Tell me."

"It makes me hungry," she replied. "Hungry for *you.*" Licking her lips, she began to move toward him but hesitated.

"Do it again, Mick," he pleaded. "Bite me."

"I don't like the idea of hurting you," she whispered. "But I can't help myself."

"Then don't try," he urged. "I like it. It's… *exciting.*"

She stared at the place where she'd bitten him before and saw that, though it should have been open and bleeding, the wound had already healed and was nearly invisible. "Wonder why—"

Groaning, he pulled her to him. "Come on, Mick," he growled. "Just do it. Bite me."

Licking him first, she tasted the salt of his sweat and was instantly lost, biting down hard, breaking the skin and then licking the wound.

"Mmm… That makes me want to fuck."

"Then do it."

"I will."

Micayla managed to keep from using her teeth to get him out of what little he had on, but even so, she ripped the fabric as she pushed him down on the bed. "I want to devour you," she growled. "All of you."

"Kiss me again," he said thickly. "I need to taste…"

I'm going mad, Micayla thought wildly. *I can't stop…* Her tongue slid into his mouth and though her eyes were closed, shimmering lights seemed to dance in front of them. His flavor reached her on a deep, primal level—setting off instinctive behaviors she didn't know she possessed—and she knew she could never get enough of it. Trailing wet kisses down his neck to his chest, she teased his nipples with the tip of her tongue and then suckled them.

Trag growled deep in his throat as his cock pulsed, sending rivers of viscous fluid pouring from the serrated edge of the head. He took her hand and placed it there. "Touch me."

It was thick and hot and slick and Micayla let out a long moan as she grasped his stiff cock and teased the coronal ruffle with her fingertips. Micayla had never seen an erect Zetithian penis before, but it didn't come as a shock. In fact, it seemed more normal to her than the phallus of human males—as though the shape was one that she recognized instinctively. Through the haze of her desire, she vaguely remembered that there was something special about that fluid, but it didn't matter. She would find out soon enough, and the discovery would be all the sweeter.

Trag gasped as Micayla tightened her fingers around his shaft and slid them to the base. Combined with the exquisite torture of her tongue on his nipple, it was almost too much for him to bear. "Oh, Mick, don't… you'll make me come too soon. I—I can't hold on much longer."

His eyes were blurry and unfocused as he flipped her over onto her back, the inferno she lit inside blinding him to everything but the deep, fiery glow of her eyes. The pain in his cock was growing with each beat of his heart, but as he pushed aside her clothing, he discovered her soft, wet entrance, and once he slid inside, he found sweet relief. She was unbelievably wet and her succulent core held his cock in a firm hug as he penetrated her. Plunging in, he took her—nothing fancy, just slowly at first, then harder, faster, deeper. She was screaming his name—did she want him to stop or keep going? He didn't know, and driven mad by her scent, he didn't care. With all his strength, he drove into her, unable to hold back.

He could feel the effect his coronal fluid was having on her; the orgasmic contractions strengthened her grip on him, and the tension in his balls tightened like a coiled spring with each thrust. Knowing he was about to snap, he blurted out: "Where do you want it?" Before she could reply, he went on, "I shouldn't… no, too late," he gasped. "Too late…"

His voice trailed off as his semen flooded her and his coronal ruffle began its sinuous movements, intensifying her pleasure as Micayla fell apart in his arms. Her eyes were wide open as he hung suspended above her and watched it happen; her glowing pupils constricted to mere slits before dilating fully, completely round and totally obliterating the iris.

She was beautiful. Her whole face seemed to glow, taking on a softness he'd never seen before. She'd always seemed so strong—her features often set in hard lines, but now it was as though she'd been sculpted in marble, flawless and serene. Long lashes rimmed her dark eyes, and her lips, full and red from both his kisses and his blood, still beckoned to him. He leaned down, tasting both her sweetness and the wild, intense flavor of her desire.

—⁓⁓—

Micayla wasn't a virgin, but she might as well have been for all that sex with Terran men had prepared her for what it was like to be with Trag. She lay helplessly beneath him, staring up into his eyes, their fierce green fire now banked down to a soft glow. Maybe she was abnormal when compared with other Zetithian women after all, because she had no intention of letting this one episode be the last—or even a rarity. Either Trag was exceptional or other women of her kind had been suffering from mass insanity—or were part of the most extensive cover-up in history. Perhaps the effect would wear off and she would feel differently, but at the moment, she had no intention of ever hesitating to say yes to him, let alone refusing him.

The ecstasy had begun almost immediately—nothing like the pain and disgust of her first experience, nor the lack of passion she'd felt when Adam had tried to make love to her. Something about him had paved the way for his penetration, making her feel not violated or merely used, but completed by the addition of him inside her. And then at the end… she had no words to describe it but was beginning to understand why it might cause someone who dealt in drugs to feel threatened. It was an incredibly euphoric high—not artificially induced or expensive, but as natural as breathing for a Zetithian. Tisana had said it was overkill for many other women, but Micayla disagreed. Every woman should experience this when she made love.

Love. The word hung in her mind like a flashing red sign, taunting her. She'd said she didn't love him—and he'd told her it was only physical—but when someone was capable of bringing you such joy, how could you not love them? And if not immediately, then surely with time?

Micayla was still trying to solve this puzzle when her thoughts began to drift even further from her grasp. She sank into a state of complete serenity—a feeling of peace and tranquility unlike any she had ever experienced. The only thought she could hold on to was that it was all because of him.

Trag gazed down into her eyes knowing that he wouldn't have missed what he saw there for anything, but he also knew he shouldn't have done it, shouldn't have let her feel the effects of his snard. She'd want more, and the more she got, the more likely it was that they would be stuck with each other for all time—whether they loved each other or not. Jack would be tickled pink, but he wasn't so sure about Micayla. Her breathing seemed a little shallow. "You okay, Mick?"

She nodded slowly after clearing her throat several times. When she spoke, it came out with an odd vibration. "I'm purring."

Trag smiled. "Yes, you are," he said, purring back at her.

"I've only done that a few times in my life," she said. "Is it normal for me to do that after… what we just did?"

"I believe so," he replied. "But I'll ask Cat just to be sure."

The subsequent pause was as awkward as it was long. "So, what do we do now?"

Trag rolled off of her with a sigh. "Damned if I know," he said, "unless you and Leroy want to trade roommates."

Micayla bit her lip uncertainly. "I'm not sure Windura would like that."

"Maybe not," Trag admitted. "But Leroy would."

She stared at him in surprise. "You really think so?"

Trag didn't think there was anything Lerotan would like more, unless it was inheriting a fortune in arms with no taxes on them. "You haven't been paying attention, have you?"

"Not to him, maybe, but Windura—well, I'm pretty sure…"

"That she likes me?" Trag finished for her. "Yeah, I know."

Micayla's expelled purr sounded a little huffy, and her next words confirmed it. "You cocky, conceited little—"

"And no, I don't think every woman wants me on sight," Trag grumbled. "I could smell it."

"Oh, yeah, right. Forgot about that," she said. "And anyway, it's true. She *does* like you—a lot. Said she'd take whatever she could get from you."

"Something tells me Leroy would take whatever he could get from *her*," Trag countered. "I've noticed him looking... Think you could say something to her?"

"Like what?" she demanded. "'Hey, Windura? Trag and I are messing around with each other—so you can't have him after all. Would you mind moving in with Leroy? He likes you—at least, Trag thinks he does.'"

Trag winced. "Sounds pretty cold, doesn't it?"

"Mm-hmm," she agreed. "I may not be much of a romantic, but it even sounds cold to me. *Very* cold."

"It may not matter what we do," Trag pointed out. "I mean, if we're going after Grekkor anyway..."

"Right," Micayla said, sounding suddenly brisk and businesslike. Trag felt a pang of regret when he realized she wasn't purring anymore. "Any idea what we'll do when we catch up with him—*if* we catch up with him?"

"I don't know. Get him to confess somehow?" Trag suggested. Shaking his head, he stretched out beside her, staring up at the glowstone-studded ceiling. "Jack will probably come up with some way to do it. She always does." Glancing over at Micayla lying there next to him, he realized something else—something he wasn't quite sure he believed, but he felt it, nonetheless. "Right now, I don't really care. I wouldn't mind just holing up here for a while. I know we need to go after him eventually, but..."

"No need to go off half-cocked?"

"Something like that," he agreed. "Maybe Veluka could track him down for us."

"Yes, he probably could," Micayla said with a nod. "But right before you came in and 'reset' him, Veluka was telling us that he destroyed the Nedwut ship that fired on us—which was probably one of *Grekkor's* ships," she added. "And then Windura found out where Grekkor was headed when he left the station."

"Oh, let me guess," he said, rolling his eyes. "Nerik?"

"Yes, and that was what made him start humming. I don't think he's going to want that job."

"Guess I'll have to fly it—his ship, I mean," Trag mused. "That is, if he'll let me."

"Or we could go in Jack's ship," Micayla suggested. "Maybe land in a shuttle?"

Something wasn't right here. Trag had just lost all semblance of control, but now Micayla was acting as if they'd just finished washing dishes together. "You know something? I'm sure this is important and all, but for pillow talk, it really sucks."

Micayla was laughing as she turned over to face him. "I told you I wasn't much of a romantic."

"No shit." He looked at her cautiously. He'd seen her physical reaction to what he'd done but knew there was more to it than that. "So, um, was it good for you?"

"No, I hated every second of it," she replied.

Trag stared back at her for a long moment. Her tone was perfectly serious, and he could detect no teasing light in her eyes whatsoever. Damn. "I guess that means you don't want to do it again." It would certainly simplify matters—if that was truly the case.

"No," she said, shaking her head. "Don't think so."

"Well, crap!" he exclaimed. His first impulse was to storm out of the room, but then he remembered that not only was he naked, but it was *his* room—though on Darconia, the nudity wasn't a problem… He briefly considered strangling her but decided against it in favor of a more reasonable alternative. "Guess I might as well go out and get myself killed," he said morosely. "Just march right up to Grekkor and surrender."

"*Don't you dare*," she warned.

"Aha!" he said, pouncing on her. "So you *did* like it!"

"Did you really think I wouldn't?"

"Well, I *hoped* you would. I'm usually more creative than that, but—"

She patted his hand kindly. "I'm sure you are, but that was lovely, just the same." Then suddenly she closed her eyes tightly and groaned.

"What's the matter?" he asked anxiously. "Are you okay? I didn't hurt you, did I?"

"No, but I just realized what you meant when you asked where I wanted it."

"And—?"

"Trag, I'm not on any form of birth control… Are you?"

Chapter 15

"ARE YOU KIDDING?" HE ASKED INCREDULOUSLY. "MESS with my reproductive capability? With Jack seeing me as one of the Future Fathers of Zetith? She'd kill me!"

"Oh," Micayla said blankly. "Does that mean you have other children?"

"Not that I know of—at least, not around here. I donated some sperm to a bank on Statzeel, but—"

"Really? There's a Zetithian sperm bank?"

"Yeah, they wanted it, and I sure as hell wasn't using it. All the other guys donated too, so, yeah, I probably do have some kids there, but if I've left a trail of bastards in my wake—though Jack would probably love it if I had—I've never heard about them. Most hookers try to avoid having kids, you know."

"So you've really only been with hookers?" she asked, shaking her head in wonder. "I find that hard to believe."

"I thought we'd established that I only get it when I pay for it."

"That's not true and you know it!"

"Yeah, well, the end result is the same, whatever the reason," he argued. "And I'm a pretty good tipper, so it's not like they're really doing me for free. Trust me, they get paid." He let out an exasperated breath. "So, how come you're not on anything?"

"I should have thought that was obvious."

"Just because you don't like men doesn't mean one of them won't take a shine to you," Trag said roundly. "What if you were raped?"

"Look, Trag," she said evenly. "It's not the having children part that I try to avoid; it's the part about having sex."

"Believe me, I *get* that part," he growled. "But what if it was someone like Hidar?"

"I don't think Scorillians and Zetithians are genetically compatible enough to produce offspring," she said reasonably.

"Yes, but you know what I mean. What about Rodan? He could probably get you pregnant."

Micayla shuddered. "I think in that case I might actually consider getting an abortion—or committing suicide."

"Jack would *really* kill you for that."

"Maybe—and I'm not saying I'd do either of those things—but remember I only met Jack recently. She didn't affect my decision—or lack thereof—as much as the fact that since I was the only female of my kind on Earth, there wasn't much of a market for Zetithian birth control pills, and I'm not sure human methods would be effective."

"They might," Trag said. "But I see your point."

"*And*," she went on, "I only just found out that the human/Zetithian cross will work—at least, the Zetithian male/human female version."

"Okay, okay," Trag said, putting up a hand. "Let's not talk about this right now. I really wish we could get back to that biting and fucking thing again."

"Does that mean it was good for you?"

Trag stared at her. She couldn't be *that* ignorant, could she? "You're kidding me, right?"

"No, I'm asking you a question."

"You can't be serious! I totally lose control, and you—" He broke off suddenly as he noted that Micayla was staring at him, mouth agape.

"*You lost control?*"

"Well, I *did* say I was usually more creative, didn't I?"

"*I* made you lose control?" she said incredulously. "I don't believe it!"

"Must have been the biting thing," Trag said, grasping at straws. "No one ever bit me before."

"Guess I'll have to keep my mouth shut from now on."

"You really don't want it—me—again?"

She shrugged. "Not really—not now, anyway."

Then he remembered what Cat said and began purring. She didn't move. Didn't blink or smile or do anything. "Shit!" he exclaimed. "You mean I only get it once?"

The blithe lift of her brows indicated that this was probably the case.

"Great Mother of the Desert!" he groaned. "The fuckin' orbit of Darconia shifts, and you don't want to go again? I can do it even better than the last time. Trust me. I promise you won't be sorry."

"Um, Trag, don't most people hold off for a few hours—or even a few days—before they do it again?"

"Not when it was that good," he declared. "I remember Kyra—"

In a flash, Micayla's expression darkened ominously; this was obviously *not* the right thing to say.

"I am not Kyra," she said sternly. "Nor am I human."

"Yes, but she and Ty used to fuck *constantly*. It drove me nuts! She smelled like sex all the time and my dick was *always* hard."

"Is it now?"

"What?" Glancing down at his cock, Trag made an interesting discovery. "Okay, so maybe not right this minute, but—"

She was already reaching for her clothes. Trag had never felt more desperate in his life. He sat up and tried to think of something—anything—to make her stay.

"Let's not push it," she said in a neutral tone. He watched, both horrified and fascinated as she put her shirt on over her head and then pulled her hair out from underneath it. That long, thick, lustrous mass of— "I mean, would you *really* want to be doing it constantly?"

Trag stared at her in disbelief, totally at a loss for words. He knew that sitting there with his mouth hanging open probably wasn't particularly enticing, but she was still the most desirable woman he'd ever seen— especially with her hair all mussed up and her lips red and swollen from his kisses. Even her eyes had a different glow to them. "You can sit there looking like *that* and still have the nerve to ask me that question?"

She stood up and pulled on her shorts, allowing Trag one last, fleeting glimpse of the most perfect ass he'd ever laid eyes on. "Aw, come on, Trag," she said over her shoulder. "Get over it."

"But I don't *want* to get over it," he said earnestly, gazing with hunger at her fully clothed but still beautiful body. "I want to stay right here and fuck you until I can't fuck anymore."

Micayla sighed. "I think we already did that."

"That's your fault," he shot back at her. "I purred just now and your scent didn't change. That's the only reason my dick isn't hard. Maybe there really *is* something wrong with you."

"I don't think so," she said, laughing lightly. "Not anymore." Leaning down, she kissed him firmly on the cheek. "Thanks, Trag. It was *very* good for me, and when I'm ready to go again, I promise you'll be the first to know."

She was leaving and, short of barring the door with his own body, there wasn't a damn thing he could do about it. "Don't you love me—er, want me—just a little?"

"Maybe," she replied. "I don't know. We'll see."

Crossing the room with a hip-swaying walk that nearly had Trag down on his knees, she lifted the bar on the door, blew him a kiss, and left.

"This is *not* going to be easy," Trag grumbled and fell back on the bed with a groan.

Trag's prediction proved true, for as Micayla exited Trag's room, the two Darconian guards were heading in opposite directions as though having just passed one another in the hall, but Micayla wasn't fooled.

"Been having fun, boys?"

Both of them stopped dead in their tracks. It seemed completely out of character for a big lizard to appear guilty, but the look Dragus gave her over his shoulder certainly qualified. "Uh, yeah," he said as she approached. "Did you, um, have fun too?"

"Sure did," she replied. Dragus was too tall to pat on the shoulder, so she opted for his forearm instead. "You two can run along now. The show's over."

"Yeah, so we heard," Hartak said, lumbering up behind her, his thick tail sweeping the floor. "Trag was right about Ty and Kyra. They really *can* fuck for hours."

"I don't believe I'd care for that," Micayla said with what she hoped was an understanding smile. "But if you're disappointed, perhaps you can hang around outside their door for a while."

Dragus and Hartak exchanged a dismal look.

"We've been banned," Dragus said.

Apparently Trag's comment that Kyra had "gotten used to it" hadn't been entirely correct. "I can't imagine why," Micayla said.

"Me either," Dragus agreed, seemingly oblivious to the touch of irony in Micayla's remark. "We were always very quiet."

"It wasn't that," Hartak put in. "It was the slippery mess you used to leave on the floor."

Mystified, Micayla darted a swift glance at Trag's doorway, noting that the flagstones in that area appeared to have been recently swept clean.

"Safety hazard," Hartak said with a nod. "He killed a guy that way once."

"But he was a traitor!" Dragus protested. "We'd all be dead now if it wasn't for me!"

"That's the whole point," Hartak argued. "The next one you kill might not be an enemy; might be Kyra or Tychar, or even one of the kids running through the corridor."

"Should have made me a hero," Dragus grumbled as he shuffled off, his broad, scaly shoulders in a miserable slump and his head hung low. "Instead, it gets me banned. Not fair. Not fair at all."

"Actually, it *did* make him a hero," Hartak admitted when Dragus was out of earshot. "He even got the Darconian Medal for Meritorious Service to the Queen—but he's still not satisfied."

"I guess a medal just wasn't what he had in mind," Micayla observed, still trying to understand Dragus's odd behavior.

"Wasn't then, either," Hartak said. "The traitor, Jataka, slipped in a puddle of semen and broke his neck." Nodding toward Dragus, he added, "His was the only medal in Darconian history to ever be awarded to a guard for jacking off at his post."

Micayla stared after Dragus's departing figure with a newfound respect. "That must have been quite a puddle."

"Oh, yeah," Hartak said eagerly. "You want to see an example?"

"Maybe later," Micayla said with a casual wave. "I, um, need to go talk to Jack about something. Which way to Kyra's quarters?"

"That way," he replied, fortunately pointing in the direction opposite to the one Dragus had taken. "Take two right turns and a left and you're there." He must have thought she'd get lost, for he added, "Want me to escort you?"

"I don't think so," she said quickly. "I'm sure I can find it on my own—as long as I don't run into Rodan."

"Oh, don't worry about him," Hartak said. "He's with one of the queen's ladies."

Micayla could only assume that the queen's "ladies" were all Darconian. The mental image alone was more than she could take. "You *really* didn't need to say that!"

Hartak chuckled softly—for a Darconian, that is. To Micayla, it sounded more like an earthquake. "I don't think he'll be bothering you again."

"I hope not," she said fervently. "Honest to God, if he shakes his dick at me one more time, I'm gonna bite it off!"

Hartak's shout of laughter was still echoing down the corridor as Micayla reached the first turn. "I really mean it," she muttered. Then she remembered having wanted to suck Trag's and her thoughts took a decided turn for the better as she wondered what it would taste like.

Trag was still in his room. All she had to do was turn around and go back. She had an idea that her current state of mind would have his cock up and running in no time at all. *Then* she would know...

"Nah, maybe later," she promised herself. "I'll just let him stew for a while."

A little time alone for some private reflection was what she needed herself. Trag had lost control? That still amazed her. He'd been with all sorts of women, some of them undoubtedly more alluring than she was. *And all I did was bite him. How weird!*

She could feel her saliva beginning to flow at the mere thought of sinking her fangs into him again. *No, I need to control that,* she thought. *He might have lost control—and I'm sure I did myself—but there's no reason why we need to do it constantly—is there?*

She hadn't been lying when she said she hadn't felt like it either. It was so odd! One minute she wanted nothing more than to keep right on going, as Hartak had put it, for hours, and the next, it was the furthest thing from her mind. It was like flipping off a switch. She hadn't felt like it when she left his room, but that seemed to change now that he wasn't with her. Perhaps the old saying about absence making the heart grow fonder was true after all...

—∾∾—

Micayla returned to the sitting room to find that the men and children had returned and Veluka was now being exhorted by all of the others—with the exception of Rodan, who was presumably still with his Darconian friend—to at least fly by Nerik to see what was going on, or to drop off someone else. He might have been scared into a humming fit before, but he didn't seem frightened any longer, just irritated and angry to the point that his scales were as flat and shiny as patent leather. Micayla stepped inside the doorway and leaned back against the jamb.

"I will not go near my world again until I know he has left it," Veluka was saying. "You can't make me. I saved your skins back there, so you owe *me* one, Jack. Not the other way around!"

"Technically, Leroy owes you one," Jack pointed out. "It was his ship."

"A minor point," Veluka said. "I will not do it!"

Jack eyed him shrewdly. "Okay, name your price."

"There is no price worth my life," Veluka insisted.

"Veluka," Micayla spoke up from her post by the door. "Where are you planning to hide? He's managed to exterminate nearly all of my people. If he's got a grudge against you, your best bet is to get to him first."

"It's a very big galaxy," Veluka said firmly.

"Yes, but do you want to watch your back forever?"

"I do that now," he said with an awkward nod. "Always have."

"'Dead meat in a can?'" she quoted.

Veluka's pupils dilated briefly—clearly displaying his reaction—whether he would admit to it or not. "That was a momentary lapse on my part," he said, squaring up his shoulders. "I am over it now. I will let you people capture—or kill—Grekkor, and then I will be safe."

Micayla couldn't argue with his logic but knew that the quote had gotten through to him anyway. She tried a different tactic. "What about letting Trag fly your ship?"

Veluka peered sideways at Jack. "That is my price," he said. "I stay here, you take my ship, and you will pay me for it if it is destroyed."

"And just what would you like as collateral in case we're all killed?" Jack shot back.

Micayla's gaze flicked to Jack. She'd obviously dealt with Veluka before and knew there had to be more to the deal.

"I will take—" Veluka paused and gazed around the room, his eyes turning completely white, "her," he said, pointing a shiny black finger at Windura.

Chapter 16

"ME?" WINDURA EXCLAIMED. "I'M NOT WORTH THE price of a ship! No way!"

"Are you not?" Veluka inquired, tipping his head to one side. "I disagree."

Lerotan stirred in his chair. He didn't get up, but Micayla hadn't missed the lashing of his tail, nor the pounding pulse beneath his tattoo. So, Windura *did* mean something to him…

"If it is truly Lerotan who owes me," Veluka went on, "then he should be the one to pay."

Windura looked confused, but Lerotan's expression was ominous. "But if Trag is going to be the one to fly your ship," he said in a voice so deadly calm that Veluka should have started humming again, "why should I be the one to, as you put it, *pay?*"

"Having you and your weaponry at his back should ensure his success. And I believe that this," Veluka said with another gesture toward Windura, "would motivate you." Turning to Jack, he added, "Or perhaps you would prefer that I take one of your sons instead?"

"No!" Windura shouted even before Jack could reply. "He'll turn him in for the bounty. Don't do it!"

"I won't," said Jack. "But know this, Veluka. Just the suggestion of that is enough to make me want to blow your scaly, white-eyed head off right now."

"Uh, Mom," Larry piped up from his corner. "Hold on a minute."

"You're not volunteering, are you?" Jack asked incredulously.

"No, but I see his point," said Larry. "I mean, it's his ship, and if something happens to it, what will he do?"

"Get a job," Jack said scathingly. "I'm sure he could find work here in the palace."

"Veluka, like it or not, you do have a stake in this," Tisana said, cutting off any of Jack's subsequent remarks. "What if we were to let it slip that you were the one who destroyed that ship? Chances are that Grekkor doesn't know it was you—yet."

Veluka's pupils widened as he began to tremble. "You wouldn't do that, would you?"

Tisana's shrug was nonchalant, almost to the point of insolence. "Hey, I'm a witch. I've been accused of a lot worse. Grekkor doesn't know me. I could walk right up to him and tell him all about it."

"She's right," Leo said. "Even *we* didn't know it was you until you told us."

"Ooo! I think we're on to something here," Jack said, her eyes dancing with excitement. "He doesn't know me either. And we aren't Zetithians. We could lure him out that way—tell him we've captured a whole bunch of Zetithians for the bounty but don't like dealing with Nedwuts."

"Jack, there's just one problem with that," Tisana pointed out. "It isn't widely known that Grekkor is responsible for what happened to Zetith, nor is it likely that he would ever admit to it—unless you *were* a Nedwut."

"Oh, God," Jack said, closing her eyes. "That means we'd have to deal with Nedwuts. Not going to do that, don't trust them, *won't* trust them—ever."

"Sort of makes you wonder how the hairy beasts have managed to keep Grekkor's secret for so long, doesn't it?" Lerotan snickered.

"It's a miracle," Jack agreed.

"So what do we do?" Micayla said. "Just walk up to him and accuse him in a public place? Windura and I are the only ones who heard him say it. No one would believe us and he's already got us suspected of killing that Norludian. We'd be thrown in jail so fast—"

"Are we going to capture him or just kill him?" Hidar asked.

"If we kill him, we'd be no better than he is," Jack pointed out.

"Hmph! Tell that to all the Nedwuts you've killed," Tisana chuckled.

"It'd be different if they weren't always gunning for my husband," Jack said hotly. "They've tried to kill just about all of the guys at some point or other. I say we blast him."

Hidar rustled his wings and waved his antennae excitedly. "Yes, yes! We should blast him!"

"Wait," said Larry. "I have an idea. What if we could get someone else to go after him for some other reason?"

"How?" asked Jack.

"Tell some Nedwuts he's been cheating them?"

"I don't know if that would work or not," Jack said doubtfully. "They probably think that already, but confronting him in a public place would certainly aim suspicion at him. And then Windura and Micayla could accuse him."

"This is going to be much more difficult than we thought," Cat observed. "Especially getting him to confess."

"Yeah, like an episode of *Mission: Impossible*," said Larry.

Micayla's wasn't the only questioning look aimed at the child, but his mother waved it off.

"Never mind," said Jack. "It's really old. But he's right about one thing: they used to get people to confess to all kinds of things on that show. They'd rig up some scenario that would get the bad guy to talk and they'd get it on tape and that would be the end of it."

"We should just find him and kill him," Hidar said, clicking his mandibles with enthusiasm. "It would be much easier."

"You know, Hidar, for a medic, you're awfully bloodthirsty," Micayla commented. "Look, I know he won't admit to it, but Grekkor is supposed to be a drug dealer, isn't he? Someone could pretend their kid died as a result of the stuff he's been selling—"

"No, wait! I've got it!" Windura shouted, jumping up from the sofa. "Not everything Grekkor does is illegal. I'd almost forgotten that the main thing that keeps him in everyone's good graces is that one of his companies manufactures the vaccine for the Scorillian plague!"

"And we have a Scorillian among us," Jack mused, tapping her chin. "It would take some serious planning—and we'd all have to play our parts perfectly—but, you know... this could work."

"Great," Micayla muttered. "Now all we have to do is find him."

"Sounds like a job for you and me, Mick," Trag said from the doorway beside her. "You can make the necessary calls and I can fly the ship."

Micayla's heart took a nosedive as she turned to meet his gaze. He'd obviously been standing there long enough to have heard at least part of the discussion involving Veluka's ship, but he hadn't made a sound. There was a smile on his lips, but the challenge in his eyes was clear—his fabulously sexy green eyes…

"And you know what he looks like," Trag went on. "So you'd be able to spot him."

"I'm sure there are photographs of him somewhere," Micayla said. She tried to avoid looking into his eyes but couldn't do it. "Lerotan has seen him too."

"Nothing like the real thing, though, is there?" Trag countered. "And we don't want to risk any more lives than necessary just to find him. It could be dangerous." Something in the way his eyes glowed suggested that the greatest danger wouldn't be from any of Grekkor's henchmen but from Trag himself—alone together on a ship flying through space…

"I just thought of something," Lerotan said, frowning. "If Trag flies Veluka's ship, who's going to fly mine?"

"I hadn't thought of that," Jack mumbled. "We're a little short on pilots these days. Veluka, you're sure you wouldn't—"

"You're forgetting me," said Curly. "I can fly it."

"See, Mom," Larry giggled. "I *told* you we could help!"

"You're kidding me, right?" said Lerotan. Aiming a skeptical eye at Curly, he added, "How old are you?"

"Seven," Curly replied. "But I can do it. I fly Mom's ship all the time."

Lerotan was shaking his head, but Jack nodded in agreement. "He's not kidding, Leroy. He really can fly."

"I'm not worried about the flying," Lerotan said, "It's his ability to *land* that concerns me."

"Well, he might have a little trouble with your bucket of bolts, Leroy," said Jack. "But he can land mine slicker than snot!"

"And I can navigate," said Moe. "Where is it we're going?"

"Great Mother of the—" Lerotan muttered.

"Oh, and you might want to take Althea with you too, Leroy," Tisana said, indicating her daughter. "Having one witch on each ship would be best."

"I'm almost afraid to ask what she does," Lerotan said, eyeing the green-eyed little beauty with a grim smile. "She doesn't shoot fireballs, does she?"

"Oh, no," said Tisana proudly. "Her talents are much more refined than that."

"What about us?" Aidan and Alrik piped up.

"Their specialty is diversionary tactics," Leo said with a nod toward his sons. "Just put them in a crowd and stand back!"

"Look, my ship is not a daycare center," Lerotan argued, his tail beginning to tap audibly. "I can't have it manned by children."

"Not scared, are you, Leroy?" Windura chided him. "I thought you never got upset about anything."

"Well, usually not, but—"

"How about if I go with you and look after the kids?"

Lerotan seemed momentarily relieved, then added, "I thought you were collateral for Veluka's ship."

Veluka shook his head sadly. "I fear your need is now

greater than mine, Lerotan. Take her, and I will keep some of your weapons instead." His scales fluttered as he attempted to smile. "That way I will be able to arm my ship when you return."

"What's left of it, anyway," Trag said. "You know, I'm not that good at landing myself…"

"Oh, be quiet, Trag," Tisana admonished. "You'll start him humming again!"

But Veluka was already beginning to vibrate. Within seconds he was in a full-fledged hum.

"Does it ever stop on its own?" Tisana inquired.

"Eventually," said Trag. "But it takes a while."

"Funny, he always seemed so unflappable before," Jack observed. "Wonder what's gotten into him?"

"I guess everyone has their limits," Lerotan said with an eye toward Windura.

"Dinner should be waiting for us in the dining room by now," Kyra said after consulting the timestones that ringed a nearby window.

"Let's just leave him here then," said Jack, motioning for the others to follow. "C'mon, gang. We've got an impossible mission to plan."

―⁓―

Rutger Grekkor was just sitting down to dinner aboard the *Valorcry* when Worell approached. He had news, and none of it was good. "Sir," Worell began, "did you ever hear of a woman by the name of Jacinth Tshevnoe?"

"You mean the one who blasts every Nedwut she sees?" Grekkor replied with a short bark of laughter as he flipped out his napkin. "Yes, I've heard of her."

"You asked me to find friends and contacts of Lerotan Kanotay and the Nerik, Veluka. She is one of them."

If anything, Grekkor appeared bored. He dismissed the minion who was pouring his wine with a casual wave. "Do you *really* think we can't handle her?"

"Possibly, but you do know about her husband?"

"Ah, yes, Cat! The Zetithian who told everyone that the Nedwuts destroyed Zetith—or so I've heard." He paused to inhale the bouquet of the wine before taking a delicate sip. "Your point?"

"Sir, they were able to spread the word about that, and everyone believed him."

The meaning was finally sinking in, wiping the smug smile from Grekkor's aristocratic face. "And those two women are on Kanotay's ship…"

Worell nodded. "Rumor has it that his pilot is Zetithian as well—the brother of the rock star, Tycharian."

Grekkor exhaled with an expression so dire Worell was amazed there were no flames.

"I fear they will spread the word, sir."

"But without proof…"

"They had no direct evidence against the Nedwuts, sir, but that doesn't alter the fact—"

"Who *wouldn't* believe that of the Nedwuts?" Grekkor scoffed. "They were the perfect scapegoats."

Worell kept his face as impassive as ever but thought privately that many would believe it of Grekkor as well. "Tycharian has many fans. If he were to accuse you publicly…"

"He wouldn't dare!" Grekkor slammed down his wineglass, splashing the pristine tablecloth with a crimson stain.

"Pardon me, sir, but I believe he would—particularly in light of the assassination attempt against him."

"Drugged-out fanatics don't frighten me."

Worell considered this foolish. "Sir, they were unarmed, and yet they tore the Nedwut assassins to pieces. I would not underestimate their strength."

Worell could almost see the wheels turning inside Grekkor's head. It was a few moments before he spoke. "We will continue on our way to Nerik to purchase more cloaked ships so that the Nedwuts will be better equipped to seek out and destroy them. In the meantime, put out the information that I am donating ten million credits to the Galactic Orphans Fund and reducing the cost of medications from Grekkor Pharmaceuticals. Oh, and Worell…"

"Sir?"

"That slave ship we were to put those two women on…"

"Yes?"

"Have someone in our fleet track it down and rescue the slaves aboard. Make it look good, and once the slaves are off the ship, blow it up. No survivors please."

"Yes, sir." Worell waited a moment and then asked, "Will there be anything else, sir?"

"No," Grekkor replied. "That should be quite enough." He took another sip of his wine before adding, "Though perhaps we should arrange a reception of some kind on Nerik to announce these new philanthropic policies."

Two servants entered laden with ornate serving trays which they set down on the table. After carefully inspecting the fare laid out before him, Grekkor nodded a curt dismissal.

"I'll see to it," Worell said, but as he left to implement these new orders, his first thought was that the only difficulty would be in finding anyone to attend the reception. Perhaps the recently freed slaves could be persuaded…

Chapter 17

THE ZETITHIANS WITH THEIR MATES, FRIENDS, AND children assembled in Ty and Kyra's dining room around the massive stone table. The first thing decided was to eliminate Kyra from the plan. "No offense, Kyra, but you're a piano teacher, not a fighter," Jack had said. "Plus, you've got three babies to take care of."

"But I've still got the rocket launcher that Leroy gave me," Kyra protested. "I know how to use it too."

"Keep it, Kyra," Lerotan advised. "You might need it someday."

And it was also decided that Tychar was too high profile a figure for a covert operation. "We don't need your teenybopper fans swarming all over the place," Trag said. "What we really need you for is insurance. If we fail, you can tell your fans that Grekkor is responsible for the plot against us. That'll teach him!"

"We ought to do that right now," Kyra grumbled. "It would be a lot less dangerous."

"True, but exposing the Nedwuts' role in the war hasn't gotten them to stop," Leo pointed out. "If anything, it's made things tougher."

"Yeah, that five-million-credit bounty has got them swarming all over the place," Jack agreed. "We've got to stop this at the source."

"Well, if you won't let us go with you, the least we can do is provide the necessary supplies," Tychar said. "Maybe we could get some Darconians to go with you too."

"I'll talk with Queen Zealon and see what we can arrange," Kyra said. "I don't mind telling you the idea of so many Zetithians being in on this has me worried. There are barely enough of you left as it is. The rest of us should do it. Me, Tisana, Jack, and Leroy's crew—Windura too since she needs to clear her name—we aren't on any endangered species list. There are only seven adult Zetithians that we know of. Granted, you've had quite a few children, but—"

"I understand your reasoning, Kyra, but we cannot allow others to do this for us," Cat said quietly. "The time for that has passed. We must do this together to save our race."

"You're forgetting something though, aren't you?" Kyra said. "This plot against Zetithians will die with Grekkor. All you really have to do is outlive him." Seeming to sense a kindred spirit, Hidar's antennae pricked toward Kyra like an alert horse's ears but drooped as she continued. "You only have to stay here or on Earth or Terra Minor until he dies. He won't live forever."

"But he'll come after us," Trag said. "We know too much to be left alive—and do you really want to leave him free to live out his natural life after what he did? I don't, and I don't think the others do either."

"Okay." Kyra sighed. "I had to give it a shot. Just don't get yourself killed trying to be a hero—any of you." She paused as her eyes filled with tears. "I—I can't stand the thought of it."

She may have included the others after the fact, but Kyra had been looking straight at Trag when she said it, jarring Micayla's memory. She too had been intimate with Trag, so she knew something of what Kyra was feeling—an attachment she hadn't felt to him before… almost as though his death would hasten her own. Perhaps Jack felt it too, and knew that having been with both brothers, Kyra would not survive if both men were lost. Kyra must have known this as well, which was why she had suggested the alternate plan. Was the attachment to these men so strong that once you found one, you truly *couldn't* live without him?

There was something about Trag that affected Micayla very deeply. On a cognitive level, she wanted to understand it, but on an emotional level, she suspected that she already did. It would be difficult to admit to him that she already wanted him again. If she had remained with him instead of leaving so abruptly, she had no doubts as to what they would be doing at that moment.

But perhaps she wouldn't have to admit it; perhaps he would just pick up her scent and know. On the other hand, a little encouragement might not be amiss. He had made a point of sitting next to her at the table; perhaps it was her turn now. She could feel his heat and knew that her own body craved his warmth, but it was more than that. There was a bond of some kind between them now—something she'd never felt with anyone. She'd barely spoken to him all through dinner, and now it didn't seem appropriate, but she'd felt comfortable in his presence all the same—as though they'd been to-gether forever…

She turned to find him looking right into her eyes and felt a smile tug at the corner of her mouth. Just look-ing at him made her feel better—like the first time she saw him—and he seemed so… *familiar* now. Perhaps it was only because they'd been intimate, but even though she and Adam had done the deed several times, she had never before felt the way she did now.

Reaching down, she took Trag's hand and squeezed it. A rush of warmth spread from the point of their contact, and she held back a chuckle of delight when he squeezed back.

"I'm sorry," she said, mouthing the words so no one but Trag would hear.

His eyes softened and she knew she was forgiven—perhaps already had been—and felt a wave of tingles dance across her skin. She longed for the shelter of his arms and wished that they were anywhere else—someplace removed from all the others where they could revel in each other's scent…

Which was something new to her, but perhaps that was why she could sit beside him without the need for conversation. She'd been unconsciously breathing him in all through dinner, the distinct and pleasing aroma of him filling her head, and she could only assume that he was doing the same.

—∿∿—

Trag fought the urge to bring her hand to his lips for a kiss but then realized that the only person in the room who would see would be Jack, so he did it, his lips at first just brushing her skin, but once he got a taste, he pressed harder, lingering on the warm strength of her.

His decision to sit beside her had been automatic; he hadn't planned it, it was simply the thing to do. If he'd been across the room from her—or even across the table—he would've missed out on her delicate aroma entirely. As matters stood, there wasn't a whole lot he could do about it, so he decided that his best course of action was simply to sit back and enjoy it. Leaning closer, he inhaled deeply. The satisfying tingle in his groin confirmed what he already knew: she wanted him. He felt like laughing out loud but managed to keep his amusement to himself.

Not laughing was easy, but it wasn't long before he discovered just how difficult it was to keep not only his feelings, but also his hands—and every other part of him—to himself. She was right there beside him; touching her would be simple, natural—his leg against hers, his hand brushing her arm, perhaps even his arm draped across the back of her chair. It was a possessive gesture in any culture—at least among those creatures that had arms—and though he'd refrained from doing it earlier, he thought perhaps she wouldn't mind it now.

No longer focused on the discussion, time seemed to stop as her scent called out to him. Trag's cock was smashed against his lower abdomen by his tight underwear; he could feel it beginning to drool and knew that when he stood up, the fact that his mind was elsewhere would be perfectly obvious to anyone. Biting his lip, he continued breathing in her glorious scent and felt it curling throughout his body, exciting every nerve ending and stimulating every muscle. His cock was so hard it hurt, and as his scrotum tightened around his balls, he let out a small groan that came out as a barely audible purr.

Instantly, he sensed her response, though it wasn't anything he could see or touch. It was pure instinct, an awareness of her he couldn't identify. Her enticing aroma intensified and Trag longed to be naked, his thick, dripping cock exposed to her eyes as well as her fingertips. He could almost feel her hands on him again—her fingers wrapped tightly around his shaft, her lips kissing the engorged head, her nails lightly scratching his balls…

"That sound okay to you, Trag?" Jack asked.

Trag felt as if he'd been jerked out of a dream; his heart pounded like a drum and his chest was so tight he could barely take a breath. "Yeah, sure, Jack," he gasped in reply. "No problem."

Jack went on with the discussion and Trag lost track again. He was drowning in Micayla's essence—could feel his entire being submerging in the ocean of her, rocking in her rhythm while waves of sensation washed over him. He began purring again and, unable to stop himself, stole a glance at her. He knew immediately that it was a mistake; he could almost feel his cock penetrating her, driving deep into her hot, wet core…

Trag surfaced briefly, catching snatches of the conversation. Windura was saying something about the plague. Then he heard Tisana laughing as she talked about aiming fireballs at Grekkor. Cat was voicing his approval while Leo mentioned a fever. Trag knew that the plan didn't concern him for the most part; all he had to do was fly Veluka's ship to Nerik, and he could do that in his sleep.

Trag hadn't gotten to do half the things he wanted to do with Micayla—like burying his face in her wet heat while he fucked her with his tongue, or delving his fingers into her while he licked her to a frenzy. Suckling her nipples until she was so wet his cock would slip into her with no friction at all came next, along with plunging his hard meat into her beautiful body, making her cry out in ecstasy. Then he wanted to fill her with his snard, watching her eyes again while he did it. He would hold her in his arms for hours, not letting her go until he could mate with her again.

Purring was only part of it. Time. She just needed time. Then he could have her again, and again, and again…

Trag was driving Micayla completely insane. As if the touch of his lips on her hand hadn't been enough, now he was purring! He had to stop before she started gnawing on his shoulder again—which didn't seem like the correct behavior for a strategy meeting. She did her best to remain attentive, but his cock—his big, luscious cock—drove everything else from her mind, teasing her with the temptation of its taste, its smell… She wanted to suck it, then suck his full, heavy balls into her mouth and tease them with her tongue. Her mouth watered and she felt the gush of moisture between her thighs. Not being used to such feelings, Micayla didn't think she could take much more before she would be pouncing on him, tearing away those ridiculous pants he was wearing. He should be nude all the time, ready to go at a moment's notice— whenever she wanted him… whenever she was ready…

She held her breath as Trag shifted in his chair but let out a sigh as he took the hand he was holding and placed it on his leg. Knowing that the height of the stone table was enough to conceal what she was doing, she stroked his thigh, feeling his sleek muscles as he moved closer to her, inviting her touch.

The children were being sent off to bed. Was the meeting over? No, Jack had more to say—things she must not have wanted to say in front of the young ones. The possibility of failure… a contingency plan in case something went wrong. Micayla knew she should be contributing to the discussion, but since she and Trag were sitting near the end of the table—some distance from where Jack sat—she doubted that anyone was paying the slightest bit of attention to them. Lerotan was on her right, but to Trag's left the chairs were empty.

Micayla trailed a fingernail across the huge bulge in the front of Trag's shorts. She didn't have to feel it to know it was there, but Trag's breathing changed just enough to let her know how much he approved. He moved again, and suddenly his naked cock was beneath her hand, his hand cupping hers, urging her to take him. From the corner of her eye she caught a glimpse of his shuttered eyes and the smile that touched his lips. He shifted his weight again, his cock thrusting up against her hand.

He was hot. Slick syrup flowed from the points of the head, allowing her fingertips to glide smoothly over his skin as she traced the network of thick veins. Leaning forward to hide him from view, Micayla rested her elbow on the table with chin in hand, looking toward Jack as though hanging on her every word. Beside her, Trag purred so quietly that she felt more than heard it, and she discovered that simply holding him in her hand was quite… *stimulating*…

But she needed to do more. Careful to hold her arm still and move only her wrist, she slid her fingers up and down his pulsating shaft, gripping him firmly.

The slow, steady strokes brought him to climax much sooner than she expected, her only warning being his sharp intake of breath just prior to the first spurt of semen. Trag cupped his hand over the head to deflect the stream, forcing the hot cream to cascade down over her fingers.

It was even slicker than his coronal fluid and Micayla delighted in the feel of it until at last, with a reluctant sigh, she let go. Raising her hand to her mouth, she leaned into it, inhaling its scent before allowing one semen-coated finger to slip past her lips. Surprisingly, it was sweet and warm—like taffy in the summertime— but she had only a few moments to savor its flavor before an orgasm struck her like thunderbolt. With an audible gasp, she lurched forward, nearly striking her head against the table, instantly capturing Lerotan's attention and effectively putting an end to the conversation.

"Hey, are you okay?" Lerotan asked.

"Mmmhmm," Micayla replied, unable to straighten up or even raise her head. "Guess I just got a little crick in my neck from sitting here for so long."

"Sorry about that," said Jack. "When I'm all fired up, I don't know when to quit! But it *is* getting late, and we've just about talked this thing to death. Maybe we should call it a night."

The others voiced their agreement, and it wasn't long before several of the party rose from their seats and said their goodnights, but Lerotan didn't move from her side.

"Are you *sure* you're all right?" he persisted. "Maybe Tisana could fix you a potion or something—"

"Oh, don't worry about her, Leroy," Trag said cheerfully. "I can fix a stiff neck. No problem."

Micayla sucked in a ragged breath as Trag's strong hands made contact with the back of her neck. They were just as hot as his dick had been, and if she'd truly been experiencing a muscle spasm, she had no doubt that it would have been relieved within moments. As it was, his touch seemed to intensify her orgasm, causing her to expel that breath with a gentle sigh.

"Better now?" Trag asked. Micayla doubted that anyone else would notice, but to her, he sounded totally *wicked.*

"Mmmmm," she replied as the euphoric effect of Trag's snard enveloped her. "That feels *so* good... you've no idea."

"Oh, I think I might," Trag said knowingly. "Maybe not *exactly*—but damn close."

Lerotan was incredulous. "You're actually letting him *touch* you?" he exclaimed. "Without hissing at him? What's going on?"

"Nothing," Trag said blithely as he continued massaging Micayla's neck and shoulders. "I'm just being helpful, that's all."

Micayla turned her head just enough to catch a glimpse of Trag's expression. He might have sounded wicked, but he looked positively angelic.

"I'm sure she'd do the same for me," Trag went on. "Wouldn't you, Mick?"

"Oh, yeah," Micayla replied, doing her best not to laugh. "Anytime."

"There, you see?" said Trag. "We're just being... friendly."

"But you two have *never* been friendly," Lerotan insisted. "Never!"

"I guess we got over it," Micayla murmured. "Oh, Trag… That feels *wonderful*. Don't stop."

"No problem, Mick," he said as he began to purr. "I can keep it up all night if you like."

"Promises, promises," she taunted.

"Do I need to sleep out in the hall tonight?" Lerotan asked, the light apparently just dawning on him.

"Oh, don't be silly, Leroy," Micayla chided him. "He's just rubbing my neck."

"Well, yeah, but he's also purring," Lerotan pointed out. "I think that means—"

"You should go on to bed, Leroy," Jack advised. "And don't worry about them. They'll be fine."

"Well, all right," Lerotan said reluctantly. "But I still—"

"Come on, Leroy," Windura said, taking his arm. "Jack's right. Let's just leave them alone."

Lerotan still seemed slightly stunned, but he went with Windura anyway. "You can stay in my room if you like," Windura said soothingly. "Something tells me I shouldn't bother waiting up for Micayla."

———

Jack didn't say another word but chuckled to herself as she headed off to bed with her beloved Cat. She'd known all along this would happen. Once they found the right girl—whether they knew it or not—there was just no stopping a Zetithian, and they needed no help whatsoever from anyone else. Lynx—and his children—were living proof of that. Not that she'd been an easy target herself…

"Do you think they will be mates?" Cat asked.

"Are you kidding?" she scoffed. "Of course they will!" Sighing deeply, she added, "They're gonna have some really cute kittens too. You be sure to let me know the moment they're conceived. No holding out on me this time."

Cat took a moment to answer, but Jack waited patiently, knowing that he was searching his mind for the vision he always had when any of his friends' wives became pregnant. "No, not yet," he said. "But I will let you know when they do."

"You'd better," Jack warned. "Or I'll—" She broke off there, completely at a loss for a suitable threat.

"You'll… what?" Cat said with a sly smile. "Beat me?"

"Yeah, right. Sure I will," said Jack. "I might try to wear out your dick, but you know very well I wouldn't hurt a hair on your head!" Glancing up at him, she added, "Speaking of dicks, is yours hard?"

"Do bees be? Do bears bear?"

"Wish I didn't have to ask that," she grumbled. "I'd have thought that here on Darconia you would… you know, when in Rome and all that? How come you aren't naked?"

"I will stop wearing clothes in public when you do it," he said, taking a swift glance at her attire, which was her usual tank top and shorts.

"Well, at least you aren't wearing a shirt," she conceded. "But I do like being able to see all of you."

"Jacinth," he chided. "If you are near me, your scent arouses me—whether you can see the evidence of it or not."

"Sorry about that, Kittycat," she said meekly. "Can't help it."

"Do you think I mind?"

"I don't know," she said truthfully. "Do you?"

"No," he replied. "If I am not aroused, then you are not at my side, which is where I want you. Always."

"Mmm, Kittycat," she said, slipping her arm around his waist. "You say the sweetest things. I think I'll keep you."

"I am yours to do with as you please, my lovely master," he purred. "I will love no other."

"Then I think I'll try to wear out your dick—that is, if you don't mind."

Cat chuckled wickedly. "Good luck."

Chapter 18

"I THOUGHT THEY'D NEVER LEAVE," TRAG DECLARED. "BUT now that they're gone, Mick, would you mind explaining…"

"I can't," she replied, knowing exactly what he was referring to. "I really meant it when I left your room. I really and truly did."

"It sure came back to you in a hurry though, didn't it?"

"Yeah." Micayla sat up and reached for a napkin to wipe the snard from her hand. "So it works even if you taste it, huh?"

"Yep," he replied. "And the other stuff—joy juice as Kyra calls it—works that way too. It even works in your—" Trag broke off there as Tychar and Kyra's little Darconian servant came in to clear the table. He worked swiftly and soon they were alone again.

"It works in my what?" she prompted him.

"Your ass," he replied, somewhat apologetically. "Any mucous membrane, actually—though I've never established whether or not getting it in your eye or up your nose has any effect."

"Not sure I'd care for that," Micayla said with a chuckle.

"Which one?"

Recalling her one and only experience with anal intercourse, she was forced to include all three. "Any of them," she said firmly.

"Oh, well, that's fine. Whatever you like, Mick. I'm easy."

"No shit."

Her skeptical tone wasn't lost on him. "Not as easy as you might think," he said. "Well… maybe I am once I get started, but I've avoided it more often than not. It's just that wherever we go, the hookers know me now, and—" He paused there, throwing up his hands. "What can I say? They want me."

"I don't blame them," Micayla said. "Even when you aren't being—what was it you said? creative?—it's pretty amazing."

"Yeah, I guess so," he said miserably.

"You don't seem very happy about it," she observed. "Is something wrong?"

"I don't know," he said slowly. "Every time I'm with a woman I think, 'Yeah, this is great, but she's not Kyra.'"

"And?"

He stopped and looked away for a moment. "I still haven't figured this out," he said. "But I know one thing. With you, for the first time in a very long time, it wasn't Kyra's face I was seeing; it was yours."

"Is that a problem?"

"No, I—well, maybe it is," he said. "You see, being in love with her has kept me from falling in love with anyone else."

"And you aren't in love with her anymore?"

"No, I don't think I am. Something happened today— maybe it was what she said about the Neriks that got to me—or something you said—but I—oh, hell, I don't know!" He gave his hair a quick yank. "Do you want to fuck some more or not?"

Micayla ignored this last bit, focusing instead on what was undoubtedly the real reason for his distress. "Trag, just because you don't love Kyra anymore doesn't mean you have to love *me*."

"Yeah, well, after the fun and games we had under the table—which I think Jack saw, by the way—everyone will expect it."

"You don't have to live up to anyone's expectations but your own," Micayla said with conviction. "Believe me, if I've learned anything in this life, it's that! Men have always taken one look at me and assumed I was some sort of seductive sexpot, and I'm not! It's always been the farthest thing from my mind—at least it was until you came along. And like you said, this thing between us is just chemistry. My being able to walk away from you proved that."

"So, what does that make us? Fuck buddies?"

Micayla couldn't help but laugh. "Maybe."

"What if you get pregnant?"

Micayla shrugged. "I'd like to have a baby at some point, and since you're the only eligible Zetithian father around, it wouldn't exactly be the end of the world. And we don't have to fall in love and get married to do it either."

Trag seemed momentarily pleased to hear this but sobered quickly. "Uh, Mick, there's something you might not have noticed. It wouldn't be just *a* baby. Zetithians always have triplets."

"Really? It's not just what happens when we cross with humans?"

Trag shook his head. "Nope. That's one thing I *do* remember about Zetith. Kids were nearly always born in litters of three."

Micayla paused to consider this new information but decided she wouldn't be the first, or the last, to give birth to triplets. "Hmm, well, that might take some getting used to, but I'm sure I could do it. And since there aren't many of us left anyway, I probably should—for the greater good and all. Besides, Trag, I *like* kids. I just never expected to have any of my own."

Trag eyed her expectantly. "So we just keep on being fuck buddies then?"

"You know, I've never really cared for that particular expression," Micayla said. "But I suppose calling ourselves 'lovers' is out of the question."

"How about *really* good friends?"

"Works for me," she agreed. "I'm sure we'd have a good time together—and it would certainly help to keep Rodan from pestering me."

"He's not still doing that, is he?" Trag said fiercely. "He'd better quit, or I'll…"

"Or you'll what?" she said, laughing at Trag's reaction. "I've already threatened to bite his dick off if he shakes it at me again—and though it was Hartak I said that to, not Rodan, something tells me it'll get back to him eventually."

Trag grinned. "Hartak never could keep his mouth shut. He may not be a slut like Dragus, but he's definitely a talker."

"Odd trait in a guard, don't you think?"

"Yes, but now that I think about it, he was never guarding anything very important; just us slaves—and then later on, he was Kyra's guard."

"You don't consider yourself important?"

Trag shook his head. "We were *slaves,* Mick. How important could we be? It's not like we were valuable to anyone but Scalia—though she did pay a bundle for us. We wouldn't have been here at all if it wasn't for her."

"You're valuable to a lot of people, Trag," Micayla said soberly. "And not just because of how much someone had to pay for you. Haven't you noticed the way everyone around here cares about you? Don't ever forget that."

Trag looked at her with a sly grin. "Everyone, huh? Does that include you?"

"Of course it does!" she said, returning his smile. "We're buddies, remember?"

"I haven't forgotten," he said. "And I also haven't forgotten that you didn't answer my question."

"Sure," she said, knowing exactly which question he was referring to. "I think it's been long enough—or it will be shortly. It seemed to help being away from you for a while."

"Guess there's no chance we could spend a whole night together then," he said, looking rather glum, "is there?"

"I'm not sure Windura was serious about letting Leroy spend the night with her," Micayla said slowly. "And I'd hate to force that on her if she didn't really like the idea."

"She did make the offer though," Trag pointed out.

"Maybe," she conceded. "But I still don't like kicking anyone out of their room. God knows that happened to me enough times when I was in college! My roommates were *always* wanting me to leave them alone with their boyfriends. I don't suppose there's anyplace else we could go, is there?"

Trag rolled his eyes. "Mick, this is a fuckin' *palace!* There are probably hundreds of other rooms! If nothing else, we could spend the night in The Shrine. I used to sleep out on the portico all the time."

"Sounds okay to me," Micayla said. "But do we need to have permission to do that?"

"Hey," he said with a cocky grin. "I know the guards—and my brother is the famous rock star who lives here. I think it could be arranged."

"Hotshot," she retorted, grinning back at him. "You wouldn't be trying to impress me now, would you?"

"Maybe," he replied. "Is it working?"

"I'll let you know in the morning."

Trag tapped the comstone which hung from a chain around his neck. "Hartak?"

"Yes," a very sleepy-sounding Hartak replied a few moments later. "I'm here. What do you want, Slave Boy?"

"Who's guarding The Shrine tonight?"

"That would be me," Hartak replied miserably. "Bretnil called in sick. I haven't pulled a night shift in ages. It's gonna be a very long night."

"Sorry about that," Trag said. "But if you don't mind, Micayla and I would like to spend the night on the portico—not under the dome, but out in the open."

If he'd sounded sleepy before, he was wide awake now. "Really?" Hartak said brightly. "That'd be great. I'd love some company! It's not nearly as much fun as the old days, you know. No slaves to talk to or anything. You just stand here all night long killing yourself trying to stay awake. It's boring as hell."

"Think you could get us something to sleep on?"

"It'll be ready when you get here," Hartak replied.

Trag held out his hand and Micayla took it without hesitation. They were nose to nose when she stood up, those mesmerizing green cat's eyes locked onto hers. Why on earth had she walked out on him? If nothing else, she could have been gazing into his eyes all evening. As it was, it was a few moments before she could even trust herself to speak.

"Um, that Hartak is a handy guy to know," she said when she finally recovered her voice. "Captures runaway women, helps you shack up for the night... Is there no limit to his talents?"

"Just don't ask him to join us for a threesome," Trag advised, his full, kissable lips curling into a devilish grin. "He might take you up on it."

"Wouldn't dream of it," Micayla said. "I want you all to myself."

"Well, that did it," Trag growled. Yanking her into his arms, he wrapped his arms around the small of her back and pulled her right up against his hard cock.

"Careful, now," she cautioned. "I bite."

"I know," he said, pushing her back against the door jamb. His breath was coming in deep, raspy gulps. "I want to fuck you right now, Mick—*really* fuck you. Hard." He dropped his head and kissed her fiercely, his fingers spearing through her hair, pulling her closer, devouring her lips, nipping at her neck.

Micayla had been the recipient of similar kisses in the past—overzealous suitors had grabbed her before, but this was different. She wanted to bite back, but when his tongue invaded her mouth, her knees turned to jelly—and she *loved* it. He was pulling her hair, biting her on the neck, ripping away her clothes, and she loved that too.

Their tattered clothing littered the floor as Trag leaned in harder, pulling her legs up around his waist.

He'd lost control the last time and it looked like he was losing it again. Straddling the door jamb, he rammed into her, seemingly oblivious to everything else.

Micayla was nearly blinded by the fiery glow from his eyes. Groaning, her head fell forward and her fangs sank into the hard muscle at the base of his neck.

With a snarl, Trag pulled her down even harder on his stiff shaft, stretching her to the limit. Micayla saw stars and let out a guttural cry as an orgasm hit her.

"Feel good, Mick?" he growled.

"Yes!" she screamed.

"Want more?"

"Oh, yes, oh yes, *please*…"

In seconds he'd carried her from the doorway and sat her down on the table. "Just the right height," Trag commented as he pulled her feet up to his shoulders. Arching his back, he pushed in until their bones wouldn't allow any further penetration. "Now I can be *creative.*"

Micayla's eyes widened as she felt him moving inside her. Their bodies were locked together like a vise, but he was still moving, sweeping his cock inside her like a spoon scraping a bowl. "Oh, my God!" she cried in a voice she didn't even recognize as her own. "How are you *doing* that?"

"This is why you didn't want a human," he said fiercely. "This is why only a Zetithian will do—and why Grekkor wants us all dead—because we can fuck better than any other men in the galaxy." He paused there for a moment as his cock began pulsing so fast it was almost vibrating inside her. "No brag, just fact."

Micayla knew he wasn't bragging. She'd never felt anything comparable—and had never heard similar descriptions from a girlfriend—of *any* species—until now. Jack and the others had said it was different with a Zetithian—that other men couldn't even begin to compare—and they, at least, had human males to use as a comparison, if no other species.

"Do you like that one, Mick?" he asked as she moaned out loud. "I learned that trick from Lynx. He was in a harem for ten years, so he had plenty of practice. He wasn't sure I could do it, but I can."

She wanted to return the favor, giving him the most pleasure she possibly could. Gazing up into his fiery eyes, she said, "What do you like best, Trag? I want to give it to you." Micayla had never dreamed that she would ever say such a thing, but offered, "Want me to suck you?"

"Oh, yeah, I love that," he purred. Pulling out, he spun her around until her head was hanging off the edge of the table. "Just as long as I can play with your pussy while I fuck your mouth."

Trag put his fingers where his cock had been, teasing her clitoris until she was aflame with need. His cock rubbed against her cheek, the slick syrup permitting a frictionless glide as he pushed past her lips and entered her mouth.

He tasted like hot, sweet love and as he moved against her, the orgasmic effect of his coronal fluid began anew, driving her absolutely wild. The angle of entry was perfect, and she sucked him in deeply, savoring his cock as though it were the most delectable thing imaginable. His tantalizing balls hung just above her eyes, and when he pushed in deeper, they bounced against her nose. A month ago the thought of doing anything of that nature would have been repellent to her, but now, not only was she aroused by the sight, smell, and feel of him, he even *tasted* good.

"Mmm, that feels fabulous," he groaned, "but I want to fuck you some more." Trag backed off and spun her around again on the highly polished surface, flipped her legs up, and then drilled his rod into her hot slit. "I can't decide which is better," he said, bracing his hands on the back of her knees.

"I guess we'll just have to keep going until you figure it out." As Micayla looked up at his face, something seemed to click into place. She had no idea what it meant, but suddenly the need to kiss him, to devour him, overwhelmed her and, in her hunger, she came up off the table, reaching for him.

The altered angle popped him out suddenly, sending the head of his penis gliding down over her anus.

"Can't go back in now," he panted. "It'll cause an infection. My first hooker taught me that much—nearly ripped me a new one when I tried it." Trag glanced around wildly, his eyes searching the room. The little Darconian servant had done his job much too well. "Damn! There's not even a napkin left!" he exclaimed. "A scrail cloth would solve the problem, but—"

Suddenly, any pain she might feel as a result didn't matter. Micayla wanted him inside her, and she didn't care where. "Do my ass," she gasped. "Just be careful."

Trag grinned delightedly. "You can count on that, Mick," he said sincerely. "It's not the kind of thing I want you to ever be afraid of doing. Trust me, when I get done with you, you're gonna like it *all*."

Trag pushed down on her legs, effectively raising her butt off the table to meet him as his hips thrust forward.

His aim was perfect and he teased her gently, pushing, stretching, taking his time until with a groan, he slid inside.

Micayla's mouth flew open and her eyes felt like they were about to pop out of their sockets. "Ohmygod," she whispered as she gazed up at him in awe. "I never *dreamed...*"

"It just takes a guy who knows what he's doing," Trag said bluntly, "and I've been with some very good teachers."

Trag moved slowly, carefully, and soon what little pain there was disappeared completely. Leaning in hard, he began the sweeping rotations again, setting off even more fireworks than when he'd done it before. Just when Micayla was certain that there could be no greater pleasure, he found her sweet spot from a different angle and took up a back and forth drumming movement that lifted her to a higher level of ecstasy. Her entire body felt like one gigantic orgasm just waiting to happen, and for one fleeting moment she almost panicked, fearing that she would simply die when she reached her climax. She had almost gained the summit when Trag arrived a split second ahead of her, growling as he sent warm jets of snard pouring into her, igniting her sensitized flesh and pushing her over the edge into oblivion.

"Hey, Slave Boy!" Hartak's voice called out over Trag's comstone. "Where in the scorching Darconian desert are you? I mean, are you two coming or what?"

"Yeah, we're coming!" Trag gasped. "Be right there. Just hold onto your tail."

"Story of my life," Hartak muttered. "Hurry up and wait. That's all I ever do."

Micayla was right in the middle of the great mother of all orgasms, but she couldn't help laughing as Hartak signed off. "Ohmygod," she wailed. "Do you think he knows?"

"He was probably just trying to be cute," Trag chuckled. "He and Dragus used to do shit like that to Ty and Kyra all the time." He paused as he backed away from her. "Think you can walk?"

"I'm not sure," she replied candidly. "Would you mind carrying me?"

"Not at all," he said. "In fact, there's nothing I'd like more." Gathering up their clothing, he dropped the pile on Micayla's stomach and then scooped her up in his arms. "Mmm," he murmured as he kissed her. "I can't wait to see the look on Hartak's face when I walk into The Shrine with a naked, freshly fucked Mick in my arms. He's just gonna up and die."

Chapter 19

IF HARTAK WAS SURPRISED, IT DIDN'T SHOW. "HEY, SLAVE Boy," he called out as they approached. "Got everything all ready for you."

Trag grinned at the big Darconian. "Thanks, Hartak. You're a real pal."

"Aw, go on," Hartak said with a wave of his huge hand. "Just have a good time and try not to think about me standing out here in torment."

"Ha!" said Trag. "But that reminds me." Tapping his comstone he said, "Hey, Leroy. Where are you?"

"In my bed," Lerotan replied. "Where are you?"

"Not coming home tonight," Trag said cheerfully. "Don't bother to wait up."

"Wasn't planning on it," Lerotan said. "So, what's up with you and Micayla? I thought you hated each other."

Trag was in no mood to explain. "We'll talk about it later." With another tap, he cut the link and proceeded to carry Micayla into The Shrine.

The light from two of Darconia's three moons shone brightly, lighting his path, though Trag could have found his way blindfolded. How many times had he dreamed of making love with a woman out here beneath the stars? He had no idea, but there had been countless nights spent alone except for the other slaves slumbering nearby. Too many. Trag had never spent a whole night alone with a woman in his life.

Hartak had outdone himself. Near the sheltered part of the portico, there was a table set with large carafes of both water and wine, a tray piled high with fresh fruit, and a stack of scrail cloths. Next to the table was a bed— and not one of the smaller types usually provided for humans and similar species when they visited. No, this one was big enough for an adult Darconian. The mattress was firm, the sheets were soft, Micayla was in his arms, and suddenly, Trag didn't care if it *was* only chemistry between them. This would still be a night to remember.

He laid her gently on the bed and tossed their clothes onto a nearby chair. They were torn in a few places, but he had an idea they wouldn't be wearing them again anyway. He'd always felt that the Darconians had the right idea when it came to their style of dress, and the way Micayla's skin shone in the moonlight confirmed it. Her hair caught the moonbeams and sparkled as though filled with gems. What had he been thinking when he resolved to resist her? He was an idiot and he knew it. When she'd hissed at him, it had set him off in a way that was so unique he should have seen it for what it was.

Trag took a moment to wipe himself clean with a scrail cloth before pouring two glasses of wine and placing one in Micayla's hand. From his own glass, he savored the sweet, potent wine, the flavor bringing back memories of the times he'd spent with Queen Scalia drinking wine and talking for half the night. He missed her presence in the palace, but less so when he recalled that if she was still alive and the reigning queen, he would be her slave and Micayla probably wouldn't be there at all.

His expression must have shown something of what he was feeling, for he looked up to find Micayla studying him curiously. "What's wrong?"

"Nothing," he replied. "Just thinking about how different things are now."

"From when you were a slave?"

"Yeah. Ty had all the luck back then—he had Kyra, and I—"

"Trag," she said gently. "Try not to think about it, okay?"

"It's hard not to," he said. "I wanted her so badly. I used to lie out here and think about him being with her. It was—"

"Torment?"

Trag nodded. Hartak's word described the feeling quite well. "Like you wouldn't believe."

Micayla set down her wineglass and held out her hand. "It won't be torment this time."

Trag closed his eyes, biting his lip. No, it wouldn't be torment—anything but that. Taking her hand, he pulled her into his arms and kissed her. "My beautiful Mick," he murmured. "I'm sure you could make me forget the worst times of my life."

"I'll do my best," she promised. Smiling, she added, "Hey, what's with you? We were having such fun and then you went and got all serious on me."

"Everybody gets serious sometimes," he said defensively. "I'm no different. Not often, maybe, but sometimes."

She nodded as though she understood. "Come to bed, Trag. If nothing else, you could use some sleep." Pulling a sheet up over herself, she added, "I had no idea it would be so chilly out here at night."

"I loved it," Trag said. "It gets so hot during the day, and then I'd go to sleep out here, finally cooling off enough to need a blanket and then I'd—"

"What?"

"Wish I had a nice, warm woman to curl up with."

"Well, you've got one now, haven't you?"

"Yes, I do," he said as he climbed in beside her. It felt very natural to do so, but at the same time it was unusual for him to be with a woman who wasn't crawling all over him, demanding that he mate with her. This was completely different. It wasn't demanding, it was more... *relaxing*.

Micayla lay on her side, her head propped up on her hand. "Back home on Earth it gets cold in the winter, but there's just something about being snug and warm by a roaring fire while it's snowing outside."

Trag shook his head. "Not sure I'd care for snow."

Micayla stared at him, her mouth agape. "You mean you've never even *seen* snow?"

"Nope," Trag replied. "Never have and hope I never do."

"You should see it at least once in your life. It's beautiful." Smiling wickedly, she added, "Plus, it makes great weather for curling up with a nice, warm woman."

"I suppose so—though that's the kind of thing I don't mind doing even when it's hot."

"I've noticed." Micayla threaded her fingers through a lock of his hair, teasing it gently. "Can't say the same for myself."

"Nope, can't see you curled up with a woman either."

"You *know* what I mean," she deadpanned. "This is a first for me. Normally I have very little desire to be this close to *any* man—and at one point I thought that included you."

Trag pulled her close for a gentle kiss. Her lips were warm and inviting, not hissing or biting, just… sweet. "I'm glad you changed your mind."

"Me too."

Her scent was delicate and pleasing as Micayla kissed him back—not urgent or seductive. Even so, it wove a spell around him, like a net that captured and drew him in, binding him to her.

As Trag deepened the kiss, images swirled through his mind—green trees, open fields, the blush of ripening fruit, and sparkling water flowing over stones in a creek bed. Blue skies, rainbows, and clouds. The peaceful glow of a setting sun and the tranquil twilight that followed. The laughing faces of children at play. Trag wrapped his arms tighter around Micayla as the images gave way to other sensations. The heady fragrance of flowers in bloom, the smell of rich, damp earth, the sound of Micayla's sweet laughter, the scent of her arousal, and the aroma of fresh strawberries…

He began purring without conscious effort and she eased onto her back, taking him with her. Trag's tongue slid past her lips, delving into her mouth as though seeking the source of the flood of imagery in his head. Trag knew the moment her scent began to alter. The change was subtle, but its effect was profound. Heat flooded his groin and his purring increased in volume as it deepened in timbre.

Micayla's hands were in his hair, running down his back and shoulders. He felt her touch on his face, her welcoming gesture as her arms and legs enfolded him in her soft warmth. As he penetrated the source of the heat, he sighed, purring loudly as he began a slow dance inside her. Breaking the kiss, he speared his fingers through her hair as his eyes swept over her face. The soft glow of her eyes captured his gaze and held it firmly; he couldn't have looked away even if he'd wanted to.

Her eyes reflected the pulsations of joy that accompanied her sighs of pleasure as he used his body to convey the depth of his feelings. Though she held him in thrall, he didn't care; he welcomed his imprisonment if it meant being able to drink in the sight of her eyes forever. Freedom was highly overrated. He longed to be a slave again. *Her* slave forever, giving her joy for as long as he lived.

Her soft cries heightened his own feelings of ecstasy and sent him on a steady upward climb. When he reached the peak at last, he felt more than his seed leave his body. Something else went with it, something he could never take back. A part of him belonged to her now, though he couldn't have said what it was.

Trag watched as Micayla's eyes became suffused with joy, and with that image firmly imprinted upon his soul, he slept.

—∽∽∽—

Micayla woke with the dawn to find Trag still sprawled across her, his head pillowed on her stomach and his hair blanketing her chest. She vaguely remembered having pulled what she thought was a sheet up over her during the night, but it must have been his hair instead. As his thick curls stirred in the morning breeze, she slid her arms beneath them, cherishing their warmth.

Gazing up at Trag beneath the moon and stars had been an experience unlike any she had ever known. The sparkling sky and his glowing eyes were mesmerizing, filling her with a deep contentment. She had lain awake for some time after Trag fell asleep, listening to the sounds of the desert as the night birds swooped through the field of stars above her head. She'd slept outdoors before, and sometimes under an open sky, but that night, she felt like part of the cosmos for the very first time.

No longer was she the lone alien being of unknown origin that she had been on Earth. She was now part of a whole with a sense of purpose and belonging that enveloped her like a hug. Wherever she went from now on, she would find comfort in knowing that there were others of her kind. Granted, they were few, but they were becoming as dear to her as if she had known them all her life.

Especially this one. She traced the line of his brow with a fingertip, knowing that this was the first and only man she'd ever been truly intimate with. There was a saying on Earth that men were from Mars and women were from Venus, but she was from Zetith, which had put her in a totally different category—or so she'd always thought. But she wasn't. She was female and not only that, she was normal! Men had always seemed like another species to her—apart from the fact that the men she'd known truly *were* of a different species—but it seemed to go deeper than that. And now she knew why. It was very satisfying to finally understand so many things about herself. Growing up as she did was worse than being an orphan and not knowing your family's medical history; she'd had no idea what to expect as she grew older. She'd had no sense of self beyond that which she'd created on her own. She was always on the outside looking in, and hardly ever with a man in her bed.

Micayla had never looked at a man the way she looked at Trag. She could understand on a cognitive level that many of them were attractive, but Trag went beyond that. She was rapidly approaching the point where she didn't want to bite him every time she laid eyes on him; she wanted to kiss him.

The cool night air was quickly being replaced by the heat of the day and Micayla was beginning to wish the bed had been under the dome. She wouldn't have been able to look up at the stars, but at least they could have lounged there longer.

"Micayla," someone said over her comstone. "Are you awake?"

"Uh, yes," she replied.

"And… decent?"

"I believe so." She wasn't wearing anything but the necklace Dragus had given her, but since that constituted acceptable Darconian dress, she didn't think it mattered. However, just to be sure, she pulled the corner of the sheet across her chest.

"Good. We're coming out there."

The doorway from the greenhouse portion of The Shrine opened and Dragus and Hartak emerged, carrying more water and fruit.

"We brought you some breakfast," Hartak called out as they approached. "Want us to move that bed into the shade while we're at it?"

Trag stirred beneath her fingers. "Should have

known you guys would find some excuse to butt in,"
he grumbled.

"Aw, just be quiet, Slave Boy," Dragus said. "We'll
take care of this." With that, the two powerful lizards
lifted them, bed and all, onto the dais beneath the dome.
"There. That should be a little cooler."

"Thanks, guys," Micayla said. "It was starting to get
kinda hot out here."

"It was pretty hot last night." Dragus snickered.
The two guards exchanged a look and both began
laughing uncontrollably.

"What's so funny?"

Trag took a deep breath and sat up. "They were
listening over the comstones," he said wearily. With a
knowing look at them, he added, "Weren't you?"

Dragus was still roaring with laughter, so it was
Hartak who spoke. "Yeah, what in the name of the Great
Mother is *snow*?"

"How does anyone keep a secret around here?"
Micayla muttered.

Trag gave her necklace a little tug. "You just have
to take them off. If someone's wearing one and you
whisper their name, they might not hear you, but the
next word they say activates the link in the other direction." Scratching his scalp, he added, "I guess I should
have told you… Sorry… I just wasn't thinking about it
last night."

"I can't imagine why," Hartak said with a smirk.

Micayla scowled at Dragus. "You didn't tell me that
when you gave me the necklace," she said accusingly.
"In fact, you told me never to take it off."

"He has a reputation for doing things like that," Trag

said. "He once gave Kyra a glowstone necklace that had a comstone set in it. It was a different color than usual— which is why Ty didn't spot it right away. He was really pissed about it too."

"I don't think I mind very much, actually," Micayla said. "I mean, how much could you get from just listening?"

In reply, Dragus made a sound that was surprisingly like Micayla's vocalizations during orgasm.

"Well, maybe there's more to it than I thought…"

Dragus grinned. "Jack sent us to find you. You two are supposed to leave for Nerik in a couple of hours."

"What?" Trag shouted, leaping out of bed. "Today? In two hours? How—? When did—?"

"Um, you must not have been paying very close attention last evening," Micayla said. "That was the plan."

"Okay," Trag said, calming down a little. "At least *you* know about it." He paused, pinning her with a suspicious glare. "Mind telling me how you managed to keep listening to all that drivel while you were playing with my dick?"

"Multitasking, Trag," Micayla said with a shrug. "Women are better at it than men."

"Yeah," Dragus said eagerly. "You know… doing two things at once? Like sucking your nuts while she jacks off your cock?"

Trag looked up, puzzled. "Did she do that? I can't seem to remember…"

"No," Dragus said, his huge shoulders drooping slightly. "Been nice if she had, though."

Micayla laughed as she sat up in bed. She would store that tidbit away for future reference as something that Trag might enjoy, but right now there were other priorities. "Set that tray down right here," she said, patting the bed. "We'd better have some breakfast before starting off on our mission."

"Mind if we stick around?" Hartak asked. He looked like a puppy begging for a treat, but Micayla wasn't fooled.

"Go away!" Trag and Micayla chorused.

"If this is our last breakfast together," Trag said. "I want it to be memorable."

"Oh, it won't be the last, Slave Boy!" Dragus said heartily. "You'll have that badass hung up to dry in no time."

"Thought about where you'll live once you've done that?" Hartak put in. "You could come back and live right here in the palace. I know Queen Zealon would love to have you."

"As what?" Trag scoffed. "Her mother's former Zetithian slave-in-residence? I don't think so." He paused, glancing uncertainly at Micayla. "Besides, Mick and I haven't talked about that sort of thing yet. We need to get Grekkor first."

"Go on now, shoo!" Micayla said, flapping her hands at the two guards. "And don't worry; we'll be at the ship on time."

Dragus and Hartak shuffled off, heads hanging low in disappointment.

"I thought they'd never leave," Trag commented as the door to The Shrine closed behind them.

"Come on," Micayla said, motioning for him to get back in bed. "Let's eat this stuff and then we'll get cleaned up and head out."

"Sounds good to me." Trag grinned. His eyes lit up as he added, "Hey, we can do each other."

"What? You mean feed each other?"

He shook his head. "Nope, I mean rub you down with a scrail cloth while I feed you breakfast."

"What's in it for you?"

"If I do it well enough, maybe you'll return the favor." Trag picked up a cloth. "Or maybe you could feed me breakfast while I get you cleaned up."

"Why do I think there's more to it than that?"

Trag shrugged. "Whatever you want, Mick," he said. "I'm easy."

"No you aren't," she said, revising her previous opinion. "You're actually quite difficult."

Trag didn't argue and he and Micayla spent a pleasant half hour preparing for their adventure. While Trag buffed her body, Micayla popped bits of fruit in his mouth. His hands left a trail of heat as they explored her skin, but even so, she didn't need to take note of her reaction to it. All she had to do was look at Trag's stiffly up-cocked penis to know that he was reaching her on a deep, instinctive, and very carnal level.

When it was her turn, she took a cloth and began with his thick, curly locks, working her way down to his toes.

"You don't have a beard, do you?" she asked as she slid the cloth over his face, noting that there was no trace of stubble on his cheeks.

"None of us do," Trag said. "Do you mind?"

"Not at all," she replied. "To tell you the truth, I've never much cared for bearded men."

Trag laughed. "Well, at least that's *one* thing you won't hold against me."

"Oh, hush," Micayla said, pressing the cloth against his mouth to silence him. No, she wasn't holding anything against him at that point, and this, like the shape of his penis, was something that seemed very natural to her.

She continued with her enjoyable task while Trag lay back against the headboard purring contentedly. His joy juice was puddling in his groin by the time she finished.

Micayla sat back and viewed her handiwork as she munched on a vreckfruit. "You know something? You look good enough to eat."

Trag smiled wickedly. "So eat me."

"What? You mean suck your nuts while I jack off your dick?"

Trag gasped and Micayla laughed delightedly as his cock instantly pulsed, sending more of his coronal fluid cascading down the shaft. She wouldn't have believed it was possible if she hadn't seen it with her own eyes, but it got bigger too.

"I like doing this to you," she said.

"What? Driving me completely insane?"

"Yeah. I like the way your penis gets all purple and shiny and wet."

He waved it at her enticingly. "Want to suck it?"

"Yes, I do," she said, tossing aside the remains of the vreckfruit. "I never thought I'd see the day…"

Pouncing on him, she took him in her mouth, savoring the slick syrup as she slid her lips up and down his shaft.

"Mmm," Trag purred. "That feels *so* good…"

Micayla's first orgasm hit, sending her head into a spin and an anticipatory gush of her own juice pouring from her core. She shook it off and went back for more.

"Oh, *yeah,* Mick," he sighed, pushing up against her. "Lick the head."

She did as he asked, running the tip of her tongue around the scalloped edge and then swirling over the broad, blunt head.

Trag came up off the bed, his back arching as his head fell back. "Great Mother of the—*ohhhh...*"

Micayla felt a tingle of delight course through her as she went down on him again—a tingle that had nothing to do with the effects of his secretions and everything to do with the satisfaction of knowing just how much he appreciated her efforts. She liked making him groan and purr and lose control. It made her feel powerful, strong—as though she could take on Grekkor and a hundred others like him and emerge victorious.

Sucking harder, she massaged his testicles, delighting in the feel of them in her hand. She never would have guessed in a million years that she would have liked having them bounce against her nose as they had the night before. Now, after Dragus's comment, she couldn't wait to eat them too.

Sipping a mouthful of juice from the head, she then dipped her fingers in the puddle at the base, spreading it out evenly over his scrotum. Smiling wickedly, she slowly lowered her head.

"You're really gonna do it," he said with a voice gone rough with desire. "You're gonna suck my balls while you jack me off. Aren't you?"

Micayla merely nodded and opened her mouth wide over his big sac, giving it a tantalizing lick. Then she sucked it in.

It was a tight fit and Trag screamed, arching his back even further, pushing her back on her heels.

Micayla's initial thought was that she'd hurt him, but his subsequent exclamations put that fear to rest. "Oh

my *fuckin'* nuts!" he yelled. "Mick, you're so—*ahhh*…
Damn, that feels good!"

She never heard the rest of that as an explosive orgasm surged through her, sending her blood roaring
through her ears. It was all she could do to keep from
biting him as her body convulsed in ecstasy. It took her a
few moments to recover and then, grabbing his stiff rod
with both hands, she squeezed.

Rivers of fluid poured over her fingers as she worked
his meat to a hard frenzy. Trag was making sounds she'd
never heard before; snarling, hissing, and purring all
at the same time. Then his breath caught and his cock
erupted, sending a fountain of his snard shooting upward. As it rained down on Micayla's face, she released
him and tried to catch it in her mouth. She was rewarded
with a large droplet on her tongue, and she savored his
sweet essence for a moment before swallowing it.

As before, the euphoria blossomed within her, sending blissful streams of joy radiating throughout her entire being. However, though it seemed more intense than
ever, she had only a moment to revel in it before Trag
pulled her into his arms, his mouth covering hers with a
possessive kiss.

"You're mine, Mick," he whispered. "Mine. All
mine. No one else's—*ever*." He broke off there, kissing
her again, his tongue filling her mouth just as his cock
had done, sending even more waves of pleasure cours-
ing throughout her body. His hands roamed all over her
as they devoured each other, but when he reached her
neck, he let out a sob of frustration against her lips.

"Trag, what's the matter?"

"This," he replied, tugging at her necklace.

Laughter from within the palace echoed over the comstone.

"I don't care," Micayla said defiantly. "They can listen all they like, but they'll never know how it feels, will they?"

"That's true," Trag agreed. "Hear that? Eat your heart out, boys. This one's mine!"

Though it wasn't the first time he'd said it, Micayla still wasn't reconciled to the idea of a man laying claim to her. It went against her nature, her history—her entire personality, in fact—but still, if Trag was the one claiming her, maybe it wouldn't be so bad...

Chapter 20

"So, WE MAKE HIM THINK HE'S BEEN EXPOSED TO THE plague," Windura was saying excitedly as Trag and Micayla approached. "Hidar could pretend to be the carrier, and we," she gestured toward Lerotan, "could say our kid died of it—even though he'd been vaccinated—and we could accuse him of selling a worthless vaccine. Everyone would be in a panic and hate his guts and, oh, I don't know, try to lynch him or something."

"Oh, and I've got a really good idea to go along with that," Jack put in. "We come in and save his sorry ass from the mob, hustle him aboard the ship, and then he's ours to do with as we please."

"I am liking this more all the time," Cat said. "But you are known to him, Windura. Tisana would be a better choice."

Chuckling wickedly, Tisana said, "And if he didn't come with us, I could always blast him with a fireball."

"That's the best part about having Tisana on our side," Jack said proudly. "She never seems dangerous until she roasts you alive."

"She could also give him a fever," said Leo. "All she would have to do is look at him."

"Hey, didn't we already talk this to death last night?" Trag commented as they joined the group gathered at the hovercars that were to take them to the spaceport.

Jack eyed him shrewdly. "How the hell would you

know?" she shot back. "From what I could see, you weren't paying very close attention."

"I *told* you she saw that," Trag muttered in an aside to Micayla.

"That's all right," Micayla said. "I was paying attention. I can fill him in."

Jack remained skeptical. "You were the one distracting him, so I wouldn't swear you heard everything either."

"I took notes, Mom," Curly said promptly. "Recorded the whole thing. I did some research on Nerik too, but I didn't find very much. I made them a copy."

"I just love my boys." Jack sighed. "They're so efficient."

Curly laughed. "You don't always think so."

"Wait a minute," Tisana said, narrowing her eyes at the boy. "As I recall, you guys were sent to bed. How did you—?"

"Recorded it over a comstone," Curly said, beaming with pride, holding up a link module.

"No point in trying to keep anything from *them,* is there?" Trag commented under his breath as he accepted the pad from Curly.

"Doesn't seem that way," Micayla agreed. "Is that the Zetithian in them, or the Jack?"

"Must be the Jack factor," Trag said. "I'm pretty sure it's the sort of thing she would have done as a kid."

Jack ignored this, tapping her chin contemplatively. "Now, who should we send with you two to make sure you don't go off on a tangent?"

Rodan was raising his hand, but Hidar stepped forward. "I will go," he said. "They may need me."

Trag stared at them aghast. He'd been looking forward to flying alone with Micayla so he could put the ship on autopilot and then kiss her for hours on end. That lovely vision was beginning to fade when Cat chimed in. "They do not need anyone to go with them. Besides, if we are to use the plague symptoms as a ploy, Hidar will need to arrive separately."

"Don't see that it matters myself," Jack argued. "They just have to find him. We'll take care of the rest of it."

"Might not turn out that way in the end," Leo pointed out. "These things have a way of taking on a life of their own."

"Okay, I guess we can trust them to keep their heads on straight—this time, anyway. Here's a list of the supplies we had loaded onto Veluka's ship," she said, handing Micayla another module. "Don't lose it. Veluka is supposed to be here to give you a rundown on the controls. Where the devil is he?"

"Don't know," said Trag, glancing around. Tapping his comstone, he called out the Nerik's name. There was no response. "Hm, wonder what he's up to?" Trag mused. "Guess I'll just have to wing it then."

"That's what you do best," Tychar said warmly. "Take care of yourself, brother."

"Don't I always?" Trag retorted as Tychar hugged him.

Kyra fought back her tears. "Trag, you better do what he says," she said, punctuating her words with a sniff. "I don't know what… I mean, if anything ever happened to you…"

"I'll be careful," Trag promised. "You take care of things around here. I'll be fine."

"You aren't still mad at me, are you?"

For a moment, Trag didn't get what she was talking about. "What? Oh, that—!" he said with a dismissive gesture. "You were right. How could I be mad?"

"Well, I think it may be a moot point anyway," Kyra said with a glance at Micayla. "But still, be careful."

Trag saw no reason to hide his feelings. Pulling Micayla up against him with one arm, he said, "I'm always careful. Besides, if I screw this up, Jack will kill me."

⁓

The *Okeoula* wasn't a huge ship—not even as big as the *Jolly Roger*—but the cockpit was spacious enough to have accommodated a Darconian. The command controls had a translator on them, making it obvious that the ship had been designed for use by different species, even though it was a Nerik ship belonging to a Nerik.

"Must be willing to sell to anyone these days," Trag muttered. "Wasn't always like that from what I hear."

"Who could blame them?" Micayla said. "In a war, you wouldn't want your opponent to have equal technology—and this stealth mode is quite a strategic advantage to anyone who has it, as we've seen."

"Still can't imagine why anyone—even Grekkor—would be stupid enough to give these ships to the Nedwuts," Trag grumbled. "They're enough trouble as it is."

"Desperate, I guess," Micayla said with a shrug. Taking a seat at the comstation, she tapped her fingers on the console. "Better com system than Leroy's too," she added. "And scanners! No wonder he wanted some collateral for this ship! It must be worth a fortune. Wonder why he didn't show up for the launch?"

"The Great Mother only knows," Trag said as he adjusted the controls. "Probably hiding out in The Shrine with Shentuck so we wouldn't make him come with us."

"That would still be the best idea," Micayla said. "He's more familiar with—"

"Are you saying I can't fly this thing as well as he can?" Trag demanded.

"Well, it *is* his ship," Micayla pointed out, "and he's used to it. All ships have their little quirks, and he didn't tell you a thing about how to fly it."

"I can do it," Trag said with calm assurance. "No sweat."

"I'm sure you can," Micayla said warmly, "but that's not the only thing I'm concerned about. Neither of us have ever been to Nerik, and he's bound to know more about his own world than any of us possibly could—no matter how much research Curly did."

"Veluka is such a wuss." Trag grinned. "A little trouble with Grekkor and he's off somewhere humming."

"Which means he obviously knows a few things about our opponent that would be worth knowing. I was up against Grekkor briefly, but let me tell you, he's not only ruthless and cunning but a little crazy too. Not a good combination."

"Sounds like your typical villain," Trag commented. "Aren't they all like that?"

"Maybe so, but he's got an awful lot of people working for him. I felt as if the entire station had turned against us after he spotted me. We couldn't trust *anyone*—except maybe the hookers. He's a very powerful man."

"That'll just make bringing him down that much sweeter," Trag said as he put the ship through a preflight test. "Besides, he'd have been dead meat a long time ago if Jack had known what he'd done."

Micayla didn't argue the point, the truth of which was patently obvious. "Speaking of Jack, I need to lock in her ship's frequency."

Trag watched her out of the corner of his eye as she adjusted the controls with nonchalant efficiency. No doubt about it, she knew her job well.

"I'd hate to miss it if Jack ever does meet up with him," Trag said. "I just hope we can find him before he heads off to some other world. He might not be as easy to find the next time."

"What happens if we miss?"

"We'll try again," Trag replied. "There is no way we can just let him go on with this vendetta against us. Too bad we didn't find out about all this a little sooner. There might have been a lot more of us left to start over again."

"Do you really think it's possible?" Micayla asked. "Starting over, I mean. There are so few of us…"

"I know," he said. "But I promise to do my part."

Micayla laughed. "Am I going to be pregnant for the rest of my childbearing years?"

"Possibly," Trag admitted. "I won't be able to keep from trying if you're anywhere around." Giving her a meaningful look, he added, "You're irresistible, Mick. You know that, don't you?"

"Me?" she exclaimed. "I thought you were the one who was irresistible."

Trag shook his head. "Not really—not to you, anyway."

Micayla looked at him in surprise. "What do you mean? Trag, I've never wanted anyone before in my life. Now I can't—"

"Keep your hands off of me? Seems like you can. You're focused on the mission, whereas I'm sitting here wishing Grekkor would just up and die of the damn plague and save us the trouble of going after him so we can fuck continuously for the rest of our lives."

Her slow, seductive smile had Trag's fingers fumbling on the controls. "Well, we can do that after we catch him."

Trag wasn't sure he believed her. "You mean it?"

Micayla nodded. "I have to make up for lost time."

Trag groaned and gave his hair a yank. "Don't *say* things like that when we've got a mission to accomplish!"

"Just a little incentive for you to pay attention to what you're doing."

"I pay attention!" Trag insisted. "I just don't—" He broke off there as the cabin alarm lights began flashing and smoke curled up from a nearby control panel.

"I don't think you are—unless that's normal behavior for a Nerik ship."

"How the hell would I know?" Trag muttered as he reengaged the safety lock. "Never been on one before."

"My, that's *very* encouraging," she said. "It's not too late to get Veluka to come with us, you know."

"Like I said, I don't think he intends to let us try, or he'd have been here."

"I don't suppose there's an operator's manual, is there?" Micayla said as she got up to look around the cockpit. Unfortunately, if there was any flight information to be had, it wasn't lying about in plain sight.

"It's probably written in Nerik anyway," Trag said. "I'll get this figured out in a minute. I always do."

Micayla chuckled. "I wish I had your confidence. I'm not stupid, but jumping into a strange ship and trying to fly it isn't something I've ever considered."

"That's because you aren't a pilot. You can work the com system, can't you?"

"Well, yes, but—"

"Same thing," Trag said with a firm nod. "Just be patient. I'll have us flying in no time."

Micayla leaned over his shoulder and pointed to a blinking switch. "What's that?"

"The self-destruct sequencer," Trag replied.

"Are you sure about that?"

"Absolutely. First rule of flying a starship: Never flip a blinking switch." Trag paused for a moment. Turning his head, his nose encountered her hair and he inhaled deeply. His cock sprang to attention so quickly he thought it would pop right through his shorts. "I'm not purring, Mick. What gives?"

"Must be your manly piloting skills," she murmured in his ear. Giving it a lick, she began purring. "I never knew this purring thing could feel so good. Sort of comforting and arousing at the same time."

Arousing was right; Trag let out a yelp as his cock seemed to fold in half as it strained against the confining fabric of his pants.

"Not hurting you, am I?" she asked, tugging at his earlobe with her fangs.

"Mick, you're killing me," he said frankly. "I never knew you to be… like this."

"The aggressor, you mean? That's funny, I thought I did that the first time I bit you."

Trag considered this for a moment. "Now that you mention it, I suppose you did. Damn! This is getting more complicated all the time. Cat just told me to purr… but it seems like there's more to it than that."

"What can I say?" Micayla purred. "You're irresistible—and you know it."

Trag took a brief moment to savor this revelation

before commenting on it. "Maybe, but enticing female Zetithians was supposed to be really hard to do."

Micayla shrugged. "Perhaps it's because I don't have the cultural background that the others did. I've been around boy-crazy girls my whole life. Just because I didn't feel the attraction to men doesn't mean I didn't want to. I wasn't taught to resist the impulse, and I tried, Trag, *believe me*, I tried *very* hard to feel it! You're just the only one it ever worked with. I think it was the hissing thing that threw me. I thought it meant I couldn't stand you rather than the other way around. It was very confusing."

"Means you like me, doesn't it?" Trag said smugly as he began purring himself.

"Means I want to suck your dick," she replied, licking the tip of his ear. "Now, get this ship into space so we can engage the autopilot, and I'll suck you all the way to Nerik."

The thought of Micayla sitting on the floor between his legs and licking his cock while he flew the ship nearly had Trag choking on his own spit. He tapped a few more spots on the console and the engines responded instantly.

Patting him on the shoulder, Micayla said, "See, you just needed the right incentive."

"What? You mean you—? Well, maybe so," he admitted. "But I'm going to hold you to that promise."

Blowing him a kiss, Micayla returned to her station. "Looking forward to it, Trag. Keep your dick hard for me."

"I'll do my best," he promised.

"I want lots of cock syrup too," she said before turning her attention to a hail from the *Jolly Roger*. "Jack says *bon voyage*."

"It will be," Trag said with conviction. "I just hope it's a really long trip to Nerik."

"Jack said it would take us three weeks."

Her tone of voice wasn't lost on Trag. No doubt about it, she was as pleased with the prospect as he was. "My dick will be worn out completely by then," Trag said. "But I'm certainly not going to complain."

"Hey, Trag," she began.

"Yeah, Mick?"

"Thanks."

"For what?"

"For being so irresistible. I never thought I'd find someone like you. I thought I'd be alone forever, but you changed that. I just want you to know how much I appreciate it."

Trag had never expected this. "Fuck buddies forever?" he asked hopefully.

"Fuck buddies forever."

—◦◦◦—

She meant it too. It was becoming increasingly clear that Trag was more than just another Zetithian. He'd said that what they were feeling was only chemistry, but it was a chemistry she'd never felt with a man before. And she liked it. He was fun. He was sexy. He made her laugh and made her feel emotions she hadn't known she possessed. It might not be love, but whatever it was, she had no intention of giving it up anytime soon.

Chapter 21

AFTER TAKEOFF, MICAYLA DID A FEW QUICK COMMUNICATION checks with the Darconian spaceport authority while Trag played around with flying the ship. One nice thing about that kind of flying: out in space there wasn't a whole lot to crash into. She knew that Trag was just getting a feel for the ship, but looking out the porthole at the rapidly diminishing planet as it spiraled off behind them was almost enough to make her spacesick.

Trag was like a kid with a new toy, which his occasional exclamation of delight proved. She could hear him talking to the ship and to himself as she set out to explore the rest of the vessel. Veluka had made a big mistake by not coming with them; Micayla suspected that Trag might conveniently forget to return his ship.

The *Okeoula* was laid out much like any other starship; command stations in the forward compartments with the galley and the common rooms in the middle, the crew quarters aft and the cargo hold below with the engine pods on either side. Even though one man could fly it, it had accommodations for a total of six. The largest compartment was obviously Veluka's—which Micayla had no intention of using—but whoever had prepped the ship for their voyage had fixed up the two next largest cabins, one with Trag's belongings and another with her own—not that she had very much. *Giving us the benefit of the doubt,* she mused. It was nice to know that she and

Trag could sleep separately if they wished, but she, for one, had no such intention.

The night she'd spent with Trag out on the portico had been a real eye-opener for Micayla. She had enjoyed every bit of it—from the fabulous sex, to falling asleep with him beneath the stars, and then waking up with him in the morning—and she was definitely looking forward to doing it again.

"Who'd have thunk it?" she muttered as she headed back to the galley. After peeking into a few cupboards, she found a number of utensils she couldn't identify, as well as some of the more familiar sort. As she might have expected, the stasis unit was filled with Darconian produce. Some of the other less recognizable provisions she took to be Veluka's. Not knowing much about Nerik cuisine, she made a mental note to leave them alone.

Sitting down at the table, she consulted the information module Curly had given them. The climate on Nerik was similar to that of Earth with a variety of biospheres, and though most of the vegetation was harmless, there were some dangerous animals. They would have to be careful. The natives she and Trag each knew something about, though certainly not everything. Not for the last time she wished Veluka had been with them.

Still, being alone with Trag for the next three weeks had its appeal, and Micayla had no doubt that her promise to suck him all the way to Nerik was at least possible, if not very feasible. Smiling to herself at the prospect, it occurred to her that the things that other women talked about made sense now—like referring to a man as being "hot" or "sexy" or a "hunk." Trag was all of those things and more. It had simply been a matter of finding a man of the same species. Simple, yes, but also unlikely as hell. The odds against having landed on the one ship that contained Trag were astronomical, and their friendship was even more so.

Micayla was still reviewing Curly's info when Trag sauntered in.

"What's for lunch? I'm starving!" Making a beeline for the stasis unit, he pulled open the latch and stuck his head inside. Micayla could tell how pleased he was by the way his butt wiggled as he did a little happy dance. "Great Mother of the Desert!" he exclaimed. "Would you take a look at this!"

"At least no one will have to cook," Micayla observed. "Unless, of course, you want fruit soup or a pie or something."

"No way!" he said, backing out of the unit with his arm stacked with two crafnets, a cluster of sporak fruit, and a bottle of water. "It's perfect just the way it is."

This observation led Micayla to suspect that Trag had never tasted blueberry crisp with vanilla ice cream. *His loss.* "Well, you're easy," she said.

Trag grinned at her. Dumping his goodies on the table, he pulled up a chair and sat down. "Not really," he said. "You'd be surprised how hard it is to find food like this in the places Leroy goes." Taking a big bite of a crisp crafnet, he chewed on it for a few blissful moments before asking, "So, what are you reading?"

"Curly's report."

"Anything interesting?"

"Yes," she replied. "But he wasn't kidding when he said he didn't find very much—though what he did find is very informative. You should read it."

"Later," Trag said dismissively. "I'd much rather do something else."

The suggestive lift of his brow wasn't lost on Micayla, but rather than make it easy, she chose to tease him. "Oh, and what would that be?"

"As I recall, you were going to suck my dick all the way to Nerik," he said. "I've got the course laid in, so now it's your turn."

"All the way to Nerik? I don't think it would survive the trip!"

"Maybe not," Trag agreed. "But it would be fun for a while."

"True," she concurred. "But I'll never have your babies if that's all we do."

Trag's eyes widened as he tried to swallow a chunk of crafnet that was a little too big. Making a quick recovery, he said, "Grekkor would freak if you walked in pregnant, wouldn't he?"

"He'd probably have a coronary on the spot," she agreed. "Then again, you almost had one yourself just now."

"No I didn't!" he insisted. "It's just that the idea takes a little getting used to. I've never thought of myself as a father. I mean, I love kids—Ty's kids, and Jack's— we've got lots of Zetithian children now—and there was this little girl on Orleon—"

"Yes?" she prompted him when he stopped.

Trag blinked and looked away for a moment. "She was… real cute," he muttered. "Gave me a strawberry."

Micayla nodded. "Believe it or not, I saw that," she said. "I was on my way to work but Windura distracted me and when I looked back, you were gone. I wanted to go looking for you, but Windura warned me to stay away from that part of the station."

"Wish I'd known that," he said. "Though I wouldn't have thought you'd notice me—unless you could tell that I was Zetithian."

"I didn't find that out until later," she admitted. "My friend Dana is the woman you spoke to in the park. She thought we might be the same species, but even before I knew that, there was still something about you…" Pausing to study his reaction, she added, "Dana said you seemed very sad. What was bothering you?"

Trag shrugged and focused his attention on the sporak fruit. He might not have been evading the question, but he was certainly avoiding her gaze. Micayla waited for him to speak, noting that he was clearly wrestling with some very strong emotions. Finally, he took a swig of water from the bottle and met her eyes. "Just… things," he replied. "And the little girl—Cara—she looked like my sister."

This was a side of Trag she hadn't seen before, though she'd felt it the moment she laid eyes on him. His usual devil-may-care attitude didn't quite mesh with it, but then she remembered what Leroy had said about him; that he had everything he could wish for but still wasn't happy. Micayla was beginning to understand why that was. "Dana told me about that too. I barely remember any of my own family, but you probably remember a lot more about yours, don't you?"

Nodding, he said, "I was about twenty when I was taken prisoner, so yeah, I remember a lot more."

"That must have been hard."

"It's *all* been hard," he said. "I know I lived through it, and I've tried not to dwell on it, but yeah, it's been tough.

I left home when I was pretty young, but at least I knew my family was still there. Then losing everyone but Ty, being captured… sold as a slave… Scalia was great, but even so…" He shook his head, looking down at his hands where he toyed with the fruit, plucking the shiny purple globes of sporak from the vine. "For a long time Ty and I thought we were the only ones left." Glancing up at her, he added, "But you'd know all about that, wouldn't you?"

"I was even more in the dark than you were," she agreed. "I never knew where I came from or even what I was. I felt out of place no matter where I went." Shaking her head, she went on, "But that's all changed. I know so much more now, and I feel… *normal*… for the first time in my life."

It was a moment before Micayla realized she was staring down at the link module without comprehending a word of the text. Looking up, she found Trag's glowing green gaze riveted to her face. "My dear Mick," he said. "You are *so* much more than normal."

He'd said it like he really meant it—with a fervor that made her feel awkward, the subsequent silence only serving to amplify the effect.

In another place and time, she would simply have left him then, not being able to identify the emotions, or to understand why they felt so alien. She'd always dealt with such instances by remaining aloof, pretending not to care if anyone teased her about her feline features or called her "Ice Queen." Trag hadn't been the first to refer to her in that manner, but he was the first to reach her on another level—delving beneath the ice to understand the reason for it. "Thank you," she said softly. "That means a lot to me."

"And thank you too," he said. "You're the first woman who didn't prefer my brother over me."

"I doubt that," she said. "Tychar is very charming, and I'm sure he's very talented, but he certainly doesn't have your personality."

Trag grinned at her. "Don't feel like biting him?"

"Not at all," she replied. This was perfectly true; though the slightest glimpse of Trag's twinkling green eyes had her salivating. "Or any of the others, for that matter. Just you."

"Aw, now, Mick," he drawled. "You wouldn't be falling for me, would you?"

"Maybe," she said with a shrug. "I don't know. Not sure how it's supposed to feel when you fall for someone. I mean, I had a boyfriend once—sort of—and I've been hearing other girls talk about it all my life, but until it happens to you, you can't really understand how it feels, can you?"

"Guess not," Trag agreed. "But then, I'm not a girl. Men don't analyze these things as much as women do." Reaching over to pop a sporak in her mouth, he added, "A guy just knows."

"Oh really?" she said skeptically. "That's all there is to it? You just *know?*"

Trag didn't reply right away, seeming to contemplate this for a moment. "I'm not sure it's in your head, though. You sort of feel it in your—"

"Dick?"

Scowling at her, he went on, "In your gut, Mick. You feel it in your gut."

"Not your heart?"

"I think that's where women feel it," he said thoughtfully. "It's more visceral with men."

"I guess I'll have to take your word for it," she said. "I barely know how a woman is supposed to feel. Men are even more of a mystery."

"Not really," Trag said. "We're pretty basic on most things."

Micayla wasn't convinced of this but let it drop. "I see you figured out the ship."

"Yeah," he said. "Would you believe it's all manual? Not even a computer to help you out. Took me forever to find how to cloak the damned thing."

A soft snicker from somewhere overhead had them both frozen in place for a moment.

"Unless it's all voice activated," Micayla suggested.

"You're kidding me, right?"

"Oh, no, she isn't," a breathy, high-pitched feminine voice said. "You only had to ask me. I would have helped you."

This was obviously the computer speaking. "And just where were you when we were looking for a flight manual?" Trag demanded.

"Waiting for you to ask," the computer said with a decided pout. "Veluka *never* asks. He makes me keep quiet until he needs me. He doesn't care for conversation." The computer sniffed as though fighting back tears. "At least, not with me."

"Great!" Trag said morosely. "A touchy computer."

"I'm not touchy!"

Micayla shot Trag a quelling look. Piss off the computer and this could be a *very* bumpy ride. "Do you have a name?"

"Not one that you could pronounce," the voice said. "But you can call me Roslyn."

"Roslyn?" Trag echoed. "What kind of name is that?"

"It's Terran," Micayla said. "And, oddly enough, her voice sounds familiar."

"Sounds like a fuckin' slut," Trag said under his breath.

"I don't *want* to sound like this," Roslyn mourned. "I was programmed that way."

Trag shook his head in disgust. "Never could stand women who talked like that."

"Obviously Veluka can't either," Micayla observed.

"I'd love to sound brisk and efficient," Roslyn said plaintively. "I can't help it that I sound like a—a—" She broke off there, dissolving into sobs.

"Dumb blonde?" Micayla said.

"Yes!" Roslyn wailed.

As her sobs increased in volume, Trag covered his ears. "Make her stop!"

"Roslyn?" Micayla said gently. "Would you like something to do?"

"Oh, yes, please," Roslyn said gratefully. "Anything!"

"Could you run scans of the communication traffic and see if you can locate someone named Rutger Grekkor? He's supposed to have gone to Nerik after leaving Orleon Station."

"I'll get right on it!" Roslyn said with undisguised enthusiasm.

"*Thank you*," Trag said to Micayla, mouthing the words. "Thank you, Roslyn," he said aloud. "We'll let you know if we need anything."

"I'll be here," Roslyn said. "Call me anytime. Bye now!"

"Wow," Trag said after a moment. "That was weird." Hunching his shoulders, he peered furtively over his shoulder as though Roslyn might have been standing right behind him. "Do you think she's still listening?"

"Probably not," Micayla replied. "Most voice-activated computers don't unless you address them directly. Though this one seems a bit unusual."

"No shit," said Trag. "For a minute there I thought we'd have to listen to her bawling all the way to Nerik."

"Don't like weepy females?"

"Not at all!" Trag declared.

"Glad I'm not the weepy type," Micayla said, "or this would be a very long trip—for all of us."

"The way I see it, it's not going to be long enough," Trag said. "I've already got the ship flying itself to Nerik and now Roslyn is busy doing your job."

"Your point?"

"That leaves us plenty of time to get to know each other better," he said.

"And leaves me free to suck your dick all the way to Nerik," she finished for him. Rolling her eyes, she added, "What was I thinking? I never thought you'd actually hold me to that."

"I won't," Trag chuckled. "But I thought we might delve into your little brain for a while." Eyeing her speculatively, he went on, "What about it, Mick? Got any hot fantasies? Something you'd like to play out?"

Her first inclination was to laugh out loud, but the look in his eyes assured her that he was perfectly serious. "You'll probably think it's silly," she began. "I can't remember if I dreamed this or saw it in a movie or came up with it on my own, and I've never told anyone about it, but I think about being in an orchard with a man. It's hot and we've been picking peaches and get to goofing around while we're washing the fruit, and we splash each other with water and then I run and he chases me. Eventually he catches me and we make wild, passionate love under the trees."

Trag's expression was unreadable. Micayla shrugged and went on, "It's not much, I guess, and maybe not terribly exciting, but it got stuck in my head a long time ago. I had a summer job picking apples, and a boy tried to get me to go off with him, but I was too chicken." Shaking her head, she added, "Though I must admit, I'd hoped I'd actually *want* him to chase me, but as it turned out, I didn't."

"Was this your 'sort of' boyfriend?"

"No, that was Adam. He and I got to be friends and he wanted more, so I tried having sex with him, but it was the most emotionless experience I've ever had. All I could do was just lie there and let him do his thing. I think he would have appreciated a little more enthusiasm because he quit trying after a while and we sort of drifted apart."

"Well, I hate to sound selfish, but I'm glad you didn't— show more enthusiasm, that is." Trag paused, running a hand through his hair. "The guy in your fantasy… I don't suppose he looked anything like me, did he?"

Micayla blinked hard and then her eyes widened. "Well, I… yeah—now that you mention it, I suppose he did. I've never had a clear picture of his face in my mind, but he had hair like yours and…" Micayla closed her eyes, trying to remember. Was she simply inserting Trag into her fantasy? She didn't think so—in fact, she hadn't thought about it for some time, but— "Green eyes," she said, opening her own. "He had green eyes."

"And he pounces on you from behind a tree, right?"

Micayla nodded. She swallowed hard as a wave of tingles tightened her scalp. "How did you know?"

"Because that's *my* fantasy," he whispered. "Or maybe it wasn't a fantasy. Maybe it was a vision."

"And we each had the same one?"

"Seems like it," he replied. "I've had that one in my head for a long time—even before the war—and I always thought it was just wishful thinking. But maybe it wasn't."

"It was the only way I knew how it was supposed to feel to be with a man," Micayla said, "even though it had never actually happened." Scowling, she added, "I always thought it just gave me unrealistic expectations."

"Not unrealistic at all," Trag said, "at least not for a Zetithian." Taking a deep breath, he went on, "I hate to admit this, but after Kyra came, I liked to imagine it was her—but it must have been you all along."

"I never had anyone to put in place of you," Micayla said slowly. "Oh, I tried it with Adam, but somehow it just wasn't right." She looked up at him as another wave of tingles rippled over her skin. "What does this mean?"

Trag smiled wickedly. "It means that one of these days, we'll be in an orchard picking fruit together and I'll nail you under a tree."

His grin was infectious and Micayla couldn't help but smile back at him. "Well, that gives us something to look forward to, doesn't it?"

Trag scratched his head. "It certainly does, but I was trying to come up with something to do right now. There aren't any trees here."

"Trag," she said with a mischievous look, "we don't need *trees*. You just have to chase me."

"Ah, well then," he said, his expression brightening, "I guess you'd better start running." He held perfectly still for a split second and then lunged at her.

With a squeal of laughter, Micayla sprang from her seat and sprinted off down the corridor. She, at least, had explored the ship a bit and knew where she was going, but it really didn't matter. Darting down a passageway at random, she ducked into a small, dark alcove that was stacked full of odds and ends.

Her heart was pounding as she waited for him to pass by. She could hear his footsteps coming closer and held her breath as he approached. He knew this game as well as she. He would stop following her eventually and she would go looking for him, but he would be waiting for her, ready to pounce.

This was the feeling she'd always derived from her fantasy—the breathtaking excitement, the hint of danger, the heat of desire in her blood as it coursed through her veins. This was why she'd noticed him in the park; he truly *was* the man of her dreams—she *had* seen him, just as Windura had suggested. She should have known, should have remembered and made the connection, but she hadn't—at least, not until now.

She slipped out of the alcove and headed in the same direction he'd taken but found nothing; there was no sound or movement to indicate where he might be. Her whole body tingled with anticipation. Was he already shadowing her movements? He possessed the same skills as she and didn't have to make a sound unless he chose to. She would have no clue where he was until he grabbed her from behind.

As she moved silently through the dimly lit vessel, he made his leap at last, seizing her around the waist. She tried to escape, but he held her until her squeals of laughter gave way to sighs. Spinning her around, he kissed her, pulling her tightly against his bare chest. She could feel him purring, could smell the scent of his passion, and could feel his engorged cock pressed against her stomach. His own clothes had already been discarded, and he stripped hers from her as he covered her face with kisses.

"My lovely Mick," he whispered. "You make me feel things that no other woman can. How did I ever live without you before? How did I even breathe without holding you, kissing you, and giving you joy?"

She had no reply to offer but knew that the reverse was also true; he made her feel complete—replenished her soul and nourished her spirit in a way that no one else ever had. Sighing, she melted in his arms, breathing in his scent as her teeth sank into his skin. The taste of his blood set her senses ablaze and she pulled him down and licked his nipples and his dripping cock, avoiding his orgasmic fluids until it seemed he could take no more. With a growl, he rolled her onto her back, nipping at her breasts before he thrust into her, his thick shaft buried up to his balls in her soft, wet heat.

Groaning with pleasure, his eyes blazed with passionate fire as he rocked into her, gently at first, and then harder as she raked his arms with her nails and bared her fangs, hissing at him and urging him on. With a kiss that promised more pleasure to come, he backed off, teasing her with a circular motion of his cock and raking her slick, inner walls with the serrated points of the head. As her orgasms began, Micayla gripped his meat with her tight warmth and Trag's climax began to build. She could feel the change as his thrusts became shorter and more forceful—stretching, reaching, climbing, until at last he gasped and his cock erupted, filling her with long, forceful jets of his creamy snard. She was still drinking in the glow of his eyes as his snard worked its magic on her, spreading the warmth and euphoria throughout her being. His ruffled corona began its slow undulations, prolonging her ecstasy, as well as his own, until, sated at last, she began to purr.

The light in his eyes softened as he smiled. "So, what about it, Mick? Did I give you joy unlike any you have ever known?"

Nodding, she reached up to caress his cheek. "Or ever dreamed of."

Chapter 22

"You're kidding me, right?" Trag said, scanning the horizon. "I know this is where we were supposed to land, but how far is it to the city?"

"About three kilometers," Micayla replied. "We couldn't risk setting down too close to civilization."

"Well, yeah, but this looks worse than the Darconian desert!"

Micayla leaned over his shoulder for a peek through the view port. The entire landscape was blanketed in soft, virgin snow. Frost glittered on the dormant plants protruding from their winter shrouds and the sky was a crisp, clear aqua. "What's the matter? It's just a little snow."

"Just a little snow?" Trag echoed. "It must be at least thirty centimeters deep!"

"Twenty, maybe," she said. "That's nothing. We have a lot more than that back home. Besides, we knew it was going to be winter on Nerik before we came."

"We did?"

"Jack said something about it at the meeting—and you said you were okay with it. Plus, it was in Curly's report. Didn't you ever read it?"

"Well, no, I didn't," Trag admitted. "Been too busy fucking you, talking to you, getting to know you, looking at you…"

While this was true, all of the above hadn't stopped

her from reading it. "You should have. Granted, there wasn't much, but we need to know all we can."

"Aw, Mick, I never read shit like that."

"Well, at least *I* read it," Micayla said. "And we'll be together, so it won't matter." She shook her head, smiling at him warmly. "That's one of the things I like about you, Trag. I have to admire a guy the always flies by the seat of his pants."

Since Micayla had been into his pants so often on the trip that he'd stopped wearing them, she knew firsthand just how enticing that part of him could be. Great place to bite him too. She paused for a moment, wondering just when her mind had been taken over by sex. She'd never been one to see a sexual reference in anything before, but she saw them everywhere now. Salivating profusely, she wanted to bite his ass so bad it was a wonder she could keep from doing it. Then she realized he was in the perfect position for her to do so. Backing away from him, she took in the view of his firm, bite-able butt with his balls hanging enticingly between his legs. The urge to pull his cock back and suck it was overwhelming.

Now is not the time for that, she told herself firmly. Giving her head a quick shake that set off a brief wave of dizziness, she went on, "We'll bundle you up good and it won't be a problem. We've come prepared—at least I think we have. Jack knew about all of this, so she'll have made sure we've got the right equipment."

"I hope you're right. I sure as hell don't want to go out in that naked."

Micayla took another look out the port. "I think it's beautiful. I've always loved snow—especially when you're curled up inside a nice warm blanket with a bowl of my mother's chili."

"Chili?" Trag echoed. "In a bowl? Is that some kind of soup?"

"Hot, spicy, rich, wonderful soup," she replied. "You probably wouldn't like it. No fruit in it at all. More like something Hidar would make."

Trag shuddered. "A few nights out in that crap and I might decide hot, spicy food is a good thing. Keeps you warm, huh?"

"Not so much keeps you warm as it warms you up when you've been out in the cold. Hot chocolate is good for that too. I'm not sure if Jack packed any though."

"There's bound to be some around here somewhere," Trag declared. "Jack sells that stuff all over the quadrant. I guess everyone loves it. Never cared that much for it myself."

Micayla looked at him as though seeing him for the first time. "You don't like chocolate? What's wrong with you?"

Trag shrugged. "Nothing. I mean, it's okay, I'm just not that crazy about it." He looked at her questioningly. "Not gonna hold that against me, are you?"

Micayla grinned and shook her head. "Nope. That just leaves more for me."

"It's always seemed to me to be more the kind of thing women like, but Leroy can't get enough of it either. Though he mainly uses it to attract women," he reflected. "He gets a load of it from Jack whenever we see her."

"A hunk like Leroy shouldn't need to ply women with chocolate," Micayla observed. "He's plenty attractive on his own."

"Yeah, you'd think a guy with two dicks would be

pretty confident," Trag agreed. "But he's not nearly as macho as he'd have you believe."

"I never could stand the macho type," Micayla said with a shudder. "Besides, women don't necessarily want men who are always in control. We like to see a little vulnerability now and then."

"Nobody's perfect, I guess." With a big grin, he added, "Especially me."

"In some ways you're not," she admitted, letting her gaze sweep down over his nude body. "But in *other* ways…"

"Yeah, and my dick's not even worn out from all the things you've put it through on this trip," Trag said proudly. With a quick pelvic thrust, he demonstrated just how eager it still was. His thick rod bounced as a gush of coronal fluid oozed from the points. "Want to suck it one more time before I get all bundled up?"

"Don't tempt me," Micayla said, doing her best to avoid staring at it. "We've got to get going if we want to reach the city by nightfall."

"Aw, come on, Mick," he cajoled. "We might not get another chance for a long time. Besides, you can get me off quicker than any woman I've ever known. It won't take that long."

Aside from the fact that he was right about the time factor, Micayla truly couldn't resist. With no further prompting, she dropped to her knees and buried her face in his groin. Licking his balls caused even more fluid to come pouring out, and she used it to caress her cheeks with his slick cockhead. Scattering kisses up and down his shaft, she fought the urge to bite it and instead moved to the head and sucked him inside. As always, he was hot, firm, and delicious and she swirled her tongue over his skin, massaging his nuts while he fucked her mouth. His coronal ruffle became a firm ridge as her first orgasm struck and Trag's purring took on a more urgent note. She felt his muscles tense and released him at the last moment, letting his cock spray her face and chest with creamy delight. Her body seemed to implode and she cried out in ecstasy as her head fell back. Trag used his cock to caress her skin once more, and the slick heat on her face and nipples soon had her moaning with exquisite pleasure. It took her a few moments to recover enough to open her eyes, and her first sight was of Trag's fabulous cock, and beyond that, his killer smile.

"See, I told you it wouldn't take long."

Kissing his cock, she licked the last spurt of his snard from the head, savoring the sweet euphoria it brought her.

"Maybe so, but now I feel like I need a nap."

"Hey, I got no problem with lying down for a while," he purred. "We could stay here another night if you want. You need to tap into the local com system anyway."

"Roslyn couldn't get much of the local stuff from space," she admitted. "Said there was too much atmospheric interference or something." Micayla took a deep breath and stood up, again feeling slightly dizzy. Trag had that effect on her, though—no matter where or when they made love, he took her breath away and made her head spin. "So far, all we know is that Grekkor landed at the spaceport at Rechred, which doesn't give us much to go on. He could be in the city or have gone somewhere else after he landed. I'll run some manual scans and see what I can turn up."

"You do that," he urged her. "I'll check on our survival gear."

———— ∿ ————

Trag went down to the cargo hold to see what was there. So far, he and Micayla hadn't done much in the way of preparations for their mission, mainly because Mick was just too damned sexy to allow Trag to think of anything else. She was endlessly fascinating and he had an idea that if the food supplies had held out, they could have kept right on flying through space forever. The Terran mates of his friends frequently mentioned feeling as though they were addicted to their men, but Trag suspected that the reverse was true in his case. He was rapidly becoming hooked on Micayla and was beginning to see his feelings toward Kyra as the result of wanting something he knew he couldn't have—not true love at all. He was pretty sure Mick would stay with him now, but though he'd done his best to keep her happy, she'd never said she loved him. Not in the heat of passion, or in the quiet *laetralance* that followed. He had an idea that she might be waiting for him to say it first, but he wasn't sure how she would react. She might like the idea—or she might not—but Mick had never been in love before, and saying I love you wouldn't come easily to her.

Exploring the cargo hold was a revelation in Nerik secrecy. Veluka must have locked down a lot of the compartments because there was only one Trag could access, which fortunately was the one he needed. He really hated the idea of asking Roslyn for assistance.

Jack had outdone herself. The compartment was stuffed with cold-weather gear of all kinds. There were heated boots, medical kits, marching rations that warmed up automatically when opened, weapons of every kind, and tracking devices. There was also an abundant supply of hot chocolate and, last but not least, a book titled *The Flora, Fauna, and Seasons of Nerik*.

"Too bad we didn't see this sooner," Trag muttered to himself. "No time for it now." He stashed it in the breast pocket of one of the parkas and gathered up all he could carry.

Time was one thing that Trag wished they'd had more of. The three weeks had passed all too quickly and Trag's initial fear that he'd only get sex from Micayla once in a while had evaporated. So far, she hadn't turned him down and had even been the initiator a few times. Trag wasn't tired of it either. He thought he might be after fifty years or so, but certainly not before then.

He wanted her to be his mate. But how to ask her was the dilemma. Being fuck buddies was close but not quite the same. He was falling for her to the point that if she left him now, he wasn't sure his mind could take it. Even now, when he'd only been apart from her for a short time, he was already feeling the loss. Trag didn't have to have his cock inside her to feel complete either. She only had to be within his reach where he could see her, hear her breathing, listen to her voice, taste her sweetness…

He had never felt this strongly toward Kyra—though he'd only been intimate with her once, and Ty had been there too. Infatuation—or a lack of options—was more likely the cause for his continued feelings toward his brother's wife, but this thing with Micayla was different. *Completely* different. He cared about Kyra, but Micayla brought out protective instincts he'd never felt before. He was very reluctant to let her leave the safety of the ship, let alone go blindly forth into a snow-covered world in search of the nemesis of the entire Zetithian race. Even before that, he found himself trying to take care of her—make sure she was comfortable, happy, and such—something he couldn't recall doing with Kyra, though he was quite certain his brother had. He'd also seen it with Cat and Jack. Sure, Jack was tough and highly self-sufficient, but Cat still looked after her, though in a very subtle way. It wasn't always something brave or heroic—unless, of course, such behavior was called for. It was the little things. Touching her, rubbing her shoulders, getting her anything he thought she might need or want. Trag knew he was doing the same thing with Mick now. She fussed at him at first, saying he was spoiling her, but after a while, she'd stopped mentioning it. Trag took it upon himself to see that she got regular meals, kept her warm, kept her company, and kept her sated. It was a pleasure for him to do these things, not a chore or a duty he felt he had to perform—more of a privilege, actually—particularly given the nature of their first encounter. Things had definitely taken a turn for the better.

Heading back up to the bridge, he found Micayla in the closest thing to a state of panic he'd ever seen her in. She was sitting at the comstation, anxiously tapping the console, muttering to herself.

Dumping the gear he was carrying in the middle of the floor, he eyed her curiously, half expecting her to start tearing her hair out. "What's up, Mick?"

"Not much," she replied, "which is a *major* problem. Did anything break when we landed?"

"Not that I'm aware of. You felt it. It was very soft."

"Well, now that we're here, nothing much seems to be working—nothing important, anyway. Oh, life support, lights, power—those sorts of things all work, but not much else. Have you talked to Roslyn since we landed?"

"I talk to Roslyn as little as possible," Trag said bluntly. "Is she pouting again?"

Micayla shook her head. "I don't think so. I can't get her to answer me, which makes me think she's either been damaged or is being jammed. The scanners don't work either, nor does the regular com system."

"I guess that means we're out of touch with Jack too, doesn't it?"

"Yeah—unless she comes close enough for the com-stones to work. They only function over a kilometer or so. Is there anything in the hold we could use?"

"Maybe," he said. "There's a ton of stuff down there. I didn't go through it all." He stopped for a moment. "So you think someone's jamming us, huh?"

"It sure seems like it, but to jam us, they'd have to know we were here, wouldn't they? We've been cloaked the whole time and we haven't exactly announced to anyone that we're on our way to nab Grekkor. Aside from that, how could anyone know that it's you and me flying this ship instead of Veluka?"

"Maybe they don't," he said. "Veluka is a crook from way back. Being scared of Grekkor might not be his only reason for not wanting to come with us."

"You think he's wanted for something here on Nerik?"

"Wouldn't surprise me a bit if he was," Trag said grimly. "Whoever's jamming us might only be after him."

"True, but it's also possible that Grekkor knows a whole lot more about all of us than we think he does. Leroy's never kept it a secret that you were his pilot, and Jack's been all over the place looking for Zetithians—and then there's Ty and all of his fans. It wouldn't be difficult for Grekkor to link all of us together—maybe even connecting Jack with Veluka."

"Yes, but I still don't see how anyone could have known Veluka blew up that ship," Trag argued. "There's just no way—"

"But what if Grekkor *did* figure it out? He could have invented a story that's got the Nerik authorities out to get Veluka. He accused me of murdering that Norludian. What's to stop him from telling tales about someone else?"

"That's possible, but from the way Tisana talks, Veluka's probably already guilty of even worse things than anything Grekkor might try to pin on him."

"Maybe, but you see what I mean, don't you?"

Trag nodded his understanding. "This could be a trap."

"And we have no way of telling Jack about it."

"Unless…" Trag paused a moment to think. "If we *are* being jammed, then we just have to find someone who isn't."

"Meaning?"

"They couldn't be jamming the whole damn planet," he said decisively. "And if they're jamming us specifically then that means they know we're here—or are at least expecting us."

"Which means we'd better get moving."

"No shit. Looks like the one ship we thought would keep us from getting caught is about to do just that."

—⁓—

The two of them worked quickly, but it was still a good hour or so before they got under way. Unfortunately, during that hour, the bright, sparkling sunny day had turned into a heavy snowstorm.

"Too bad Jack didn't think to give us a speeder," Trag grumbled. "Would've come in real handy right about now." He braced himself as he stepped outside and the first blast hit him in the face. He staggered against the wind, nearly being blown off the gangplank. "Holy shit! And to think I ever wanted to leave Darconia!"

"Come on, Slave Boy," Micayla said, shouldering her pack. "If you keep moving, your nuts won't freeze."

"Maybe, but that doesn't mean the rest of me won't."

"You've got enough gear on for a polar expedition," Micayla pointed out. "And it's not all that cold—only a little below freezing."

"You just had to say that word, didn't you?" Trag said with a shiver. "It's that *freezing* thing that has me bugged."

"Wuss, wuss, wuss," Micayla chided him. "Don't worry. I'll warm you up the first chance I get."

"Promise?"

"Promise. Now let's get going. Which way to the city?"

"I have no idea whatsoever," Trag replied.

Micayla stopped short, glaring at him. "Well, isn't that just ducky? We're about to blunder forth into a snowstorm and you don't know which way we're supposed to go?"

"I'm kidding," he said. "When I landed, it was that

way." He pointed out the direction which, Micayla noted, was into the wind.

Shaking her head, she said, "This is *not* going according to plan."

"Plan?" he echoed. "We had a *plan*?"

"Yes, we had a plan," she replied. "We were supposed to find out where Grekkor is and then call Jack. It doesn't look like we're going to have much luck doing either of those things." Visibility was extremely poor due to the snow, but she stared off in that direction anyway. "I think I see something up ahead. Maybe it's the city."

Trag peered into the wall of swirling flakes. "How the devil can you tell?"

"I can't," she replied. "But it's in the direction you pointed, so that's where we're going."

"Got your comstone on?" Trag asked.

"Yeah, why?"

"Oh, no reason," he replied, "other than the fact that I won't be able to see you if you're more than half a meter away from me. Good thing they still work."

"That's the advantage of having a communicator that no one understands. If they knew how they worked, they could jam them too." She trudged forward, wading through a deep snowdrift. "If Jack got that last message we sent about what city we were going to, they should be here soon. I wondered why she never answered us."

"Now we know. I just hope it wasn't intercepted."

"C'mon, Trag! Give me a little credit. I encoded that sucker like you wouldn't believe. If anyone did intercept it, it will sound like an ad for Weyolin's Wonder Fertilizer."

"Which is?"

"Sheep shit, basically," she replied. "Nothing that could be traced back to us anyway."

"I dunno," Trag said dubiously. "Sounds like something Jack would sell."

"Yes, but you know Jack pretty well. Grekkor doesn't—we hope."

They trudged on in silence for a time. What had begun as a relatively deep snow was getting even worse. Micayla was used to slogging through snowdrifts, but she was a little worried about Trag. Even though she'd teased him a bit, she knew just how poorly he tolerated the cold. They'd just reached a stand of tall conifers when Trag spoke up. "Is it just me, or is it snowing harder?"

"It's not just you," Micayla replied, brushing the accumulated snow from her goggles. "It's getting colder too."

"And darker. It was morning when we got here. How could it be getting dark so soon?"

"Beats me. Got that book on you?"

"The one about Nerik? Yeah, I've got it here somewhere," he said, slapping his pockets. "Here it is. Good luck reading it, though."

"Maybe it's got an audio feature," Micayla suggested. "Most of them do."

"It looks pretty old," Trag said, pushing aside a snow-covered branch so Micayla could get through. It swung back with a crack as soon as he let go of it. "I mean, it's even printed on paper. Might not have that feature."

Micayla stopped and looked about her. No doubt about it, the sun was just about gone. "Well, we know we're not in one of the polar regions where they only have a few hours of sunlight in winter, but it really is getting dark. Maybe it was later in the day than we thought."

"Crazy planet," Trag grumbled. "Cold as hell, snow up to your ass, dark in three hours. No place I'd ever want to live, that's for sure."

Micayla shook her head, still not quite able to figure him out. "Where *do* you want to live, Trag?"

"Is that a rhetorical question, or do you really want to know?"

"I really want to know."

"Well, to hear Jack tell it, I think I'd like to live on Earth, or barring that, Terra Minor. But that's probably just me wishing for something else I can't have."

"Maybe when this is all over…"

"Doesn't matter," he said abruptly. "Might not live through this anyway."

Micayla's response was automatic, but the vehemence of it surprised her. "You'd better!"

"Aw, Mick," he said with a grin. "Would you miss me if I was dead?"

"I'm sure I'd die of a broken heart." She had enough of a grip on herself to try for a casual reply, but though the words were spoken lightly, the shocking truth of them hit her like a pulse blast. All of a sudden, living without him didn't seem possible.

"Then I'll try to stay alive." Trag stopped and turned toward her. Even through the thick snowfall and growing darkness, she could still see the glow of his eyes. "Promise me you'll do the same, Mick."

"I will."

"Then come on. I think I see something through the trees up ahead. Might be someone there who could help us."

Micayla blinked a few times as though trying to reset her brain into a more practical, working mode. All that talk about dying had her normally well-ordered mind going off on all sorts of tangents. Clearing her throat with an effort, she said briskly, "I've been trying to figure out why anyone *would* help us. After all, we're offworlders and no one would have any reason to trust us—or stick their necks out for us."

"Guess we'll have to rely on charm then," Trag said cheerfully.

"Good thing you've got plenty of that," Micayla said. "I haven't got a drop."

"You'd be surprised, Mick. Just don't hiss at anybody."

"I'll try not to."

The building Trag had seen turned out to be an old, abandoned shed of some kind—abandoned by the Neriks, that is. Strange birds flitted toward the ceiling as Trag forced the door open and then switched on a flashlight. Inside, it was dome-shaped and spacious, but its support beams tilted at precarious angles and unidentifiable bits of machinery lay in a rusty stack in the center. Various plants had made a futile attempt to grow up from the dirt floor, and something rustled in the dry leaves—a sound that brought rattlesnakes and rats to Micayla's mind. Remembering Curly's report, she could only hope that the dangerous animals were either hibernating or had gone south for the winter.

"Think we ought to stay here for the night?" Trag suggested, shining the beam of light over the interior. "It's at least dry in here and we're out of the wind."

"I don't know," Micayla said doubtfully. Pulling off

her goggles, she added, "If anyone's hunting us, this might be the first place they look."

"True, but if we keep wandering around in the dark we might wind up so lost that no one will ever find us— not even Jack or Leroy."

"Or we could be in someone's backyard," Micayla pointed out. "I think we should keep going." A large bird soared down from the overhead beams and landed on the ground in front of her. "That's funny," she said. "It looks sort of like Veluka."

Covered with black scales and possessing huge white eyes, it did, indeed, look like the Nerik. "Except Veluka can't fly," Trag said. "Wonder if they hum when they get upset."

The bird pecked at the ground and fluttered its wings. "Doesn't matter," Micayla said. Reaching into her pack, she tossed out a few sporaks which the bird promptly ate. "It's not going to help us any to know that."

"Nothing can help you now," a voice said as two Neriks armed with pulse rifles seemed to materialize from the surrounding walls.

Chapter 23

FOR A LONG MOMENT NO ONE SPOKE. "WELL, THAT TOOK longer than I thought it would," Trag said, breaking the silence. "What kept you?"

"Very amusing," one of their captors said, but he wasn't laughing and he made a point of not lowering his weapon.

"Mind telling me how you did that?" Trag went on.

If Trag was trying to lull them into a false sense of security, or make friends with them, it wasn't working. The Nerik merely blinked at him.

"Didn't think so," said Trag.

"Would you at least tell us how you knew we were here?" Micayla asked. "We went to a lot of trouble to avoid being seen."

Ignoring this as well, the Nerik said sharply, "You spoke of Veluka. Where is he?"

"He opted not to come with us on this trip," Trag said dryly. "And I'm beginning to understand why."

Micayla studied the two Neriks. At first they appeared to be identical both to Veluka and to each other, but as she looked more carefully, she began to discern the differences. One was taller than the other, and his shorter companion had scales and eyes of a slightly different shape—more hexagonal than oval. Another thing she noticed was that, despite the cold, neither of them wore clothing of any kind. Apparently their

scales were all they needed to preserve their body
warmth. Veluka must have worn his tunic simply as a
courtesy to others.

"Why would you think Veluka was here?" Micayla
inquired. "I mean, aside from the fact that I mentioned
his name."

"We know the ship," the tall Nerik said. "We have
been looking for him."

"Yes, but how did you even know to look for it?"
Micayla asked. "It's been cloaked the whole time."

"It was stolen," the Nerik replied. "There is an anti-
theft device embedded in it. Not removable or alterable
in any way. It sends out a constant signal which we
began to receive when the ship landed."

"So only you guys can pick up on it?" Micayla persisted. "Not anyone else?"

"Only us," he replied.

"They don't know anything about it, do they,
Slurlek?" the smaller Nerik said.

"Should have known Veluka couldn't have gotten
a ship like that through honest means," Trag muttered.
Drawing himself up to his full height—which was taller
than either of the Neriks—he said firmly, "We aren't the
ones who stole it. It was on loan to us from Veluka. We
just needed to get to the city unseen by a certain someone."

"Still, we must impound the ship," the one called
Slurlek said.

"Help yourself," Trag said with a shrug. "We don't
need it anymore, but if you're looking for Veluka, he's
not here."

"He could be hiding," said Slurlek's sidekick, glancing around the shed.

There was no place for anything bigger than a rabbit to hide—and the best Micayla could tell these two had appeared out of thin air. Suddenly, the connection became clear to her. "Cloaked, you mean, don't you?" she exclaimed. "Your scales! That's why you aren't wearing clothes because we'd be able to see them! The technology in your ships is based on your own abilities."

"Clever girl," Slurlek said with a scaly smirk. "But you are not the first to realize that."

"So it's not one of those things where if I figure it out you have to kill me?"

Trag was shaking his head in bewilderment. "What are you talking about?"

"The Nerik ships," Micayla said excitedly. "The scales on them are what makes them capable of becoming invisible—just the way the people of Nerik can. That's why no one else has the technology." Turning back to Slurlek, she asked, "So, what do you do, put real scales on the ships?"

"Not exactly," Slurlek replied. "They wouldn't withstand the temperatures during atmospheric reentry—but that's where the idea comes from."

"So you really can disappear?" Micayla marveled. "I thought only Treslanties could do that."

"We don't advertise it," Slurlek said shortly.

While Micayla had been focusing on the ship's technology, Trag was more concerned with its owner. "That son of a drayl knew he'd get caught if he came back here!" he grumbled. "No wonder he wanted collateral for the ship! He's probably already sold the weapons Leroy gave him and scrammed off of Darconia."

"So, he is on Darconia?" Slurlek said, showing a decided interest.

"Well, he *was*," Trag said. "Didn't show up to see us off either, the little scumbag. All that crap about being afraid of Grekkor must have just been an act. He probably knew about that tracking device and decided this was a good way to unload the ship."

"Grekkor?" the smaller man echoed. "Rutger Grekkor?"

"You know who I'm talking about?" Trag asked eagerly.

"This is an enemy of Veluka's?" Slurlek inquired. "What do you know of him, Orlat?"

"You've heard of him, haven't you?" Orlat said. "The head of the Commerce Consortium in this sector? He's here on Nerik."

"Well, that answers our next question," Trag said. "Any idea where he is?"

"He is in the city for a reception," Orlat replied. "A philanthropic event of some kind. I don't remember all of the details."

Slurlek rounded on his cohort, demanding, "And just how did you know that much?"

Orlat shrugged. "What can I say, Slur? I listen to the news. You should too. You'd understand a whole lot more about interplanetary politics if you did."

Slurlek's eyes dimmed slightly. "As if that sort of thing is important to us," he scoffed.

"Sure it is, and I know lots of other things besides that. Like these two," Orlat said, indicating Trag and Micayla. "They're Zetithians. Bet you didn't know that."

Slurlek seemed unimpressed. "So?"

"They're an endangered species," Orlat said informatively. "Which means there aren't many of them left. One of them's a famous rock star named Tycharian Vladatonsk."

"Oh, here we go again," Trag muttered.

"And this is his brother!" Micayla exclaimed, realizing that they now had a potential ally. "And I'm... his girlfriend."

"The rock star's girlfriend?" Orlat said, his scales beginning to rise with apparent delight. "Really?"

"No," Trag said, gritting his teeth. "She's *my* girlfriend. Ty's already got a mate."

"Sorry," Orlat said meekly. "Didn't mean to make you mad."

Micayla patted Trag on the shoulder. "He's a little touchy about having a famous brother," she explained.

"Probably gets him laid, though," Orlat said with a shrug. "Wish I was related to someone famous. I *never* get laid."

Trag looked like he was about to explode. "She is not my girlfriend just because of my brother!" he shouted. "I got her all on my own."

Orlat rolled his eyes. "Sure you did."

"Tell him, Mick," Trag growled.

Seeing a Nerik rolling his eyes made Micayla feel slightly dizzy again, but she managed to form a reply. "I—I'd never even heard of Tychar until after I met Trag—well, I'd *heard* of him, but I'd never met him, or seen him."

Trag stiffened as he turned to peer at Micayla. He had a look in his eyes she'd never seen before. "But you never slept with me until after you met Ty," he said accusingly. "Couldn't stand the sight of me before that. Are you sure he didn't have anything to do with it?"

Micayla stared at him open-mouthed for a moment before irritation finally took over. "Oh, for the love of—" she said with an exasperated stomp of her foot. "Trag, will you just get over it? So what if you've got a hot rock star for a brother? Big deal!"

"Uh, I don't think she's all that impressed," said Orlat. "She might be telling the truth."

Trag tried to yank on his hair but couldn't because it was tucked into the hood of his parka. "Can we please talk about something else, like whether you guys are gonna let us go or help us out or kill us or what?"

"We're only supposed to impound the ship," said Slurlek. "You two don't fall under our jurisdiction."

"Well, thank the Great Mother for that!" Trag said. "But could you at least point us in the direction of Rechred? That's where Grekkor is, right?"

Orlat nodded. "The reception will be at the Palace Hotel. Very fancy."

"Formal wear was the one thing Jack didn't think to pack for us," Micayla snickered. "We'll be *so* underdressed."

"Doesn't matter," Trag said. "We'll be crashing the party anyway."

Orlat blinked and his pupils dilated with apparent interest. "I've never crashed a party before," he said. "Mind if we come along?"

"Thought you had to impound the ship," Trag said.

"We've already locked it down," Orlat said, dismissing the argument. "Party crashing sounds like fun."

Something didn't seem quite right to Micayla. In her experience, policemen didn't usually crash parties unless they were there to arrest someone. "Aren't you two lawmen?" she asked. "I don't know how you Neriks feel about it, but on Earth, party crashing is frowned upon—maybe even illegal."

"We're private enforcers," Orlat said, puffing out his chest a trifle. "Hired by the ship's owner."

"Ah, I see," said Micayla. If they were hired thugs, it might be best to have them on their side. "I don't suppose you'd consider working for us, would you?"

"Sure, why not?" said Orlat, looking to his companion for confirmation. "You okay with that, Slur?"

Slurlek nodded at first but then eyed Trag suspiciously. "Got any credits?"

"Some," Trag admitted. "But we could pay you more when the job's done."

Slurlek hesitated for a moment. "And just what are you planning to do when you find this Grekkor?"

Micayla opened her mouth to reply, but Trag beat her to the punch. "I'd like to kill him," he said fiercely.

"That's *not* what we're supposed to do, Trag," Micayla chided him.

"Okay, so we just need to find him," Trag said. "Does it matter what we want him for?"

"Not really," said Slurlek. "Just checking."

Slurlek obviously didn't mind aiding and abetting a murder, but Orlat was more cautious. "Why do you want to kill him?"

"Because he's the one responsible for destroying my planet," Trag replied. "The Nedwuts were working for him when they rammed Zetith with an asteroid and they've been hunting down the survivors ever since. I think he deserves to die, but the plan is to get him to confess and then get him locked up for the rest of his life." Trag clearly didn't think the punishment fit the crime, and the Neriks seemed to agree.

"Don't blame you for wanting him dead," said Slurlek.

"It's what I would do," Orlat said with a nod.

It hadn't taken much to win them over, but Micayla suspected that killing wasn't something they shied away from very often. "Bloodthirsty lot, aren't you?" she observed. "But if we don't get going, we're liable to miss the party."

"It's not until tomorrow night," said Orlat. "We've got plenty of time."

"Uh, one more question," said Trag, holding up a hand. "Speaking of time, what time is it right now?"

"Nighttime?" Orlat ventured.

"But we just got here and I'd swear it was morning!"

Orlat shook his head. "You're thinking about other planets. This one rotates the wrong way. Drives everyone who visits us nuts."

"One of the few planets in the known galaxy that does it," Slurlek said proudly.

"I guess every planet has to have some claim to fame," Trag said. "I really wish I'd read that book."

"See, I *told* you we should have done something besides…" Micayla broke off there, realizing it might not be a good idea to discuss such things in front of a couple of Nerik thugs. Might give them ideas.

"Besides what?" Orlat asked eagerly. "How long have you been in space?"

"Three weeks," Trag replied.

"Bet I can guess what you've been up to," Orlat teased.

"Later," Micayla said as the entire building seemed to swim before her eyes. "This whole planet makes me dizzy. Must be that backward rotation thing. Either that or I've been in space too long."

"Or both," Trag agreed. "So what do we do now? Hole up here for the night or go on?"

"Better stay here," Slurlek advised. "We've got to report in to the ship's owner, but we could come back in the morning."

"I'm almost afraid to ask this," Trag began, "but just how long is it until morning?"

"I dunno, twelve, thirteen hours?" Slurlek replied, scratching beneath the scales on his chin. "Something like that."

"This is a damn strange planet," Trag griped. "Not sure I could go back to sleep right now. We haven't been up that long."

"Well, if you want to keep going in the snow, go right ahead," Slurlek said. "But as poorly as you tolerate cold, I wouldn't recommend it."

"What do you mean?" Trag demanded. "I thought we were doing pretty well."

"Maybe you are, but she isn't," he said, pointing at Micayla, who was shivering and having a great deal of difficulty remaining upright.

"Mick!" Trag exclaimed. "What the hell's the matter with you?"

"No idea," she gasped. "Haven't felt right since we landed. It wasn't too bad while we were moving, but now—it seems to be getting worse... Maybe I'll just sit down here for a while." She staggered to the side of the building and sank down with her head between her knees. Despite the cold, she could feel beads of perspiration running down the middle of her back.

"Ever hear of this happening to anyone before?" Trag asked Slurlek.

"No, but I doubt if any Zetithians have ever visited this world," he replied.

"Doesn't seem to be bothering me any," Trag commented. "Well, you two go on. Maybe she's just hungry or thirsty or something. We've got plenty of provisions with us. She'll be all right."

"See you in the morning, then," Orlat said. With a swirl of snow the two Neriks pushed through another door and departed.

"I thought they'd never leave," Micayla said. "Think they'll be back?"

"Who knows?" Trag replied. "My guess is that we've seen the last of them."

"I hope so—for tonight, anyway."

Trag leveled a chastising glare at her. "Mick, why didn't you tell me you didn't feel well?"

"Wasn't any point in it," she replied. "It wasn't like we'd have done anything differently."

"True, but next time you feel like crap, I'd appreciate it if you'd tell me."

Micayla wasn't in the mood for a lecture. Wiping the sweat from her eyes, she said irritably, "What, so you can pick on me for being a weak female? Thank you, but I think I'll pass."

"Trust me, Mick, there's nothing weak about you. Matter-of-fact, I figured you'd be the one keeping me warm on this trip."

Since this was precisely what Micayla had assumed would happen, she didn't argue the point. "Funny how things turn out, isn't it?"

"Yeah," he agreed. "You just sit tight and I'll get this place warmed up."

Micayla nodded but immediately wished she hadn't moved her head. The interior of the shed seemed to come to life, swirling around in her visual field until she had no choice but to close her eyes and wait for the dizziness to pass.

"This is damned inconvenient," she grumbled when she opened them a few moments later. "You can plan for just about everything else, but the possibility of getting sick never occurs to you."

"Don't worry about it, Mick," Trag said. "Even if we don't get Grekkor this time, we know the truth now. We'll catch up with him eventually."

"I suppose you're right," she said with a sigh. "He can't hide from us forever."

Trag pulled the heating unit out of his pack and set it up nearby. "This'll have you warm as toast in no time," he said.

"Sounds good—at least I think it does. I've never felt like this before; I'm freezing cold but sweating at the same time. Very strange."

"Want something to drink?"

"Yeah. Maybe some of that hot chocolate."

Trag fixed a cup for her and heated it up with his pulse pistol set on the lowest stun level. "Hidar taught me how to do that," he said, handing her the steaming mug. "Wasn't something I ever needed to do on Darconia—didn't have a pistol either—but as cold as I've been ever since I left, it's been very helpful."

"Thank you," she said gratefully. "It's perfect."

While she sipped her chocolate, Trag laid out their sleeping bags. Even engaged in such a simple task, Trag still drew her eye; just looking at him made her feel better.

"These things are heated too," he remarked. "But there's nothing quite like another warm body, is there?"

Micayla agreed, wishing she dared to undress completely so she could spend the night in his arms. Suddenly, the need to have Trag's skin next to hers was overwhelming. Maybe if he just undid his shirt so she could lay her head on his chest. That might be enough…

"Hungry?" he asked.

"A little," she replied. "Though it might make me feel worse, depending on what it is. Something tells me these rations don't include fresh fruit."

"Probably not," Trag said. "And knowing Jack, they could be from anywhere." Trag pulled out a few packages and inspected them carefully. "Would you believe they're actually Terran? We've got something here called meatloaf and mashed potatoes, and another that says turkey and dressing. Sound okay to you?"

"Sounds fabulous," Micayla said. "I was afraid we'd be getting sun-dried Kreater beast or something equally horrible."

"Jack should have given some of these to Hidar while we were at the palace," Trag remarked. "Then he wouldn't have had to fly to McDonalds all the time."

Micayla shrugged. "I think he likes his Big Macs too well to ask for anything else. He's a strange one, isn't he?"

"And touchy as hell when he's molting," Trag said with a nod. "He looked pretty ragged when we left, though. Should be done with that pretty soon."

The heating unit put out more warmth than a campfire, and soon Micayla had stopped shivering. The hot food helped, but she felt even better when Trag sat down beside her and put an arm around her shoulders.

"I think I could come out of this parka now," he said. "What about you?"

Micayla nodded and with Trag's help she was soon snug inside their combined sleeping bags, leaning up against the wall with Trag's parka behind them and hers covering them. As she'd expected, the heat of his body was far more soothing than anything else. Until he began purring, that is.

"This is what I was talking about when I said I liked cold snowy nights," she said. "The only difference is that I had to imagine what it would be like to be snuggled up with another person."

"Now you know."

"Yeah, now I know."

"Like it?"

"Mm-hmm," she replied, wrapping her arms around him. "Can't think of anything better."

"I can," Trag said. "But we'll leave that for when you're not feeling so rotten."

It was slightly drafty inside the shed, but for the most part, the howling wind was kept at bay. The heater was highly effective, if somewhat lacking in atmosphere. "Too bad we don't have a real fire," she said. "I went camping a lot when I was a kid. There's nothing quite like sitting around a campfire in the winter. It feels cozy and warm and makes a nice crackling sound. Smells good too."

"I'll take your word for it," said Trag, giving her a squeeze. "This feels pretty perfect to me."

She didn't argue, and Trag decided it was as good a time as any to ask her some questions that had been plaguing him. "So, Mick," he began. "What are you going to do when this is all over? Just supposing everything turns out right; Grekkor is brought to justice and the Nedwuts aren't hunting us anymore—and no one thinks you killed that Norludian. What will you do then?"

"I don't know," she replied. "I could go back to Orleon—might even be able to get my old job back—but I'm not sure that's what I want now."

"Any idea what you *do* want?" he asked.

"Not really," she replied. "There are a lot of possibilities."

Trag swallowed hard. Since she obviously wasn't going to broach the subject, it was up to him to take the plunge. "Do any of them include me?"

"What do you mean?"

"I don't want to lose you, Mick. I—I think we should stick together."

"We should *all* stick together," Micayla said. "But I doubt if Jack will ever truly settle down."

"She tried it for a while," Trag said. "Couldn't stand not being on her ship, though."

"What about you?" she asked, her warm gaze searching his face. "You seem to be something of a wanderer yourself."

"Not sure I need that anymore," he said. "While I was a slave, all I could think of was how much I wanted to get back into space and feel free again. Now that I'm there, I'm beginning to see the advantages to settling down."

"Such as?"

"Such as not having to watch my back all the time. Not having to kill every Nedwut on sight before they get the chance to kill me. Having decent food and a warm bed and someone to share it with. I never cared about those things before."

"Oh," she said, her voice sounding unsteady. "W-what changed your mind?"

Trag took her hand and pressed it to his lips. "You did," he said. "I never wanted it until I found you."

"Trag, I—" She looked delightfully confused—a circumstance which made him long to pull her into his arms and kiss her until she knew exactly what he meant, but he would try words before actions this time. He wanted her to understand him beyond a shadow of a doubt.

"Look, I know you don't love me, but honest to God, Mick, if anything ever happened to you, I'd—well, I don't know what I'd do! You mean a helluva lot to me. Promise me you'll think about it."

Her expression of confusion persisted. "Which part?"

"Staying with me. I don't care where we go or what we do. I only know that whatever I do, I want to do it with you."

Chapter 24

MICAYLA DIDN'T KNOW WHAT TO SAY. HAD HE JUST asked her to marry him, or what? She thought she should say something in response but didn't know what it would be, particularly when she wasn't completely sure she'd understood the question.

"You don't have to answer me right now," he went on. "I just want you to think about it. We've had a pretty good time together these past few weeks and I don't want it to end. In fact, I want it to grow into something more—a *lot* more. We make a good pair, Mick. There's not many women I could spend this much time with without screaming at them."

"You don't have a very high opinion of women, do you?"

"Just haven't met the right kind, I guess," he said with a shrug. "Been hanging out with hookers and such for too long. Then there was the time I was a slave. Can't say I was abused or anything, but maybe I was sort of... used."

She thought she understood and nodded, but something else was bothering her. There was one little thing she needed to be absolutely sure about. It wouldn't do to marry a man who was still harboring amorous feelings toward his sister-in-law. "What about Kyra? You said you loved her. Are you sure you're over that?"

"Yes, but it took you to make me see it," he said. "What about you? You didn't care much for men before. Are you over that too?"

"Maybe," she replied, smiling wickedly. "I don't mind you a bit."

Trag chuckled softly. "It's not much, but I guess it's a start." He pulled her closer. "You know something? I'm really enjoying this trip."

"Me too," she said. "Cozy and warm with my Trag here with me. What more could I want?"

"Oh, I dunno, this all to be over and done with so we could go home?"

"Sounds nice, but we aren't there yet."

"Nope," he said sadly. "But at least I've got something to look forward to."

Trag truly did have something to look forward to now. *My Trag,* she'd just said. He still wasn't sure he'd heard her correctly. Even though she hadn't said, "Yes, Trag, I'll be your mate," it came damn close. The trouble was, neither of them had much experience when it came to being in love. All the endearments that rolled so easily off of other tongues were hard for either of them to put into words. Trag toyed with the idea of just blurting out, "I love you, Mick! Please be my mate!" but somehow managed to hold his peace. There would come a time when he could say it without it sounding forced or contrived, but that day hadn't come yet. No, asking her to stick around for a while had been best. Even that had shaken her a little—at least, he thought it had.

He wanted to make love with her, to show her how he felt. Not just being creative or going through the motions of sex to prove she could arouse him. No, it was more than that, and he was finally beginning to understand it. Maybe just kissing her would be enough…

Purring, he dipped his head down to taste her lips and felt the magic there—a potent and lasting magic that he knew he'd never grow weary of. Just feeling her warm body in his arms, her smooth skin beneath his hands, her soft lips and wet kisses on his face were enough to prove it was real. He loved the sound of her voice, delighted in her laughter; fell completely apart when she cried out in ecstasy…

"Mmm, kiss me, Mick," he said between nibbles. "You see what I mean? I want to kiss you every day for the rest of my life—until we both grow old and our children are all grown up and have children of their own. Could you do that, Mick? Could you stay with me forever?"

Trag's heart nearly stopped when she pushed away from him. "Forever's a long time, Trag," she said hesitantly. "Are you sure you want to commit to that?"

"Mick, I've been from one side of this galaxy to the other, and I've never found anyone I want to be with forever—until now." He shifted slightly in an attempt to relieve the pressure on his cock, which was considerable. "Want to know how much I want you, Mick? Just feel my dick—and what you feel there, multiply that by about a million, maybe even more than that."

"My, how romantic that sounds," she said with a soft laugh, but Trag felt a jolt of pure sexual electricity when she put her hand on his groin. "Well, there's a big lump there, but I can't really tell if it's your dick or not with your pants on. How many pairs are you wearing?"

"Three," he replied. "Guess I'd better take them off then—and while we're at it, let's get rid of yours too. That is, if you're feeling okay."

"I feel better after eating a little something and resting for a bit. Maybe it *is* Nerik's backwards rotation," she said, "but it seems odd that it would bother me when space travel doesn't—at least, not much."

"Might be something in the air," he said as he pushed off all three layers of his clothing at once. "You never know how you'll react to new planets."

"True," she agreed, smoothing her hand over his hip. "That's *much* better. I'll have to say, the Nerik winter may be good for snuggling, but Darconia is the best place for boywatching."

Trag couldn't believe it. "You? Boywatching? Really?"

"Yes, really," she grumbled. "Okay, I'll admit it. I do like to look, but I'm very careful about it."

"No kidding. I'd have never guessed."

"I learned a long time ago how not to get caught. Guys catch you looking and they get all cocky and think you want more."

"Oh, I'd never make *that* mistake," Trag said facetiously. With a wide grin, he added, "Take a good, long look at me, Mick. Do you like what you see?"

Micayla took a deep breath and pushed back the parka that still covered his chest. "Mmmm," she said as she ran her fingers lightly from his neck to his groin. His penis bloomed as she reached it, the corona becoming even more stiffly engorged, the syrup flowing freely from the ruffled points. "You make me wish I was the most romantic woman in the universe," she said, "or at least a poet, but I'm not. Never had much practice at saying sweet things to a man—but I do love the way the hair grows on your belly, leading down to that fabulous cock. Your glowing eyes and thick, curly hair. Sleek muscles… Yeah, I like what I see. You make me drool, Trag," she purred. "You bring out the animal in me… make me want to suck your dick and bite you…"

"I just love it when you say things like that," he said with a sigh. "Makes me want to give you something to sink your fangs into."

Rolling over, he pushed himself up on his hands and knees and backed up to her face. She obviously needed no further encouragement, and he let out a growl as her fangs penetrated his skin. The feel of her teeth pulling at his flesh tightened his balls and they threatened to ejaculate right then, but he managed to control his response somehow. After the initial bite, she moved over his butt, trailing kisses across his skin until she reached his balls. With a guttural growl, she sucked them into her mouth and pulled his dick back with her hand. He didn't know which felt best—her hand on his cock or her tongue on his nuts. Then there were the light touches on his penis and hard bites on his ass. She was driving him insane. He'd meant for it to be romantic, but she was right—that wasn't the way they were. They weren't romantics; they were more like animals. Sure, they could be soft and loving at times, but though this moment had begun on a gentler note, it was rapidly escalating into a sexual feast.

And she *was* feasting on him. Eating his meat and driving him wild. She pulled his dick up and into her mouth and he began rocking back into her, fucking her hard and fast. He wanted to come in her mouth, coat her tongue with his snard and fill her with joy.

"Oh, yeah. Suck my dick, Mick." Chuckling softly, he added, "See, I'm the poet. I rhyme every time."

"Ha, ha," she scoffed. She may have stopped sucking him, but she was doing almost as good a job with her hands. "You're not a poet; you're a big, sexy beast that I can't get enough of. Besides, though I can't speak from experience, I'd be willing to bet that poets are highly over-rated as lovers. I'd much rather have someone like you."

Trag nearly passed out from the shock. *Great Mother of the Desert!* She'd said it. *Lovers*. Trag savored the word, just the sound of which had him about to come in her face. Biting his lip to regain control, he backed into her again, bumping his cockhead against her lips. "Guess you'll just have to stay with me until you get enough," he said.

"But what if I decide to go home?"

"I'm sorry if it sounds selfish, Mick, but I hope you never do."

Then suddenly it hit him. Home wasn't a place; it was a state of mind, and for Trag, home was wherever Mick was, and not only that, it was inside her.

Spinning around as quickly as a cat, he seized her by the waist and flipped her over onto her stomach. Pulling her hips up, he knelt behind her and drove his dick into her with wild abandon. Oh, yes, this was home—inside her, where it was soft and warm and delightfully carnal. Where he could fuck as hard as he wanted and plant his seed where it would grow.

And he hoped it would grow. He wanted to watch his babies make her belly swell with life and then watch them grow up after they were born and then do it all over again. What was it about her that brought out his paternal instincts so strongly? Sure, she was young and strong and healthy, but there was more to it than that. He'd met plenty of women who fit that description and he hadn't wanted to plant babies in them. It wasn't even just that she was Zetithian. What made her so different?

He loved her; that was the difference. Really, truly loved her. The fire in his loins pushed him on. He wasn't just fucking her for the pleasure of it; he had a purpose now. He pulled out and rolled her onto her back and plunged into her once more. Had there ever been a woman like her? Would there ever be again? Trag thought he knew the answer to that and the answer was no.

His mind seemed to reach inside himself, and as it did, he pulled out a bit of his soul and passed it through to her, sending it on to where it would become new life and new love. Shuddering as his seed spewed forth into her waiting womb, he didn't have to have a vision the way Cat did; he knew she had conceived beyond a shadow of a doubt.

Even so, he wanted to see the joy in her eyes. "Look at me, Mick," he said, surprised at how different his own voice sounded to him—ragged and rough, as though he'd run a hard race and hadn't recovered yet.

She opened her eyes and Trag saw it all right there before him—the rest of his life with Mick. It was similar to what he'd seen before—trees and fields and children at play—but now he knew it for what it was. There was no way to prove it other than the sense of complete truth he felt deep within his heart. If asked, he'd have sworn he'd never had a true vision before, but he was absolutely certain he was having one now. He saw young faces and old, all smiling and joyous, lined up before him and continuing on beyond his sight. Then he realized who he was seeing. They were his descendants, stretching out before him and on into infinity—and he was seeing them in her eyes.

Chapter 25

HE WAS STARING INTO HER EYES AS THOUGH HE'D SEEN a ghost. "Trag?" Micayla whispered. "Are you okay?"

It was a long moment before he responded. "I—yeah, I'm okay," he said at last. "At least I think I am. I just saw the most amazing thing…" His voice trailed off as he continued to gaze at her, dashing the sweat from his eyes and pulling the hair back from his face as though attempting to recapture the previous moment.

What she was seeing was quite amazing in and of itself; Trag's face suspended above her own, his expression now soft and suffused with happiness and contentment. She'd never seen him like that before, not in all the time they'd known each other. Trag had always seemed like such a restless spirit. What he'd said earlier about settling down had seemed out of character for him, but she could see it in his eyes now. The commitment to her was very clear; if he said he would stay with her forever, then that was exactly what he would do.

A heartbeat later he was kissing her like he'd never kissed her before and she felt the shock of it all the way to her soul. He loved her—he might not have said it aloud but he didn't have to. Closing her eyes, she felt her mind expand as she floated higher, out past the confines of the small building and into the storm that continued to rage on while they were snug and warm inside. She was like a bird soaring over the countryside past rivers and farms and fields that lay fallow in their winter shroud. Then she saw it: the city of Rechred was laid out before her like a grid and her mind was centered on one spot, one person—one terrifying bit of humanity that was focused intently on her—as though they were standing face-to-face.

It was Grekkor, gazing up into the storm as though challenging the heavens to stop him in his determination to see his vendetta through to the end. Terrifying because she knew where he was and also knew it would take all of them to stop him and put an end to the madness.

"I see it too," she said aloud. "We don't need those two Neriks to guide us. I know where he is."

The magnitude of their combined thoughts should have ignited even the dust motes that drifted through the space between them, but nothing happened. For a moment, neither of them spoke, but then Trag shifted back onto his heels, leaving her momentarily bereft of his warmth and the strength of his passion. "That's not what I saw," he said flatly.

"So it wasn't a joint vision after all?" she said. "What did you see?"

Trag shook his head, sending his dark curls flying back over his shoulders. "Nothing to do with Grekkor," he said, "though, on second thought, maybe it did. I think I just saw proof that he will not succeed in destroying us completely."

"That's comforting," Micayla said. "But to make your vision come true, we need to act on mine. I can get us to the city; I know *exactly* where he is."

"We'll head out as soon as it's light," Trag said.

"You don't understand," Micayla persisted. "We can go now. I can find him."

"In this weather?" Trag screeched. "I'll be damned if I let you go out now! It can wait until morning—for that matter, *he* can wait until morning. If you know where he is now, he won't get far."

She was beginning to feel desperate. "But I've got to go now!" she exclaimed, attempting to push him off of her. When he wouldn't budge, she took a deep breath and said calmly, "Really, Trag, we need to start right now. I've never been more certain of anything in my life."

"Never try to stop a Zetithian with a vision," Trag grumbled, relenting at last. "I liked my vision a whole helluva lot better."

"What was it exactly?"

"I'll tell you someday," he said. "Someday when we aren't about to walk blindly forth into a blizzard."

"We aren't blind," Micayla assured him. "Trust me. I won't get lost."

"You might not, but what about me?"

"I'll tie a rope around my waist and you can tie the other end around yours," she said. "That way we won't get separated. But really, Trag, we need to get dressed and get out of here."

"Aren't you sick anymore?"

"What? Oh, you mean the dizziness. Must have just been hungry. I'm fine now."

"You're also pregnant," he blurted out.

"What?" she said again. "I'm pregnant? Since when?"

"Since right now," he said. "That was part of my vision. Cat will confirm it eventually, but I'm sure I'm right about this."

"Odd that we'd have to get Cat's input rather than a

doctor's," Micayla said dryly. "Or Hidar's—at least, I guess he could do that."

Trag shrugged. "No idea, but Cat is one hundred percent reliable on this sort of thing."

"Too bad we can't ask him now," Micayla said briskly, "but there'll be plenty of time for that later on." Taking Trag's hand, she gave it a meaningful squeeze. "Trust me, Trag. We need to do this—whether I'm pregnant or not—and if I am, I'll be just as pregnant in daylight."

"I can't argue with that," said Trag. "Wish I could, though. Don't suppose your vision includes knowing whether we make it or not—no, wait, mine did that." His expression brightened as suddenly as the sun popping out from behind a dark cloud. "Okay then. Let's get moving."

Even with a trail to follow that was as clear to Micayla as a path carved in the snow, it was still tough going. They marched on through the night, never seeing a single soul. If the two Neriks were coming back in the morning, she thought they might pass them along the way, but she hoped not. Trusting anyone on this strange world was probably a mistake, especially two hired thugs that could just as easily have been hired by someone like Grekkor.

There wasn't much opportunity for conversation, which was just as well, for Micayla already had a lot to think about. If Trag was right—and with the strength of her own vision to use as an example she had no doubt that he was—she was going to have triplets. And they were Trag's. Just the thought of having his children warmed her heart, but how soon? She didn't even know the length of the gestation period for Zetithians. It might be shorter or longer than that of humans and was yet another thing she needed to ask Jack about. She wished she could be more precise about Grekkor's location and therefore send Jack on ahead, but even though the Neriks had supposedly locked down Veluka's ship, they still couldn't get the comlinks to work.

"Must be the snow," Trag said, shouting over the howling wind.

"Could be," she said, "but I doubt it. I've never dealt with anything that wouldn't work at *all* because of the weather. I mean, it might be spotty or intermittent, but not totally dead."

Trag laughed. "Maybe the snow is different on Nerik; disrupts the signal or something."

"It wouldn't surprise me if that was true, but it doesn't seem any different from the snow on Earth, and even my phone would work in snow. Back home there was no such thing as being out of touch due to the weather unless there was a major catastrophe like a hurricane or a tornado."

If his expression was anything to go by, Trag had a different opinion. "Snow isn't a catastrophe, huh? It is to me! Never had anything like this on Darconia," he grumbled. "Sandstorms, maybe, but not snow. Try the comstone again."

Micayla reached inside her parka to tap the bead on her necklace. She called out Jack's name. "Nothing," she said. "Of course, if they landed in Rechred, they'd still be out of range."

"I'm almost afraid to ask this, but do you know how far it is from here?"

Micayla closed her eyes. She could still see the whole thing from a bird's-eye view and could even judge the distance. "At least another half kilometer before we're in range. We should be passing through the outskirts of the city pretty soon."

"At least it's still dark," Trag said. "I hate to admit it, but going in under cover of night probably *was* the best bet. Just wish it wasn't snowing."

Micayla glanced up at the sky. The flakes were still falling in a thick, swirling haze but were getting smaller. "I think it's letting up a little."

"Really? How the devil can you tell?" Trag said. "I can't see a damn thing."

"I can," she said. "My night vision must be better than yours."

"Yeah, well, my nose isn't so hot either. Don't know why you'd put up with such a poor excuse for a Zetithian."

"I believe we've been over that," she said with a wry smile—which, of course, Trag probably couldn't see. As far as she was concerned, his nose and vision had nothing to do with how she felt about him. "You're a fine specimen—and you know it."

Trag chuckled softly. "Just making sure." He dropped an arm around her shoulder and they headed off into the snow.

As they reached the outskirts of the city, it had nearly stopped snowing and the streets had already been cleared. They took in the deserted pavements and strange buildings dimly lit by lamps that seemed to hover high in the air.

"Guess everyone's got sense enough to stay inside on a night like this," Trag commented. "They must have one helluva street crew."

"No piles of snow anywhere either," Micayla observed. "They must not use speeders here; otherwise they wouldn't have to clear the roads. We quit bothering with that on Earth ages ago when everyone switched over to speeders."

Trag eyed the vast expanse of snow behind them with distaste. Clearly, the very last thing he wanted to do was to trudge through any more of it, and the fact that the roads were open probably suited him right down to the ground. Micayla suspected that getting him to enjoy snow would be difficult, but then a mental picture of sledding with him down a snowy hillside with his arms wrapped around her popped into her head and she thought she might have to revise that notion. He'd probably end up laughing his head off and throwing snowballs at her. Then they'd go back inside, curl up beside the fire with some hot chocolate...

"What? You mean nobody ever walks on Earth?" he said, bringing her thoughts back to the present.

"Oh, of course they do!" Micayla said. Enjoying snowball fights with Trag would have to wait for a while—unfortunately. "They clear the sidewalks for foot traffic, but everyone usually takes care of that on their own property. This was obviously done by someone else." She shuddered slightly as all thoughts of snow sledding and hot chocolate evaporated. "They could be all around us and we'd never know. Gives me the creeps just thinking about it."

"Their scales only let *light* pass around them," Trag said. "I doubt it would work with blowing snow—I mean, you'd see the snow being diverted by them—wouldn't you?"

"I'll be damned if I know," Micayla said. "If light can slip around something, maybe snow can do the same thing—though snow is visible, and light particles aren't."

Trag shrugged. "All I know is this is one strange planet. Look at those buildings. Don't you think that's weird the way they stand on end like that? Must take some kick-ass structural engineering to keep them from falling over."

Micayla had to admit, they *were* odd. Some of them looked like pyramids standing on the point, rather than the base, while others were perfectly spherical. "I wonder if they rotate."

"What, to dump the snow off the top?"

"Maybe. Then again, the bottom base could just be invisible."

Trag walked up to the edge of one of the larger structures. There wasn't any snow there, nor did the light from the hovering globes which illuminated the rest of the street reach the ground beneath it. Tentatively putting out a hand, he came up against the solid but completely invisible side of the structure. "There's your answer," he said. "Snow doesn't make them visible, except for the fact that there's no snow underneath them."

"Why would anyone design a building to be partially concealed like that?"

"Purely for fashion," Slurlek said, suddenly materializing beside Micayla, who let out a shriek and leaped forward into Trag's arms.

"Don't *do* that!" Trag exclaimed. "Gives me the— what is it Jack calls that?—the willies?"

"Probably," Micayla replied. "Couldn't you guys warn people when you're about to appear?" Though it *did* get her closer to Trag—which was a plus in any situation.

"But we like to make people jump," Orlat said, suddenly appearing behind Slurlek. "It's fun."

She could understand the appeal, but it was bound to get old eventually. "Yes, but you guys probably don't even notice it, do you?"

"True," Slurlek said. "Happens too often."

"Have to wait for offworlders to come around," Orlat added.

"So, how did you know where we were?" Micayla asked. "Obviously you didn't track us through the snow." The wind had already obscured their trail from the ship, piling it into sloping drifts behind them.

"Trade secret," Orlat replied. "Can't tell you everything."

"I suppose not," Micayla reluctantly agreed. "It's just that I know where Grekkor is now—or where he'll be when we get there." Frowning, she added, "It's hard to explain, but we may not need you guys after all."

Orlat looked hurt—at least, Micayla thought he did, though with Neriks it was difficult to tell. "Not even for moral support?"

"Well, maybe for that, but not much more." She paused for a moment remembering her earlier thought that these men could just as easily have been working for Grekkor and had been sent back to capture them and turn them in for the bounty. "Didn't rat on us, did you?"

It might have been a Terran figure of speech, but Orlat obviously understood it. "To Grekkor?" he scoffed. "Like we'd ever work for someone like him. That is one scary son of a leckler."

"What the devil is a leckler?" Trag asked.

Orlat's upper lip clicked into an expression of distaste. "A flat, slimy thing that lives in ponds," he replied.
"Not a nice thing to be."

Trag nodded. "Just checking."

"So the buildings are like that for fashion?" Micayla
asked. "Kind of expensive, isn't it?"

"Terribly," agreed Slurlek. "It's a measure of high
status to have a house that can be completely cloaked.
Not everyone aspires to that, though. Far as I'm concerned it's a waste of credits."

"Well, you certainly wouldn't need to put up cur-
tains," Micayla mused as she studied the buildings.
"Some people would see that as an advantage. On the
other hand—" She broke off as another thought struck
her. "Hey, do you have any idea why our comlinks still
don't work? I figured you two were jamming the ship,
but why don't they work now?"

"It's the snow," Slurlek said, shaking his head sadly.
"Messes up *everything* on this planet. Something about
the shape of the dust particles in the atmosphere that
alters the crystalline nature of the flakes. Most signals
are distorted by it. We can make things disappear but
can't get decent reception in a snowstorm—well, some
things work, like beacons and such, but nothing very
complex can get through."

"Nobody's perfect," Trag said with a shrug. "So the
snow's different from that on other worlds? I'd have
thought snow was the same everywhere."

"Not here," Slurlek said. "Lots of things are different
here—and some things are too much the same."

"What do you mean by that?"

"Every life form on this planet has black scales and

white eyes," Slurlek replied. "The birds, the other land animals, the fish—everything except the plants."

"Whew! Talk about your lack of biodiversity!" Micayla exclaimed. "Can they all disappear?"

"Nope, only us bipeds can do that," Orlat said smugly.

"What about lecklers?" Trag asked.

"Flat, slimy, with black scales and white eyes," Orlat replied. "We just *wish* they could disappear."

"Must have missed that chapter in the book," Trag muttered.

"You never *read* the book," Micayla reminded him.

"What?" Orlat said.

"Never mind," said Micayla. "We've got to keep moving if we want to get to Grekkor in time."

"In time for what?" Orlat asked.

"In time for him to meet his destiny," Trag said grimly.

"Destiny?" Slurlek echoed.

"Just deserts, perhaps?" Micayla suggested.

"Yeah, all of that," said Trag. "Oh, and just to be sure, which way is it to the Palace Hotel?"

Micayla, Orlat, and Slurlek each pointed in the same direction at once.

"Well, at least you all agree," said Trag. "How far?"

"Might get there by midday," Slurlek said. "It's a big city."

"And catch him just sitting down to lunch," said Trag. "Perfect. Nice, crowded restaurant—you *do* have restaurants here, don't you?"

"Of course we do," Slurlek said stiffly. "What kind of planet do you think this is?"

"I dunno," said Trag. "You've got weird snow, no biodiversity, the buildings are mostly invisible, and the planet spins backwards." He tapped his chin as though giving this careful thought. "Screwed up?"

"Well, you've got that right," Orlat admitted. "But we do have restaurants—and pretty good food in most of them." He paused for a moment, considering. "Well, *you* might not think so, but—"

"Doesn't matter," said Trag. "We've got our own food anyway."

"Might be best to get to him before the big reception," Micayla agreed. "And a restaurant would be a great place to do it—lots of people around to hear him confess."

Trag nodded. "Security won't be as tight either. I'll bet even a leckler couldn't squeeze past the guards at that hotel."

"You've obviously never dealt with lecklers before," Orlat pointed out. "They can squeeze past anything."

"I didn't mean that literally," Trag said with a withering glance. "Come on, then. Let's get going."

The snowfall picked up again and as they journeyed through the city, the reason for the lack of snow on the streets became clear.

Micayla stifled a shriek as a giant scaly worm with brush-like teeth emerged from a hole on the side of the road and vacuumed everything within its reach. Then it disappeared back inside the hole and the lid snapped shut.

"What the devil is that?" Trag exclaimed.

"Snow sucker," Orlat replied. "Just ignore them."

Trag figured that they were yet another reason why there weren't many people out on the streets, aside from the late hour, for the only warning the snow suckers gave was a soft beep whenever they were about to pop

out. Trag had to pull Micayla out of the way more than
once and shuddered to think where the thing would have
spewed her out—if, indeed, it ever did. He also found
out the hard way that the streetlights weren't actually
hovering; they were set on poles, *cloaked* poles.

"Why would anyone *do* crap like that?" he said
after he'd run into the second one. "It makes no
sense whatsoever!"

Orlat shrugged. "I thought it was a stupid idea too,
but nobody asked me. The city planners thought it
would be cool to have the lights there with no visible
means of support."

"Well, I hate to tell them this, but the technology for
hoverlights does exist," Micayla said. "We have them
on Earth."

"Must be where they got the idea," Orlat said. "Too
bad they didn't think to buy any of them."

"Probably wouldn't work in the snow," Trag commented. "Hey, if I end up with a concussion, you guys
just drag me along behind you, okay?"

"Sure," said Slurlek. "No problem, but if you look
for those little round shadows on the pavement, you can
avoid them."

"Important safety tip." Micayla chuckled.

They tried their comstones at various intervals but
still got no reply from Jack. Trag was beginning to doubt
that they were even on the planet yet, but Micayla was
fairly certain they were just out of range.

Trag would have preferred to carry Micayla after rescuing her from a snow sucker the second time, but figured she'd fuss at him for trying. It was still something
he wanted to do, though. His protective instincts kicked

in every time she slipped or hesitated and he wondered if it would be like that all the time or just while she was pregnant. If it was constant, she was bound to get pissed at him eventually.

Slurlek and Orlat were chattering away to Micayla, but Trag kept his thoughts to himself. The question of where they would go and what they would do after this adventure was plaguing him mightily. He went over in his mind all the planets he'd been to and couldn't come up with a single world he wanted to live on—and not so much himself as his children. He wanted them to grow up on a world as they could play outside without him having to worry about them every second of the day and night. A world like Zetith had been. Not remembering his homeworld would have been a blessing at this point, he decided, because then he wouldn't be so choosy. Even though he'd never been there, Earth was his first choice, but there were other worlds with similar climates—Terra Minor was one that came to mind, particularly because it hadn't been colonized for long and wasn't densely populated. Plus, if his information from Bonnie and Lynx was correct, it was a good place to raise children.

Jack and her shipmates didn't seem to mind having their children grow up on a starship, but Trag had misgivings and wondered if Micayla was having similar thoughts. Granted, Jack and Tisana's kids had seen more of the galaxy, but there was a lot to be said for a nice home with green trees to climb.

Then there was Darconia. It wasn't as out of the question now as it had been in the past, but a desert world was no place for Zetithians either. He knew there were verdant spots on Darconia, but living among reptiles wasn't such a great idea—certainly not the place for them to find mates when they grew up, as he knew from personal experience.

If only Zetith still existed! He imagined taking Micayla home to a world where they both belonged and would be welcomed. Too bad there wasn't another planet quite like it in the galaxy—at least none that he'd seen or heard tell of—and the fact that there wasn't made settling down somewhere else seem second best. Then it occurred to him that as long as Micayla was with him, it truly didn't matter. Home was wherever she was, whether it was Earth, Darconia, or even—though he didn't care much for the idea—Nerik.

Chapter 26

GREKKOR LEANED BACK IN HIS CHAIR, THOUGHTFULLY sipping his wine. The trio of Neriks sitting across the table from him disgusted him excessively, but then Neriks always had. In his mind, they were even more hideous than Norludians, though most people would have disagreed. Neriks were notoriously treacherous creatures; he'd hired a number of them in the past and knew from experience that they couldn't be trusted. Having to deal with them at all went against his better judgment, but they possessed a technology that no one else could duplicate—and since they made you pay through the nose for it as it was, it wouldn't do to tick them off, especially these three, who were all high-ranking officials. Ilegret was the *sklarth* of Rechred, which, if Grekkor understood correctly, was a post similar to that of mayor. Tularnek, whom he had met before, was the local Consortium representative, and Narelna was the government agent in charge of approving the sale of starships—not easy men to get together. It had taken several hours of diligence on Worrell's part to arrange this particular meeting.

"My dear Ilegret," he said pleasantly. "What delightful wine you have here. Is it produced locally?" It tasted worse than pond water, but Grekkor wasn't about to say so.

"Why, yes," the elderly Nerik replied. "It comes from a vineyard not far from the city. This is said to be the best vintage in a century."

Grekkor suspected that Ilegret could have made this judgment himself, for he appeared to be quite old. His scales were ragged and snagged the smooth fabric of his tunic at the shoulders and he had the foulest breath of any being Grekkor had yet encountered. Of course, that might have had more to do with the Nerik cuisine than age. Everything on Grekkor's plate tasted as bad as the wine—and some of it appeared to be moving.

Just how the denizens of Rechred would welcome him, Grekkor hadn't been certain. So far as he could tell, the news that the two women from Orleon Station possessed hadn't traveled. He could only hope that Worrell was wrong and that they wouldn't be believed if they ever told anyone—especially since all efforts to track them down had failed. Still, he was certain that this plan to donate large sums to charity was a good one. It never hurt to boost public relations, particularly in his line of business, and a positive image was imperative to allow him to maintain control of the Consortium. He'd seen others booted out of power on a whim, let alone the charges that those two women were capable of leveling at him.

"This plan you have," Tularnek began, diverting Grekkor from his thoughts, "I still don't understand why you chose Nerik for that particular honor."

Tularnek may have appeared to be a fool on the surface, but Grekkor knew better. Smiling disarmingly, Grekkor shook his head. "I chose Nerik because of its unique position in the Consortium. It is centrally located and has the potential for becoming one of the richest planets in the sector. I'm sure there are many here now who would benefit from these charities."

"Are you insinuating that we are a poor, underdeveloped world?" Tularnek said, his scales flattening to a dull sheen.

Grekkor laughed softly and waved his hand as though it would erase the notion from Tularnek's mind. "I would never be so unkind. This world has vast resources. I am merely attempting to aid you in tapping into them."

"We come to the point now," Narelna said, his enormous white eyes veiled by half-shut lids. "Our cloaking technology. You would have us sell it at more, ah, competitive prices, shall we say?"

"It *would* enable you to sell more ships," Grekkor said, inclining his head in assent.

"Meaning to yourself?" the Nerik suggested.

"Come now, Narelna," Ilegret said, his scales ruffling with laughter. "Do not antagonize our guest. He will purchase the ships he requires at the normal cost." Turning to Grekkor, he added, "That *is* why you are here, is it not?"

Grekkor had to hand it to the old Nerik; he didn't miss much. "Perhaps," Grekkor said cautiously. "But first we must finish with the more altruistic business at hand."

"I wonder," said Narelna, "just why it is that you require ships with cloaking capability? Surely a businessman of your stature would not require that your dealings be so… covert?"

"My business?" Grekkor echoed. "Did I say the ships were for my own personal use?"

"No, you did not, but I wonder…"

"You see, my dear, *dear* Grekkor," Ilegret said with so much emphasis on the use of Grekkor's own

endearment that it sounded like a curse. "We have recently heard some rumblings about your... *business*."

"Oh, and what sort of *rumblings* would that be?"
Grekkor's tone was casual and he was certain there was
a smile on his face, but a sense of danger was beginning
to curl around his gut.

"I can't be certain," Ilegret went on, "but perhaps you
could elucidate—no, wait. I see they have arrived!"

Grekkor watched as Ilegret waved a hand in greeting
to someone behind him.

"Greetings, my friends," Ilegret said warmly. "We
have been advised of your visit. As the *sklarth* of this
great city, allow me to welcome you to Rechred."

—∞—

Micayla's vision had been a true one. Until she laid eyes
on him, she hadn't been sure. But there he was, sitting at
a table in a restaurant that would have been considered
posh by anyone's standards and sipping wine as though he
hadn't a care in the world. It was all she could do to keep
from screaming, "Murderer!" When she'd seen him before
she hadn't realized the full extent of his crimes, but now
she saw him for what he was: the one man responsible for
the death not only of her family, but of her entire world.
The urge to kick his blond butt all the way from Rechred
to Darconia and back was overwhelming—so overwhelming, in fact, that she now found it difficult to move. To be
in the presence of such consummate evil—the depth of
which she could only guess at—was horrifying.

Trag, however, had no such fear.

Waving back to the Nerik, who seemed to know him
for some strange reason, Trag stalked right up to the table

where the nemesis of his world sat. He didn't need Micayla to point him out now; something in the insolent set of his shoulders told him that this was, indeed, the one. Out of the corner of his eye he could see Lerotan, Hidar, and Rodan slipping in the side entrance—no doubt Jack and her crew were also somewhere nearby, though how any of them had found the right place was a mystery—but this was something he felt he needed to do on his own. Tapping his comstone, he activated the link to Jack and—hoping she was listening—stopped right behind Grekkor's chair.

"I've got a bone to pick with you, Grekkor," he said, putting on his most pugnacious face. "Rumor has it that you killed a Norludian on Orleon Station and blamed two women for it. Is that right?"

"What business is it of yours?" Grekkor said lightly, turning to face him. He might have been intending to laugh it off as a joke, but then he saw who—or what—it was that was addressing him. It was quick, but Trag caught the expression of murderous intent as it swept across Grekkor's casually amused features.

"It means a lot to me," Trag said roundly, "because I'm going to marry one of them and I don't want her getting locked up for murder on our wedding night."

"You're going to *mate* with one of them?" Grekkor's face displayed his disgust. "Which one?"

"Why, the Zetithian, of course," Trag replied with a nod toward Micayla. Crossing his arms over his chest, he added smugly, "We're gonna be mates and we're gonna have a million pure Zetithian kittens. She may even be pregnant already; in fact, I'm pretty sure she is—and then we're gonna spread 'em across the whole fuckin' galaxy, so you can just get over it, asshole."

The glare of pure, venomous hatred Grekkor leveled at Trag should have killed him where he stood, but Trag's taunt had the desired effect. "I will never get over it!" he shouted as he lunged to his feet. "You horrid cats all deserve to die. I destroyed your world and now I want you to die—in fact, I *intend* that you will die—like anyone who gets in my way, including that Norludian."

"You're sure you mean that?" Trag taunted. *"Really* mean it?"

"Yes, I mean it, and I'll increase the bounty on you just to make sure of it!" Grekkor snarled. "Ten million credits for each one of your stinking Zetithian hides!"

Trag smiled. "Sure you don't want to soften that up a little?"

Grekkor's handsome face was now deep red and contorted with hatred. "*Twenty* million for *you!*"

"No, I guess you wouldn't." Trag said. Smiling, he added, "Did you get that, Jack?"

"You're damn straight I did," Jack replied over the link. "Your ass is grass, Grekkor. The good guys are gonna win this time."

Grekkor glanced frantically around the room. The restaurant was filled with rich, influential people, and his bodyguards were all being held at gunpoint. There was no escape.

Trag caught the desperate look in Grekkor's eyes and made a dive for him, gripping the hand that now held a deadly weapon. The other patrons were screaming as the pistol swung in all directions, blasting the walls and the ceiling before knocking out an enormous light fixture that crashed right in the middle of the dance floor. In the confusion, Micayla darted in behind Grekkor, neutralizing him with a choke hold that soon had him gasping for mercy.

Driven to his knees, Grekkor released his hold on the weapon, which Trag then tossed aside with distaste.

"Why don't you just kill me?" Grekkor said, glaring at his captor with ire. "It's what I would do to you."

"That would make us too much alike," Trag replied, "and I don't think I want to be *anything* like you." He stood back then and began laughing at the spectacle before him. The bane of his world was nothing but a gasping, red-faced, quivering lump of flesh. "Man, you are *so* screwed."

"But I have had my revenge," Grekkor panted. "Your species will not survive. There are too few of you."

"That's what you think," Trag said with an amused smile. "You just watch us." Glancing around the room, Trag called out: "Are any of you ladies willing to be surrogate mothers to some Zetithian kids? You'd have some really cute kittens, plus you'd be saving an endangered species from extinction. We seem to cross best with Terrans, but I'm sure other species would be compatible." Pausing a moment to grin at Grekkor, he added, "How about it? Any takers?"

"I will!" shouted one.

"I'd *love* to!" shouted another.

"No you won't," Grekkor seethed. "Because I will hunt you down and kill every last one of you—starting with *her*."

Trag's perception of the entire scene slowed to a crawl. Micayla was standing right behind Grekkor, having released her hold on him. He saw Grekkor's fluid movement from sprawled on the floor to a swirling image highlighted by the flash of a blade. Trag realized, too late, that a knife must have fallen from a nearby table during the struggle. It was in Grekkor's hand and time stood still as he plunged it into Micayla's chest.

Trag was on him before the sound of Micayla's scream died. His arm snaked around the murderer's neck, giving it a quick twist, breaking it with a sharp snap. Killed instantly, Grekkor's nerveless body fell in a heap, pulling Micayla down with it.

Trag's heart nearly stopped as he watched her fall. "Oh, God, Mick," he sobbed, dropping to his knees at her side. Slipping his arm around her, he lifted her head, cradling her in his arms. "I'm so sorry. I should have gotten to him quicker."

"You... killed him?" she gasped. The knife protruding from her upper chest made breathing difficult and blood was already staining her shirt.

"Yes, I did," Trag replied. "I know I shouldn't have, but after he—"

"Good," she said hoarsely, attempting to smile. "That's my Trag... my hero."

"Not if I let you die."

"Doesn't matter," she whispered as her eyelids fluttered shut. "Love you anyway."

Trag felt as if the whole world had just stopped spinning. "Don't you dare die on me!" he roared. "You promised to stay alive!" He stared down at her inert form, unable to think, unable to reason. The only thought in his head was that he loved her and would probably die without her. He was vaguely aware that a crowd was gathering—diners disrupted from their meals, the occasional Nerik having gone into a hum, Jack's shout of outrage from across the room.

"Stand aside, stand aside!" Hidar shouted, fluttering his bright, newly molted wings as he passed through the crowd. "I must attend to her!"

Trag's eyes were bleak as he looked up at the tall Scorillian. "I don't know, Hidar," he said, choking on the words. "I think she's—"

"Not dead," Hidar said firmly as he crouched beside her.

Trag watched in horror as Hidar clutched the knife handle in his claw-like hands and began to push the flat side of the blade against the edge of the wound, creating a gap.

"I didn't think you were supposed to do that with a stab wound."

"You aren't unless you're a Scorillian," Hidar said. He made an odd, choking sound and then spat into the opening he'd made. His foamy spittle hissed as it made contact with her blood. Then he pulled the blade out slightly and spat on it again before pushing it back in.

"What the hell are you doing?" Trag shouted.

Micayla's back arched suddenly and her eyes flew open as she sucked in a huge breath. Her body then began to convulse, and though the seizure only lasted a few seconds, it seemed like hours to Trag.

"You killed her!" Trag exclaimed as she finally collapsed in his arms.

"No," said Hidar. "Only time or disease will do that now—or perhaps some other wound."

"What?"

"She will recover," Hidar insisted. He said this with such firm conviction that it seemed irrefutable, but Trag still didn't believe it.

"That's impossible!"

"No it isn't," someone said, but the voice wasn't Hidar's.

Trag looked down at Micayla in dismay. He'd never expected to hear her voice again. But he had—unless he was dreaming, and if he was, he never wanted to wake up. He'd thought she was dead, and now, there she was, looking up at him and even trying to smile.

"Mick?" he whispered. "Are you really—?"

"Going to live?" she said. "I think so."

She was looking at him, moving, and breathing, but— "With a *knife* stuck in your chest?"

Hidar's mandibles were clicking with irritation. "Of course she will not have a knife in her chest forever," he said waspishly. "It must stay there for an hour or so and then I will remove it. Take it out before the healant has had enough time to work, and she'll bleed to death."

"Healant?" Trag echoed. "What the devil is that?"

Hidar shook his odd, triangular head, displaying his impatience with Trag's ignorance. "Did you never wonder why I was aboard Lerotan's ship more as a cook than a medic—*and* why I resented your criticism of my cooking?"

"Well, no," Trag admitted. "Not really—"

"On Scorillia, I was regarded as an excellent chef," Hidar said. "But not a doctor. It's not like I ever went to medical school."

"But—"

"I saved Lerotan's life that way once," he said with a gesture toward Micayla, "and he rewarded me with the position of medic aboard his ship. This ability is innate among Scorillians. It doesn't heal our own wounds, but it works very well on mammals."

"I didn't know that!" Trag sputtered. "How come I didn't know that?" He was beyond bewilderment. Glancing around at the curious crowd, he went on, "Did any of *you* know that?" Receiving only negative responses, he turned back to Hidar. "You Scorillians are only known for spreading the plague!"

Hidar waved his antennae dismissively, much the way a human would brush aside an insignificant speck of dust with their fingertips. "Unfortunate, isn't it?"

"Yes, it is," Trag said. He still couldn't quite grasp the fact that Micayla wasn't dead or dying. Whether or not she lived or died, she was alive at the moment and there was something he had to say. "I love you, Mick. Promise me you won't ever let anyone stab you again."

"I'll try not to," Micayla said. "And if it's all the same to you, I'd much rather you didn't die either." She drew in a ragged breath and added, "Don't think I could stand that."

Trag was almost afraid to ask, but he had to know the answer. After all, he was a big boy; he could take it if she said no. "You said you loved me. I know you probably thought you were dying, but did you mean it?"

"I love you to pieces, Trag," she whispered with tears in her eyes. "I can't imagine loving anyone else. Promise you won't die on me. Live a very long life and keep me pregnant until I'm too old to do it anymore. I want to have millions of babies that look just like you."

Trag felt a rush of warmth spread throughout his body, tingling all the way down to his fingers and toes. Tears filled his eyes. "I'll do my best," he promised. "Now that this bastard is dead," he said with a nod toward Grekkor's body, "I don't think we'll have to worry about anyone trying to kill us."

"Nice feeling, huh?" Micayla said. "Um, did you really mean that part about us getting married?"

"Sure did," Trag replied. "How about it, Mick? Think you could stand being my mate?"

"Oh, yeah. I'll do it right now if you like."

"Doesn't matter," Trag said. "You said yes. That's enough for me."

Cheers went up through the crowd as Trag kissed her, but he never heard them. Micayla was purring and that was all that mattered to him—all that would ever matter. For now, and for the rest of his life, he would be content with whatever happened. Just as long as Mick was beside him.

"Ha!" said Jack as she approached along with the rest of the gang. "I *knew* it would happen! Pay up, Leroy."

Lerotan looked grim but handed over the credits anyway.

"Wait a minute," Trag said. "You two had a *bet* on this?"

"Leroy was so sure you wouldn't do it after she hissed at you," Jack said with a nod. "Bet me a thousand credits you'd never mate with her—but I knew better. Dammit, Trag, you're a total hottie! She'd be an idiot not to fall in love with you!"

Trag laughed softly. "Be that as it may, I fell for her first—at least, I *think* I did."

Tisana stepped up just then, nudging Jack in the ribs. "Told you so," she murmured.

"Don't tell me you had a bet on that too?" Trag exclaimed.

"Yes, and she now owes me *two* thousand credits," Tisana said with a nod toward Jack.

"I do not!" Jack insisted.

"Double or nothing?" Tisana chided. "Remember?"

"Oh, yeah, right," Jack admitted. "Came out behind on that deal, didn't I?" Jack may have been down a thousand credits, but she was still smiling.

"So, how did you know where to find us?" Trag asked. "We've been trying to contact you ever since we landed but haven't had any luck."

"Who *wouldn't* know?" Jack retorted. "When we didn't hear from you, we came on ahead. Soon as we landed all we heard about was some fancy reception Grekkor was planning. After that, it was only a matter of asking a few questions and here we are!"

"Guess you didn't need me and Mick after all," Trag said.

"Nonsense," Jack insisted. "The way you handled Grekkor? It was downright masterful, Trag! I doubt if anybody else could have gotten him to spill his guts like that. You pissed him off good and proper."

Trag winced. "My claim to fame?"

"Something like that," Jack agreed.

"Too bad it almost got Mick killed," he said.

"'Almost' being the operative word there," Jack said heartily. "Good thing we had Hidar with us, though. He's even better than Tisana!"

"Want to trade medics?" Lerotan suggested.

"No way!" Jack protested. "I'm never giving up Tisana."

"Oh, and why is that?" Lerotan asked.

"I… well, I'm pretty sure she's better at treating humans for one thing," Jack said hesitantly. "I mean, how often have any of us been stabbed? And for another, I've got an idea she's a better cook." Jack looked at Trag expectantly. "Am I right?"

"I'm not saying a word!" Trag said as he held Micayla tightly in his arms. "As far as I'm concerned, Hidar can do all the cooking he wants. I'll never pick on him again!"

Chapter 27

"OKAY, SO HOW DID YOU KNOW WE WERE COMING?" Trag asked Ilegret as several Neriks with some sort of official insignia on their tunics carried Grekkor's body away. "Did Jack tell you, or what?"

"Uh, actually, it was us," Orlat said. "We had a little stake in this too. Not that we didn't want to help you or anything, it's just that Veluka is our cousin."

"You're kidding me, right?"

Slurlek shook his head. "No. He stole the ship from us."

"*Borrowed*," said Orlat. "The three of us had joint ownership of it."

"But he encoded a message on the ship for us to help you out," Slurlek went on after a brief quelling glance at Orlat. "Not that you needed any help. You were doing just fine all on your own."

"If that isn't just like Veluka!" Jack declared. "He's got an angle for every deal there is! He got you guys—and Grekkor—off his case in one fell swoop."

"So, where *is* Veluka, anyway?" Micayla asked. "Still on Darconia?"

Jack shook her head. "No clue. He'll turn up again somewhere, though. Mark my words."

"Uh, Hidar," Micayla began. "How long did you say I had to keep this knife in me?"

"About an hour," Hidar replied. "I will put more healant in the wound to make sure before I remove it."

Jack was shaking her head. "Spitting in a knife wound to heal it," she muttered. "Never in all my born days…"

Hidar turned to Jack, his antennae waving gently. "You have seen for yourself that it was the appropriate treatment," he said stiffly. "But she should not be moved."

Since she was lying in Trag's arms, Micayla really didn't have a problem with that, but her butt was getting numb.

"No problem," said Trag, wrapping his arms more tightly around her. "I'll sit here with her all night if I have to."

"That will not be necessary," Hidar said.

"Hidar?" Micayla said gently. "Thank you for saving my life."

"Make that *four* lives," Cat said with complete confidence. "And yes, Micayla, there are three of them, but very young as yet." He paused, scrutinizing her closely. "You have been feeling… strange… for the past day or so?"

"Been dizzy ever since we landed," Micayla replied, "that is, until Trag and I…" Glancing up at Trag, she felt heat flood her face, in spite of the fact that everyone already knew what they'd been up to. "I guess that was significant, huh?"

Cat nodded. "That is a sign of fertility when a Zetithian female is with the right man." Reaching out to shake Hidar's claw, he said, "You have our neverending gratitude, my friend."

Hidar's antennae were beating so fast he seemed to lift off the floor for a moment. "You are welcome," he said. Glancing around the room, he said, "Shall we have lunch now?"

Having noticed what was on the plates of the other patrons, Micayla had an idea that Hidar would probably lose a wing if he were to eat any of it. "Wait, Hidar," she said. "See if you can reach into my pack." Shifting sideways against Trag's chest, she added, "There's some stuff in there I think you'll like a lot better."

Hidar reached into her pack with his claw-like hands. His wings fluttered in excitement as he read the label. "Oh, my Maker's Wings!" he exclaimed. "White Castles!"

"What's the matter with the food here?" Rodan said, scratching his bald head. "Looks great to me."

"Which is why none of us should eat here," Trag whispered in Micayla's ear. "You probably shouldn't eat anything with that knife in your chest either."

"I hadn't planned on it," Micayla said. She shifted her weight slightly to relieve some of the pressure on her hip. "This feels really weird."

"Does it still hurt?"

"Oddly enough, it doesn't, but I feel like I'm only using part of that one lung to breathe."

"Well, just rest easy then," he said. "It'll be over soon."

Micayla tried to take a deeper breath and immediately decided it was a bad idea. "I probably shouldn't talk either, but I just wanted to say... I saw what you did, Trag. I've never seen anyone do that. I mean, I've seen it demonstrated, but never actually—"

"Don't think about it too much," Trag said quickly. "I just reacted, that's all."

Taking a quick glance around the room, Micayla saw no evidence that a SWAT team was about to pounce on him. "Obviously no one is going to throw you in jail for it. In fact, I'll be surprised if they don't give you a medal."

"Whatever," Trag said with a shrug. "At the time I wasn't thinking about anything but what he'd done to you."

"He deserved it whether he'd killed me or not," Micayla said. "We all know that. *They* all know that too," she added with a nod toward the throng of beings of all kinds that had gathered.

The babble of excited voices had grown to a dull roar as the story was being retold from a hundred different points of view. It was anyone's guess as to how the official report would read, but since the *sklarth* of Rechred had been sitting at the same table, it was safe to say that at least one eyewitness would get it right. Of course, having Grekkor confess and then try to murder Micayla had been pretty damning evidence against him. Ilegret was already proclaiming Trag a hero—and Hidar right along with him.

"Never saw anything like it!" Ilegret was saying. "We must have more of you Scorillians visit here—perhaps to remain as healers." Ilegret was patting Hidar on the back like an old friend while Hidar's wings rustled with pleasure.

"What do you know?" Trag muttered. "Hidar might actually get laid because of this."

Micayla bit her lip. "Don't make me laugh," she gasped as the knife jiggled in her chest. "Bad idea!"

"Sorry," Trag said contritely. "But it's true."

She felt him move behind her. "What are you doing?"

"Just looking around," he replied. "Speaking of getting laid, take a look at Leroy and Windura."

Micayla turned her head slightly to the right just in time to see Windura, who had apparently been waiting outside, take a flying leap into Lerotan's arms. The kiss that followed should have set the nearest table-cloth on fire.

"That turned out rather well, didn't it?" Trag commented.

"Sure did," Micayla agreed. "Think she'll reform him?"

"I doubt it. Something tells me Leroy will be playing with guns forever."

"*Toy* guns, maybe," she said. There was no question that the two of them were lovers, and what the results would be… "They should have some interesting-looking children."

"Mmm, so will we," said Trag. "Ours will be cuter, though."

"Well, if they're even half as cute as the rest of the gang's kids, I'll be happy," Micayla declared. "They're all adorable. Can we have—?"

"You can have as many as you like," Trag purred. "Don't know about that million kittens thing, though. I might have been exaggerating slightly."

"You're making me laugh again," she warned. "Ordinarily that's a good thing, but right now it might be fatal."

"I'll shut up then," he said. "I just want to sit here and hold you anyway. No need to talk."

———

True to his word, Hidar was able to remove the knife without any further bleeding or damage. "I can breathe almost normally," Micayla marveled as Trag helped her to stand. "You're a miracle worker, Hidar."

Trag took no notice of either of these comments and proceeded to scoop Micayla up into his arms.

"I think I'm okay now, Trag," she said. "You don't have to carry me."

"You told me that once before," Trag reminded her. "I didn't listen then either."

"Gonna be my hero whether I like it or not, huh?"

"Yep," he replied as he headed purposefully toward the door. "You have absolutely no choice in the matter."

"Don't go getting all macho on me," she warned. "You know how I hate that macho stuff."

"You'll get over it. I'm not like that most of the time anyway. Allow me my moment now and then."

"I will if you'll let me be a—what was it you called me? a hissing, spitting bitch?—once in a while."

"Mmm, I love it when you hiss," Trag said. "And the way you *bite*…" He broke off there as a thrill of delight shot through him. Rather than disliking the idea, he was looking forward to being gnawed on for the rest of his life.

"Any idea where we're going?" Micayla asked as they left the building.

It was snowing again. Trag surveyed the swirling mass with distaste, not having the first clue as to which direction to take. All he knew was that he wanted to find someplace warm and comfortable to spend some quality time alone with Mick. "Dunno, but Jack's ship is bound to be around here somewhere, don't you think? Leroy's too. Just have to find it."

"Well, yeah, but we're probably a long way from the spaceport."

"Good point." The thought of trudging through more snow didn't appeal to him in the slightest, though the snow suckers were doing their best. "Totally ruining my exit, though. You know how the hero always rides off into the sunset with the girl—"

"I think you've been watching too many of Jack's old movies."

"Never watched a one of hers," Trag declared. "But Hidar has quite a collection."

"I'll bet those are interesting," Micayla said with a sardonic smile.

"Not half as interesting as watching them with him," Trag went on. "He points out all the women he'd like to fuck. And just for the record, he wants to do all of them."

"Hey, where are you going?" Jack called after them.

"We're riding off into the sunset—er, snowstorm," Micayla replied.

"Well, don't go too far," said Jack. "We've got rooms at the Palace Hotel—recently vacated by Grekkor and his crew. Nice rooms, they tell me."

"I'm sure they are," said Trag. "Just point me in the right direction."

"Never mind," Micayla said as she closed her eyes for a moment. "I know the way."

"Looks like I'll never have to ask for directions again, will I?"

"Probably not."

"We'll make a great pair," Trag said cheerfully. "Me flying, you telling me where to go…"

Micayla choked back a giggle. "What did I tell you about making me laugh?"

"Can't help it," Trag said. He was completely un-apologetic. "I love making you laugh and hearing you laugh. *Feeling* you laugh is pretty nice too."

"Am I going to get to make love with you when we get to our room?"

"We probably shouldn't," Trag said with marked regret. "Guess I should have asked Hidar about that, but it hardly seemed like the time. What if I promise to be very careful?"

Micayla feigned a pout of disappointment. "Not creative?"

"Not this time—although I'm sure I could be careful *and* creative if I put my mind to it."

"I'm sure you could," Micayla said with a nod. "Go for it."

———

The celebration that took place later that evening had originally been intended as Grekkor's reception, but it turned out to be more of a wake for him than anything—except that no one present was truly going to miss him.

It was a reunion as well as a celebration. The crew of *The Equalizer*, along with that of the *Jolly Roger*, joined in with Trag and Micayla and Veluka's cousins. Ilegret even dropped by for a while. Micayla was feeling much better by that evening and didn't even mind seeing Rodan again—as long as he kept his clothes on.

The high point of the evening was a speech given by Ilegret which proclaimed Micayla and Windura's innocence and Trag's heroism, plus another little perk that had everyone buzzing with excitement.

"Well, Trag," Micayla said as she handed Trag the document that Ilegret had given her. "Looks like you're not just my hero, but everyone else's too."

"What are you talking about?" Trag asked. "And what the devil is this?"

"I couldn't say for sure," Micayla replied. "But it looks pretty much like a ticket to anywhere you want to go."

Ilegret had done it up right. Covered with official stamps and seals, the document proclaimed one Tragonathon Vladatonsk to be an *"Upstanding Citizen of the Galaxy and a Hero of the Highest Order."* It was signed by no less than twenty Nerik officials. At least Trag *thought* they were officials; they had more letters after their names than anyone he'd ever seen—even Queen Scalia hadn't had as many.

"Well, I'll be damned," Trag whispered. "Do you think this means—?"

"That you can live on Earth? Yes, I think it does."

"Yes, but it's from Nerik," Trag pointed out. "Think it'll carry any weight anywhere else?"

Micayla shrugged. "If not, there's always Darconia."

"Speaking of Darconia," Trag began. "What do you say we get married there?"

"And have Shentuk perform the ceremony?" Micayla said with a smile. "I think she'd like that."

"I guess she could," said Trag, "though I don't think marriage is something they actually have on Darconia— at least, not that I've ever been able to tell."

"Did Ty and Kyra ever get married?"

Trag shook his head. "No," he replied. "And now that you mention it, I don't think Leo and Tisana are married either."

"Do we need to be?"

"No," he replied firmly. "There was no such thing on Zetith. When Zetithians mated, it was for life. There was no need for a ceremony."

"You never told me that," she said. "I had no idea…"

"Doesn't matter," said Trag. "We're already mates. The rest is just for show."

"But you did bring it up—even told Grekkor we were getting married—"

"That was more to get him riled up than anything," Trag said. "But I did mean it."

"What about a double wedding with Ty and Kyra?"

Trag grinned. "Want to make sure there's no chance I would ever try to leave you and steal her from Ty?"

"No," she said. "It's just a thought. Kyra might like it."

"We can ask, but I don't think she would." Trag paused for a moment. "Besides, you'd probably want the wedding all to yourself. You should have seen Manx and Drusilla's wedding. It was a pretty lavish event— Drusilla's friend, Ralph, did all the planning—even though it *was* on Jack's ship, but I'm not sure all that was necessary."

"We could talk to Shentuk," Micayla suggested. "She sort of prophesied this whole thing, and if there *is* such a thing as a wedding ceremony on Darconia, I'd like her to perform it."

"And if there isn't, we can always start a new tradition."

"We'll be starting lots of new things," Micayla said thoughtfully. "We've got a whole new population of Zetithians to produce. What we do now could turn out to be very significant in the future."

"Let's see now…" Trag said. "We'll get married in The Shrine of the Desert on Darconia—won't be any need for you to buy a wedding dress because they don't wear clothes there. We'll have a big party and then we could spend our wedding night under the stars on the portico—"

"We've done that," Micayla pointed out.

"You see!" Trag said triumphantly. "It's already a tradition!"

———∿∿∿———

Arriving on Darconia with the news that Grekkor was dead and that Micayla and Trag were not only expecting their first litter, but were also intending to wed, had everyone excited, Dragus in particular.

"I'll plan the entertainment," he said eagerly. "I know just the thing! We've been practicing ever since you guys left."

"I'm almost afraid to ask what it is you've been practicing," Micayla said. "Care to enlighten me?"

"It's a secret," Dragus said with a wag of his head.

"Now *there's* a scary thought," Trag muttered as Dragus hurried off, his tail swinging wildly behind him as he ran. "Wonder if it has something to do with that video Jack gave him."

"That's even scarier," Micayla said with a shudder. "But we might as well let them have their fun. If nothing else, I'm sure it'll be interesting."

Trag laughed sardonically. "Oh, it'll be interesting all right, but have you ever been to a Darconian event before? No, of course you haven't," he said, answering his own question. "They don't clap their hands or whistle when they get excited; they thump their tails, and trust me, it's loud enough to—" Trag broke off there, clearly attempting to come up with an apt simile and failing.

"Wake the dead?" Micayla suggested.

Trag nodded his agreement. "Even the dead that have already turned to dust."

"Well, apparently Manx and Drusilla had a very nice wedding when they let someone else do the planning," Micayla said. "And who knows? We might get lucky."

"Yes, but Dragus?" Trag scoffed. "Come on, Micayla! His idea of a good time is to—well, maybe I'd better not say."

"I already know," Micayla said, laughing. "Hartak told me."

"So you see what I mean then?"

"He's not going to do that at a wedding, Trag. And if we're in The Shrine, I'm sure he'll behave himself."

Trag looked doubtful. "I'm not worried about the ceremony," he said. "It's the party afterward that has me worried. Get enough wine into a crowd of Darconians and some of us humanoid types are liable to get squashed!"

Kyra and Tychar may have declined the offer of a double wedding, but to Micayla's surprise, Windura indicated that Lerotan had an interest in the idea.

"Leroy asked you to marry him?" Micayla exclaimed. "I don't believe it! Somehow he doesn't seem like the marrying kind."

Windura smiled grimly. "That's not exactly how he put it," she said. "And you're right; he's not what you'd call romantic—though he does surprise me sometimes. He just said that you and Trag might not be the only ones looking to get married."

"That's all?"

Windura nodded. "Not much to go on, is it? But you know how low-key he can be. Anyway, when you mentioned the idea of Kyra and Ty getting married along with you, that's what he said."

"Not another word?"

"Nope."

"But you're—lovers, right?" Micayla asked cautiously. What with one thing and another, the two friends hadn't had much time to discuss things; the opportunity for a private chat simply hadn't presented itself.

Windura nodded. "Figured that out, did you? He actually did spend the night with me when you and Trag told us not to wait up, and I've been on the ship with him ever since—looking after the kids and such, though they really didn't need much looking after. Tisana's daughter, Althea… that girl is amazing! You wouldn't believe the things she can do! And Curly really *can* fly—and land! Even Leroy never complained, and you know how touchy he is about his ship."

Micayla knew this to be true but had other questions that had nothing to do with scratching the paint on *The Equalizer.* "So, Windy, tell me, what's it like with Leroy?"

"It's, um… different," she replied.

"That's all?" Micayla was astonished. "For a guy with two tools I'd have thought—you mean it's not mind-blowing or multi-orgasmic or anything like that?"

"My, how you've changed," Windura said mildly. "There was a time—"

"When I wouldn't have cared, let alone asked?"

Windura nodded.

"Well, I *have* changed," Micayla said. "I'm *normal,* Windy. Really and truly normal! Not warped or man-hating or frigid or any of the stuff guys used to say about me. Turns out the hissing was a good thing—and the purring! Oh my God, the purring! It drives me absolutely wild!"

Windura nodded sagely. "Most Terrans probably don't purr."

"Well, Terran *cats* do, but not Terran men."

"I'll bet some of them would have tried if they'd known it would make a difference."

"I'm very glad they didn't. Trag was definitely worth waiting for."

"Happy?"

"Extremely."

"So what are you two going to do after the wedding?"

Micayla shrugged. "Trag wants to go to Earth. Don't know if we'll stay there or not, but I think he only wants to go just because he can. After the wedding, Jack's going to pick up her babies on Terra Minor, so I'll get to meet Lynx and Bonnie and then we'll visit Manx and Drusilla when we get to Earth—and my stepmother. Bet she never dreamed I'd ever bring a guy home to meet her."

"Too bad you're not all going to be living on the same planet," Windura said wistfully. "It's going to be hard to keep in touch."

"Maybe someday," Micayla said. "But in the meantime, we just need to be somewhere that our kids can grow up and find compatible mates. Humans seem to be the best choice for that, so we need to live wherever they are."

"There are lots of Earth colonies," Windura pointed out. "You just have to find the one you like best."

"Jack knows them all too," Micayla said with a nod. "I'm sure she'd love to keep us on her ship for a good long while, but Trag—of all people!—seems to want to settle down someplace where he can grow fruit. Would you believe it's his ambition to grow strawberries?"

"That doesn't sound like him at all," Windura admitted. "But maybe we don't know him as well as we think we do."

"He's a puzzle sometimes," Micayla agreed. "I plan to spend the rest of my life figuring him out."

"Have fun."

Micayla smiled. "I believe I will."

———

Micayla had been to a variety of weddings on different worlds but was convinced that her own ceremony had them all beat. After all, what other bride could say afterward that she had married the last known—and totally hot!—Zetithian man in existence, that the ceremony had been performed in The Shrine of the Desert, that clothing had been optional, and that a hundred Darconian guards had danced the Macarena at the reception?

Probably not very many.

Epilogue

"ANY WORD YET?" CAT ASKED.

"None," Jack replied. She sat at the helm of the *Jolly Roger* feeling more despondent than she'd been since Lynx's problems had made her feel so down. They were on their way to Terra Minor, but even the prospect of seeing her babies again didn't lighten her mood completely. "I really thought we would have heard something by now. Those stupid Nedwuts can't have eradicated all of you! They just can't!"

"I had hoped the lifting of the bounty would bring out more survivors, but if there are any of us left, they may be hiding out somewhere that the message wouldn't reach them," Cat said reasonably. "Remember how isolated Manx was on Barada Seven? He would never have received the news."

"And it's only been a month or so since we—er, *I*—eliminated the problem," Trag reminded her. "You just need to be patient."

"Patient?" Jack exclaimed. "I've been waiting for this moment ever since Cat and I first met! I've had no *choice* but to be patient."

"Plus, I only sent that message out right before we left Darconia," Micayla said. "It will take a while for it to reach all the known star systems."

"True," Jack admitted. "But I still think—"

"Hey, Mom," Larry said as he and his brothers

dashed onto the bridge. "We've got something here you need to see."

"In a minute," Jack said. "I—"

"No, really, Mom," Curly chimed in. "You need to see this. Now."

"It's from Lynx," Moe said, handing her the message pad. "You're not gonna believe this."

Lynx's message was brief and to the point.

A woman by the name of Amelyana Grekkor has arrived at Terra Minor in a starship filled with over a hundred Zetithian refugees. They have been in space for twenty-five years and are requesting permission to land.

Better hurry up, Jack. You don't want to miss this.

Acknowledgments

My heartfelt thanks go out to:

All of those readers who have so anxiously awaited Trag's book and have also offered their suggestions and encouragement.

My friends and family for putting up with my moods and doing their best to help me get this book written.

And the people at Sourcebooks for believing in me.

I couldn't have done it without you!

About the Author

Cheryl Brooks has been a critical care nurse since 1977, graduating from the Kentucky Baptist Hospital School of Nursing in 1976, and earning a BSN from Indiana University in 1986. Cheryl is an avid reader of romance novels and has been a fan of science fiction ever since watching that first episode of *Star Trek*. Always in need of a creative outlet, she has written numerous novels, with *The Cat Star Chronicles: Hero* being her sixth published work. She lives on a farm near Bloomfield, Indiana, with her husband, two sons, three horses, one dog, and six cats. You can visit her website at: http://cherylbrooksonline.com or email her at: cheryl.brooks52@yahoo.com.

ROGUE

"I WILL NOT KEEP YOU MUCH LONGER." SHE PAUSED, calling out to a servant in the next room before taking another delicate sip of her wine and continuing, "But before you go, you must see my cats."

"Your cats?"

Nodding, she said, "I'd like your opinion of them."

That sounded odd. What did it matter what I thought of her pets? The little toad creature was told to fetch the cats, so I had a little time to think. Okay, if this was a desert planet with intelligent life forms that looked for all the world like dinosaurs, what kind of cats would they have here? Saber-toothed tigers?

On that thought, the door opened again, and the two cats entered—but they weren't cats, at least, not in the ordinary sense. They were tall male humanoids—undoubtedly more of Scalia's "exotic slaves"—and they certainly were exotic! Separately, each one would have been stunning, but together, they took my breath away—would have taken anyone's breath away, even Nindala's. For myself, I was just glad I happened to be sitting down when I saw them for the first time. Staring back at them in awe, I had barely managed to take another breath when one of them turned his startlingly blue eyes on me and, no doubt noting my open-mouthed expression, lowered his eyelids ever so slightly and sent a roguish smile in my direction.

And I had an orgasm.

Scalia probably thought I'd choked on my wine, but that wasn't it at all! I felt a fire begin to burn deep inside me when I first laid eyes on him, and his smile sent me over the edge. I'd never felt anything quite like it before in my life—nor had I ever seen anything to compare with him.

"They are my most prized possessions," Scalia said. "Very beautiful, are they not?"

I'm not entirely sure what I said in reply, but it was affirmative, though undoubtedly inarticulate.

Scalia smiled. "I hoped you would like them."

I took another sip of my wine—actually, it was more of a gulp than a sip—and asked, "W—where did you find them?"

"The slave traders in this region know of my penchant for interesting specimens and brought them to me," she replied. "You would not believe what I had to pay for them! The trader said that there had been a bounty placed on them, which, of course, meant that I was required to pay about twenty times that amount in order to get them—and also to keep him quiet as to their whereabouts! Apparently, someone holds a grudge against their kind and set out to exterminate them entirely—which would have been most unfortunate, as I am certain you will agree."

I think I nodded, but sitting there trying to imagine a whole planet full of these guys nearly made my uterus go into another spasm. I decided that a group of jealous men must have gotten an army together and plotted against them, for certainly no female in the known universe would have gone along with such a scheme. I mean, Scalia was a lizard, and even she liked them!

"But they are safe here," she added firmly. "They are kept under lock and key at night, and no one beyond the palace walls knows they exist. And, unlike my other slaves, even my daughter has never seen them."

The fact that they were both entirely nude except for jeweled collars around their necks and genitals might have been one reason Zealon had never been permitted to see them. She was much too young for such things, though I didn't think that anyone under the age of—oh, I don't know, a hundred, perhaps?—could look at them and not be affected.

"These two are brothers," Scalia went on, as though she were truly talking about a pair of pet cats who happened to be littermates. "I would dearly love to breed more of them, but they are a mammalian species and will not cross with our kind. Nor are they… aroused… by our females."

Which, of course, made me wonder whether or not they liked humans. I, for one, certainly liked them, especially the one who'd smiled at me. The other one didn't seem terribly pleased to see me—not quite scowling, but certainly not smiling.

As they had positioned themselves on either side of Scalia's chair, across the table from me, I had an excellent view of them both. They didn't seem particularly shy, either, not minding a bit that I couldn't take my eyes off them. The blue-eyed one was fair-skinned with the most spectacular hair—jet black with a thick streak of white running through it near his temple—hanging to his waist in perfect spirals. The other also had black hair which curled to his waist, but with a similarly placed orange stripe, green eyes, and more tawny skin. They both possessed upswept eyebrows and pointed ears, as well as vertical pupils that seemed to glow slightly. The green-eyed one yawned just then, revealing a mouthful of sharp white teeth with canines that looked downright dangerous. All in all, they put me in mind of Earth's tigers—the one Bengal, and the other Siberian—but they had body hair more like that of human males, not the fur you would expect to find on a cat. Neither of them had beards, but I wasn't close enough to determine whether or not this was natural. Both were tall, broad-chested, and lean, with smooth, rippling muscles and perfectly proportioned limbs. It was no wonder Scalia had paid a fortune for them!

All of this possibly wouldn't have mattered if they hadn't had one other notable attribute: they were both hung like horses. A crass description, perhaps, but it was accurate, nonetheless. Unfortunately, they were not, as Scalia had mentioned before, aroused. The mere thought of what they might look like if they were aroused made my mouth go dry, and I attempted to take another sip from an empty glass.

"My guest needs more wine," Scalia said, crooking a finger toward the Siberian tiger.

Nodding, he collected a flask from the sideboard and came around the table. When he leaned over to pour the wine, his cock was just below my eye level, but as my eyes were slightly downcast, I had an excellent view of it. Among other things, I noted that the jewels on his genital cuff were every bit as blue as his eyes. Scalia, it seemed, was not the slightest bit color-blind and had paid attention to detail when decorating her slaves.

"Thank you," I said hoarsely.

"You are very welcome," he replied. "It is my pleasure to serve you."

His deep voice was like melted butter and, even though polite, his choice of words had me envisioning all manner of pleasurable things—none of them having anything to do with food or drink. I couldn't help but look up at him, and, when our eyes met, he smiled again and blinked slowly. Then I watched, fascinated, as his nostrils flared with a deep inhalation—and his smile intensified, as did the hot blue of his eyes.

"Oh, excellent!" Scalia said in hushed tones.

Yes, he is! Excellent, perfect, amazing, unbelievable—and just about any other superlative you'd care to use. Still gazing up at him, I felt as though I were about to melt into a puddle and slide off my chair. Honestly, if I'd ever felt a more overwhelming sense of desire for any other man in the galaxy, this one would have made me forget it.

I felt something wet drop onto my hand. Glancing down to see if I was, indeed, melting, I saw what Scalia had undoubtedly been referring to, for the tiger's penis was now fully erect. As thick and long as a well-endowed human's would have been, it also had a wide, scalloped corona at the base of the head that was obviously there for one reason only: to give the greatest possible pleasure to any woman fortunate enough to be penetrated by it. Looking closer, I noted that the clear fluid that had fallen on my hand appeared to be coming, not from the opening at the apex, but from the starlike points of the corona.

I tried to swallow and couldn't. I looked up at him

again with what must have been an expression of raw hunger mingled with guilt written clearly upon my face. In return, what I saw on his face was the most open invitation to partake of anything I'd ever seen. His mesmerizing eyes beckoned, his full lips promised sensuous delights beyond my wildest imaginings, and his provocative smile assured me of his knowledge of every possible way to drive a woman wild. He was offering himself to me—completely—without saying a word.

Unfortunately, just as I was about to take a taste of him, I suddenly remembered where I was. We were not alone, and he was a slave who belonged to the lizard queen sitting across the table from me. Reaching awkwardly for my wineglass, my sleeve slid across the head of his cock, soaking it with his fluid and drawing a barely audible groan from him.

Trying desperately to ignore his reaction, I looked away from him and saw that Scalia was watching us intently, but she had her hand on the Bengal tiger's thigh, stroking him, though without any erotic response on his part whatsoever. I would have thought that such a pornographic vision right across the table from him would have been enough to stimulate him, but apparently, it wasn't.

Then I remembered the blue-eyed tiger inhaling as though he was taking a whiff of me. It was something to do with scent, then—though it was surprising that I was clearheaded enough to figure that out at the time. What was also surprising was the fact that my "scent" hadn't reached the other man, because if the way I was feeling was any indication, it had to have been pretty heavy on the sex pheromones.

Breaking the silence, the Queen's voice was now brisk and businesslike. "You will require a personal attendant during your stay with us," Scalia said. "I believe he will suit you very nicely."

"Who, him?" I gasped. As I sat staring at his cock, I decided that if anyone could "suit me," it would have been him, but he was far more... man... than I'd ever so much as touched in my life! He could turn me to mush in a heartbeat—and, of course, in that state, I'd never play piano again... "Oh, but I don't really need—" I protested, before she cut me off with an imperious wave of her hand.

"Yes, you do," she said firmly. "You are new to this world, Kyra. He will be able to help you... adjust."

Adjust. What an interesting choice of words! He probably could have helped me adjust to just about anything—even daily torture—if only he were to hold my hand for the duration. And speaking of hands, I wondered if I'd be able to keep mine off of him when we were alone together. Having been within a hairbreadth of licking his cock just moments before—and in full view of two other people, I might add—I thought I'd probably have some difficulty with that. I also wondered if he'd go running to Scalia to complain if I did something of that nature—or what he would do if I didn't.

To be honest, I doubted that I needed a servant of any kind, though due to the scarcity of water and fabrics, it was a given that there wouldn't be any easy way to wash my clothes. I wondered if my bed would have sheets on it, or if I'd be sleeping on a bed of stones or sand. Hopefully, Zealon had done some homework in that area as well.

My tiger was still standing next to me, flanking my chair just as his counterpart did for Scalia—quite slave-like behavior, despite his persistent erection—and it occurred to me that he might like to have some say in the matter.

"What about you?" I asked, looking up at him curiously. "Do you think I need a personal attendant?"

"Absolutely," he replied, his luscious lips curling in a smile. "There are a great many things I can do for you."

I'll just bet you can, I thought grimly. "But do you want to?" I said aloud. For some reason, I felt it was important that his service to me be voluntary. Not that he wouldn't have done whatever he was told to do by his owner; after all, he was a slave, though a very valuable one. What would happen if he refused? I doubted that Scalia would punish him—doubted that she ever had, for neither of them had a mark on him, nor did they have the cowed expressions of people who were habitually abused or bullied. In fact, they appeared to have been well cared for, if not cosseted, by their owner—truly more like cherished pets than slaves.

"I can think of nothing I would like more," he assured me.

"Because you have been told to." I said this not as a question, but as a statement.

He seemed uncertain about how to reply to that, glancing at Scalia out of the corner of his eye as if for direction, but she gave him none that I could see.

"Because you smell of desire," he said finally. "Being near you pleases me… and I have no doubt that I can please you."

"An honest answer," Scalia asserted. "You may believe what he tells you. They are both very truthful."

I nodded. "Yes, I can believe that much," I said.
This man undoubtedly could please the most stone-cold
woman imaginable, but I secretly wondered if it was
my desire which pleased him, or if any woman's desire
would do.

Sighing deeply, I relented, knowing that while I
might regret my decision in the end, if I refused, I'd
regret it even more.

"It is settled, then," Scalia said to my tiger. "You may
escort Kyra to her rooms." Turning to me, she added,
"Your quarters have been adapted to suit human needs.
I believe you will find them to your liking."

"I'm sure I will," I replied, "but, if you don't mind
my asking, how are you going to keep him a secret
if he's with me? The Princess, or someone else, may
see him."

"We will take that risk," Scalia said with conviction.
"I believe it to be worthwhile."

And her word was law. After all, she was the queen.

Now Available